Forever Sheriff

OTHER FIVE STAR TITLES IN THE HIGH MOUNTAIN SHERIFF SERIES

Founding Sheriff
Fugitive Sheriff

THE HIGH MOUNTAIN SHERIFF SERIES

Forever Sheriff

Edward Massey

FIVE STAR
A part of Gale, a Cengage Company

Five Star Publishing, a part of Gale, a Cengage Company

LIBRARY OF CONGRESS CATALOGING-IN-PUBLICATION DATA

Names: Massey, Edward, 1942– author.
Title: Forever sheriff / Edward Massey.
Description: First Edition. | Waterville, Maine : Five Star, a part of Gale, a Cengage Company, 2022. | Series: The high mountain sheriff series
Identifiers: LCCN 2021048039 | ISBN 9781432892302 (hardcover)
Subjects: GSAFD: Western stories
Classification: LCC PS3613.A819327 F67 2022 | DDC 813/.6—dc23
LC record available at https://lccn.loc.gov/2021048039

First Edition. First Printing: May 2022
Find us on Facebook—https://www.facebook.com/FiveStarCengage
Visit our website—http://www.gale.cengage.com/fivestar
Contact Five Star Publishing at FiveStar@cengage.com

Printed in Mexico
Print Number: 01 Print Year: 2022

Anne
Unconditional Love
Lived with Boundaries
Great Cook Greater Companion
Partner

ACKNOWLEDGMENTS

John Nesbitt, Tiffany Schofield, Hazel Rumney, and editors at Five Star Publishing, members of the Just Write Chapter of the League of Utah Writers, Western Writers of America, Western Fictioneers, Lieff Cabraser Heimann & Bernstein, classmates, friends, and three grandfathers who gave me these stories.

Neither biography nor history, simply stories. In the blunt words of Sheriff Mark Willford, I hope damn good ones. They are the stories of a grandfather, a great-grandfather who evaded the U.S. Marshals and refused to escape to Mexico, and a great-great-grandfather apprenticed as a cooper in Derby, England, who left his errant ways behind when he emigrated and helped settle the Summit Mission.

These grands acted as each believed a man should, even in error, with certain conviction that his actions molded and shaped future generations.

Sheriff Luke Willford Simms, sworn in 1854
Sheriff John Willford Simms, sworn in 1883
Sheriff Mark Willford Simms, sworn in 1918

★ ★ ★ ★ ★

I. Deputy Simms Pins on His Star

★ ★ ★ ★ ★

Chapter 1

October 12, 1905, Coalville, Utah

"Do you swear to uphold the laws of the State of Utah and the County of Summit?"

Before Mark Willford Simms could answer, Sheriff John Willford Simms squinted up Main Street in the direction of the north end of town. Mark Willford's mother continued to hold the family Bible as she turned to follow her husband's urgent gaze.

"Say, I do," barked the sheriff.

The deputy-to-be felt October's chill mountain air in his struggle to bring the words from deep in his throat. "I do."

In the six years since New Year's Day when his father told him to trade school for work, not once did Sheriff John Willford Simms say a word about the day he would administer the oath to create once again a Sheriff Simms and a Deputy Simms. Coming up on eighteen, Mark Willford remembered his father's instructions to ask, but that felt like testing the very limits. A little less direct seemed more prudent. "When you gonna tell me I can be your deputy?" he asked after church on the Sunday before his birthday.

"Hell, boy," said Sheriff Simms in the boom that was the family's voice of affection, "it ain't enough to wait to be told. You got to ask for what you want."

"Well, I'm asking," he said and now he wondered if he needed to ask whether he had been sworn in.

"Get Woodside," the sheriff shouted. "That's Charlie McCormick, and he's carrying a body in that wagon behind him."

The new deputy decided he had his answer and started scouring the small crowd. Deputy Woodside brushed past him on a dead run.

His mother pushed his deputy's star into his hand, clasped the family Bible to her chest, and followed his father down the steps into Main Street, calling out, "I'll meet you at the Merc."

By the urgency in her voice, Mark knew she meant the two rooms above the Mercantile that served as the town's hospital. Deputy Simms swung his eyes from his mother's back to see his father grab the reins of the second horse from Charlie McCormick. The sheriff waited a scant moment while Deputy Woodside reached the other side of the horse. The deputy's hand steadied the boy's body, and they started walking the horse toward the Merc.

Mark Willford stood on the steps of his grandfather's jail, holding the star in his hand, trying to be sure he had said, "I do." He banished his moment of indecision. His father would have no patience for such a thing. His father expected him to know what to do without being told.

Deputy Simms pinned on his star and ran down the steps into the churned-up dirt of Main Street. His long strides took him past his mother. He needed to make it to the door onto the stairway before his father and Woodside arrived with the slumped-over rider.

He threw open the door. In the same instant, "Good," came the sheriff's voice from behind. "Let's take this boy upstairs."

Deputy Simms held the door with one hand and the reins of the boy's horse with the other. The sheriff and Deputy Woodside lifted the boy and started up the steps. Without a glance, the sheriff said, "Charlie, this here's Deputy Simms. You met his grandpa. You might as well meet him. He'll be having some questions for you."

Charlie McCormick offered a hand. The deputy tipped his eyes at his occupied hands and said, "I'll shake later."

"Sure," said Charlie. "Pleased to meet the third in the line of Sheriffs Simms."

"Only a deputy," said Mark Willford, "and only since eight o'clock."

Charlie chuckled, "Sorry to interrupt." He pointed to the star hanging on the deputy's chest, "Just a matter of time."

"Or being involved with a McCormick," said Sheriff Simms.

"Now, you know my boy didn't have nothing to do with your dad's death," said Charlie.

"Only the robbery that brought it about," said Sheriff Simms. "And what about this?"

"Not Lester," said Charlie. "A new hand. He's a bit jumpy."

The sheriff lifted his left hand, causing the body to shift. Deputy Simms let go of the door and caught one side of the boy. The sheriff pressed a finger to the wound in the right shoulder. "That's from a rifle. How do you get jumpy a half mile away?"

"I didn't see it," said Charlie. "Lester told me the new hand shot a kid rustling cattle. Son or no, I didn't spend no time asking questions. I rode out and found the kid. Then I brought him straightaway to you."

Deputy Simms gentled the boy back into the sheriff's hands. Now he had a question. He looked back and forth between the two men. After a moment's hesitation, taking the sheriff's words as permission, he asked.

"This new hand left the boy out there? Shot?"

McCormick glanced at the deputy. "A Simms, all right." He paused a moment and looked at the sheriff. "I'm just sayin' I went out to find him."

"This new hand have a name?" asked Deputy Simms.

"Tom Hixson."

Chapter 2

Sheriff Simms and Deputy Woodside carried the boy upstairs. Deputy Simms, holding the door, paused to consider the sheriff's comment to McCormick. *He* would be asking questions. The deputy fingered the badge pinned on his shirt and remembered he had not thanked his father or mother. His father had made the badge and that morning his mother baked biscuits and handed them to him on a plate resting on a soft package wrapped in tissue. His father had made the star in a circle badge out of tin he had found somewhere. His mother had made his swearing-in shirt from a bolt of cloth purchased out of her wages earned working at the mercantile. Like everyone in the Simms family, neither mother nor father said, "I love you." His father made him tools. She made him biscuits and shirts.

Deputy Simms vowed to thank them both as he climbed the stairs. The sheriff emerged from the room and started down. The deputy pressed back against the wall and watched him, tall and square, more a monument than a man. The sheriff stepped off the boardwalk and turned to look back. He surveyed his deputy's badge, shirt, heavy cotton pants, and hat. The deputy knew never in God's heaven would the sheriff say he liked what he saw. Not as tall, more solid and broad, more a barrel than an oak tree, he felt pride in Charlie's comment, but if the deputy wanted to hear approval, he knew he would have to learn how to listen to himself. Mark Willford smiled. He trusted the fact his father demanded truth-telling. The sheriff must have liked what he saw. For damn sure, if he didn't, that he would say.

Sheriff Simms nodded, put on his hat, and said, "Get a move on. You got work to do."

The deputy heard in the sheriff's words the faint suggestion he would be relied upon. Yet no word suggested when he would be given the tools to do his job. He had the badge, but no horse and no gun. They had a shooting to tend to, and he did not know how he could hold up his end of the bargain. The sheriff appeared to believe he had said everything he needed to say. He waved a hand in dismissal and turned to go back across Main Street to the jail.

"So, when do I get my gun?" asked Deputy Simms.

Sheriff Simms continued toward the jail. His answer floated over his shoulder. "Whenever you want. I bought my pistol after I became sheriff. I wouldn't advise that."

Mark Willford took a breath. He had faced this dilemma before. The sheriff expected him to stand up for himself and what he thought. The father expected him not to talk back. "I had to ask you to make me a deputy, and now I have to buy my own gun?"

The sheriff continued his purposeful march across Main Street. He stopped at the foot of the steps to the jail, turned around, and looked, for a noticeable moment, at his son. He answered in his normal, booming voice, "You're a deputy now, aren't you?"

Deputy Simms could see that he and Woodside needed to ride out to McCormick's spread, even take McCormick with them. He had to figure out how to do that without asking more stupid questions.

The sheriff reached in his vest pocket and brought out a key. He took one step forward and threw it toward the deputy. "As far as guns go, I taught you how to shoot. You can use one of the county rifles. That's the key to the cabinet. If you buy a pistol, Trueman will give you good terms, but not today. You got your hands full with that boy above his store."

Deputy Simms picked up the key from the dusty Main Street. "Thanks. I figure Woodside and I will go out to McCormick's place."

The sheriff turned and walked up the steps.

"I'll pick up the rifle before we go." Deputy Simms put the key in his back pocket.

The sheriff stopped at the jailhouse door. "Good. No need to take risks that don't need taking."

Woodside came out of the room and dove down the steps waving an impatient arm. "The sheriff expects us to be on our way already."

Deputy Simms nodded toward the senior deputy and said, "Right. I already told Pa, we'll go out to McCormick's ranch, but it's north of Wahsatch. What am I supposed to do for a horse?" The deputy kicked his boot in the dirt and looked up. "I suppose Pa'll make me buy that, too."

"Could do," said Woodside. He stepped down off the boardwalk and started across the street. He motioned to the deputy to keep up. Without warning, he stopped and looked up at the rooflines of the five buildings that lined the street. After a moment's pause, he said into the air, "I wouldn't want to set you to thinking anything unrealistic, but your grandfather gave your pa Indigo. Maybe he'll give you a horse."

"Fat chance," said Deputy Simms.

"Don't go judgin' the man 'cause he makes you do for yourself," said Woodside. "That horse is still alive. It's about all he has of his father."

"You think that matters to him?" asked Deputy Simms.

"He don't say much about what matters to him, but he rode that horse hard back to town when he found out your grandfather had been shot. I couldn't keep up. And he lived with

Indigo when he hid out from the U.S. Marshal."

"Like you said, best not to get my hopes up." Out of respect Deputy Simms fell behind as he walked up the steps with Woodside. At the last step he reached to open the door and said, "It's embarrassing."

After Deputy Woodside stepped inside, Deputy Simms followed him to the sheriff's desk. "When we take McCormick out to his ranch, I'll need a horse. Am I supposed to buy that, too?"

"The job requires one," said Sheriff Simms. "You asked to be a deputy."

"Okay. So, is this a lesson? Answered prayers?" asked Deputy Simms.

"Ah, Matthew," said Sheriff Simms. "Your grandfather loved the book of Matthew."

"I know. Ma told me that's why I'm named Mark," said Deputy Simms. He looked at the sheriff. His father had a test going on. He could not back down from it. "So, I'm asking if the county can arrange for a horse?"

The sheriff laughed. "Sounds reasonable to me. I took you down to Seth Parker's livery before. Until you have your own, Seth'll loan you a horse. Good idea, too. His livery is the place for news. Everybody in town'll know you're a deputy by nightfall."

Deputy Simms didn't particularly want everybody in town to know he was a deputy without a gun or a horse, but he'd have to face that. "That don't tell me he'll loan me a horse."

John Willford put down his pen and simply looked at Mark Willford.

After a moment, "I know," said the deputy, "you got to ask."

Seth set up Deputy Simms with a horse and saddle and bridle on a week's loan. He arrived back at the jail to find Clive Orson, his grandfather's friend and deputy.

"Are you the only one here?" asked Deputy Simms.

"Seems so," said Clive.

"Didn't you retire somewhere around my tenth birthday?"

"Thereabouts," said Clive. "Stopped taking the county's two dollars a week in ninety-eight, at sixty-five."

"Eleventh birthday," said Deputy Simms. "But you bring breakfast every morning?"

"Frances can't break the habit. She makes breakfast for four, then tells me it'll go to waste if I don't bring it over here," said Clive. "Sheriff left before he could eat it."

"Leaving you in charge," said Deputy Simms.

"I just stand around when he does that," said Clive. "Until one of you comes back."

Mark Willford noticed the "one of you." Clive had said nothing about his swearing in today, like he'd always been a deputy. "You know, I got a lot to learn."

"So did your grandpa, but he started a few years older than you. Still, there weren't any sheriffs out here before him, so he was learning while he was doing."

"That's how I feel," said Deputy Simms.

Clive Orson handed Deputy Simms a breakfast sandwich. "Frances'll have to make five now." He smiled and patted the forearm of the deputy. "He's in you. You'll do all right."

"Thanks." Deputy Simms motioned with the sandwich in his hand. "I'll eat this on the way." At the door, he turned and said, "If you're sticking around, give the sheriff a message. Now I have a horse, Woodside and I'll take McCormick back to his son's ranch and come back with some answers."

"I expect he knows," said Clive Orson.

Chapter 3

Deputy Simms walked his loaner horse out of the livery, lengthened the stirrups of his borrowed saddle, and climbed up to ride north on Main Street past three buildings to the Mercantile. It felt like a frustrating precursor to his urgent need to start the thirty-mile trip to Lester McCormick's ranch. Without any direct words making it official, he sensed his father had put him in charge of investigating this boy's shooting. Like everything that passed between them, not much of it passed with words. He had not expected to be put in charge of anything on his very first day. He would have liked it better had the sheriff told him he was in charge. No matter, best to say nothing and watch how Woodside proceeded.

The deputy climbed the stairs and found two rooms; one door closed. He opened the door with care. Deputy Woodside looked up. Nurse Bullock continued working on the boy lying in the bed. Drawn curtains darkened the room. The mood told him his normal voice would be too loud. He tried to whisper, "Who is he?"

"Don't know," said Woodside.

"Some boy from Deseret Land and Cattle." The voice rose out of a shadowed corner, not in a whisper.

"That's Lester's pa," Woodside thumbed back in the direction of the corner.

"The sheriff introduced us," said Deputy Simms. "Who shot him?"

"It was an accident," said Charlie McCormick. "A new hand. Jumpy."

Woodside looked back into the darkened corner. "Like the sheriff said, an accident from half a mile away don't wash. Jumpy or plain mean, either way, your new hand's dangerous."

Deputy Simms still held the door, caught up in this exchange. The door at the bottom of the stairs opened.

"What happened? Who is he?" Sarah Jane Carruth's words reached them before her footsteps brought her.

"You interested in the guy who shot him?" asked Deputy Woodside.

Sarah Jane shot a blazing look at Deputy Simms. She said nothing and edged close to watch Nurse Bullock pull the sheets tight across the bandaged chest. The silence drew out. She looked up at Woodside and asked, "Why do you say that?"

"You're here," said Deputy Woodside. "It's either him or the boy."

Mark Willford looked at the boy in the bed, not so much a boy now that he looked at him close, probably older than Mark Willford. He knew from yesterday in Ma Carruth's barn that Sarah Jane had not come because of her interest in the boy.

"Ma tells me," said Sarah Jane with slow emphasis as she stepped through the open doors of the barn while Mark Willford harnessed the buckboard for Ma Carruth, "you're a deputy tomorrow. Gettin' such an important job ought to be well rewarded."

He finished the last buckle and looked up to ask her how could he be well rewarded? He had not even asked how much the county bargained to pay him. Before he spoke, he noticed her blue work shirt opened down the throat. Perhaps she had lost a button. She stepped up close to him. He could see three buttons sewn in place up to the collar. He looked away from what the open fabric left uncovered and sputtered, "Truth to tell, I don't know how much they'll pay."

She giggled and gripped his hand, tugging him, "Whatever it is won't be enough."

He planted both feet and tried to make his full bulk resist her. He found it easier to stand rooted in the earth than not to look at her. She may have simply forgotten those buttons, but she did not forget to pull that blue work shirt tight and tuck it in under her belt. He tried to find something to say but remained mute and made to turn back to the buckboard.

Sarah Jane reached up, stretching her body close to him, and caressed his cheek. "Don't you think you deserve a reward?"

Mark Willford said nothing. Speaking, saying anything, meant he lost this duel. Nevertheless, he didn't want his silence to imply, well, anything. He jerked away to gain separation between their bodies. "Sarah Jane, I don't . . ."

"Oh, don't worry," she laughed. She punched his shoulder. "I'm spoken for."

Deputy Simms breathed easier with that news. Caution told him still say nothing.

Sarah Jane did a little wiggle and put her hands on her hips. "You might could be fun, I'll admit, but it'd end there. My new guy works for Lester McCormick. McCormick's a rancher not a farmer. Tom is McCormick's top hand. His prospects are a lot better than a deputy."

"And I don't think it's the boy," said Woodside. "I don't know how many hands are up at McCormick's spread now, but Elsemore can't do nothing, let alone shoot somebody. Lester may not be as smart as his pa. For damn sure, Charlie wouldn't let him do it." Woodside paused a moment, then pointed in the corner. "And his pa's over there. Charlie said their new hand shot the boy. Called him jumpy."

"That's not fair," Sarah Jane said.

Deputy Simms could feel the tension and see the fear in her face as she looked in at the bed. "Fair's not the question," he said.

Deputy Woodside stepped close to Sarah Jane. "You know this guy, Tom Hixson?"

"Is he the Tom you told me about?" asked Deputy Simms.

Nurse Bullock spread her arms and motioned them forward to shoo everyone out the door. "Leave this boy be. He lost a lot of blood. No tellin' how long it took before Charlie brought him in here."

"Soon's I could," said Charlie stepping out of his corner.

"Well, not soon enough," Nurse Bullock snapped. "Looks like someone left him out the better part of overnight."

"That's the first I heard of it," said Charlie. "And I brought him here."

Nurse Bullock stood with her hands balled into fists on her hips. All four visitors waited. She glared at Charlie and said, "We'll take care of him."

"Good to hear, Nurse Bullock," said Deputy Simms. "For the boy's sake and for ours. We don't want no murder to deal with."

The deputy could feel Nurse Bullock appraise him, the neighborhood boy, for a moment but she ignored his comment. "You'll deal with what God gives you." She pulled the door closed behind them.

Deputy Simms took Sarah Jane by the elbow and held her back in the doorway until McCormick and Woodside reached the bottom. Before he guided her down the steps, he said, "Your ma's included in that, too."

"What's that supposed to mean?" asked Sarah Jane.

"You think he's a prize. Maybe. I ain't met him, but I'm doubting." He dropped her elbow. "Ma Carruth don't deserve to have her daughter involved with no murderer."

"She approves," said Sarah Jane. "She loves Tom and she'll love her grandson."

Mark Willford suddenly had two questions, but one far outweighed the other. He grabbed Sarah Jane's elbow again and pulled her into the street with him. "You start a baby coming?"

Sarah Jane twisted her head over her shoulder and gave him a defiant look. "We're working on it."

"Jesus, girl, if Ma Carruth approves, which I doubt, marry him first." He took off his hat, and his face reddened up. He put his hat back on again. "How long you known him, anyway?" With the words barely out of his mouth, he held up his hand. He didn't want her to answer that.

"Gotcha goin'," said Sarah Jane, and she laughed.

"Best if you did," said Deputy Simms. "Don't you go gettin' a baby goin'. Don't you even go gettin' started with him. I don't know Hixson, but I am gonna find out for honest what Ma Carruth thinks. I don't know why that boy in there is shot, but he is. That don't sound like a good start for your top hand. We're gonna show up with him down at the new county courthouse before you and him show up down there. You best don't start with him at all."

Chapter 4

"Willf!"

Deputy Simms paused before he put his foot in the stirrup to climb on his loaner horse for the trip out to the McCormick ranch. He looked across the saddle. His friend from grade school, Lon Crittenden, ran from the jailhouse steps, long legs and long arms flying in his black suit. When he stopped, he leaned in close to inspect the new deputy sheriff's badge. With a step back, he grinned and saluted.

"Lon," said Deputy Simms, "I thought you was down at the university."

"Well, I am, sort of."

"Why you back here?"

Lon opened his arms in a grand gesture to encompass all the town. "I came to watch you takin' on the job of protecting us good folk."

Mark Willford had seen Lon Crittenden half a dozen times since leaving school to work the silver freight, enough to count him a friend, not enough to believe this story. "Crittenden, not an hour ago, I took an oath to arrest people who don't tell the truth."

"You'll be busy in this town," said Crittenden, drawn out slow, voice and pace the same from word to word. He fingered the shirt Simms wore. "Present from your special girl?"

"As a matter of fact," said Deputy Simms. "Now, why are you here?"

"I had a pretty big decision to make," Lon said. "I rode up here to talk it over with Dad. I figured I could miss a class or two to talk to him."

Confidence wore well on Lon. Most people who tried to look confident came across like a skin filled with air in danger of bursting. Lon Crittenden filled up his tall space, a mighty thin one, with the weighty matters of his life.

Deputy Simms could think of only one thing Lon's words might mean. He reached again for Lon's hand. "My god, you're fixin' to get married."

Lon pushed the outstretched hand away with a laugh. "No. Not it at all. I don't go around much. Not much time for that."

Deputy Simms waited. What Lon wanted him to hear, he would be told.

"Truth is," said Lon, "my pa's a banker."

"I know," said Deputy Simms. "Mother told me of an offer he made to help my father when they arrested him."

"He might have," said Lon. "Never mentioned it to me, but that's his way. Anyway, he wants me to join him. I don't want to be a banker. I want to be a doctor."

A foreign language, the language of wanting to do something different from what his father did. In each of the five years since that New Year's Day of the new century when his father told him to trade school for work, not once, never, did the sheriff say a word about his son becoming a deputy. Mark Willford breathed in that Sheriff Simms wanted his son to be a deputy and, someday, a sheriff. That suited fine. All Mark Willford wanted to do, forever, was what his father did.

"Hey, Crittenden," said Woodside, nudging his horse over to them, "I heard what you said. We could use you right now, there's a shot boy up there above the Mercantile in bad shape. If you want to go up to offer your help to Nurse Bullock, I'd be obliged while we go out to McCormick's land."

"Not a chance," said Lon. "I might could survive my dad, but not her." Lon touched his right index finger to an imaginary hat and stepped back into the street.

Deputy Woodside leaned over and handed the reins to Deputy Simms. "Here, you take the boy's horse down to Seth Parker's livery. I'll take McCormick and we'll meet you up at the north end of Main Street."

Returning from the livery, Deputy Simms noticed the blue roan at his grandfather's jail. He thought for a moment. The urgency lay in that bed above the Merc. A few more minutes before he met Woodside to go to McCormick's ranch wouldn't make any difference. He hitched his loaner horse and walked into the jail. His father sat at his desk, hands around his coffee mug.

Deputy Simms nodded toward the mug, "I just saw Clive. Did he make that coffee?"

"You know, I miss Clive," said Sheriff Simms. "He didn't drink coffee, and couldn't make it, but at least he made it hot and reliable."

"Miss him? He still brings breakfast from Frances, and he still makes coffee for you, first thing," said Deputy Simms.

The sheriff held up the mug. "Cold. Not that it's your fault." The deputy shrugged. The sheriff asked, "What'd you find out?"

"Like Charlie said, they shot the kid."

"He said a new hand shot him. Thomas L. Hixson. Bad blood?" asked the sheriff.

"Dunno. Charlie said he found him early this morning," said the deputy. "All we know."

"Uh-huh." Sheriff Simms dropped his chin to his chest and thought for a moment. "Well, this isn't the first time Charlie's told us what's going on. I'll believe him." He walked over to the stove and poured the coffee back in the pot. "It's what he never told us that led to all this."

His mother had taught Deputy Simms that his grandfather established justice in this empty wilderness and his father fought for justice. She never mentioned his father's courage had made his birth possible. His father never mentioned he had not solved the mystery hanging over his grandfather's murder. "You mean the money?"

"Yeah," said Sheriff Simms. "Charlie's smart, and he works it. He persuaded his boy to give up, and like he predicted, the territory let Lester out in four years. They lived up there on Porcupine Mountain in that cabin Charlie built. Going about their business. They kept that up for a year longer than Lester's parole, nine years."

Sheriff Simms hefted the pot and poured a little coffee into his mug. He sipped it. "Ah, better." He filled his mug and took it back to his desk. The sheriff took another sip and shook his head. "No way Charlie could plan this, but a year after Lester's parole ended, the powers back in Washington figured we had all changed our behavior enough—Americanized was the popular phrase—they could let Utah become a state. He figured to sit out that year to be safe, then the McCormicks could start acting different."

The sheriff stopped and looked up into the ceiling beams. He brought his gaze back down to his son and deputy. "Come to think of it, Charlie might have seen all that coming. He knew they couldn't take any risks with Lester on parole. We had it bad down there at the penitentiary in Sugar House the year they paroled Lester, same month you were born, but everybody knew we were headed for statehood."

Mark Willford's father rarely talked to him except to tell him what to do. The deputy bobbed his head to encourage the sheriff to continue.

"He knew." The sheriff drew the words out as he rocked his shoulders back and forth with each nod of his head. "He knew.

The railroad and the mines and all the ways to make money out here made everybody start to believe life in the mainstream had its advantages. Keeping the faith is all well and good, but everybody knew the government couldn't treat a state the way they treated a territory. Everybody wanted statehood to start making some money. After that, nobody noticed when Lester started buying land.

"Charlie always looked out for his son. He stopped by the day he traveled to Sugar House to pick up Lester. You know why?"

Mark Willford shook his head.

Sheriff Simms smiled. "He never said it, but he wanted to make sure there were no hard feelings, to leave his son alone. From that day, until after they started buying land, I never saw him again, a solid eight years, maybe nine. Those two never strayed off Porcupine Mountain."

"Pa, don't you think that was mighty cheeky? His son's robbery caused Grandpa's killing."

Sheriff Simms shook his head and took a moment or two before answering. "To us, maybe. But you're not a father yet. He looked at the facts through his eyes, a lens ground to protect his son, so to speak. Charlie wasn't around when Lester's gang robbed Bromley's express up in Echo and that includes when we caught the three of them up to his cabin. If I'd a asked him, he'd've told me he wasn't so bothered when we caught Lester.

"But when they broke Lester out and Hopt shot my father, he wasn't having any part of that. Charlie set it up with Rabbi Slonik so I could go out there and bring Lester in. He even waited out in the field for me and offered me coffee. Making the best of a bad thing, he never thought it cheeky. He didn't see anything better to do."

"D'ya ever think he mighta been behind it all?" asked Deputy Simms. "The land they bought is up in Pine Meadows. I never been to either one, but it must be a lot better than Charlie's on Porcupine Mountain."

"And more of it," said Sheriff Simms. "That land goes all the way up into Wyoming. But Charlie wasn't behind the robbery. Hopt took that idea to Elsemore. They needed Lester." The sheriff paused, leaned forward in his chair, "Now, there's a lesson, boy. Lester was smart enough to pull it off," the sheriff paused again, "and dumb enough to do it. No, Charlie didn't have anything to do with the robbery, but when he saw his son had to go to jail, he undoubtedly asked him if he knew where the money was."

"So, back then, did you think he knew where it was, all along?"

"Not Charlie. Truth is, I never even thought about what you just made me think. Charlie only wanted to know that his son knew. He didn't want to know. 'Course all along Lester said Hopt took the money and hid it. Hopt said he didn't, but if he did, it was more than just stubborn. He was perverse enough to take the secret with him. Either way, Lester's built up quite a ranch. Enoch Pike told me they've laid hold of a square mile, some all the way down south of Wahsatch, beyond the ranch house where they shot the boy."

"Don't Charlie hightailing it in here tell us Lester did it?" asked Deputy Simms.

"He says Hixson," said the sheriff. "Once again, like I said, I'll believe him. He didn't want that boy to die on their property." A pause with a dip of the head across the street. "Or above the Merc for that matter."

"We'll find out," said Deputy Simms.

"That you will," said Sheriff Simms, and he smiled.

The deputy looked a second time to convince himself he saw a smile. He had no idea what to expect. He hesitated, then asked, "What do you mean?"

"You're a deputy. It's your job to find out. Consider this your case," said Sheriff Simms. "Woodside can handle it. He's been a deputy since exactly your age, hired by your grandfather, like me. You can tag along, but that ain't no way to work. Think of it as your case. You don't need to tell anyone you're in charge."

Chapter 5

Deputy Simms rubbed the nose of his loaner horse before climbing into the saddle. This loaner brought him closer to having his own horse than ever. For now, his horse, even if he didn't own it. Mark Willford could ride well enough to compete in the Pioneer Days rodeo, but they weren't his horses. It was a she, and he could not keep calling her a loaner. Seth Parker had called her "Number Two." So, Two she would be.

Swinging his leg over Two's back, Deputy Simms told himself he would ride better if he'd grown up on a ranch or even a farm instead of in town. Not counting the rodeoing, Deputy Simms could count on one hand the number of times he had ridden a horse. Staying atop a bucking horse in the rodeo didn't count for more than sport, like playing on the town baseball team. He commenced up Main Street. It felt all right. He promised himself to practice at night in the foothills above the cemetery. *Don't make promises you can't keep.* It wouldn't be possible. And right now, he had to connect with Woodside and McCormick to ride out to McCormick's ranch. Winning a ribbon in the rodeo wouldn't keep those two older men from seeing he had no skill as a horseman.

He had left the senior deputy at the Merc with the boy. Seeing no horse in front, he continued Two at a walk past the Mercantile, continuing all the way to the ledges at the north end of town, looking for him. Damn, he had lost track of Woodside.

"Bang, you're dead."

The voice startled Simms. Sitting in his saddle, he had found Woodside. More the other way around.

"I was always good at that game," chuckled Deputy Woodside. "We played it all the time up in these ledges as kids. Evidently you didn't play it."

"Didn't play many games as a kid," said Deputy Simms.

Woodside smiled. "You might say it shows."

"Could do," said Deputy Simms. "You've known my pa longer'n I have, he ever teach you any games?"

Woodside smiled again. "Seriously, Deputy, you'll want to take better care not to let anybody sneak up behind you."

Deputy Simms picked through a swirl of thoughts before he spoke. Best to leave them all unsaid and leave it simple. "Thank you, Vernon. Keep it up. I'm gonna need to learn everything I can from you."

Deputy Woodside laughed aloud and clicked his tongue to start his horse forward. "I been training a Sheriff Simms since the first one hired me at eighteen."

"Say?" asked Deputy Simms. "Where's McCormick? Ain't he ridin' with us?"

"Since he had the wagon in town, said he had things to buy. We can find it without him."

The deputies set a good pace to Lester McCormick's ranch. They rode in silence out the north end of town, up the valley with the river on the left and the low, rising foothills on the right. At the railroad crossing above Echo, Deputy Simms stopped to look up and down the line.

"You know," he said, "I came up here before, first with my pa and then alone, on the silver freight. Always seemed like somebody'd be killed at this crossing."

"Somebody was," said Deputy Woodside. "Heber Wells and his wife and two daughters. Left an eight-year-old boy at home looking after five kids. Before you were born. Sheriff Simms did the best he could to investigate it, but he had his own problems. Even so, they promised to put up the light."

Deputy Simms looked at the dark light on his right before they crossed the track. "Even if it works, might not be enough."

After crossing and continuing parallel to the tracks to Wahsatch, they veered more north toward Park Meadows. The tracks headed east toward Wyoming.

"What d'ya expect we'll find out there?" asked Deputy Simms.

"Dunno," said Woodside. "Charlie made it to town about eight and it must've taken him a good two hours to make it. Coulda happened early this morning."

"Maybe last night," said Deputy Simms. "Nurse Bullock said he had lost a lot of blood."

The deputies continued with long silences interrupted by short questions that created small puffs of fog in the cold mountain air.

"Think he looked like he could handle a gun?"

"The boy? A long gun, maybe."

The deputies continued at a pace calculated as best they could to preserve their horses and cover the distance.

"They tell you his name?"

"Nope."

Another mile.

"What call did he have to be out here?"

"No telling."

A few more steps in silence.

"No, that's not exactly right. There's been some rustling."

"He don't look like a range policeman."

"That boy doesn't look like any kind of policeman," said Woodside.

After another hour, Deputy Simms noticed the land begin to

lose all trace of plant life, even sagebrush, and the ground took on the steady, light brown color of the stone and the sand it created. He had not been this far outside Coalville before. One look at this changing landscape, and the brown land brought a question to mind. Just how do you make a ranch pay?

"Think he's living off the money he stole?" asked Deputy Simms.

"To buy the land," said Deputy Woodside. "Maybe not day-to-day."

"All of it," said Deputy Simms. He waved his hand at the great expanse of brown land. "First, you have to have enough to buy it. Then, you have to make enough to keep it going. Make it pay. Think he does?"

"I think he dug it up," said Deputy Woodside.

Deputy Simms turned a quizzical look on Woodside.

Expressionless, Deputy Woodside said, "Thirteen years after he stole it."

Deputy Simms nodded. "How much'd he need to buy a square mile?"

"It'd take a bite out of twenty thousand dollars."

Continuing side by side in silence, both spotted a double-wide opening in the middle of a few lengths of post. Rail extended a few feet on either side and angled into the dirt, not exactly a fence and no barbed wire. Two rough-hewn poles rose high up to a lintel that bore McCormick's brand. The arrangement announced the entry to McCormick's ranch.

They passed under the high lintel and stopped. Deputy Simms surveyed the half mile to the front door and asked, "Do you think Charlie McCormick's behind all this?"

"Not particularly," said Woodside. "You can trust him to make the best out of whatever hand he's dealt, but he don't create these messes. He flat out gave his son to your father. I heard him say, 'Best he faces twelve years for robbery than the firing squad for murder. He'll be out in four.' And, by God, he was. Lester spent Christmas with Charlie, out on parole, but two months after you was born. Charlie aimed to keep him out. He did not let him go near that money. Wherever they hid it, it stayed hid. By the time Lester's parole ended, everybody knew statehood had been all scheduled to come the very next month. He made Lester wait another year before he let him dig up the money."

"That's what my pa said."

"Testin' me, huh?" said Deputy Woodside. "Well, Sheriff Simms and I mighta talked about it some." Deputy Woodside nudged his horse to start walking toward the ranch house. "What's for sure, it's no coincidence Lester started buying land in ninety-seven. It fits right in with their story. When you ask Lester, he'll say he worked hard for ten years to save up enough to start buying."

Deputy Simms let his eyes follow this great expanse of brown land all the way to the ranch house. "Then I'm guessing you think Charlie had no hand in shooting this kid?"

"Not a chance." Woodside repeated. "No hand." He shook his head. "Same as he did in eighty-three. When they shot that kid, Charlie tried to make the best of a bad situation."

Chapter 6

Deputy Simms fell back into his thoughts and counted Deputy Woodside's silence to mean the same. They rode the half mile from the gate to the front door. Deputy Simms tried to figure any way he could believe this ranch to be an honest operation. He calculated Lester at about thirty-two, most thirty-three, when Woodside said he started buying the land. That included the better part of ten years Lester spent working his father's barren desert land on Porcupine Mountain. Mark Willford started working at the turn of the new century, five years straight. He'd saved some, but no way Lester could save enough from a workingman's wages to buy all that land. Once he had the land, he'd have to have money to work it. Into the bargain, rumor had it the McCormicks owned one of the largest herds in the state. Deputy Simms had never thought about ranching. Except for earning his pay with hard work, Mark Willford had never thought of how you go about making money before today. Now a deputy, the shooting that brought him out here made it his job to think about it. A forthright review of all he should know reminded him of his inexperience. He doubted he had tracked down all the questions. The ones he had come up with about making money seemed obvious. Why would anyone be dumb enough to shoot that Deseret Land and Cattle boy seemed even more obvious.

Woodside's voice broke into Mark Willford's thoughts. "Don't ask him where he hid that express money."

Deputy Simms stuck his tongue out the side of his mouth to make a silly face. A prudent caution, and Deputy Woodside's age bestowed wisdom, but Simms counted he could figure that out for himself.

They had drawn near enough to be seen by anyone looking out the front door. Deputy Simms kept an eye on it as he drew close to Deputy Woodside. "Who owns that money?"

"I'd guess Wells Fargo," answered Woodside, "but they stopped looking for it about the time we buried Sheriff Simms."

"You mean they stopped looking a week after the robbery?"

"Sounds about right," said Woodside. "That's a bank. They're dealing with somebody else's money. Your father never stopped looking for it."

"Does the sheriff's office still have an obligation to find the money?"

"Dunno," said Deputy Woodside. "Remember, that money put his father in the ground."

"Sheriff," hailed Lester McCormick from his porch.

Deputy Simms looked up at the late afternoon sun. Even if he had grown up in town and not on a ranch, he had worked a lot of years in his life. At this time of day, a workingman ought to be working, not standing on his porch.

"Deputy," Deputy Simms said. "Sheriff Simms is at the jail."

"Congratulations," said Lester McCormick.

"Lester," said Deputy Woodside, "your pa here?"

"Nah," said McCormick. "Workday. He comes sometimes on weekends."

Deputy Simms had not expected Charlie McCormick to be there. He had been at the ranch that morning and in town when they left. Woodside's question had surprised the deputy but now it made sense. He stepped down from Two and tied her to the post, all the while looking around. Not much of a yard, not much in it, either. He looked up at McCormick. "We thought you mighta had company. It's a little early to be done work."

"No company," said McCormick. "I quit when I saw you coming . . . To be hospitable."

"Uh-huh," said Deputy Simms, noting McCormick's blue shirt and brown pants. He continued to take in the surroundings. No surprise, the house looked bigger than the little yellow house he lived in with his mother. The barn looked bigger than the one Sam had built for Ma Carruth. Simms also saw a stable and another building, maybe a bunkhouse. "No need to knock off work on account of us. Looks like this spread takes a lot of work."

"It does."

"We didn't really come to see you," said Woodside. He nodded his head toward the possible bunkhouse. "We came to see your help."

"Which one?" asked McCormick.

"How many are there?" asked Deputy Simms.

"Couple o' men," said McCormick.

"Uh-huh," said Woodside. He shrugged his disbelief.

"And maybe a couple o' more out," said McCormick.

"How many all told?" asked Simms.

McCormick made something of a production, even counting on his fingers. "Five."

"Bigger than your old gang," said Woodside.

"Ahhh," said McCormick, drawing out the word in a long breath, "days long since gone." He gave a relaxed little laugh. "You know that because you helped put an end to 'em."

Deputy Simms found himself agreeing with the implied meaning. This man looked more like one of the self-assured businessmen he had seen around town than the leader of a gang.

"Elsemore one of your five?" Woodside asked.

"You're right," said McCormick. "Forgot him. Should'na done that. He's been here since ninety-eight. You on his heels for something? He the one you want to see?"

Deputy Simms noticed the misdirection and marked it down as a learning. McCormick knew why they were out there. The deputy said, "The lot o' ya."

Woodside remained in his saddle. He peered down at McCormick and said, "You tell us."

McCormick stood at the edge of the porch, two steps up. Deputy Simms stood in front of the porch on the hard dirt. He had never had the experience of looking up to anyone save his father, and he determined not to move or speak.

"Like I said," chuckled McCormick. "I knocked off early. Want to come in for a cup of coffee? Or do you not partake?"

"Coffee'd be fine," said Woodside.

"Good," said McCormick.

Simms accepted the offer of a chair at the kitchen table. His head was pointed at McCormick, watching him make the coffee, but his eyes roamed. He saw no sign that a woman took care of the place. "Could use a woman's touch," he said.

"Don't Mrs. Elsemore offer much help?" asked Deputy Woodside.

"What's that mean?" asked McCormick, frowning. He took the coffee pot off the stove as it started to percolate.

"A Relief Society lady told me Elsemore's wife has arrived back in town," said Deputy Woodside. "I hear she found her way out here to join her husband."

"Is that why you took better part of a day to come out here?" asked McCormick.

"You know better'n that," said Woodside.

"Can't say as I do," said McCormick, "But as for Elsemore, he's served his time. I told him, if he earns his keep, he can stay. This is a working ranch."

"No extra cash for him to dig up," said Deputy Simms. "So to speak."

McCormick forced a full laugh. He filled two mugs with coffee, gave one to Woodside, and took a seat at the table directly across from Deputy Simms.

"So, you're gonna pick that up," he said. "I told your pa. Hopt took that money to his grave. Your pa put him there. For me, I have no idea where Hopt hid the money. My pa has always been on my case to save money and buy land. He's the one convinced old man Phillips to sell me this land for a note."

"Been making enough on it to pay the note?" asked Woodside.

"Well, for right now, he's just asking interest."

"Eight years?" Deputy Simms could hear the smug note in Woodside's voice. He had a lot to learn. Woodside knew things he did not. He wondered how he would ever learn it all. He heard his father's advice, keep his mouth shut and listen.

"Ten," said Lester.

"And you keep buying up the land around."

"When I can," said Lester. "We're a state. People are optimistic. I might pay a little too much if they'll take a note, but I want to work the land and those people want to have something for all the work they put in pioneering and such."

"With all those note payments," said Woodside, "you make enough to pay five hands?"

"Like I say, they earn their keep."

"Does that include Tom Hixson?" asked Woodside.

Deputy Simms noticed the slightest change in McCormick's eyes, but his answer still flowed out smooth. "He's new. We'll have to see."

"Uh-huh," said Deputy Woodside. "How'd you buy all the cattle? People aren't selling you cattle for paper, that's for sure."

Lester stiffened up.

"You got no call to come out here, asking me these questions." He remained seated at the kitchen table holding the coffee he had not touched, but his voice raised a level. "This is land I bought with money I worked hard to earn and save. I kept my nose clean twenty-two years now and you got no right to hound me."

Deputy Woodside took a sip of his coffee and said, "You said you bought it with notes." He leaned forward, close in on Lester, "And your clean nose led to a boy shot on your property, last night or this morning."

"That's why you're out here," said Lester, at once leaning back and trying to hold his ground. "Well, Charlie took care of that. He'll be all right."

"Charlie took care of it by taking him to the hospital above the Merc," said Woodside. "As for being all right, that don't say why you shot him. And as . . ."

"For rustling cattle," interrupted Lester. "And I didn't shoot him."

"You interrupted me. As for being all right, he ain't doin' too well."

Lester remained silent; his finger crooked through the handle of the mug. He maintained a steady gaze at Woodside. The deputy kept both hands palms down on the pine plank table and returned the gaze. Simms felt the silent tension rise in the room. He let it go another uncomfortable moment, then asked, "Who did?"

McCormick seemed to regain his confidence. "Pa told you already, that new guy."

Deputy Simms thought the response sounded strange. Woodside gave a slight shake of his head. Simms took the sign, said nothing.

"He go by 'the new guy'?" asked Deputy Woodside.

"I meant the one you mentioned. Hixson. Tom Hixson."

"We want to see him," said Deputy Woodside.

"I told you. It's a working ranch. He's working. He won't be in till supper."

Deputy Simms gauged about two hours left till dusk. He judged they would come in before then. "We'll wait."

"Good," said Lester. "Have supper with us. You'll have to take care of yourself for a little while. I got work to do. If you think it's too late to go back after supper, you can stay in the bunkhouse overnight. When you end up out here, there's nothing around for miles . . ."

"Nothing around but your land," interrupted Woodside.

Deputy Simms watched. Lester McCormick continued.

". . . more the reason to be hospitable."

Not an hour later, Charlie McCormick rode the buckboard ahead of another rider through the gate and to the corral in the back of the house. Charlie came in through the kitchen, dressed the same as he had been that morning, in his overalls, not dressed the prosperous businessman like his son. The man behind him, about five-ten and a little soft, wore denims and a checked shirt. He carried a rifle. It looked new or well oiled.

"Tom," said Lester. "These men are here to see you."

The man looked at them, half smirked, and followed that with a nod. "Charlie told me they would be."

"I imagine he did," said Woodside. "We haven't seen him since he told us you shot that Deseret Land and Cattle boy."

Hixson smirked again, said nothing.

"Did you?"

"Saw somebody in our cattle. I figured him for a rustler," said Hixson. He made a decided survey of all four men standing in front of him. "Just doing my job."

Hixson's words and attitude triggered Deputy Simms. He took a careful look. He could not be sure what he saw. He saw no rider in the soft frame. He saw no worker in the hands. For sure, no cowboy looked out of those eyes. Deputy Simms could not even be sure he saw a Westerner. Sarah Jane had been like an older sister to him until he turned twelve. Then something about her made him nervous. For the next three years he didn't feel comfortable being alone with her, then even worse when she turned twenty. This Hixson seemed to fit into the silliness and wildness that had been going on for three years now. Deputy Simms couldn't tell how much older Hixson looked, not much. He might have been younger than Sarah Jane. He wondered how Hixson came to show up at the McCormick ranch. More, he couldn't figure how Hixson came to show up in Sarah Jane's life. He knew about the Wyoming Livestock Association from his father's Uncle Frank up in Rock Springs, but he doubted Hixson had come down from Wyoming. He didn't look like a killer. He looked like a sneak.

Rustling had been a problem since his father became deputy in 1862. His grandfather had dealt with it also, as Territorial Governor Alfred Cumming had reported "the northern part of the territory is infested by bands of cattle thieves." In fact, the robbery of Bromley's express station that led to his grandfather's murder amounted to a routine, petty theft by three young punks compared to the Indian troubles, vigilantes, and cattle rustlers that consumed the sheriff's time.

Serious though rustling may be, that a boy from Deseret Land and Cattle came up to Park Meadows to rustle didn't ring true. Mark Willford knew nothing about how a big, church-sponsored company operated, but before he became deputy, his sense of adventure and his rodeoing had led him to study up on rustling.

Cattle rustling amounted to a complicated business. It took brains and men and cunning. Rebranding the cattle or altering the existing brand so it would not be recognized took more skill than picking up mavericks and branding them with a running iron. Better still, being patient proved the best strategy. A man with plenty of open range could build up a herd of cow-calf pairs without worrying too much about rebranding. Driving them out of Utah or even to the nearest railroad siding provided plenty of opportunities to sell cattle. A big enough operation could avoid altogether the risk, the work, and the loss of weight on the hoof of driving cattle if they set up to sell slaughtered and quartered beef to the public. Between cow-calf pairs and a slaughterhouse, a lot of cattle, branded or not, could go misplaced without a trace.

That didn't sound like work for one boy out in a herd. In fact, it sounded more like a ranch on the shady side out to build a herd.

That thought brought Simms's rolling mind to a complete stop. He had gone about all this learning by doing the chores around two houses, not a ranch, and reading about cowboys. All of them, like Butch Cassidy, lived in other counties and they seemed to work their way up from cattle rustling to robbery. He knew about Robbers Roost, and he had read all about that Castle Gate payroll robbery.

Deputy Simms calculated the $7,000 Butch Cassidy took in that payroll job amounted to what McCormick turned each year on his ranch. Mark Willford had been good at arithmetic before he stopped school, and if the deputy had his numbers right, eighty butchered and sold cattle would bring more than that payroll job.

Cattlemen rode right over meaningless acts of the legislature by creating livestock associations and offering rewards for the capture of rustlers. Those damn rewards brought out a bunch of people who knew how to shoot a rifle better than they knew how to use their heads. Worse still, shooting a rustler proved a better defense for murder than self-defense.

Deputy Simms felt good about making sense of all this, except he didn't know what the Deseret Land and Cattle boy was doing in their cattle. He couldn't shake his conclusion that Thomas Hixson didn't look like a gunfighter. He wondered what Woodside thought.

Deputy Simms had leaned his rifle against the wall when he entered the ranch house. When Tom Hixson came through the door, like the deputy he wore no pistol, but he did not set aside his rifle. He carried it to the table, sat down, and rested it between his legs, butt touching his right boot, the barrel rising under his left arm. He helped himself to the food.

"Do you always bring your rifle to the table?" asked Deputy Simms.

"When I need to," said Tom Hixson.

Deputy Simms fought back his annoyance and listened hard for an accent that might tell him where they came from and how long ago. He heard too few words to tell. He asked, "And why do you need to today?"

"My job around here is to keep the varmints down," said Hixson. "I shot one this morning. Could be that's the reason you're here."

"Glad we're not one of your varmints," said Deputy Woodside.

With that, Hixson raised the rifle from between his legs to lay it on the table. Deputy Simms watched. The barrel faced straight across the table, but he knew it could be readily rotated. He looked at Woodside, not sure what he hoped to see. The deputy smiled, maybe at his own joke, picked up his fork with his left hand, and started to eat. Deputy Simms couldn't see his right hand.

Charlie McCormick ate at a leisurely pace. "So, the sheriff sent you out here to check on our new hand?" asked McCormick.

"Seein's you told us he shot that boy," said Woodside. He nodded toward the rifle on the table. "What's he have to do with your cattle business?"

"Nothing," said Lester.

"Well," hastily corrected Charlie, "nothing except like he said, to keep the varmints down. We're livin' hand-to-mouth, and we been raising cattle this way since the 1870s. Leastwise I have, and Lester can't afford to lose any now he's started."

"You never supported five head of cattle on that scraggly homestead on Porcupine Mountain," said Woodside. He reached for the bowl of potatoes with his left hand and speared two with a fork. "And you know it."

"I did better'n that," laughed Charlie McCormick. "True, I thought my boy could go me one better if he looked for land up here in the grassy pastures."

"Pa's right," bristled Lester McCormick. "Lots of natural grass. We almost never need to feed them hay."

"Tell me how you make all this work," said Deputy Simms.

"No different from anywhere else," shrugged McCormick. He lifted his knife and started cutting his beef, as casual as could be. "Calves are born in spring and we send them out to pasture with their mothers 'til fall. In the fall, we sell the steers and the smaller heifers to feedlots for cash before winter sets in. We keep the best heifers for breeders to replace the cull cows, and we use the cash to live on."

Simms looked down to the end of the table, expecting to see McCormick's father guide his son in this conversation.

"Is that what Charlie told you to say?" asked Deputy Woodside.

"No," laughed Lester. "It's what Charlie told me to do."

"I didn't see you at the auction last year," said Woodside.

"It depends. If the price ain't right, we graze 'em out," said McCormick. "We rotate the cattle through the pastures. Then, whenever we sell one, we sell them one at a time."

"Perfect way to sell branded cattle."

"All we ever sell." Lester gave a smile.

"I meant someone else's brand."

"Deputy, I know there's no love lost for me because there's a history, but like I said you got no call to talk like that. I even joined the Summit County Livestock Association." Lester leaned out across the table, earnest now, no smile. "You know they're working a program to keep from stealing cows. You go over there and check with the Hazenauer farm in Kamas and the Compass ranch in Coalville, you'll see we're working together on this rustling problem."

"That's why we hired Tom, here," said Charlie McCormick.

"Fox guarding the henhouse," said Deputy Simms.

"What's that you say," asked McCormick. "I didn't hear you."

Deputy Simms felt hesitant. Maybe he should mention he was new on the job before putting his opinion out there. He heard his father's words, *You're a deputy now, aren't you?* He said, "Cattlemen want bigger herds. Rustlers want bigger herds. That don't make for much distinction when shooting starts."

Charlie McCormick nodded in agreement and spread his arms to encompass both sides of the table. "That probably explains that Deseret Land and Cattle boy's accident."

"He was rustling," said Tom Hixson. He reached his right hand out to the grip of the stock. "He was in our herd, cutting them out. My job was to stop him. I did."

Hixson's words told Deputy Simms what had happened. He knew he couldn't prove it. Hixson also knew, same as him. Simms eyed the hand on the grip. Hixson could rotate the barrel to point at his stomach. He kept an eye on Hixson's hands and said, "Or he inspected the brands. It takes skill to change a brand. He coulda been inspecting your herd for his brand."

"No chance," said Lester McCormick.

"He cut them out," said Hixson.

"I can see how you might say that," said Charlie. "More likely, nothing but a misunderstanding. Tom here's a bit of an artist and a little jumpy. He made a mistake. True, the boy mighta been inspecting our herd. There's an auction coming up. He wanted a leg up on the quality. We sell them a lot of cattle."

Deputy Simms watched Lester and Hixson relax under Charlie's clever words. He chuckled and said, "Easy enough. We best go out and look for ourselves."

"Can't do that," said Lester.

Charlie jumped in. "Nobody's stopping you, mind you, but what Lester means is we put the herd out on the open range today. You're free to stay over tonight and go out tomorrow. 'Course you'll be doing a lot of riding to see them one at a time." He looked from Deputy Simms to Deputy Woodside and added, "Or you can come back next week. We'll have most of 'em rounded up for the auction."

Lester McCormick said, "We like to do our own butchering."

He appeared to answer a question not asked. Deputy Simms saw Charlie McCormick glare daggers at his son.

"A whole beef will weigh out at six hundred pounds," continued Lester, "and we'll charge fifteen cents a pound hanging weight. Butchering beats the lousy prices we're getting on the hoof. Of course, our price includes everything, butchering, cutting, and wrapping, for whatever you want, a quarter or a half, even a whole beef."

"Nobody sees the brand that way," said Woodside.

"You know it's illegal to sell unbranded animals," said Lester McCormick. "I was a big supporter of that legislation."

"Sure you were," said Deputy Woodside. "Seein's you sat in the territorial prison at the time."

"You know what I mean," said Lester. "I believe in it. I told you I joined the livestock association. I support everything they do, but it's still a lot more profitable to butcher 'em. I looked into Herefords. They're popular out here, but in today's market, a Hereford steer don't bring but around five-six cents a pound. Lucky, I decided on Angus."

"Where'd your original stock come from in the first place?" asked Deputy Simms.

"Like everything good in my life," said Lester. "My pa. He built up a herd by trading with the emigrants. They're from Scotland, you know. Lot of our people are, too. He could always trade one of his strong cattle for two, sometimes three, of those trail-weary stock. He's the one told me to buy the Angus bull. You want to see the papers from my bull?"

Woodside raised his head and with a sociable air asked, "You know Enos Mendenhall?"

"No," said Lester.

"Sure we do," said Charlie. "He's the head of the Mormon co-op. An old friend."

"I wonder if they ever come up short after their summer count?" mused Woodside to no one in particular. "I'll remember to ask him next time I'm out at the co-op."

A silence ensued, some eating, some sitting, until Woodside spoke up again, "I still say you never had more than five head. Where'd you sell your beef?"

"When he had some to sell," said Lester as cool as if he and his father had practiced the answer, "he sold beef over to Park City and Alta. Miners don't grow much beef, so there's always a ready market, and a little bit of work carting it up there never bothered Pa. These days mostly he sells to the railroad."

"He selling his cattle? Or your cattle?" asked Woodside.

"Different brands," said Lester. "And I told you, I like to sell my cattle dressed."

"Not many folks can come all the way up here to get a quarter beef," said Deputy Simms.

"I take some down to Echo," McCormick waved his hand to downplay Simms's comment. "From time to time."

"Do you sell to the passenger trains down there?" asked Simms.

"You know better than that, Deputy. I'd have to sell to Big Man Anderson or go all the way to Ogden."

Deputy Simms didn't know better than that, and the answer told him to investigate it. "Sounds like it's all figured. True, you'd be closer to Evanston."

McCormick smiled.

Deputy Simms calculated silently in his head. "It still makes for a hardscrabble life."

"I never said we made any money," said Lester.

"We?" repeated Deputy Simms.

"I include my pa in everything I do."

"I guess I'll have to sit down with a pencil," Deputy Simms said. Not a deputy twelve full hours yet, he knew Lester McCormick used the money he had stolen from the express office in 1883 to buy and run the ranch. He knew Lester ran rustled cattle. And he knew Charlie enjoyed this chess game, his son the king and everyone else a pawn. "We came here to find out why Hixson shot that boy. Something doesn't work out right," Simms said.

Deputy Woodside pushed his chair back and stood up from the table. Tom Hixson jumped the moment Woodside moved. Woodside's hand went to his holstered pistol. Charlie McCormick's hand came down on top of Hixson's rifle before he could lift it off the table.

"Day's done, Tom," Charlie said. "Sit a spell."

Chapter 7

Woodside looked at Charlie and Tom and around the table. He held steady a moment, then looked out the window. "It's comin' on dark outside." The words carried over his shoulder. "That offer still good?"

Charlie continued to rest his hand on top of Hixson's rifle.

"Sure," said Lester. "After a good breakfast, we'll go out to look at our cattle."

"I'll go with you," said Charlie. "Everyone else has work to do." He folded his hand around the rifle and picked it up. He stood up and stepped close to Woodside. " 'Course, you'll spend all day to see one beef, maybe two. You'd do a lot better to come next week when we have them all rounded up."

Deputy Simms had learned a lot about Charlie McCormick that day from his father and Woodside. He figured he knew why Charlie held that rifle in his hand, *making the best of a bad situation.* He felt better with Charlie in control of it, but he still wished he had a pistol. He thought Charlie's suggestion made sense, but why had they rounded up the cattle once already and dispersed them again after the Desert Land and Cattle boy found his way into the herd and they shot him. That's didn't make sense to him.

He stood up, looked around the table, and stepped to the end next to Woodside. He leaned in, with his back to Charlie McCormick, and whispered in Woodside's ear. "I need to see

Trueman. I'd as soon talk to him and that boy first thing in the morning."

Woodside gave no hint that he'd heard. He spoke over the deputy's shoulder to Charlie. "Seein's we're up here to investigate you shootin' that boy, not your cattle rustling that brought him here, I'll take your suggestion. With a good hour before dark and comin' on to a full moon, we'll be going down tonight."

"Fine by me," said Charlie. "But I didn't shoot that boy. Hixson did."

"That why you're holding his gun?" asked Deputy Simms, knowing full well the answer to his question.

Charlie nodded, smiled, and spoke with a tone of sharing confidences. "In a sense, it is. I told Sheriff Simms this morning Tom's jumpy. I don't aim to have no accidents in my house."

"Your house, huh?" Deputy Simms regretted his exclamation the moment it came out his lips. Charlie's comment may have been a simple figure of speech. And maybe a slip of the tongue that told them something until then denied. The deputy felt foolish for letting them know he had noticed.

Charlie didn't want them anywhere near the cattle today. He recalled what both the sheriff and Deputy Woodside had told him, and what he thought he'd learned. Charlie made do with what he had. Deputy Simms began to understand. At times that worked better than bending the world to his will.

Simms picked up the county's rifle from next to the front door. He carried it outside and shoved it down the sleeve of the scabbard on Two. Woodside joined him. The deputies rode through the posts and lintel gate before either spoke. "You know, I never finished the seventh grade. Ma taught me at home every day since I quit to start working."

"You didn't miss much," said Woodside. "She was the only schoolteacher in town some of those years."

"Hadn't thought of that," said Simms, nodding. "She taught me about Cache Valley up in the north end of the state. You can stash twenty-thousand dollars in a cache."

"Clever," chuckled Woodside. "I see. A stash of cash. Buried it or cached it in a cave, he woulda had to do it before Sheriff Simms thumped him. I asked him in the prison. Maybe he told the truth. Maybe Hopt took that money to his grave."

The harder he concentrated the more Two slowed her pace and Woodside carried on ahead of him. Deputy Simms called, "I don't believe Hopt ever knew where it was. Why did he stick around if he could put his hands on the money and leave the other two behind?"

"Not much of a surprise to think McCormick hid the money." Woodside made no effort to slow down or turn around to talk to his junior deputy. Abruptly he stopped and looked up in the sky and asked, "Really think this is a good idea?"

"Why not? Look, the moon's already up." Deputy Simms pointed over their shoulders. "And the sun's not even set." He waved his hand toward the blanket of gold turning to silver on the sagebrush-covered land. "It's a full moon tonight. We'll have plenty of light to see."

Woodside nodded. "Ain't the light concerns me. We asked these horses to go out here once already today."

Deputy Simms's sense of urgency overruled the slight feeling of being chastened by the senior deputy. "So, we'll walk 'em. That'll be enough to go see that boy and Trueman at the Merc in the morning."

"Walking all night," said Woodside, shaking his head. "I'm dealing with a Simms."

Simms and Woodside walked their horses side by side down the broad valley shimmering with moonlight. At Wahsatch, Deputy Simms broke the lingering silence. "They rested a couple of hours at the ranch and now we've walked them a couple more; if we can find water at the siding, think they'll be all right?"

"Better'n us, probably," said Woodside, "but you remember, that's how to keep you and your horse alive."

Mounting after the water trough, Deputy Simms said, "Pa once told me his father conducted a good part of the sheriff's business just by thinking. Pa musta thought about that day Hopt and McCormick had before Grandpa caught McCormick, not to mention the time they spent together before Pa caught McCormick the second time."

Woodside stopped and leaned forward in his saddle, holding the pommel with both hands. "Not much time that second time, they were on the move, but you're thinking that second time wouldn'a happened if Hopt had the money. He wouldn'a sprung McCormick and he wouldn'a shot Sheriff Simms if he'da had the money."

"And after Pa caught Hopt, wasn't he in prison with McCormick?"

"We had only the one territorial prison. They were in it the same time for four years, but no telling how much they saw each other, what with McCormick careful about good behavior and Hopt maneuvering his stays and delays and whatever kept him alive until 1887. Your pa and me never thought about McCormick at the time. Hopt wanted to believe he'd beat the whole thing. Charlie never thought Lester'd be in there more than four years. Lester probably told Hopt he'd use the money to hire lawyers to get Hopt off."

"Well, we know he didn't do that," said Deputy Simms.

"Because Lester's parole took until a couple of months after the sheriff finally executed Hopt. Not that Charlie woulda let Lester touch that money, but it coulda worked. Damned near did without the money. In the mid-eighties the judges were federals. They figured if a sheriff had come out here as a

Mormon pioneer, dead was as good a state as they could hope for. They didn't think justice for a dead sheriff amounted to all that important a thing if it meant helping a sheriff who was a polygamist. Truth be told, judges were more sympathetic to murderers."

From the railroad crossing to home, Deputy Simms led the way, his eyes half closed on the route he had driven the silver freight so often. After midnight, he separated from Woodside at the corner of Fifty East and One Hundred North and dismounted. He walked Two into the shed behind the little yellow house. Finishing his first day as a deputy, even at this late hour, brought a thrill matched only by caring for his own horse, even her being a loaner. Next morning, with the resilience of an eighteen-year-old body, he shook off the effects of five hours of sleep and walked with his mother to the Mercantile.

"Young Simms," Mr. Trueman said reaching for a hearty handshake. "The sheriff said you'd be over, not sure when. I thought you was out to Park Meadows lookin' for the guy who shot that boy upstairs."

"Was . . . Am . . ." Deputy Simms stammered a little, not sure of how to answer. "Did . . . Found him. That had something to do with my decision to come here as soon as I could."

"Sensible. The sheriff said to set you up the same way I did for him. That'd be an 1873 Colt Single Action Army Revolver."

"And why's that?" asked the deputy.

"Like I said, it's the same as I set him up with, but the real reason is it's chambered same as your rifle."

Deputy Simms looked at the rifle in his hand and said, "County's."

"Good for you," said Trueman. "Progress. I'm sure he told you he had to buy his."

"No," said Deputy Simms and he chuckled. "I'm a little

surprised he didn't. Speaking of which, how am I going to pay you?"

"Same way," said Trueman. "Two bucks a month until you're paid off."

"I don't even know how much the county's paying me."

"Well, when the county tells you, tell me. We'll work it out."

Mark Willford took the pistol, holster, and belt from Trueman and strapped them on. As he hoisted his rifle to go upstairs, his mother came by.

She looked at him a long moment and asked, "Are you going out to practice?"

"Hadn't thought of it. I was going upstairs to see the boy."

"Well, he'd never tell you, but your father did."

Deputy Simms had only heard about how Deputy Woodside persuaded Sheriff Simms to buy a pistol, but his mother's comment sounded about right. His father would practice until he was good enough. Maybe not the best, but good enough, and he'd never mention it to anyone.

Deputy Simms bent down to kiss her check, "Thanks, Ma."

She reached up and touched his face, her eyes moist for no reason he knew. "Your father was a deputy when the bishop introduced us. I never had much choice in that." She dabbed her eyes. After a moment's pause, she looked up at him. "I never had much choice in you being a deputy, neither."

Deputy Simms enfolded her in his arms. "Oh, Ma, if you're worrying about me, you don't need to."

"Oh, but I do," said his mother. "If you could ask him, I'll bet that boy upstairs told his mother she didn't need to worry."

Deputy Simms pushed his arms out straight, holding his mother, and looked at her. Without the need to ask, he knew what he had been told. He ran to the back door and up the stairs. Tom Hixson's shot had killed that boy. Now the new deputy had a murder to look into.

Chapter 8

Deputy Simms took the steps two at a time and burst through the door to see Sheriff Simms at the foot of the boy's bed and Nurse Bullock at its head. Her hands held the sheet she had pulled to its complete length to cover the boy. Nurse Bullock signaled the deputy's presence to the sheriff with a nod.

The sheriff showed no recognition he had seen her. He made no move before he started to speak. "The sheriff made me a deputy in 1862 right in the middle of the Civil War going on back East. Nobody up here, including him, ever had much of anything to do with that war. Still, the Mormons rounded up a battalion to fight for the Union. It marched all the way down to San Diego. Whatever for is beyond me. Somebody must have pointed them in that direction, but nothing happened. He wanted to join up, but he never did. He pretty much thought it stupid to send young boys off to die like that—like this. Still, that battalion made everyone a Yankee. Where people came from, if not from Europe, they probably were Yankees.

"I'm telling you this because it has to do with a ranch almost as big as the McCormick ranch. If they'd had fences, it might have made all the difference. A young boy was killed who didn't need to be.

"After I caught Hopt, I still had to stay out of the hands of the marshals so I could put Hopt before the firing squad, I heard that a real-live Texas Ranger lived down in Price, Utah. Two things I knew for sure. First, I had a lot to learn. Second, disappearing down to Price made about as good a place as any to stay away from those marshals.

"Straight off, that Texas Ranger, Jack Watson, told me he didn't like no Yankees. It didn't matter none that I wasn't in the battalion. It didn't even matter that my father was English, or that I was English born, too. From the first words out of his mouth, I expected to be sent packing, except Jack Watson took a shine to the thought of a full-grown adult man riding a horse a hundred sixty-five miles across three or maybe four counties, depending on your route, to learn something from him.

"He made it plenty clear to me that he still didn't like Yankees, but—to use his words—since I had rid all that way I could go ahead and ask him some questions.

"He either felt like a hero or he liked me, but they were making up a posse to go after Joe Walker, a boy who thought he'd been wronged by his uncle, a man name of Whittemore. Walker claimed Whittemore took what was rightfully his, his ranch, so he'd been launching raids on it. The sheriff and his deputy were going to put a stop to it. With a posse of nine, Jack Watson invited me, and I made ten.

"It turns out Joe had happened upon a passing cowboy and invited him to camp for the night. Hospitable."

Lester McCormick's, "hospitable," from yesterday, gave Deputy Simms a sense of foreboding.

"So, the sheriff or his Texas Ranger deputy, Jack Watson, had some inkling where the camp would be, and in the darkness our posse surrounded it. Everybody assumed Walker's companion was in on it. The posse waited until light broke. When Walker and the cowboy stirred, they let go. A stranger, and not all too sure I had been sworn in as a deputy, I didn't want to create any new problems for that sheriff. So, I watched.

"Lucky, too. That cowboy died along with Walker, and he turned out to be innocent."

Deputy Simms looked at his father staring at the sheet. He asked, "You think this boy is innocent?"

"Of rustling," said Sheriff Simms. The sheriff turned and pointed to the pistol on his deputy's hip. "Trouble is, rustling's a better reason for shooting a man than self-defense. I talked with Charlie. Everyone out there will say this boy was rustling."

"Same songbook," said Deputy Simms. "It don't ring true. They complain about rustling and their herd keeps growing."

"So, what was this boy doing out there?" asked the sheriff.

"I think he was checking brands," said Deputy Simms. "Not rustling, just the opposite. That's why Hixson shot him. That's Hixson's job. Changing brands, not shooting people, I mean."

"Hixson?" repeated the sheriff. "He the same guy who's involved with Sarah Jane?"

"How do you know about that?" asked Deputy Simms.

"Ma Carruth told your mother Sarah Jane has a new beau who works for Lester. You know she's worried about how old Sarah Jane is."

"That's a better worry than what she might have on her hands," said Deputy Simms.

"You say you don't think he's their hired gun?" asked the sheriff. He nodded toward the pistol. "You better make sure you can handle that."

"Don't worry," said Deputy Simms, "he can't handle a rifle better than me, and he won't be able to handle a pistol better neither."

With no indication he doubted his deputy, the sheriff said, "You best make that true."

"I will," said Deputy Simms, "but he's not a hired gun. I think he's their artist. He fixes their brands. It looks like he might do other things for 'em, too, but that ain't right. He shot the boy because of the brands."

CHAPTER 9

April 1906

Deputy Simms opened the door of his half-brother's music store. Sheriff Simms played his organ at James's music store when he wanted to look available and open to all the county yet in truth sought to hide and concentrate. Cooled by the rush of an April breeze around his back on a bright sunny day, the deputy nevertheless hesitated when James waved him into the heated room. He doubted the wisdom of piercing the sheriff's cocoon. He couldn't figure anything else to do. "You'll never guess who's looking for you."

The sheriff looked up at the deputy, his face concentrated on some other thought, perhaps even his continued playing. Deputy Simms winced again at interrupting the sheriff. He knew his father had not carried the organ around on his back to play in public, except for one July 4th, since the day he became sheriff. In fact, James William, the sheriff's second son from his marriage to Elizabeth Jensen, had kept the organ in his store. Since the first Manifesto[1], the sheriff had played his organ down at the music store for his own enjoyment and for the benefit his

1 The "1890 Manifesto" officially advised against any future plural marriage in The Church of Jesus Christ of Latter-day Saints. Issued by church president Wilford Woodruff in September 1890, it paved the way to statehood and stopped the harrowing life of a fugitive forced on Sheriff John Willford Simms.

music and having the organ on display brought to his son's business.

His interruption already a fact, the deputy stepped into the little shop and closed the door to settle back to watch and listen and wait.

"How did you know I was here?" asked the sheriff, his eyes on his keys.

Deputy Simms rolled his eyes. "I stood in the street and listened for the organ."

The sheriff continued to play, "Do I need to be interrupted?"

"Not for my part," said Deputy Simms. He put his hands out in mock defense. "And you're not looking forward to it. Charlie McCormick is looking for you to complain about Deseret Land and Cattle."

"Let me guess," said Simms, his head and body keeping time to the music. "They're getting back at Lester by running sheep on his land again."

"Probably." Deputy Simms sat in one of the wooden chairs that James kept in his store to make his customers comfortable. James had once told Mark Willford, the longer they stay and the more comfortable they are, the bigger the sale. "Keep playing. I'll listen. What is that?"

"I found an old 1835 hymn book. Words and all. This one's *Every Soul Is Free,*" said Sheriff Simms. "Now what's bothering Charlie McCormick."

Deputy Simms moved out to the edge of his chair. He knew what his father expected. Looking too comfortable wouldn't do. He needed to look alert. "You know McCormick put a fence up. Last October, they claimed that fence was one of the reasons that boy should'na been in their herd."

"I know," said Sheriff Simms, "Charlie didn't wait. Not long after Deseret Land and Cattle started buying so much land up in Morgan and Rich Counties, he started putting up that fence.

Before Deseret started buying in Summit County, too. My guess is they needed to run their sheep, so they cut the fence and ran them through. That it?"

Sitting on the edge of his seat may have been enough to demonstrate his attention to the sheriff, but his energy forced Deputy Simms to stand up. "He didn't say. He started blustering about how you, well, we, were out harassing his boy last year when they were in the right. He said you should have been going after Deseret for trespassing 'cause that's right when they started running sheep, despite that boy being shot."

"What?" Sheriff Simms stopped playing. "The McCormicks got off scot-free with that rustling claim. Now what's Charlie going on about? Deseret's cattle operation? Or the fact they've started running sheep?"

"Evidently both. Charlie's saying if you weren't always after his son because of your pa, you'd see that was a big corporation out to ruin his son's little farm."

"A good many people can't see the difference between a corporation using other people's money," said Sheriff Simms as he pushed the organ up against the wall where James kept it while the sheriff performed his county duties, "and Lester using stolen money." He finished positioning the organ and turned back to his son, "But there is one. A big one."

The deputy wondered if he should make any response. After a moment's wait, he said, "The difference won't matter if a range war starts up."

"It won't happen like up in Wyoming," said the sheriff. "Charlie will make sure of that."

"Is that where Hixson came from?" asked Deputy Simms.

"Nah," said Sheriff Simms. "He's from Ogden. I checked up on him down in Weber County. He mighta spent some time in Denver, but you had it right. He's more of an artist. The deputy down there told me more of a conman than a gunman, but they're glad he's our problem now, not theirs."

Sheriff Simms sought James and thanked his son for the pleasure of playing his own organ. Before he reached his deputy at the door, Clive Orson pushed it open.

"Who the hell is watching the jail?" asked Sheriff Simms.

"Following orders," answered Orson, a suspicious-looking smile on his face. "You said no need to watch the jail when no one's in it."

Deputy Simms looked out the window at the clear blue sky. April but not April Fools' Day. That fact did not overshadow Deputy Orson's smile. He had come from England and crossed the plains from Kanesville with his grandfather, and he had the manner of a seventy-seven-year-old trickster.

"I locked it to keep everybody out," said Orson. "Besides, I'm retired, but we best go back. Somebody's waitin' for you over there."

"What're you hiding under that hat?" asked Sheriff Simms.

"Not hiding nothing," said Orson. "Nor nobody. Left Lester right out in plain sight with a tied-up trespasser."

"Lester? How's he involved with Charlie looking for me?"

"Told me he waited up last night and rode his horse to the fence line and lassoed himself a trespasser."

"I'll bet he did," said Sheriff Simms. "At least, he didn't have Hixson shoot this one."

Sheriff Simms and his deputy and his retired deputy left the music store and walked three abreast two blocks down Main Street. They could see Lester McCormick sitting on his horse a safe distance from the jail with a rope around the neck of a young man, hands tied behind his back.

"Take the rope off that young man's neck," yelled Sheriff Simms.

"Sheriff, I want him cuffed and throwed in the clink."

The sheriff looked to Deputy Simms and pointed to the

young man, "Take care of that."

The sheriff stepped up to McCormick's horse. "Now give me that damn rope. The last lynching in this county was on my father's watch in Wahsatch and there ain't going to be another one, for damn sure not on my watch and not in Wahsatch."

"That's why I want him locked up," said McCormick. "You teach Deseret respect for our property and I won't have to do it myself."

"Not sure I can do that," said Sheriff Simms, "but thanks for not shooting him. You near didn't make it stick when you shot that DLC boy. You might not pull off a second time cryin' rustling."

"Hixson shot him, and he works for us, but I still would have been within my rights with this guy. He's a trespasser and he destroyed my property. He's been cutting my fences and running Deseret livestock right across my land."

"Livestock, huh? Cattle? Not sheep? Or both?"

"They bought all the land I been trying to buy, right up and down, land right next to mine. Who knows what they're running? Whatever they fancy."

"Don't bring this to me," said Sheriff Simms. "McCormick, what you need is a lawyer to tell you what to do. Or me, for that matter." The deputy could see the sheriff's sour look. He could see it galled the sheriff, doing even that much to respond to McCormick's complaint. It could be Deseret buying land drove up the price, but he guessed the real problem was Deseret paid cash and might even have received a lower price.

"They damn near bought up the whole Heiner Canyon. I hear they plan to graze more'n a thousand cows and nursing calves next summer."

"I heard sheep," said Deputy Simms. "Ten thousand."

"So, bigger than you?" asked Sheriff Simms. "That the problem?"

"Just do your job. You let sheepherders roam the county without any regard to who owns the grazing land and now they been buying steers and they're stealing from me directly when they graze them on my land."

"I thought you said they were driving them?" said Deputy Simms. He looked at the rope in his hands and lifted it over the young man's head and dropped it in the dirt on Main Street.

"Same difference. Can't drive them without feeding them," said McCormick.

"Looks to me like the biggest problem is you came up against someone who ain't impressed by a little cash and a lot of promises," said Sheriff Simms.

"I paid my debt. Because you had me in Sugar House, I missed my opportunity to sign up leases in the 1880s. It took me until ten years ago to start my ranch and because of statehood, land prices went against me and now the market's gone so bad, but I pay my bills. I didn't put anyone out of business. I gave them money when they wanted to go out of business."

Deputy Simms expected an explosion from his father. None came. He wanted to know how much of that twenty thousand dollars remained, but he knew no question would bring him the answer. "No way you can build up a herd of twenty-thousand head with twenty-thousand bucks."

McCormick pivoted from the deputy's father and said, "You are the sheriff's son. You're both against me. My goal is five thousand and I got a long way to go. A long way that I won't make if you and your pa let these Deseret people trample all over me."

"Shoe's on the other foot," said Deputy Simms. "I been here but six months, and the low man does the paperwork. You've been filing claims all over the county on water holes Mormon ranchers been using for fifty years."

"And the court has sided with me," said McCormick.

"Doesn't mean anything except the judge is a gentile," said Sheriff Simms. "You know you're taking advantage of a long tradition of judges being anti-Mormon."

"Sheriff, I'm a Mormon, too."

"Aren't we all," said Deputy Simms.

"God takes care of them that takes care of themselves. That's our preaching," said Lester.

"Yes, it is," said Sheriff Simms.

"You can't say I'm getting anything by foul means. I'm using my head."

"For foul deeds," said Deputy Simms.

"Nothing I can prove," said Sheriff Simms.

"Sure, you can," said Lester. "Right now, with my testimony, you have an obligation to lock up this trespasser."

"I already told you, you'll need a lawyer or a judge." Sheriff Simms looked past Lester and his horse to Deputy Simms. "Untie the boy."

"That's not a wise idea," said Lester.

"Only," said Deputy Simms, "if you let Hixson shoot him."

Lester laughed. "Hixson won't be shooting anybody. He's busy building a shack on the land we gave him for a wedding present. Why'd you think I'm the one brought this lout here?"

"Wedding present?" asked Sheriff Simms. "Or pay for shooting the last one?"

"Sheriff, you know we been to court. Judge said we're in the right." Lester's voice carried a calm, superior tone. "Maybe you'd believe it more if my father told you. Hixson's good with his hands, and he's getting married next month. We done right by him."

Deputy Simms asked Lester, "Who's he marrying?"

"Sarah Jane Carruth."

Chapter 10

May 2, 1906

Thoughts of Emma Carruth and her daughter, Sarah Jane, flooded Deputy Simms's mind. A hand from the Deseret Land and Cattle Company rode into town before dawn to tell the sheriff they were losing cattle, not only from rustling. His manager thought a natural pond on the ranch had been poisoned. The sheriff sent his deputy. His destination, near the Wyoming border, lay three miles northwest of Wahsatch, and his mission brought Ma Carruth's son-in-law to mind. He saddled Two for his trip to DLC's home ranch and gauged Ma Carruth lived sort of on the route, close enough to stop by on the way. He emerged with Two from the shed behind the little yellow house and looked up, into the clear cold sky, already sunup. No doubt Ma Carruth would be awake. His life as a deputy occupied every waking moment and he had not paid enough attention to Ma Carruth. That wouldn't change.

"Your father goes," said his mother when he told her he had not been over to see Ma Carruth since the day of his swearing in. In the past ten years, since Sam died, his father had insisted he make regular visits to Emma Carruth and her daughter, Sarah. The visits had a practical side. John Willford made Mark Willford responsible for keeping up Ma Carruth's property and taught his son how to do the tasks of a grown man by doing them. As she saw him out the door, his mother kissed him on the cheek and handed him a sandwich for the trail made of venison his father had brought them. She said, "Families fill in the holes. Your father knows what the calling demands."

He walked Two to the street before he climbed in the saddle. Mark Willford could see Ma Carruth's property behind the white fence Sam had built and he had tended, not half a block away. At the corner, he looked left, the direction he would take, before turning right to stop and pay that visit to Ma Carruth.

"Sorry about being scarce since October," he said when Ma Carruth opened the door.

"Oh, land's sake," she said, pulling him in the house. "Only one to suffer is you. These chocolate cookies been waitin' for you since then." She continued to pull him through the living room into the kitchen. Still holding his arm, she reached the plate and held it up in front of him.

Mark Willford took one and felt its warm softness at first touch. He smiled and waggled the cookie at her. "You do know I'm a deputy? And the law don't abide false witness no more than the Lord."

"No more fibs, huh?" Her eyes twinkled. Her smile accentuated every round and oval feature of her face.

"The truth tastes even better," he said, and he took a second cookie.

"Oh, that's clever. Very clever. Most days you sound like your father, but that was your mother, through and through." She pointed to a pitcher on the table, "Milk?"

He shook his head. "I'm headed to Deseret Land and Cattle. Since that takes me out to Wahsatch, it reminded me of my bad manners, not seeing you. So, I stopped by, but I can't stay."

"Ah, Wahsatch," said Ma Carruth. "How's your mother?"

"Fine. She's worried about you. So am I. Maybe for different reasons. We hear there's a wedding coming up, and she wants to help."

"I heard there's a wedding coming up," laughed Ma Carruth,

"but Sarah wants to do it all on her own. It's fine for her to take the burden of the work off me. It don't take my suspicions."

"You mean?" Deputy Simms didn't know how to ask the question that came to mind. "You think . . . ?"

Ma Carruth laughed again. "No, I don't think she's pregnant. Don't mean I don't think she's tried, but I'm suspicioning she wants to marry him because she's twenty-three, almost on to twenty-four. She's scared off all the boys around here, except you, and you dawdled and didn't catch up to her quick enough."

Mark Willford didn't know what to say. He decided it best to put another cookie in his mouth and say nothing.

It didn't work. Ma Carruth also said nothing and waited. Mark Willford swallowed and said, "You worried?"

"Well, she ain't marrying the right man. That'll come back to haunt her. So, maybe I'm not worried for right now, but yeah, I'm worried."

Deputy Simms understood yet tried to keep a blank face, thinking it best not to acknowledge he too had worries. He took the cookie plate out of her hand and put it on the table, then he took her hand. "Ma Carruth, I ain't my pa, but I'll do everything I can to keep him on the straight and narrow. Hixson, I mean. No need to tell Sarah anything about our talk."

"Why not? You think we got worries? She's gonna have big worries. Tom Hixson's good with his hands, but they're the kind of hands gonna get him in trouble. I think she's gonna need to believe there's someone she can turn to."

"If you think so." He leaned in and kissed her on the forehead. "Think she'll invite me to the wedding?"

"I don't think she'll invite me," said Ma Carruth.

Deputy Simms took Ma Carruth in his arms, kissed her on the forehead again, and left out the back door. He walked around to the front to mount Two. He did not want to be the one to put Sarah Jane's husband in jail—or worse.

Brad Feltingh had sent a hand down to the sheriff to carry his complaint against the McCormick ranch for poisoning his water hole. The sheriff worried that Charlie may have lost control of that new man, Hixson. Deputy Simms worried that no one could control Hixson, and he barely noticed the ledges, the valley, or the railroad crossing, landmarks he used to gauge his trip. He recalled what he'd heard about Deseret buying land first in Rich County, then in Morgan, and now in Summit. He calculated all those purchases added up to more than 20,000 acres. He'd met Brad Feltingh, a displaced Texan, married, and about a year older, once. Somebody must think him solid. They seemed to have given him a mighty big responsibility.

Now almost seven months a deputy, the sheriff had told him to investigate Brad's concerns. He wondered if he could count that as a responsibility. Like almost everywhere else out of town, this trip would be the deputy's first time up to Deseret's home ranch. As he neared it, he recalled his family's involvement with Wahsatch started before Emma's missions of mercy from her work camp base. His grandfather had some problems with the freewheeling hell-on-wheels town. Long since gone by, still its history brought smiles to the deputy at the thought those Deseret cowboys, all good Mormon boys, rode ten miles east to cross the state line to take advantage of freewheeling Evanston. He chuckled. Butch Cassidy had been a cowboy—and a good Mormon boy—once.

The first time he had visited Wahsatch he and his mother rode with Ma Carruth in her buggy to see all the places in the story about how Emma Wilde, not yet married to Sam Carruth, saved the Saints, including his mother, who floundered in the snows in Hilliard, Wyoming.

He had visited a second time, in truth multiple times, with his friends who hitched on the freight slowed by the grade. When they reached the wye track, they jumped off to play games on the switching trains. The railroad complained to his father in his official capacity as sheriff and he allowed as how he had wished he knew how to jump off moving trains when it came time for him to do that in his escape from the U.S. Marshals.

Wahsatch had long since become a virtual ghost town. The original Union Pacific railroad station still stood, long since empty. A quick look around showed three lived-in houses, probably for a section crew and their families, maybe a population of a dozen.

Deputy Simms crossed the U.P. track that ran north-south through Wahsatch. All the buildings and homes, empty save those for the section crew, nestled in a 200-yard strip of land off the railroad track. After the Golden Spike, the railroad camp became a stop for a period, and the early residents planted those trees, all the life that remained. Grown into thirty-five-year-old silver poplars, elms, black willows, and weeping willows, the trees provided cool shade to empty streets.

Near the station stood a red water storage tank, and to the south, a long warehouse. Deputy Simms noticed a set of corrals alongside the track. He could visualize the operation in full swing, shipping livestock—cattle, horses, and sheep.

He followed parallel to the track until he found in the center of this wide and dry and tan high mountain valley the turnoff to the Deseret ranch. Finding his way after the turn required little thought. Mostly he thought about the meaning of a poison water hole.

Maybe Lester McCormick had sneaked a step without his father's knowing or let one of his hands do it. Deputy Simms had been hoping for it.

That wouldn't do. Maybe onto something that could finally

expose McCormick, all the better, but when you started to hope for it, you started to stop seeing clearly.

Simms tried to empty his head. He trusted he could keep riding until he started to see clearly again. His hope for something on McCormick ran up against the truth. Even poisoning a water hole would give Deputy Simms only some young hand, probably his own age, not Hixson, not McCormick, and not enough to stop McCormick's whole operation.

Across a mile of dark brown land dotted with low scrub oak, he could see the main house built on a hill rising into the foothills behind. A rider pushed along fast toward him. Deputy Simms watched the rider and continued his pace until he heard, "Yo!"

The deputy pulled up and waited. Brad Feltingh arrived. The deputy asked, "What's up?"

"I didn't want you to ride to the door without company," said Brad. He spread an arm across the entire horizon. "And everybody's out working. Least I could do is ride out."

While they rode together back to the house, Brad told him some about their operation, including they had six hundred yearling Hereford heifers summering in Heiner Canyon.

"That's about what McCormick said where you been buying land," said Deputy Simms.

"No secret," said Brad. "Every deed's recorded. He been complaining?"

"As a matter of fact, he has," said Deputy Simms.

"He figured he had to go on record against us, after he poisoned our water holes. Clever."

Deputy Simms looked at Brad Feltingh. Polished boots, clean pants with a crease, a leather vest, and the shirt looked ironed. He seemed to talk as cleanly and crisply as he dressed. The sheriff had sent him out here to find out what lay behind all of this, not to make up his mind based on appearances. He stayed silent.

"Well, we won't set it right tonight," said Brad. "Nor on these horses. You can wash up. It's time to eat."

Brad's wife cooked almost as well as Mark Willford's mother. Deputy Simms took a close look at her and convinced himself she was his age. He'd worked hard since seventh grade and lived with his mother and never had time nor interest in girls, but this seemed like a surprisingly good arrangement.

"Is this your normal evening?" he asked over apple pie.

"Well, we do have a fair number of visitors," answered Brad. "Easy for them to travel to Wahsatch with the train and then we bring them out here. Alice makes a fine hostess, and as you can tell, she cooks a good meal."

"Yes, I can tell," said Deputy Simms.

"But mostly they're out here to talk, so we stay here after dinner and talk."

"My guess is there's two hours of daylight left," said Deputy Simms. "Can we make it out to those water holes and take a look at them, tonight?"

"We'll be out about five miles north, about where the hills break off into McKay Creek."

Deputy Simms had heard his father tell of riding every inch of his county. He felt embarrassed that he didn't know the territory Brad referred to well enough to find the water hole. He didn't want to let that out.

Brad continued with no hint of suspecting what Deputy Simms thought. "We'll proceed east, staying to the ridge on the south side of McKay. With dusk coming on, we'll have to keep moving down on McKay Creek and across to the north side. There's some lush green grass over there, and you'll be able to see a hundred or so Hereford cows with their calves."

"Will we be able to make it out there before dark?" asked

Deputy Simms.

"For sure, but we might want to stay there and see what happens in the morning," said Brad. "That poisoned spring is on the north slope. Now we know it's poisoned, I don't let any of my livestock drink it, or at least we try to keep them out. Of course, I don't let any of the men drink the water."

"How do you know it's poisoned?" asked Deputy Simms.

"Late April, we moved the cattle up from winter grazing and the sheep shipped from the desert. Collecting the herd, we bedded them down for the night close to that spring. Next morning, we had two hundred dead cattle from drinking that poisoned water."

Almost to the border, with Crane Creek on one side and the plateau dropping down an exposed rock face to a grass covered flatland, the terrain created a natural corral about four miles from the ranch house. They dismounted and started to walk. Deputy Simms followed Brad north a hundred yards to an open spring.

"You say you have six hundred here, now. You mean you lost a quarter of the herd?" said Deputy Simms, a question that was a statement.

"Well, not a quarter of the herd, but you're right about them we shipped up here. We lost one out of every four."

Simms surveyed the lush grass and the purple hue given the landscape where the sagebrush crowded out the grass. "So, why haven't you put a fence around it?"

"I told all the men not to use it," said Brad.

Simms saw more than beauty. He could see the cattle a hundred yards away and his eye followed the manure right up to the edge of the spring. It didn't look all that old to him. He could also see deer tracks at the spring and droppings and some other tracks. Tracking had been among the skills his father taught him a man needed to know, but these tracks were too deformed to make out.

He did not see dead animals.

"What'd you do with the dead cattle?"

"Burned 'em," said Brad. "Poisoned cattle are not fit to eat."

"And the deer?"

"What deer?"

"Look. Tracks. Right up to the spring. You found dead cattle. I'm guessing you had dead deer, too."

Brad slowly moved his head back and forth. "I'll ask my men. They didn't say anything."

In amongst the grass and the sage, Simms could see high stalks with white flowering clusters at the tops. He recognized the mountain lily that wasn't a lily. He knew well the stories of surviving the early winters on sego lilies. To make use of those lifesaving bulbs, you had to be taught about the poisonous lilies, bulbs that look like an onion, but are poison onions.

"Looks to me like there're some poisonous plants around here," said Simms.

"Not that I know of," said Brad.

"Where you from?"

"Texas," said Brad.

Deputy Simms nodded with half a laugh, "Truth to tell, I knew that. You must be the only one with Deseret not from Utah."

"Don't know about that," said Brad. "They sent a land recruiter all the way down where I live, hiring for a foreman. I had cattle experience and Alice and I wanted to get married. Time to move up."

"Evidently your cattle experience was enough to land you the job," said Deputy Simms. He considered how to say the next and decided he only knew one way, direct. "I never been down to Texas, so I don't know what kind of mountains you have down there. Don't seem like you have mountain experience.

Leastwise, not mountain plants."

"What you talking about?" asked Brad.

Simms pulled his gloves out from his back pocket and put them on. He reached over and snapped off a long stalk with bunches of white flowers atop it.

"Some people mistake this for the camas lily," said Simms. He held it up and twisted it around slowly to display all aspects of the plant. "The camas lily, the sego lily, others like them, kept our people alive in the early years. Not this one. This one's a poison onion."

Brad reached out for it.

"Best not," said Simms, jerking the plant back. "Best you put your gloves on. Every part of this plant is poisonous. Bulb especially. One bulb'll kill you."

Brad put on his gloves and took the stalk from Simms. He pulled the stalk apart and then broke open the bulb and smelled it.

"You called it poison onion. It doesn't smell like onion," said Brad.

"No, just looks like one. If your cattle ate some of this during the day, they could have died from it at night."

"So, you don't think it's poison?"

"The onion is, but not the water," said Simms. "If your cattle grazed in this stuff all day, that'd be plenty. Even half a day. Easy for cows standing around like this. If you were moving them through, a mouthful or two wouldn't do more than make 'em sick."

"We had some sick cattle," said Brad. "But it still looks like the water to me. I gave them sick cattle fresh water and the next day they all recovered."

"Woulda done," said Simms, "flushed 'em out." He threw the rest of the stalk to the ground and brushed his gloves but did not take them off. "You might still think it's from the water, but it's not. I'd sorta wished it was, but it's not."

"Can you take a sample and have it analyzed?"

Simms recognized that the prospect of finding out McCormick had poisoned the water hole was one he had silently enjoyed. He breathed a sigh of relief that Brad had not asked about his slip. Even though he knew a sample and a test to be unnecessary, he said, "Sure can. Then you'll know for sure."

"So, you don't think we need to bed out here overnight to watch that spring?"

"Can we get back to your house in time for breakfast?" asked Simms.

"Sure can," said Brad. "Alice won't ring the first bell till six o'clock."

"Then let's stay. Not for the spring. Nobody's coming to poison it." Deputy Simms hesitated, then plunged ahead assuming the truth of what he said. "This is beautiful territory, but the new moon leaves it dark and makes it treacherous. If we wait till twilight, we'll make it for breakfast, and I'll see where I'm going."

Chapter 11

May 9, 1906

Deputy Simms stood in the first row on the aisle in the Summit Stake Tabernacle, his mother standing next to him. His half-brother, James, stood across the aisle with his five half sisters. Their mother had taken to bed with their grandfather's funeral, and she said she certainly was not getting out of bed for their grandmother's. Deputy Simms did not know Elizabeth Jensen Simms, and he tried not to judge her, colored as his thoughts were by her choice to remain bedridden and her status as the first wife. Judgment or not, as he surveyed the six hundred souls filling every seat, she had made the wrong decision about not attending this funeral. A hush settled over the murmur as Sheriff John Willford Simms walked through the side door and took his place under the white plaster ceiling in the soft, somewhat blue, light created by the stained-glass windows. He held the silence a moment, then delivered the eulogy for Mary Ann Opshaw.

"All the facts are on the piece of paper handed out at the door."

Deputy Simms could feel the sheriff's eyes. He thought everyone in the pews felt them. They read the piece of paper and watched him pull out the railroad watch. He glanced at its sweep hand and gave them one more minute.

"My mother will never have a book written about her. This is all she'll get.

"A son's effort.

"Perhaps because she is my mother, it seems an inadequate tribute.

"My mother lived her life in three periods, each different from the other.

"First, she came here from England with my father when she was twenty-four years old, already a mother at age nineteen, a leader among the young adults. They all looked up to her, none more than her husband, three years younger. Mother and Father joined one of the first wagon trains. They did not know Brigham Young until they arrived in Salt Lake City. Their meeting set the course of my mother's life because it set the course of my father's life.

"Like her, I have no desire to adorn the facts. She led my father to the church and then followed him all the way across the plains and up into these mountains.

"Ours was not a house that talked about the privations of walking across the plains. She applied her wisdom to each challenge and made the most of it. One example. She made our small allowance of flour each day into gruel. She preserved our ration, yet gave us a little something warm three times a day—better than having it all at once with nothing more until the next morning.

"She thought the trek here trained her for living here, her second period of life.

"We didn't feel all that special. After all, by the time we arrived about five thousand had already come the same way and ten times that were still to come.

"And like everyone else, we arrived in Salt Lake City on a Monday. I think my mother said November 26, 1849, but I was five. I couldn't swear to that.

"My mother might have held on to that date because three months later Brigham sent my father up here to be the cooper and to help settle the Summit Mission. He wasn't here a month before Brigham made my father constable.

"For thirty years, way too few as she recounted them in the following twenty-three years, she made a home for the sheriff and the county as well as for her husband and her son. To hear her tell it, it was easy having my father underfoot. What wasn't easy was having him out days and weeks at a time.

"This is not about him. We buried him twenty-three years ago, and she might disapprove of this eulogy. She allowed no eulogy for him, saying his life spoke for itself. She asked me to say a word, and she allowed the bishop to give a prayer at the graveside.

"She spoke far more eloquent words: 'I pray I will be with you soon.'

"Upon those words, my mother entered her third period and lived here without my father another twenty-three years. She waited to join my father, but she did not take to her bed to wait. Active of character, mind, and spirit, Mary Ann Opshaw served as Relief Society President, held Fast Day meetings and other church gatherings at her home, and boarded the schoolteacher to save all the other families in town the cost of putting her up."

Sheriff Simms stopped. He looked at his son and deputy and then at all 600 faces, each person taking in his look as if one at a time.

"Now at eighty-nine, a fourth period, the one when her prayer is answered."

After the hymn, the bishop asked everyone to remain seated while Sheriff Simms and his two families formed a receiving line at the door of the tabernacle. Deputy Simms held back to allow his mother and his father's other family to precede him to the door to join the sheriff in honoring their grandmother.

Before he started his short walk to join the receiving line, he saw Emma Wilde Carruth, tearful and looking even smaller in the great doors that framed her. He could not be sure whether she had arrived at that moment in the doorway or had left her pew early to join the family. He could understand if she had done that, almost a member of the family.

Deputy Simms's mother swooped over to put her arm around Emma. She then intercepted him before he reached his place. She put Emma's hand in his.

He had no idea what his mother knew that he didn't nor what question to ask. Emma saved him.

"I didn't want to miss the funeral, and then I started crying."

"Were you very close to my grandma?"

"Of course. Everybody was. But she's where she wants to be," said Emma. "I didn't want to interrupt Elizabeth at a moment like this, but I'm afraid I'm selfish."

Deputy Simms looked around. He started guiding Emma through the door. "Why don't we go sit down." He led her out to sit in the May sunshine on one of the benches that lined both walkways to the tabernacle door. "I know you're not selfish, so what's up?"

"Sarah Jane didn't make it to the funeral because she's run off to Evanston to marry Tom Hixson." Her chest heaved as she sobbed more and dabbed her eyes. "Yesterday."

Deputy Simms nodded. He held still for an extra moment, then reached for her second hand. He said, "Ma, you know they planned to get married. This month, too. Don't worry about Grandma. Sarah Jane always said she wanted things to be exciting."

"Well, this might be a little too exciting," said Ma Carruth amidst her sobs.

"I'll admit I'm not too sure about this Tom Hixson, but I know they want to have kids, so that'll straighten him up."

"Well, she does at least."

"You're right. I don't know what he wants, but she usually gets what she wants, so my bet is it'll go that way."

"Mark, you're a good boy," Ma Carruth said, and she patted his cheek. "You shoulda had something going with Sarah, but you didn't. Now I'm worried about who she's settled for."

"Settled is a little harsh, Ma. When I talked to her, she said he had a lot better prospects than a sheriff's deputy."

"She mighta said the same to me when she thought he was a rancher. Now he's in meatpacking."

"Meatpacking?" interrupted Deputy Simms. He recalled his conversation with Lester months ago about butchering, but meatpacking sounded like a whole lot bigger operation. He realized he had interrupted Ma Carruth and didn't know exactly how to turn the conversation back to her. She apparently had not noticed.

"Yeah, meatpacking. I was gonna say I ain't seen better prospects in him than anybody else, leastwise, you." The spirit that lit up her entire life showed through again. She let no more sobs come but added, "I'm worried."

Deputy Simms ran through the list in the eight or so months since he had come across Thomas L. Hixson, the dead Deseret Land and Cattle boy, the threatening incident with the rifle, and the cut fences. Yet his list didn't add up to what he thought Tom Hixson really did for Lester McCormick. The trouble being, if he was the artist on the brands, he was good at it. There had been complaints, but not a single beef or cow presented as evidence. And now if the butchering destroyed the altered brands, he could see Hixson's smart aleck logic in telling Sarah he was in charge of meatpacking.

The deputy chided himself that he should not approve of Hixson's lying to Sarah. He justified it with the knowledge that Charlie McCormick did not approve of those Ogden boys. He held a steady rein on his son. He'd never play out enough line to let Lester go beyond hiding stolen brands by butchering and go into meatpacking. Lester'd be competing with characters tougher and more vicious than the Mormons at Deseret Land and Cattle. He felt confident Hixson's claim amounted to a dose of exaggeration with Charlie around,

Deputy Simms reached over and wiped Ma Carruth's cheeks. Then he kissed her on one. "Don't you worry. I will keep an eye on him. He'll do good by Sarah. I promise."

Chapter 12

October 1906

"Go talk to Curtis Brimville at the Imperial Hotel." As usual, the sheriff spent no time explaining his order. Deputy Simms had long since learned to ask if he thought he needed more information. Sometimes scowls greeted his questions in disapproval of the supposedly approved asking. With the sheriff still in embrace on the porch of the little yellow house when he gave these instructions, Deputy Simms thought he'd wait before he added the risk of asking why he needed to go to Park City.

The deputy could see the sheriff watching him, waiting for a question. The deputy waited him out. After a long moment, the corners of the sheriff's mouth began to turn up in the threat of a smile. The sheriff said, "Ask Brimville what he's serving over there." Pause. "We know what he serves in his bedrooms. I want to know what he serves in his dining room."

Mark Willford had asked his mother why his father refused to sleep in or even step inside the little yellow house. She told him she had not discussed it with his father, and she wasn't about to discuss it with her son.

The deputy guessed at what that meant the same as he guessed at the sheriff's assertion that he knew what the Imperial Hotel served in its bedrooms. The question about the dining room seemed more straightforward. Last spring Ma Carruth told him that Tom Hixson now ran the meatpacking operation for the McCormick ranch. Deputy Simms had taken it as a big city word for butchering rustled cattle. Something had happened, though. Maybe Charlie had worked some compromise or order. In the past five months or so, the sheriff's office had not heard any complaints about rustled cattle, not even from Brad Feltingh and his people.

His first year as a deputy coming to an end and the three of them knew little more about Lester's herd than they did when Hixson shot the boy. The sheriff in Weber County had told them the meatpacking operation[2] in Ogden grew larger every month. The meaning of that fact lay beyond their grasp and seemed almost as distant as everything else that happened in the big city sixty miles away. Emma's comment, originally taken as her son-in-law's effort to put a high gloss on whatever he did at the McCormick ranch, now brought all three members of the Summit County sheriff's office to suspect she had told them something Lester didn't want known. He had undertaken to transform his little butchering outlet for rustled cattle into a full-scale meatpacking operation.

"I can't believe Charlie will let them tie up with the meatpackers," said Sheriff Simms. "Lester's been hankering for it since they started butchering, but ever since that meatpacking book came out, Charlie's tried to steer clear. He knows those guys do things in their own way."

"But ain't our question where all the beef comes from?" asked Deputy Simms. "Judging from how quiet it's been, something else is going on besides rustling."

"I read the book," said Sheriff Simms. "Judging Tom Hixson, if he's read it, I'd guess he likes those Chicago tactics."

2 Meatpacking operations began in 1900 with five plants, thirty-four employees, product value of $343,444. It increased to twelve plants, ninety-nine employees, product value of $1,690,447 by 1910. ($52,302,000 in today's value). It continued to grow at an even accelerated rate until the end of 1918.

"If you mean strong-arm, I'd wager he does," said Deputy Simms, "but why you sending me over to talk to Brimville?"

"Speculation," said Sheriff Simms. "I want to know more about where Lester sells that packed meat of dubious origin."

More gentiles relative to the population lived in Summit County than in any other county in the state. Salt Lake housed more gentiles, but it housed half the people in the state and fewer than one in five were not Mormon. Except for his father's true friend, "that annoying lawyer" Rabbi Slonik, Deputy Simms did not know that he even knew any other gentiles. Most of the county's outsize number of gentiles lived and worked in Park City. On that subversive goal, Colonel Connor had achieved a small measure of success.

Colonel Connor's goal of finding riches in those mountains had been achieved. His goal of attracting a horde of non-Mormons—they did not call themselves gentiles—had been achieved to the extent a couple of thousand Chinese and Slavs and assorted other Europeans could be called a horde. The Mormons were Europeans, too, and the deputy had learned that his grandfather reminded everyone that once again the Church outflanked Colonel Connor. It accepted all these new mining Europeans as potential converts. The Church sent its missionaries to proselytize in Park City, saving the long trip to all those distant lands.

Curtis Brimville looked at that cosmopolitan population and saw the vision of a great commercial empire built around a grand hotel. He named it the Imperial Hotel. It had been open two years and had drawn no attention from Sheriff Simms until now.

"Single miners are no longer required to live in company-owned boardinghouses," said Brimville, "not since the Mine Boarding House Bill."

Deputy Simms took in this information as new news. He had

no idea what the Mine Boarding House Bill said nor when it passed. Like so much in this job as deputy, he made a mental note to study up on it.

"The sheriff and the city fathers never expected that bill to change anything, certainly not their accommodation with Mother Urban." Brimville smiled for an effect that Deputy Simms missed. "Excuse me," he said. He turned away to hand a key to a man who had stepped up to the desk trailed by a woman. Brimville turned back to the deputy. "It works the same."

Deputy Simms began to comprehend what Brimville was saying. His father had carefully crafted a compromise between righteousness and reality. The deputy didn't like the way Brimville disdained it.

"How does it work?" asked the deputy. He had his dander up. Even before he turned to the question of the dining room, he felt like withdrawing the compromise from the Imperial Hotel. He wondered where his father had learned to put up with people like this.

Brimville took on a very patient tone, like he was talking to a child. "You're here to tell me the rules against prostitution in the mine boardinghouses really are rules, and you're going to enforce them." He lowered his voice for effect. "Now that the boardinghouses are in town."

Deputy Simms felt the bite of that comment, and he didn't like the tone. He spent a moment wanting to find a way to make Brimville regret being so cheeky.

"You leave Mother Urban to the sheriff and me," said Deputy Simms. He had not asked for it, but he realized patience was the answer. Brimville's kind find a way to take themselves down all by themselves. "Make damn sure you don't have her girls in here."

"I rent those rooms. So far, no woman has rented one, and I

can't control what the men do in their rooms."

"You damn well can. What you can't do is turn a blind eye on something illegal in your establishment."

"If fornication was illegal, the Mormons'd all be in jail." The two stood looking at each other, Deputy Simms wanting to move on to the next subject, but not wanting to take the pressure off Brimville. Brimville broke the silence, "You'd do well to remember your father had his problems." And then Brimville laughed. "And here you are."

"Here I am, doing my job." Deputy Simms glared at Brimville, determined not to let a moment's hesitation pass. They had steered clear of discussing the real reason he came. "Where do you buy your beef for your dining room?"

"What?" smirked Brimville. "From meat in the bedrooms to meat in the dining room? Selling steaks to miners is illegal now? When did they pass that law?"

Deputy Simms recognized he had some to go on learning his job, but there was nothing he could do with his inept transition other than accept his blundering and plunge ahead. "You know, I been on the job about a year now, with still a lot to learn, but I think that law's been around since last century. The one about butchering stolen cattle."

"I don't butcher nothing," said Brimville. "If you're trying to shut me down, you can't make that one stick. You got the wrong man."

"I'm not trying to make anything stick." Deputy Simms chided himself. What Brimville charged him with had never occurred to him. "I'm not trying to shut you down, Curtis."

"Just saying," said Brimville. His smile grew bigger. "No *Jungle* here."

Deputy Simms tried to imagine how his father would handle this. Not many men could rattle Sheriff Simms. He knew of none. His father had only one course, stay true to his calling.

For Deputy Simms, that meant continuing to focus on his job "Where're you buying the beef?"

"Oh, that's all you want?" Brimville's voice sounded surprised.

"Are you thinking I'm asking for money?" Even asking Brimville that question exceeded Simms's tolerance for what he allowed people to think of him. He wanted this cleared up, fast. "Mother Urban pays her fines to the city, that's it."

"Same difference," said Brimville. "City pays you. You're all hypocrites."

"County pays me, and you best keep your mind on what you're doing. Providing rooms only." Deputy Simms heard his own words and said, "You haven't answered my question."

"Your prescription for staying in business?" asked Brimville.

"More my father's," said Deputy Simms. "But good advice. One thing you can trust. If there's no trouble, there's no trouble. Now answer my question. That is, if you want to keep the Imperial Hotel open."

Curtis Brimville let a big smile escape as he stepped from the registration desk to the cash register. A loud ring signaled his press on the zero key to open the drawer. Brimville pulled out a piece of paper and handed it to Deputy Simms.

"There you are," said Brimville with a certain triumph. "The invoice shows what we bought and paid for—in cash." He handed it to Deputy Simms. "Wasatch Meatpacking Company, but otherwise no address. I doubt it's Chicago."

"You don't say," said Deputy Simms. "So, who sold you this?"

"A man named Tom Hixson," said Brimville. "Told me he runs the operation."

"Told me that, too," said Deputy Simms. Ma Carruth's words came easy but brought a heavy blanket of concern.

Deputy Simms stood at the front desk, held the invoice in his hands, and let the moments pass while he thought, what next?

"You know Wasatch is owned by Lester McCormick?"

"Lester McCormick? There's history between you and the McCormicks."

"You mean like he got my grandfather murdered?" asked Deputy Simms. "Yeah, there's history, but we treat him right."

"So?" asked Brimville. "So, he owns a meatpacking company. Sounds like he's straightened up."

"So long as Hixson pays attention to Charlie the way Lester does. Ain't you concerned where that beef comes from?" asked Deputy Simms.

"Why? It smells fresh, and no one's sick," said Brimville. After a moment's silence passed between the two, he asked, "That it? I got work to do."

Deputy Simms handed the invoice back to him. "One thing you need to remember. If there's any trouble with one of Mother Urban's girls, you're the one's gonna be fined."

"That ain't fair," said Brimville.

"Sure it is," said the deputy. "That's how it works with Mother Urban."

Chapter 13

February 23, 1907

The Union Pacific Railroad tracks' grade crossing through Yellow Creek Road from Porcupine Mountain to Wahsatch lies about three-quarters of a mile northeast of the rail siding and business center of Wahsatch. On the Wahsatch side, the road links to a tee that passes down the broad high valley into the narrow Weber Canyon and continues through the towns next to the river all the way to Ogden. In the opposite direction, the road goes up to the McCormick ranch, further on to the Deseret Land and Cattle ranch, and all the way to Evanston. Both ways, it didn't matter; man, horse, or wagon had to use the grade crossing.

Deputy Simms rose into the dark morning of the last Saturday in February. His bare feet on the cold planking decided for him first among his chores to bring in the wood. One step toward the storage shed, he saw the heavy snowfall. He snuggled into his wool coat. After loading in wood for the potbellied stove and the fireplace, he started on the kitchen stove. No surprise, he saw his father coming down the walk for breakfast. The sheriff maintained his vow never to step foot in the house again. He also came for breakfast every Saturday. He sat with Elizabeth Tonsil outside on the porch. Mark Willford respected his father's will, but he left it there lest he start to judge it. He thought what he couldn't change, he shouldn't judge.

Wood for the kitchen stove all stacked, Deputy Simms said

goodbye to the sheriff and his mother. He left for the jail, hoping to arrive before Woodside, who had the duty up to Park City the night before. Woodside had already made the coffee.

"I wanted to beat you here," said Deputy Simms. "I guess this means George Washington's birthday isn't a very big holiday in Park City."

"Not too rowdy," Woodside laughed, "but the snow started last night. It blankets over the partygoers so to speak. Even miners. Truth is, I didn't want to be in it, so I slept over in the jail. I came back early this morning. I haven't even been home yet."

"Not much doing here, either. I'll take a walk over to the Mercantile and have a look at the *Deseret News.*" Before he could lift his hat off the hook, the wall phone clanged its hammer against the brass bell.

Despite the telephone's arrival in town almost a year and half ago, the device continued to strike him as strange and wondrous. He picked up the black horn and held it away from him.

The words streamed through as if from his hand. "There's been an accident at the grade crossing." Deputy Simms jerked to press the horn hard against his ear. "The Los Angeles Limited Number 27 comes through here every day, lickety-split. It's due in Los Angeles by nine at night. Railroad gives them an hour for the commissary in Ogden. They can just make it. They're hauling. This engineer laid on that whistle all the way from the signal box."

"Where?" asked Deputy Simms.

"Wahsatch, at the crossing."

"He still there?" asked Simms.

"Yep, he says in the snow he didn't even see the wagon until he hit it."

"That the accident?"

"Yeah, the Limited hit a wagon."

"You talk to the engineer?"

"Yeah. He pulled the cord as soon as he knew he had trouble, stopped her almost to the siding, maybe shorter, two thousand feet or so. We never heard the crash. We heard that train screeching and sliding on the tracks, but we never heard the crash."

"Who are you?"

"The section crew. We were here at the maintenance shed for breakfast. We ran up there and asked him what happened."

"Don't let him go nowhere," said Simms.

"I told him to wait while I called you."

"Go find him and put him on." Simms could hear the earpiece being passed. A hesitant voice came on the line.

"Sheriff?"

"What's your name?"

"Harrington."

"You been drinking, Harrington?"

"Why? Because I'm Irish."

"Because I'm the sheriff's deputy. Did you answer me?"

"No."

"No, you didn't answer me. Or no, you haven't been drinking?"

"We're not allowed to drink while we're operating a train."

Deputy Simms noticed the engineer still had not answered. After a split second, he decided to ignore it.

"Harrington, you stay put."

"How long'll that be? I got a schedule to keep."

"You're already off schedule. I'll be there as soon as I can. We're about thirty miles away."

"That's the better part of five hours," said the engineer.

"Straightaway," said Simms. "Even if it's six. Now find whoever was on the phone."

After a moment, Deputy Simms heard the same voice he had

talked to first. "Yes, sir." He wasn't used to that. It spoke well of the caller.

"What's your name?"

"Folger."

"Well, Folger, find someone to help you to take care of these people."

"Not but one man."

"One man? Who was it?"

"A rancher from around here." A long pause occurred before Folger resumed. "I know him. Knew him. Met him at the loading pens. I saw him around here a lot. Charlie McCormick. I don't think his son knows yet."

Deputy Simms had met Charlie McCormick the once with the investigation of the Deseret Land and Cattle boy's shooting. He knew from his father and Woodside that McCormick kept his son from bringing on worse trouble than he already had. The deputy immediately began to think that a man regularly at the loading dock would never have an accident at the railroad crossing. His instinct told him not to expose his doubts. "Look, Folger, you think you can call your crew chief."

"I am the crew chief."

"Oh, well, good. Stay there. Find someone else to go up to McCormick's ranch and bring Lester down to you. I don't want Charlie moved, and I don't want any of them touching him. I want somebody responsible to watch over him. Whoever goes up to McCormick's ranch, tell 'em to bring a wagon. We'll need to bring him down here to Mr. Kidner as soon as we can."

Two could have carried Deputy Simms to the accident in less than five hours. Except, in the sixteen months since Seth Parker made the loaner available, he had grown to cherish her. Maybe he shouldn't have named her. He had forgotten to think of Two as a loaner. She had been the deputy's companion for as long as his star. He knew one hour out of five made a big difference.

Charlie was dead; he would let Two set the pace.

Deputies Simms and Woodside stopped at the yellow house to tell the sheriff about the accident. Charlie McCormick had smoothed over his son's outlaw actions that brought tragedy to the sheriff, yet the two had forged a bond of magnetic attraction found in opposites over the twenty-four years.

Sheriff Simms said nothing upon hearing the news. Deputy Simms stood with his mother and Woodside mute in the knowledge that only Sheriff Simms could break his own silence. "It is like losing a real friend," he finally said, "but there's more than a hole there where Charlie used to be." He looked away from the porch, out into the snowfall. "I don't know if Lester can find his own way without Charlie, and I," he turned back to the three on the porch. "I don't know how Lester's going to handle this Hixson guy."

"Do you want to go up with Mark and talk to Lester?" asked Woodside.

Sheriff Simms looked at the horses and his deputies. He took no time to consider his answer. "Naw, Lester didn't do it. You go. Take what time you need. Look into Charlie's accident. It ought to put a damper on that bunch up at the McCormick ranch—for a little while." From his chair he picked up the extra coat he had worn against the snow and the chill. "A February day like this does my job for me. I'll see you back at the jail."

Woodside set the pace and Deputy Simms mulled over the phrase his father had used. Finally, he said, "Ought to? I don't see how Charlie could have an accident like that. You think Pa was saying that, too?"

"Well, first off, I know he thinks all accidents have causes," said Woodside. They had reached the ledges at the north end of town. He pointed up to the top of the closest one, the one with the sheer face right down to the road. "You played up there as a kid. If you'da fell, it'd been an accident, but for sure it had a cause."

"Ought to," repeated Deputy Simms. "That sort of suggests somebody caused it who ain't smart enough to pretend he's shocked."

"That wouldn'a been Lester. From the day Charlie stepped in to take Lester's trouble in hand, I'm quite sure he knew he needed his pa," said Woodside. "For sure, your father trusted him right off. Maybe it was instinct. Charlie wasn't one of the early pioneers. Like Sheriff Simms and your grandfather, Charlie was born in England, not sure exactly what year. He showed up in Coalville sometime in the 1870s. I wasn't but five or six, maybe seven. Sheriff Simms was a deputy then and, for sure, he knew him. His father expected him to know every newcomer."

"What'd he do? Test him?"

"I worked for your grandfather for one month, and he was always testing people, just not the way you think." Woodside rolled his head back. Snow collected on his face as he smiled with his recollection. "It wasn't that Sheriff Luke Willford quizzed him, but for certain a week after any newcomer arrived, if your father had not yet brought the new arrival to Sheriff Luke Willford's attention, he would ask, 'Can you help me with the name of that new member of our community?' or 'Remind me the name of that new family. We need to ask if they need any help.'

"When Charlie came is important. Those converts who came on the train clear to Great Salt Lake City were not pioneers. That made him and his family separate. There might have been too much pride in that thought. I think that's why he settled out on Porcupine Mountain. That and not having any money at all when he arrived.

"Somehow Lester took care of that. Once Charlie let Lester start buying land for his ranch, Charlie became a man of substance. He's been a county commissioner for two terms, but he's never stopped farming that desert up to Porcupine."

They reached the grade crossing and followed the road to its tee, down to Echo, up to Wahsatch. As Simms turned up, he wondered what he would see at Wahsatch, how the debris covering the rails would disclose more than the horror of the accident and tell the full story. "You know what don't make sense," he said. "Before or after the Golden Spike, it don't matter, Charlie was one of the survivors in this county. How could an accident like this happen to a survivor? Nobody ever talks about his wife."

"She died with Lester," said Woodside.

"Whenever he lost her, Charlie continued," said Simms. "Even if he did it with Lester's money, Charlie prospered. Stolen money don't exactly make him a survivor, but it took special spirit to keep going through all of that."

Woodside didn't answer. Deputy Simms kept wondering. Like a spring, the subject of that special spirit had no bottom. Its mysteries kept flowing the more he thought. Almost two hours later, they saw a knot of people milling around the rails off the side of the road. Snow covered the high, flat desert but neither hills nor vegetation impaired the view. A wagon broke free of the group and rolled down the road to meet them. Deputy Simms recognized Lester McCormick.

"What happened here?" asked Woodside.

"Why the Hell you asking me?" answered Lester. "I don't know any more than you do." He stared at Woodside. Woodside held the stare. "I told him he didn't need to go, but he insisted."

"Go where?" asked Woodside.

"Charlie planned to take half a steer down to Big Man Anderson. We slaughtered it for him yesterday."

Big Man Anderson, so tall and so large that no one ever thought to call him Darrell, owned and operated the Echo Cold

Storage. Big Man Anderson slaughtered and packaged livestock unloaded at the rail siding in Echo. He started his business before Ogden Provision and Packing Company started in 1902 and he had resisted their irresistible offers to sell out.

The deputies urged their horses forward again toward the crowd that awaited them. Lester turned his rig around and caught up to their side.

"You doing business with Big Man Anderson?" asked Woodside. Deputy Simms looked off into the crowd, hoping to spot someone who looked like a section chief.

"Well," said Lester, with a notable pause before the next word came, "we're trying. These days, we've loaded some beef already slaughtered and halved at Wahsatch for him to take off in Echo and package."

"Uh-huh," said Woodside. He stopped this side of the crossing and remained in his saddle. He wasn't exactly looking at Lester when he asked, "and what's the problem?"

"No problem."

Now he turned to look full on Lester. "Not what 'trying' says to me."

"Just business," said Lester, "but these things come up all the time."

"And these things are?"

"We're hoping to ship him more packed cuts," said Lester.

"Isn't that Big Man's business?"

"Only part. He's storing it, too. He don't need to go to all the bother he has. Buying the beef on the hoof and slaughtering them as well as cutting and packing the cuts. We can do that and save him a lot of time."

"What's he think of that?" asked Woodside. "Seems to me what he wants is to sell more. All you're gonna do is cost him more for what he sells."

"Well, that's not what you're here to look into," said Lester.

"My father was killed by a train and your job is to find out why."

No matter how accurate Lester's statement might have been, Deputy Simms saw him trying to steer away from the Big Man Anderson question too quickly. All knew the circumstances of Charlie's death. A freight train hadn't killed him. They rolled by so slow boys hitched on them. Passenger trains with a schedule to keep took advantage of this broad valley with few curves and none too sharp. The engineers pulled maximum speed, barely slow enough to stay on the track. Simms didn't know what the rules were yet, but the engineer had to give a blast on his whistle at that first signal light. With five miles before the grade crossing, that'd be five minutes, more or less. Why did Charlie McCormick take five minutes, or even more, to clear the tracks? And what did it have to do with Big Man Anderson?

Deputy Simms whispered in Woodside's ear and they dismounted. Both deputies looked up at Lester on the bench seat of his wagon. Deputy Simms asked, "So, who was with him? Your father had to leave Porcupine Mountain at four in the morning to make this trip. If he was going down to see Big Man, did he bring someone with him?"

"Dunno," said Lester. "He told us to load half a beef in his wagon before supper last night. I knew he was going to see Big Man."

"Why?" asked Deputy Simms.

"To help me."

"No surprise," said Deputy Woodside.

"Help you do what?" asked Deputy Simms.

"Tom had been negotiating," said Lester. "Big Man charges less for cutting and wrapping than we do, and we have no storage to offer. We have the beef. Big Man needs to buy beef. Hixson was negotiating to sell it to him."

Once again the words Deputy Simms took in spoke of a world

he knew nothing about. *Don't say anything until you know what you are talking about.* The tension built up among the three men. He let it build until he understood, and at length, he said, "Sounds like Tom was selling Big Man something he didn't want to buy."

"And Charlie was doing what he always did," said Woodside. "Making the sale."

"Big Man's customers needed the beef cut and wrapped, so it amounted to a matter of price," said Lester. "Tom might not a understood as well as Charlie. Charlie planned to go talk to Big Man about how it could all work out. The side of beef was a little gift."

"More a peace offering," said Deputy Simms, remembering the threatening rifle put on the kitchen table. "And it must've riled Hixson." He flicked his head toward the knot of men at the crossing. "Let's bring the section chief over here. I'd like to know if somebody's shipping more and more from Wahsatch."

"No need to," said Lester. "Tom's been doing a good job building the sales."

"Packed meat," said Deputy Simms. "Deseret ships live animals to Ogden. By the way, where is Tom Hixson?"

"Working, of course. I told him this was my father; I'd take care of it."

"Where'd you tell him that?"

"At the ranch, when he brought me the news."

"He brought you the news?" Woodside shook his head in disbelief.

"The section chief called us," said Deputy Simms. "He didn't call you?"

"Coulda done. Maybe called Tom," said Lester. "Tom brought me the news."

Simms couldn't square his suspicions with Lester's total calm. Maybe the territorial prison had taught him how to show nothing. For sure and certain, Tom Hixson had a hand in this. Nothing in Deputy Simms gave credence to the thought that Lester did. Simms thought to ask how he planned to deal with Hixson. All he could muster was, "Uh-huh."

Lester had driven his wagon to meet them at the point where the locomotive came to a stop, about two thousand feet down the track from the crossing. Woodside pointed up the track. "Go up there and stay until we finish. After Kidner takes a look at him and tells us what he finds, you can take care of the body."

Deputy Simms and Woodside stepped to the tracks to take their first close look. The shafts remained attached to the horse. Broken and partial remains of the wagon, horse, and McCormick's body clung to the stopped locomotive.

Deputy Simms looked to see if he could find half a beef in the remains of the wagon bed. More severed than smashed, most of the wagon bed must lay up track. He said, "Tom Hixson did this."

Woodside found the shafts that somehow held the horse and the wagon on the locomotive partially unhooked from the horse. He pointed to the upper half of McCormick's body, facing the horse's flank, pinned between the shaft and the locomotive. "You really think Hixson could have done something to put Charlie in this position and not get killed himself?"

"Don't know yet, but I know he created this mess. Charlie had in mind to persuade Big Man that McCormick would make it worth his while to buy only from him as a matter of price, not muscle."

Woodside continued his inspection without looking up, "That was Charlie's style."

"And Hixson's style," said Deputy Simms. "He was trying to muscle Big Man."

They continued to piece together an explanation from what they saw and guessed and understood of the men in their mountain county. No surprise that Charlie had little concern for a late February snow. After he set out, his horse and wagon probably plowed more snow than he expected. By seven-thirty, Charlie reached the crossing at Wahsatch, and the snow had made the crossing indistinct from the rails.

"Wouldn't matter," said Woodside. "He figured he could follow straight ahead on where he thought the road to be, up over the built-up crossing and over the rails. With all those people up there and part of the train still at the crossing, we'll never find anything." Woodside stepped back and looked at the missing rear wheels and the crushed left front wheel of the wagon. "I'd guess the front wheels slid a little or the horse spooked, and Charlie tried to correct. The back wheels might have slid, or the angle might have caused the bed to veer a little to the left behind him. That smashed left front wheel veered off the edge of the ties that formed the crossing. It sank through the snow onto the roadbed and locked between the rails."

"No telling how long he tried to coax it back and forth," said Deputy Simms. "You can bet he heard the whistle. He musta known he had five minutes. I can understand he wasn't about to leave a good horse to die in front of that train."

"Seems so," said Woodside. He pointed to the wagon. "He tried to unbuckle the shafts."

The Los Angeles Limited roared down that broad valley into the narrow canyon pouring on the speed for a few short miles through a straight stretch of track on the way to its first stop, Ogden. Not that it mattered, but Deputy Simms knew that train traveled well above its safe rolling speed of 65 miles per hour. Even if late to react, the engineer had hit the Westinghouse air brakes to slow it some before it crashed into the horse and wagon and Charlie.

"You got to ask why he didn't have time," said Deputy Simms, He rolled his head back and forth. "No, you best ask why he stayed there when he knew he didn't have time."

"You ready to let Lester take care of his father's body?" asked Woodside.

Deputy Simms thought more about why Charlie had remained on the crossing to let the train hit him. He walked back to inspect the mangled wagon, horse, and body. Over his shoulder, he answered, "No, let's keep him in Kidner's hands until they close the casket," said Simms. "The sheriff might want to look at him before Lester buries him on the ranch. Kidner might find something on the body we missed. With that five-mile whistle, for sure that train didn't surprise Charlie. What with the train hitting him, it's hard to tell, but maybe something on Charlie's body'll tell someone had a hand in keeping him a few seconds too long at that crossing."

Deputy Simms pulled his coat tight around him and stepped over to Two. He looked up at Woodside before climbing in the saddle. "This snow's treacherous, but Charlie's lived out here in it for more'n thirty years. From what you and Pa have told me about him and from what I saw him do with Hixson the first day I was deputy, makes me wonder who's gonna tone down Lester and his bunch? That's why I got my suspicions. Somebody don't want to be toned down."

Chapter 14

June 1908

"Pa, who owns horseless carriages around here?" The deputy's question preceded him through the door of the jail.

"Getman and, maybe, one other," said Sheriff Simms. "There's not but two. Did one wander into the middle of the sheep?"

"No, Deseret drove the sheep through without any trouble," said Deputy Simms. "Looked like Lester made a path for them. Musta been six hundred."

"Good. Lester's learning from the ghost of his father. Deseret's up to three thousand. Moving them to summer pasture'll take five more drives like that. If Lester keeps it up, things'll calm down. Let's hope so."

"Brad tells me there's profit on the hoof with sheep," said Deputy Simms. "I got my doubts a Texan like him likes being a sheep man, but he's smart. The profit in raising cattle has been drained out by the meatpackers."

"Once Lester set them to butchering to make the rustled brands disappear, Hixson pushed them to grow into meatpacking. Charlie wanted to stop that when he saw what was going on down to Ogden. There was a clash brewing and, for sure, he was happy to see Deseret go heavy into sheep. Made it easier for him to keep Lester on a path to steer clear of 'em."

"I still got my doubts about Charlie's *accident*," said Deputy Simms. "Best I can see, since then, the McCormick ranch has gone from butchering to full-scale meatpacking."

The sheriff looked up at his deputy and nodded, "Seth Parker'd know."

"About Charlie's accident? If somebody else was involved?" asked the deputy.

"Who owns horseless carriages. He sells gasoline and fixes those things."

"How'd he learn to do that?" asked the deputy.

"The way most men learn things around here, by being quiet about it until he can do it, then doing it."

"Well," said the deputy shaking his head, "he's the last one I'd ask."

"Why? You need to keep it a secret?"

"Best do," said Mark Willford. "It involves a young wisp of a thing. One of them contraptions about ran her down today."

The sheriff smiled, "And?"

"I rescued her."

The sheriff smiled again. "And you think Seth'd make it all around town?"

"Don't you?" asked Mark Willford.

"Of course, he would," laughed John Willford. "And judging from your behavior, well he should."

"My behavior?" Deputy Simms put his hat on the peg and sat down at the deputies' desk. "Nothing special happened. I yelled, 'Watch out, there,' and first thing I know, she froze in the middle of the street. I had to run out and pick her up and carry her off the street. She didn't even thank me. Told me I was the cause. Said she didn't know anything at all about that big box on wheels bearing down on her."

"Who is *her*?"

"A little thing. I grabbed her up and planted her on the sidewalk. She seemed limp. Said her name's Elizabeth Pike."

The name caught the sheriff's attention. "Limp doesn't sound right. She'd be James Pike's granddaughter. I imagine the trail captain's granddaughter is made of pretty stern stuff."

Mark Willford couldn't figure his father's information. It contradicted what he thought he had experienced. "Dunno, maybe she fainted."

Sheriff Simms laughed. "Yeah, I'll bet she fainted."

"She needed help outa the street and onto the boardwalk. I helped her. And I warned her horseless wagons take some getting used to."

"With all you know about horseless carriages, I imagine you telling her about them was more help than carrying her off the street."

Mark Willford puzzled at his father's comments. After a moment, he grinned. "You're pulling my leg. Fact is, I been studying up some on horseless carriages. Way things are going, I'll own one of them before I own a horse." Deputy Simms stopped and waited for the sheriff's response. None came. The deputy shrugged and said, "I don't recall that I ever met her before. That bothers me some."

"You should be bothered," said Sheriff Simms and then with emphasis, "Hell, I should be bothered. A deputy's first job is to know everyone in the county. Not too much to ask in a county of five thousand souls."

Deputy Simms squirmed in his desk chair. "If I'd a worked harder at it, I'd a known her."

"True," said Sheriff Simms. "True about most things. It's not much of a help to learn it after the fact." Mark Willford could hear the rebuke, but his father continued with no change in tone. "I told you her grandfather was a trail captain. It was a handcart company. Her mother came here in Pike's company, six or seven years after us. She was a Rawlings, one of the last families to come here pushing a handcart."

Deputy Simms thought about little Ebby Pike and that made

it hard work to concentrate on the sheriff's words. "Well, she's a tiny thing. Not five-three in her shoes. She stood right up and said, 'No, sir, we have met. At my high school graduation.' She stepped right back in the street after I had put her on the boardwalk. She hardly took up any space, a speck in the center of the grid. It was hard to see her and the entire street at the same time."

"Sounds bad," said Sheriff Simms.

Deputy Simms pretended to ignore his father's piercing eyes. "Don't go making nothing of it," he said. "I was just protecting the safety of one of our citizens."

"A deputy's job. That's all."

Deputy Simms saw the twinkle. "That's all," he said. "And by the way, you neatly ignored my reference to the horse and the horseless carriage."

"Didn't ignore it all," said Sheriff Simms.

"I get it," said Deputy Simms. "I got to ask."

The sheriff smiled.

Deputy Simms said, "Well, I want a horse for my twenty-first birthday."

Sheriff Simms nodded. "My pa gave me one."

Chapter 15

1909

Deputy Simms settled Two with fresh hay and water in the shed behind the little yellow house. He had ridden her hard all day with the Cattlemen's Co-operative, inspecting the brands in McCormick's herd. He rubbed her flanks with his hands. Amazement filled him once again at how different she seemed since his father had made her his birthday present. He had no doubt the difference lay entirely in her. He had already cherished her, but now she seemed less distant, more affectionate. He liked not needing her tonight, putting her to rest until the morning.

He looked forward to his rounds tonight, checking on the stores up and down Main Street. He'd walk the half block from home to Main and take the east side down about a mile and cross over to walk the west side back. Most of the stores had built on the west side of Main to gain some small measure of protection from the hot summer sun. One, next to last at the end of his planned return, held his attention. His mother still worked at the Mercantile. Trueman couldn't do without her, but she wasn't the reason he thought of the Merc. His hopes for what would happen at the door told him to walk down the east side first.

"Hey, Deputy!" Halfway down the east side, Deputy Simms reached the tabernacle, with only the jail and the livery before he could start his return trip. Terry Holcombe stepped out of the shadows. His call and his smile pierced the gloaming of the early February evening.

"You can call me Mark," chuckled Deputy Simms, "seein's we know each other since grade school."

"Not tonight, Deputy." Terry put his smile away and brought out a formal tone.

"We got a problem?" asked Deputy Simms.

"Your grandpa's problem," said Terry. "Vigilantes."

Deputy Simms often had no idea what Terry meant, this time like many before. Terry had been the one in grade school to tell him about his grandpa's problem with vigilantes and then told him to ask his father if he didn't believe it. The problem in question happened twenty years before Deputy Simms's birth. A good many people lived with it as part of Coalville's history and maybe that was the reason the sheriff had never told him anything about it. Deputy Simms had no idea what Terry's warning meant when he asked, "Where?"

Terry pointed to the large double doors of the tabernacle. The building had often been used for community meetings since its dedication, but this seemed irreverent.

"Vigilantes in the tabernacle?"

"Soon. There's a committee fixin' to meet in there."

"Committee?" repeated Deputy Simms. He recognized the word his father used in relating that Grandpa Simms could not save Ike Potter from murder at the hands of vigilantes. "What for?"

"To deal with the cattle rustling," said Terry.

Deputy Simms nodded. He and his father had watched the rustling start up again and grow from the spring after Charlie McCormick's death. It had occupied him all day. He craned his neck to recognize the men when the light shone on each as the door opened to allow entry.

"Charlie," he mumbled.

"What?" asked Terry.

"Remember Charlie McCormick? When he had that accident a couple of years ago, we thought it might lead to some troubles. Some rustling then but looks like these might be more troubles than we were expectin'."

"We had a good three or four years without much rustling around here," said Terry.

"Before Charlie died," said Deputy Simms. He recognized most of the men, all good cattle farmers and ranchers. No one carried a gun, not even a shotgun. He turned to Terry and registered for the first time that he wore a suit and tie. "I was fixin' to ask where you fit in all of this, but I remembered, you work for Crittenden, at the bank."

"More'n a year," said Terry. "He made me vice president at Christmas."

"Wow, vice president of a bank? Ain't you my age?"

"Crittenden thinks people are happier talking to a vice president than a teller. Besides, he pays more in titles than he does money."

Deputy Simms laughed. "Maybe he's been talkin' to my pa." The deputy pointed toward the doors of the tabernacle. "What do you make of that?"

"The meatpackers been drainin' the profit out of raising cattle for years," said Terry.

"Like I said," chimed in Deputy Simms, "Pa credits that to Charlie. He was smart enough he didn't need rustlin' and he didn't allow Lester to do it."

"Maybe," said Terry in one slow word contrasting to his normal rapid torrent, "but those meatpackers put up so many slaughterhouses, seventeen now. Nine years ago, they had four. That gave the cattlemen and farmers the idea they hold some advantage keeping the beef off the market for higher prices."

Deputy Simms looked at Terry for a moment, trying to

understand the complexity explained to him, marveling that Terry did. "Price is pretty high now," he said. "Four and a quarter a hundred."

"Not as high as it's going," grinned Terry. "Statehood mighta come thirteen years ago, but it really kicked in the last three years, what with all the mining and industry in the valley."

Deputy Simms noticed the growing darkness. "Have you seen my pa go in there?"

"He's not there. He's the reason I set to looking for you." Terry pointed down to the jail. "I walked down to see him, and he seemed to know all about it. Told me to find you. He had some place to go but didn't tell me."

"Never does."

"Whatever it was, he told me to find you and tell you to go to the meeting."

"To do what?"

"Dunno. He didn't say."

"Never does."

Deputy Simms and Terry Holcombe walked up the long, concrete walk to the imposing building, completed the last year of the last century. Simms asked, "Everybody there?"

"Everybody I know," Terry stopped. "No, I didn't see McCormick there." He nodded as they reached the towering doors. "Deseret's not here, either."

"Deseret's mostly sheep now," said Simms. "Brad's not growing their herd."

"We don't see McCormick's herd growing neither," said Terry before he opened the door. "Crittenden keeps a good eye on those things. The growers have to borrow the money from him to keep going."

"I don't believe McCormick ever borrows anything," said Deputy Simms.

"He doesn't," said Terry. "He doesn't put much in the bank, neither."

"No surprise. Prob'ly buries it, but there's plenty. He's shipping a lot of beef from Wahsatch."

"Where's it all going?" asked Terry.

"First off, Big Man sells only their beef now," said Deputy Simms. His father had taught him never to say more than he needed to, and he didn't even notice he was doing it. "Started right after Charlie died last year."

"No, he doesn't," said Terry. "I see the paperwork, invoices and checks. Everything Big Man sells comes up from Ogden, Ogden Provision and Packing Company."

"Somethin' a banker don't know," Deputy Simms chuckled. "That's rich. Same difference. Soon after Charlie died, two guys from Ogden visited Big Man. They convinced him it would be more profitable to buy packaged from them than buy on the hoof and slaughter the cattle. They might have even bought his slaughterhouse since it wasn't going to be worth anything. Anyways, McCormick ships everything to OPP and OPP ships it back to Big Man. On their own, McCormick pretty much sewed up Park City."

"I wouldn't know about that," said Terry. "The bank over there's owned by some gentile down in Salt Lake."

"Brother," said a man in a heavy coat and a heavy beard, "step inside and close the door. You're lettin' the all of outdoors come in."

Deputy Simms stepped further in and Terry closed the door he was holding. "That salesman of his must be pretty good."

"Tom Hixson?" Typical Simms, a question that was a statement. He walked up the center aisle to the last unoccupied pew behind the men who had come to the meeting. "It looks like he is. And then it looks like a couple of guys from Ogden help him whenever he needs it. But we don't have many people up here in this mountain desert. Hixson's making more sales going to Ogden than what's here in Summit County. To keep that going, he needs Lester to worry about supplying the beef—or worry about it himself."

Terry scooted into the pew after the deputy and turned to him, holding his hand in front of his mouth. "You think Lester's into rustling? Or letting Hixson?"

"Lester's older'n me, but I'm hopin' I can be the best sheriff ever after Pa's gone. I'm guessin' he thinks that way about Charlie."

Terry continued to hold his hand in front of his mouth and whispered, "Meaning?"

"Meaning," the deputy made no effort to hide his words with his hand or to hold his voice down from its normal all outdoors volume, "he's worked out something. Somebody, maybe even somebody in this room, is doing the rustling and he's buying. I mean really buying with a bill of sale but for half the beef at the market. Today, it's four and a quarter a hundred going to five even five fifty. I'm saying he buys one for five a hundred and makes up an invoice. The trick is two beef are delivered. He slaughters them right away and ships before you know your herd's been hit."

Noticing that the deputy's voice had attracted attention, Terry dropped his hand. Before he could speak, Joshua Shanklin broke in to ask, "How we gonna stop it?"

"For damn sure, not with no committee," said Simms. "I'm only deputy. Ask a businessman to take care of this."

"Who?" asked Shanklin.

"Ask Terry."

"Can't," said Shanklin. "He's a banker."

"You think he's lending to Lester?" Deputy Simms knew he and Terry had discussed the subject, but he asked, "Are you?"

"No," said Terry.

"Thought so," said Deputy Simms. All the men at the meeting had turned to face him, but he continued his private conversation, making no attempt to address them. "I coulda guaranteed that. Lester don't borrow money."

"Except on notes for land," spoke up Robert Whitby from the front row of the men grouped around Terry and the deputy. "He's always after me to sell my ranch for a note."

"What I know o' you, it don't do him no good," chuckled Deputy Simms. "But I meant for cash. What I'm sayin' is have Terry talk to people down to Ogden and Salt Lake. He's vice president of the bank, they'll talk to him. Maybe there's somebody who can help."

"What do you mean, help?" asked Whitby.

"All I know is what I heard growin' up and what I learned since I became deputy, but McCormick wants money," said Deputy Simms. "Any of you know my family know that's how this all started. I don't think Lester had a hand in Charlie's accident, but I think somebody did. I think Lester's doing the best he can, but he's hanging on for dear life. If somebody offered him a good price, I think he'd sell and let somebody else worry about the problems."

"So, you think we should hire Terry here," asked Whitby, "to go down to Ogden, or even Salt Lake, and find someone to buy out the McCormick ranch?"

"I don't know about hiring," said Deputy Simms.

"Hirin'd be a very good idea," interrupted Terry before the deputy could continue.

"Best way to do that," the deep voice came from behind the knot of men. Terry flinched and Deputy Simms looked through the crowd to see who spoke.

Brother Crittenden emerged, tall, lean, black suit, and bearded. The father of his best friend, and yet Deputy Simms had never formally met the man credited by his father with organizing the invisible hand of the community to aid his escape from the train carrying him to court on charges of being a co-habitator. Deputy Simms counted Brother Crittenden as one more person to whom he owed his ultimate birth.

"Mr. Crittenden," stammered Terry. "I didn't know you planned to come to this meeting. You told me to come."

"I did both," said Crittenden. "And I wanted the sheriff here. Deputy's as good. We can't afford to let a committee taint Coalville again. When that happened, I didn't yet have the bank, but a lot of people believe there's a curse on the town from that vigilante murder. Something like that's not good for my bank."

Shanklin said, "Easy for you to say, Crittenden, you got the mortgage on my ranch. What I don't have is the cattle."

"As I started to say. The deputy has a good idea. Best way out of this is to find somebody to buy McCormick's ranch," said Crittenden. "The best way to do that is to buy it ourselves."

"Buy it ourselves?" exclaimed Whitby. "I'm in, but how we gonna do that?"

"Right," said Shanklin. "Nobody around here's a big enough businessman to do that. Leastwise young Deputy Simms."

"Joshua, why don't we do what this group came to do, form a committee," said Crittenden. "Only this time, the committee's work is buying McCormick's ranch."

"Do you know how to do that?" asked Whitby. "I'm always for buying more ranch land."

"I doubt it's any different from organizing to do anything else we need to do," said Crittenden. "But you'll all have to join in."

The deputy watched a general clamor arise. He had no idea how to help. He knew his father respected Crittenden's invisible hand, so he figured he best watch and wait. He noticed that Crittenden did the same thing. Shanklin smiled and pulled his relaxed slouch up straight, still a head shorter than the banker. He raised his baritone voice above all the rest, "Only if you're in charge. You don't have to do anything, just be chairman." Shanklin smiled and then jerked back around as if catching himself, "Oh, and only if we don't need to chip in cash money."

"Sure," said Crittenden. "Providing all of you join. As to cash money, that is way too far away to talk about. First thing, we are going to do what Deputy Simms said. We are going to send Terry down to Ogden to say he wants to buy McCormick's ranch. He will tell them he knows OPP has bought many businesses in the last, well, call it nine, really five, years. If they are not interested, he will say he would like to buy it and he would like to make sure they will keep doing business with him. Of course, if they are interested, he will ask what they are offering. If it is too much, he will just walk away. He will tell them he does not want to enter into any price war."

"So, you think they'll buy it?" asked Shanklin.

"You mean the story or the ranch?" chuckled Crittenden. "The story, for sure, and the ranch, maybe not this time around, but they will buy it."

To see the bearded, black-suited banker's demeanor amused Simms. For such a serious endeavor, Mr. Crittenden seemed to be having a lot of fun.

"So, if they don't buy it this time around, how are we going to buy it?" asked Shanklin.

"The bank will lend the committee the money," said Crittenden with a calm smile. He looked at Whitby, "Only, this time around, we will call it a co-op."

Deputy Simms stepped into the aisle and walked up to Crittenden. He shook his hand. "Mr. Crittenden, I know what you did for my father, and I got no doubt you'll always be helping this town. Thanks for turning this committee to good use. It'll help me do my rounds."

"Thanks for coming," said Mr. Crittenden.

"Terry can catch me up tomorrow and let me know where we stand."

By the time Deputy Simms closed the great tabernacle doors behind him, everyone sat in the pews. Mr. Crittenden stood in the front and explained what had to be done next.

Seeing the evening on the verge of darkness, a little beyond twilight, Simms crossed over to the west side of Main Street and resumed his rounds. Respect for his calling, or some instinct simply to do it right, did not allow him to skip any of the buildings on his rounds, but he figured he could be quick about it, until the Merc.

He stopped at the door of the little insurance office next to the Merc and took a deep breath. With a purposeful step, the deputy approached the front door. In the dark, he could see a lamp aglow inside.

He rattled the handle of the door. The door remained firm. It appeared to be locked. He rattled it once again.

"I know you're in there," Deputy Simms said through the glass pane. "Why don't you open this door?" From rounds, month upon end, he knew Ebby Pike worked late. "I been calling you three months through this door."

Ebby opened the door a crack, not enough to let him in, and said, "Not much of a compliment. Seeing as how you're the deputy on his rounds."

He thrilled at the thought she'd been keeping track, too. "That don't alter the feeling."

"And what feeling is that?"

"You are a trouble," he said through the door.

"Well, if I'm so much bother, why do you . . . bother?"

"For sure because I never met a person named Ebby before," he said. He looked at the door as if following his words through it and then stepped in closer, but still raised his voice louder.

"How'd you get a name like that, anyway?"

To that question she opened wide the door. She planted her feet firmly in the doorway, as if to do battle. He noticed she had come to the door with her coat on. "Elizabeth, but my grandfather took to calling me Liberty. My little sister turned it into Libby and with one final twist, Ebby—my name for life."

She made a show of looking up and down the street, and said to him, "Not much to do. Best we get on with it."

She turned around and locked the door. They walked together to her parents' little white house, the first one across the Chalk Creek bridge. Getting on with it meant walking together and planning rides in the buggy, going to the church dance, even attempting a picnic in the snow.

Their initial effort failed. On the first warm April Sunday afternoon, they made a second attempt at a picnic. They found a hollow full of light breezes and sunshine down the road from her house, on the quiet banks of the Chalk Creek. He built a fire. She brought chicken, deviled eggs, and potato salad. He noticed right away she had baked bread rolls that morning. They sat huddled together under a blanket in front of the fire on the bank where a little pool eddied under thin sheets of ice away from the current of the creek.

They kissed.

He could feel the warmth of her skin. He wanted more. He dared not hope she wanted more, but she snuggled into his arms.

He kissed her again and she slid her mouth around to his ear.

"If you keep going, I'll call the sheriff."

Her words and her voice sounded flirty, but he didn't consider he had much experience at this, and his mind filled with concern that she was telling him he had gone too far. He separated and tried to look her square in the eyes, an effort not all that easy to keep up.

Desire met in equal measure with fear for what he wanted to do next. Discussing his desires or his fears wasn't his way. Not being his way, he figured it wasn't Ebby's, neither.

"You know, I'll bet thousands of people are out on a creek, trying to stay warm on a chilly day like this one," he said.

"Think they're thinking what you're thinking?" She stuck a finger in his ribs.

"Might be," he laughed. "I just keep wantin' more."

"If that's what you're thinking, we'd best get married."

Deputy Mark Willford Simms didn't know how to tell his mother. He wished he could be as informal as Ebby. She bubbled over with excitement as she told him about telling her cousin, Karen Bullock now Hinckley.

Saturday morning, he asked his father about it. Sheriff Simms laughed. "It must be in the blood. I had a hard time telling my mother our first baby was coming, and I'd already been married awhile."

"No, Pa," said Deputy Simms as soon as he heard the words. "It ain't nothing like that. We decided on Sunday and we ain't done nothing. I haven't told Ma yet about gettin' married."

"Nothing to it," said Sheriff Simms. His smile told Deputy Simms what was coming. "Be a man. Stand up and tell her."

"Yeah, right." He waved his hand in frustration at his father's advice and left the jail to walk across Main Street. Headed to the Merc and one step on the boardwalk told him Mr. Trueman's ability to draw traffic with newspaper headlines had solved his problem. Facing the street for all the town and county to see, the *Summit County Bee*'s headline read:

Angling on the Chalk Creek,
Deputy Simms Caught a Pike

Deputy Simms felt embarrassment turn to shame as he started to think about what it meant that he had not yet faced up to his mother to tell her. He walked down the aisle of canned goods to the office in the back. There he found his mother, Elizabeth Tonsil, giggling with his soon-to-be wife, Elizabeth, Ebby, Pike. His mother spotted him and said, "That Karen has a way with news, doesn't she?"

Before Mark Willford could notice that his embarrassment and shame had disappeared, Sarah Jane Hixson burst in, talking, taking no notice, ignoring that Ebby and Elizabeth and Mark Willford had their heads tight together in the delight over the news.

"Nineteen years old and getting married to the sheriff. Getting on to be an old maid had its good side," said Sarah Jane.

"Deputy sheriff," said Mark Willford.

"You will be sheriff," said Sarah Jane. "You been deputy now almost five years. Only a matter of time."

"Three and a half," corrected Mark Willford.

Sarah Jane waved her hand and tossed her head, "Speaking of time, that happened fast."

"Oh, I don't know," said Ebby. "We've known each other better than two years."

"Better part of a year," said Mark Willford.

"I'll bet it took more than a picnic down at the Chalk Creek," sniggered Sarah Jane.

Ebby turned to look directly at Sarah Jane. "The man does have his appetites," she said.

No discussion of love or family or children or future had ever passed between Ebby and Deputy Simms. He knew both recognized it was rough country, and nobody wanted the problems brought by excitement lived out before marriage. And they wouldn't discuss it with anyone else, either. He stepped up to the two of them, "We're gettin' married."

Sarah Jane ignored what he said, even his presence, and spoke to Ebby. "I'll grant you, he's a handsome buck. Of course, we have a special relationship." A smile crossed her face. "I remember the day he became deputy. All the same, I wouldn't want him for a husband."

Deputy Simms could not quite figure these two women. He stood there and yet they talked about him as though absent. "Why would you say something like that?" he asked. He wanted to protest more and took in a breath.

Ebby placed a hand on his arm and squeezed. Without turning her head from Sarah Jane, she said, "You already have a fine husband in Tom Hixson."

"Exciting, maybe. Not so sure about fine," said Sarah Jane. "But exciting is what I wanted. That's why I waited till I was twenty-six. Now I'm waitin' some more. If I'd a known you had to wait for a baby, I wouldn'a been so careful all those years."

On the day of the wedding, Deputy Simms entered the jail to find the sheriff looking out the window, away from a visitor standing at his elbow. The deputy read the language of the sheriff's rigid back and stiff neck.

"Normally the first snowfall makes me very happy," said the sheriff. "This year, it came late, in December, the day Mark Willford was supposed to get married, and brought you with it. The two cancel each other out." The sheriff planted a long look on his visitor and then continued. "My horse died last year. For ten years before that, because I was loyal to Indigo, I rode a loaner. It doesn't matter if I'm still riding a loaner. Until outlaws have cars, I want a horse."

"Go to Salt Lake. Outlaws have cars now," said County Commissioner Lavely. "They had so many cars down there last year, they had to register 'em to keep track. Over three hundred as a matter of fact. They got those new Fords now from Detroit, and I think our sheriff's department needs one. I'm gonna campaign for that."

"Talk, just talk," said Sheriff Simms. "The year's coming on an even number, so, you're out doing what county commissioners always do—promising people something they don't need and won't get. Once you're elected, it'll all be forgotten." Sheriff Simms waved at papers on his desk and glared at Lavely. "They make me do a report here—on roads. The more modern we become, the more reports I got to do, and the less sheriffing I do. The job I really have right now is to marry off my son."

Sheriff Simms stood up. Deputy Simms could read the finality of the movement, and the sheriff left no room for misunderstanding. He took the county commissioner by the elbow and walked him to the door. "Anthony, I'll allow as how I need to be reelected, too. Difference is, I don't aim to do it by asking the county to spend more money."

"The perfect time. No one's running against you," said Lavely.

The sheriff stopped at the door. He still held the commissioner's elbow. Deputy Simms wondered, push or persuade?

"So what? I'm bettin' there aren't but a thousand cars and trucks in the whole state. Half of them aren't working at the same time." Deputy Simms knew the sheriff had finished persuading. Action, walking the county commissioner to the door, maybe even a gentle push, amounted to the sheriff's explanation, yet his final words surprised his deputy. "When the need arises, we'll talk about it."

The sheriff closed the door behind County Commissioner Lavely. With the first step toward his desk, he started talking. "So, you think Emma's son-in-law is behind the rustling?"

"Always did," said Deputy Simms. "Didn't you?"

"Well, I know you don't have much use for him, so I'm asking if your judgment's good here. What you're talking about sounds bad, at least for Ma Carruth."

"Problem is, it's getting worse. Somebody's gonna get hurt."

"I thought you believed in Crittenden's plan."

"I do. In fact, I think Hixson does, too. That's why he's pushing the rustling . . . even harder than before. He knows it'll end. Hixson's not good for Sarah Jane. I bet that's what Ma Carruth thinks. Talk to her. She's not going to say that to me, leastwise not until I'm sheriff." Deputy Simms had let *until I'm sheriff* slip out and immediately recognized it as pride before the fall. He tried to keep an expressionless face and added, "Someday," in hopes of fending off the sheriff's reaction.

"So, what's Hixson doing with meatpacking down in Ogden?" asked Sheriff Simms. "It's rough down there on Twenty-fifth Street. I'm not so sure he can hold his own."

Deputy Simms felt a shock of surprise and gratitude that the sheriff did not admonish him. "Since we first came across Hixson, when he shot that Deseret Land and Cattle boy, the question's been how he's involved in Lester's business. Charlie called him an artist. That means fixing brands to me. Lester claims he's butchering only his own herd and only because of price."

Sheriff Simms nodded and said, "Makes a lot of sense. It was probably Charlie's idea."

"Probably was, probably both, fixin' brands and butcherin'," said Deputy Simms. "I found that muckraker book in the library and read it. We got no complaint yet about working conditions, but Lester's gone way beyond butchering. With that slaughterhouse he built up there, he's trying to use the meatpacking business to hide the rustling. Both Lester and Hixson say Hixson's in charge of sales. For my money, that explains Charlie's accident, but still, I agree with you. Hixson ain't tough enough to stand in with those boys on Twenty-fifth Street."

Sheriff Simms smiled and nodded.

The deputy expected no word of praise, but the sheriff's silent approval filled him. He continued. "What I don't know is who's squeezing the dairy farms. Somebody is."

"Maybe," said Sheriff Simms. "You best guard against seeing him behind every problem. Doing too good a job, producing too much milk, all by itself, squeezes dairy farmers. I think we might be getting there with the sheep farmers. If they don't kill the lambs, they're in business for the wool. Nobody likes mutton."

Deputy Simms laughed, "Leastwise, you, but if Lester was raising sheep, Hixon'd be muscling them, too."

"And he's not?"

"Dunno. Doubt it. I haven't talked to Brad Feltingh in a while. Best I can tell, he's been growing his sheep a lot faster than his cattle. He sees the market for wool is going up, but he also calculates the cost of losing his stock in cattle. He still believes someone poisoned his cattle."

"But poisoned cattle don't give McCormick any beef to sell," said Sheriff Simms.

"Feltingh might not be so happy with me for seeing it different. That's where the guys from Ogden come in. They're in and out of your county before you know it." The deputy breathed in before saying his next thought. It pushed the edges some, but that's what he'd been taught. Stand up. "And, Pa, I don't know if they got cars, more likely trucks, but they will as soon as the roads are good enough."

The sheriff lifted his eyebrows and raised his head. He gave a slight smile. "Not much evidence for that. Some complaints from the cattle farmers, but nobody's seen them. When we go out to count, we still can't prove what they really had."

"Like Lester's butcherin'. Hixson moves 'em right on to OPP and they're packed for shipment the next day. He's prob'ly still Lester's muscle, but he's not gonna cross those Ogden boys. He might not a had any real trouble yet, but that don't mean Ma Carruth don't have a problem with her son-in-law."

The sheriff continued the small smile he had been carrying and let it expand a bit. “Yeah, you might be sheriff, someday.”

Mark Willford Simms married Elizabeth Pike that afternoon. With barely two weeks’ notice, he had asked Sheriff Simms to be his best man.

“Where’s Lon?” asked the sheriff. “You’re stuck with me, but you wouldn’t want to lose a friend by leaving him out.”

Deputy Simms felt stuck. No matter how he answered, his father would come out second. Explaining never worked with the sheriff, so the deputy tried to answer without making excuses. “Can’t leave out someone who ain’t there. In fact, he’s the one suggested it. He told me he had exams in December, and I should ask you. It never came up if I was going to ask him.”

John Willford held his son in his gaze for so long Mark Willford began to doubt his father believed him. At length, the sheriff said, “Seems a waste, but I’d be honored.”

Mark Willford took a deep breath. “There’s one more thing.” He plunged ahead before his father could ask a question. “We’re going to be married here.”

Both father and son knew that meant just one thing, Mark Willford and Elizabeth Pike were not going to be married in the Temple[3], at least not now.

“Now or later, there’s time,” said John Willford. “You’ll do what’s best for Elizabeth.”

His father left it at that. Deputy Simms breathed relief. His father’s no debate, no question, no persuasion surprised him none, but the man had spent eighteen years in peril because he had been sealed to his two Elizabeths on the same day. His

3 In the Church of Jesus Christ of Latter-day Saints marriage in the Temple is a special religious ceremony.

father's reaction removed the initial fear of facing the subject with him.

Mark Willford smiled broadly, his father, the sheriff, on his right, his wife, Ebby, on his left, in the receiving line.

County Commissioner Lavely stepped up and shook the sheriff's hand. "I see a black Ford parked out there to take the newlyweds away." Lavely bent in close to the sheriff's ear, firmly holding the sheriff's hand. "One of the county's?"

"You know damn well it's not," said Sheriff Simms, using his strong right arm and the commissioner's firm grip to guide Lavely on his way to Mark Willford.

"Wouldn't bother me none," said the commissioner as he released his grip and turned his smile on the deputy sheriff.

"Seth Parker loaned it to us as a present," said Deputy Simms, taking the commissioner's hand, squeezing, smiling, and guiding him to Ebby.

Deputy Simms turned to see the next guest, Emma Carruth, rolling her eyes and tossing her head. With a broad smile wreathing her wrinkle-free face, she grabbed the sheriff's shirt at the button front and pulled him down for a kiss on the cheek.

"Emma," said the sheriff as he nodded to the departing Lavely, "you make a habit of saving my family."

"You needed saving."

Sheriff Simms's face clouded. "Like Tom Hixson. How's Sarah faring?"

"No time for that here," said Emma. She pointed to the line behind her, held up by their talking. "She wanted an exciting, younger man."

"Maybe not the right kind of exciting," said Sheriff Simms.

Emma pulled him down. Deputy Simms could see she was

about to whisper in his father's ear when she placed another kiss on his cheek and said, "Not the right young man."

Penury and hard work had served as the guardians of chastity and created an awkward wedding night. Deputy Simms and Ebby learned together in a continuation of their family's ways. They discussed no intimacy, neither feeling nor act. Without a word between them the awkwardness smoothed out with each passing day.

On a snowy afternoon, Deputy Simms marched through the front door of the one-room log cabin on the lot at the corner of One Hundred East and One Hundred North. The labor to help him build it had been the sheriff's wedding present.

"What you doing here?" asked Ebby, surprise in her voice.

"Sneaking around." He put a finger to his lips and made an exaggerated gesture of looking over his shoulders. "Learnin' how we can live with my schedule." He reached for her. As usual, she almost completely disappeared in his arms. He kissed her.

She rolled out of his arms and swatted him. "Right. Learnin'? The more you learn, the more you want."

He scrunched up his face. "Never thought about that." He reached out again to enfold her in his arms. "I been sort of thinkin' about how to balance being on duty twenty-four hours a day with wanting to spend twenty-four hours a day with you."

After that afternoon's balancing, the railroad clock he had purchased surplus from the Union Pacific struck three. Ebby lifted her head from the soft pillow of his shoulder and whispered, "Do you think we're wanton people?"

Chapter 16

1911

Six families, one street, and a different name made up the town when the founding fathers laid out the grid. They defined how the months-old outpost would grow to a county seat housing one thousand souls with the serious industrial name of Coalville. They named that one street, Main Street, and determined it should be wide enough to turn a team of oxen hauling a freight wagon in one continuous arc. From the open door of the jail now located on it, Deputy Simms watched Robert Whitby and Roger Thompson, members of the Coalville Cattlemen's Co-operative, engaged in animated conversation in the center of that continuous arc. More precisely, Deputy Simms corrected his observation, Whitby engaged in animated conversation and Thompson soothed in response. From time to time, Thompson nodded his head crowned in white hair. The deputy knew they would be coming to see him and waited.

"Where's Holcombe?" Whitby's voice sounded like a growl and preceded him by more than half the distance of the wide street.

Deputy Simms stepped off the stoop. He continued on the concrete walk to the boardwalk and answered in his normal boom, "At the bank, I imagine. He's a workingman, not like you wealthy gents."

Thompson lifted his eyes and spread his hands to respond, and Whitby spoke over him, "Well, he ain't workin' to make me any money. He gave OPP the idea, and now they beat us and bought out McCormick."

Whitby's reaction surprised Deputy Simms. "Congratulations. Like you said, that was the idea in the first place. Took two years, but you wanted them to buy out McCormick."

"Not my idea," said Whitby. "I don't pull my gun unless I aim to shoot it."

"You didn't tell me that last week," said Deputy Simms. "You said McCormick's ranch with his meatpacking operation hid the rustlers."

"Like I've said before," Thompson put his hand on Whitby's arm, "Robert leans to the colorful. Consistency isn't a high point with him."

Deputy Simms nodded. "We were trying to stop the rustling. It seems to have worked from the moment you asked McCormick to join the co-op."

"Some," said Thompson. "Better than none. We can't complain. Our problems have eased some since we formed this co-op, goin' on two years now."

"Yeah," sneered Whitby, "that's gonna end now." He stamped his foot. "Those Ogden fellows put Hixson on the co-op. The fox in the henhouse. The state's growing, and the demand for beef will continue to grow. The growers should receive the better part of any price increase that comes. Those meatpackers want to ignore the price increase and only talk about keeping the source of cattle cheap enough. Free's cheap."

"True enough, Robert," said Thompson, "but that doesn't mean you'll see McCormick ranch involved in a lot of rustling. Lester won't want that. He's a bishop now."

"He's what?' exclaimed Deputy Simms. "Don't the source of that money make it hard for them to do that? I never thought he was all that religious."

"Maybe he's not," said Whitby.

"He lives the life," said Thompson with a calm smile. "Like all of us, he believes the Lord helps them who help themselves."

"I'm not all that religious," said Deputy Simms. "Still, that might could be distorting it a bit."

"To your mind maybe," agreed Thompson with a nod. "Lester's been working on this since we put the bee in his bonnet about selling. They organized the Wahsatch Ward last May, runs north and east all the way from Echo to the Wyoming border. He put up the money. No one doubts it. The whole seven thousand dollars. Most folks in the county couldn't afford that for a house, let alone a meeting house. A pretty penny. They're building it right now, expect to finish it next year. Go look, not far, about three miles north of the Wahsatch loading dock."

"He's out of the cattle and meatpacking business?" asked Deputy Simms. Thompson nodded. The deputy thought for a moment. "You know, no surprise. Not even that about the bishop business. I bet Charlie'd approve. I bet that's why he did it. I knew he was wanting money. Now I see he had to sell. He couldn't a used the money from the express robbery. He had to sell."

Deputy Simms stepped back and waved the two members of the co-op toward the bank across the street. "If you need to see Holcombe, go to the bank. Crittenden's out drummin' up business. He pretty much leaves Terry in charge now."

Deputy Simms took the steps two at a time with an extra bounce on the top step. He had to figure what OPP's takeover of the McCormick ranch and Lester's new life as a bishop meant for the county and the Simms family.

"One of Hixson's men robbed a pawnshop and killed a man in Salt Lake last night," said Sheriff Simms.

The sheriff's words stopped the deputy at the door. "Did you know Lester got himself named a bishop?" he asked.

"I knew about his plans." The sheriff didn't appear to think it mattered a whole lot.

"Shouldn't that stop this kind of thing?" asked Deputy Simms.

"Lester never had much influence over Hixson, not the way Charlie did over him, or over Hixson for that matter," said the sheriff. "That's why Charlie had to have an accident."

"Maybe I'm wrong," said Deputy Simms. "It mighta been what caused this."

"You mean the bishop thing?" The sheriff asked. "I don't think Hixson had anything to do with this pawnshop thing. McCormick moving on probably means OPP'll put him in charge. He'd be a fool to be involved in something like this."

"Who says he ain't?" asked Deputy Simms. His father made no response. He said, "A fool and involved."

"Nah," said Sheriff Simms, smiling for some reason the deputy could not figure out. "I grant you. He could be faulted for the kind of men he hires."

"And the way he runs them," said the deputy. "His brand of leadership sets a bad example."

"That, too," said the sheriff, still smiling. "But it's not our county, not our problem." Still with that smile, he asked, "Say, don't you have something you want to tell me."

"About what?" asked the deputy.

"C'mon," said the sheriff. "You forget what makes me your father. I'm married to your mother. I'm told that's a process you have figured out."

Deputy Simms's face flushed. This was not a subject he had ever talked about with his father. "Uh, oh, that. We were, uh, sort of waiting to make sure no problems come up. Ma only knows about it because Ebby had some questions."

"And because she's your mother. She knew."

CHAPTER 17

November 1912

Deputy Simms jumped up the moment the hymn ended. His father stood slowly from the pew in front of him and walked to the front of the church. He touched Elizabeth Jensen's open casket and stretched his arm out to take his place one arm's length distant. Six of his seven children from that marriage arrayed beside him. Once his father and his father's family were in place, the deputy allowed the mourners to pass by the open casket to the receiving line.

The sheriff shook the hand and listened to the words of each person who had come to pay respects to his first wife. What a strong woman. What a difficult life. How good a mother. The sheriff nodded, offered no objection, and added no agreement. Deputy Simms still had a way to go to master his father's ability to agree with things that don't matter. *Doesn't cost anything.* The deputy did not really know this woman. The son did not really know how his father felt about her. He never would. His father and this woman and his mother married in June of 1869 after his father had married this woman in 1865. Elizabeth Jensen took to her bed after Mark Willford's grandfather had been shot and killed. There she remained until removed by her burial today. From the day she told him of Mark's coming, his mother had been kept distant by his father. Mark knew to his bones that his father loved his mother. That distance had been imposed in his father's belief it preserved her life. Mark also suspected that each murmur of condolence on the death of Elizabeth Jensen brought his father an added measure of emptiness.

Deputy Simms grew up with one sister, born five years after the diphtheria robbed him of three older sisters. He had not known the five half sisters born to Elizabeth Jensen beyond the community knowledge of their existence. Nonetheless when he visited to offer his help with the funeral or in any other way, his oldest half sister, Anna, responded, "What are we to do? He has told us to do the speaking for Mother."

Deputy Simms could not remember ever having talked to Anna before, seventeen years his senior and already into child-raising when he became aware that he had half sisters. He smiled. "I can imagine. Most times his requests come by telling. He considers it a duty exclusive to a child to give a parent's eulogy. He gave his mother's." The deputy reviewed a scene he could now see but never witnessed. "She probably thought the same. She asked him to say words over his father when he was a fugitive."

Now their turn, Mark Willford followed Ebby and heard nothing as he progressed through Elizabeth Jensen's receiving line. He grappled with the reality that her death meant his father no longer lived as a polygamist. His father never talked about what started as a bishop's calling and turned out to be a threat to the United States. Now he no longer needed to defend it.

As Deputy Simms thought about that, he began to doubt it would change anything in life. His grandfather's death had made his father a fugitive sheriff. Had his grandfather lived, his father would still have been a fugitive. Lester McCormick would still have lived out his plan to use the stolen money to build the ranch that he sold to OPP to create the wealth that made him Bishop of Wahsatch Ward. He would still preach the Gospel inside the ward house and outside preach his personal gospel by telling all who thought it advantageous to listen that he had been railroaded by Hopt, that it had all been Hopt's doing. And OPP would still have put Hixson in charge without even knowing the man. Nothing would change.

Mark Willford watched his father and he realized why the sheriff showed no surprise and no interest in the news Lester had sold out and become a bishop. Because Charlie had died at that railroad crossing. Deputy Simms had been suspicious of that death but could never prove from the mangled body that Charlie had somehow been subdued before the crash. Hixson had put that plan in place. In the passage of time, OPP had delivered. OPP simply did not know the person they had acquired with the land. Deputy Simms chided himself for believing he saw past things so clearly when he knew he had no idea what to expect. He expected OPP to run the ranch the way they wanted it run. He knew Hixson would have his own ideas, and he could not see whether Hixson would stay in line. One thing sure, Hixson would do what OPP wanted him to do, or they'd find someone who would.

They stepped up to view Elizabeth Jensen, and Ebby squeezed his hand. Mark Willford came back to the receiving line and put thoughts of the McCormick ranch and OPP and Hixson out of his mind. He held out his hand to his father.

"You'll be the last one," said Sheriff Simms.

"What?" Deputy Simms wondered if his mind remained preoccupied.

The sheriff extended his left hand and held his son's hand in both of his. Mark Willford had no recollection of ever shaking his father's hand.

After a quiet moment, the sheriff looked up the receiving line. "Did you see John, anywhere?"

"Pa, I've never seen John, ever," said Mark Willford. "Why would you expect him here?"

"It was his mother who died," said John Willford. "He can be angry with me, but he ought to stand up to me. I did not do my job with him. He's making a whale of a mistake. I lost my father when I was thirty-nine. I've wished I had him longer every day since. He thinks he disowned his mother and me when he was fourteen. I can't see why he figured we needed to be punished, but he's the one who became an orphan; he's the one who lost his parents."

Mark Willford also could not remember his father speaking three sentences in a row to him and none about his other family. It took a moment to respond. He asked, "Want I should go find James?"

"No," said Sheriff Simms, looking down the line to see his son, James, at the end.

"The procession's lining up out there. I think Seth made sure everyone brought a wagon, no cars. You better go."

"I'm not going with them," said Sheriff Simms.

"To your own wife's graveside?" said Deputy Simms. "You have to."

"Oh, I'm going to the grave," said Sheriff Simms. "I'm not riding."

Seth Parker took Kidner's place to drive the stately black wagon to the cemetery. Deputy Simms climbed up next to him and twisted around in his seat. All the way from the church to the cemetery in the foothills, he watched his father, John Willford Simms, walk behind his wife, Elizabeth Jensen Simms, to her grave.

Chapter 18

August 1915

Deputy Simms burst through the door of the jail full of energy to right a wrong. Filled with righteousness or not, he remembered to stop and survey the room before he spoke. He saw the sheriff's newspaper spread in front of him. The sheriff read it, peering over his mug while he sipped his coffee. He paid no attention to the commotion caused by his deputy. The deputy filled his lungs and stabbed his finger on a headline at the top of the sheriff's page. He exclaimed, "Pa, we got to do something."

Sheriff Simms leaned back, ran his thumb down the seam of the newspaper, took notice of his deputy standing urgently hunched over, and said, "My father objected to being called 'Pa.' " He searched for his article. "Since he did that objecting because I called him 'Pa,' I suppose I can't object." He bent to reading.

"You know Joe Hill didn't shoot that grocer," said Deputy Simms.

Sheriff Simms picked up the newspaper and leaned back from his desk, stretching some. "That's about as much our business as the speed racing out on the Bonneville Salt Flats."

"It's right there in the newspaper. He's gonna be executed in November."

"Not my county, didn't see it," said Sheriff Simms. "I'm reading about Bonneville. Tetzlaff set a record last August, and he's trying for a new one this month."

"Serious, Pa. You know that ain't as important as how they're trying to railroad Joe Hill for that grocery murder."

"What I know is I'm damn glad it happened in Salt Lake County," said Sheriff Simms.

Deputy Simms wanted to ask why, but he knew the sheriff would tell him he could figure that out for himself. Certain his father had not considered all the facts, he said, "Might's well a been in your county. It was one of Hixson's boys again, like that pawnshop four years ago."

"Not how the court saw it," said Sheriff Simms. "The jury never believed that story about the woman and why Hill got shot."

"That's because he'd never tell them the name of a married woman, and the prosecutor railroaded him. Look Pa, I know Joe Hill. You knew him, too."

"Being that much in the jail over in Park City doesn't make him a guest," said Sheriff Simms.

"Maybe he wasn't exactly my friend, but after a couple of arrests when the Workers of the World were organizing the miners, I knew him pretty well and liked him a lot."

"Don't see how," said Sheriff Simms, shaking his head. "Joe was a Wobblie, and they caused a lot of trouble."

"But he wasn't no labor organizer," said Deputy Simms. "And he was a ladies' man. He'd be more apt to mess around with that man's wife he said shot him than kill that grocer and his son."

"An interesting way of putting it," said the sheriff. "I'll allow as how he was an artist. I always thought he was the one smudged the Wobblies sign on the wall."

"See, even you thought he was creative," said the deputy. "And you know that lot Hixson has is just thugs and ruffians."

"Could be, but it has nothing to do with what the jury

decided," said Sheriff Simms.

"Sure, it does," said Deputy Simms. "Like you with cars, only reversed."

"That clears it up," said Sheriff Simms.

The deputy leaned into his argument with enthusiasm. "From last year you looked forward to this August knowing they would try to drive even faster. Still, you insisted on an oath of secrecy when you asked Seth Parker to teach you how to drive."

The sheriff folded the paper and put it on his desk. He looked at his deputy. "It's no secret that I know how to drive now, but how did you find that out?"

"Pa." Deputy Simms made a face, scrunching his eyes as if in pain. "You asked Seth Parker to keep a secret."

"So what?" asked the sheriff.

"So, you kept it a secret but it's out in the open about you and cars and speed records. You even refused to let them stencil *Sheriff* across the side of your car, but you love patrolling the county. You can drive everywhere in the county and back in the same day," said Deputy Simms. "Same as OPP only reversed. That pawnshop murder caused so much looking into who they really are that it almost blew the whole deal. They couldn't deny that one, but they still had to spend a lot of money on it. Now this murder of the grocer. I say it's by another one of Hixson's men. That grocer's shot didn't hit him. Then Hixson went to OPP to cover it up."

The sheriff nodded with a shrug and asked, "How do you explain it was the doctor who notified the police about the gunshot wound?"

"Doing his job," said Deputy Simms. "But it wasn't from the grocer's gun. OPP probably already had a man at the police by the time the doc called it in. They heard the bad news about the wound and went to work right away to pin it on Joe because he lived there. They got what they wanted. It diverted attention.

Nobody even thought about looking for anyone else. The labor organizers used him, and OPP used him."

"That's some theory," said Sheriff Simms in a voice that held none of its normal boom, "but I think it best to remember we aren't in a position to have an opinion . . ."

"But I do have an opinion . . ."

". . . and" in a voice still quiet and firm, "it is best to remember we have no responsibility for organizing Joe Hill's firing squad."

"But Pa," Deputy Simms pushed.

The sheriff held a hand up. "The murder occurred in Salt Lake County. Salt Lake Police arrested him. Salt Lake County will take care of him down at Sugar House. That's about as much as I care to think about that case."

Deputy Simms thought he might be pushing some harder than reflected his best judgment, but he did not want somebody else paying for another of Tom Hixson's deeds. "You know Governor Spry. You knew him well when he was a U.S. Marshal. He respects you. You could ask him to do something."

"William Spry wasn't one of the marshals back then. Besides, my relationship with the marshals was never what you'd call a friendship," said Sheriff Simms. "I saw the headline. I read the article. President Wilson and Helen Keller pushed Joe Hill's last appeal. I doubt the governor respects me any more than he respects President Wilson, and they didn't matter to Governor Spry. The appeal still failed."

"That's right," said Deputy Simms. "They're gonna give him the firing squad in November."

"All those big people?" The sheriff shook his head. "I can't do anything."

"Well, I can," said Deputy Simms. "I'm gonna go up there to Park Meadows right now and talk to Hixson."

"Ask him to give up his man?" chuckled Sheriff Simms. "No,

no you won't do that."

"If you won't let me take the county car, I'll ride Two."

"You're welcome to do that on your day off, but you'd be better off taking your wife and kids for a ride. This is not our crime. Salt Lake hasn't asked us for any help."

"Pa, you know I don't have a day off." Deputy Simms realized he had never pleaded his relationship before. "Sheriff, I mean."

"Nor no overtime pay," chuckled the sheriff. "Remind me, there will come a day, I'll give you the day off."

Deputy Simms couldn't figure a new argument. His interactions with his father had always been teaching. Just suggesting a day off brought enough distance to recognize he might have been a little impulsive. Grab his rifle and drive out to the McCormick ranch, puffed up and ready to apprehend whoever it was who really shot that grocer. Not a good place for the deputy to be. Some defense of his foolishness seemed necessary. "Hixson and Elsemore have rounded up a pretty rough bunch."

The sheriff nodded and said, "The Cattlemen's Co-operative hasn't come to us about rustling since OPP bought the ranch."

The sheriff had made his point. Deputy Simms said, "So, we can't arrest them for being rough?"

The sheriff nodded again.

"But we got to bring them under control," said Deputy Simms.

"No, our job isn't to control anybody. If they do something, we need to stop them. Sometimes, stop them before they do something; if anybody needs to control them, it's OPP."

"Fat chance," said Deputy Simms. "It's years and they're still stringing along with Hixson. Must suit their purpose. Whatever he's doing for them, they want him to keep doing. They're not gonna dispose of him as long as he suits their purpose."

Chapter 19

November 26, 1917

Deputy Simms drove the county car to Old Seth Parker's garage. Seth Parker had been Old Seth Parker since the day in the new year of the new century when Sheriff Simms walked his son around town introducing him to people. In the seventeen years since that meeting, Old Seth Parker had gone from fixing wagon axles and feeding horses to fixing transmissions and selling gasoline. Like all men in the community, he went about it without comment. When he decided to learn something new, he made no show of it. He made every effort to hide it. Something sinful lay at the center of being imperfect. What greater proof of imperfection than being unable to do everything? For a man who never talked about his skills or his talent or himself, he sure did gossip. A shrewd business sense and a compulsive need to meddle made the garage the place for town news.

"Seth, there's a rattle in the engine we need checked out," said Deputy Simms.

"Ludendorff has launched a new offensive over there," responded Seth.

Deputy Simms considered repeating his request, then, some in amusement and some in wonder, took to his morning rounds on foot. He forged up the west side of Main Street in the cruel November blow until he reached the Mercantile. Trueman had made a concession to nature and racked up the newspapers inside his store.

German Breakthrough Threatens Our Boys

The headline hooked Deputy Simms. He marveled at the clever Trueman as he stepped inside to read the article. He had not seen Tom Hixson in the back of the store behind the dry goods shelves.

Simms read of the British failure at Cambrai: three American Expeditionary Force units, engineer units, brought to disastrous results in the first meeting with the enemy in battle. Mark Willford was no engineer. He was a deputy sheriff, and he knew what he was going to do.

"All them dumb bastards gettin' kilt over there," Tom Hixson's voice interrupted Mark Willford's growing resolve.

The deputy looked at Sarah Jane's husband. It being early, he took some shock at seeing Hixson up and about, in town, hair all slicked back and wearing a vest to boot.

"Say again."

"Sure enough," said Hixson swaggering in closer. "I said all those soldiers gettin' kilt over there have to be volunteers. The draft didn't start but last May. They's dumb bastards."

He had Tom Hixson pigeonholed in his mind and this level of reasoning ability surprised Simms. He considered a moment. "It says here, our soldiers were engineers. That don't make 'em dumb but it ain't fair. I'd be better fightin' those Germans. If the country must go to war, I figure we have to go, too."

"You maybe," said Hixson, "not me. I got war enough just runnin' that ranch. OPP's the biggest employer in the state. We're just a little piece. We should be bigger, but OPP has its ways, and they want it their way. Elsemore agrees."

"Considering that lot you've hired, you're gonna have more trouble still," said Deputy Simms, itching to bring up Joe Hill. "No wonder OPP don't want you any bigger."

"You don't need to like 'em," said Tom Hixson. "They do what I tell 'em. That makes 'em a good crew." Deputy Simms wanted to pursue what was going on at the ranch and why Hixson was down here in town so early and all dressed up, but he said, "I s'pose you're one of those folks don't think it's America's affair?"

"It don't matter to me," said Hixson, paying at the counter. "It don't seem worth fightin' a war over wherever your ma came from."

Deputy Simms wondered what he meant by that and surmised he meant England. That was pretty much where they all came from, though judging from his name, Hixson might have been one of the Scandinavians. "I know we was all against it out here. That changed once they declared war. Seemed like I had a duty. I shoulda signed up."

Deputy Simms paid for his newspaper at the counter, almost oblivious to the fact his mother took the money. "When they passed that draft law, it kind of embarrassed me. I ran right down and registered."

"You're a damn fool. Didn't embarrass me none. I registered, too. You had to, or they'd a sent the sheriff after ya," said Hixson. He gave a little snort. "Leastwise, after me."

"I tried to volunteer,' said Deputy Simms. "They told me ten million men younger than me had registered. Now, I don't care what they say."

"Sure," said Hixson. "You're looking to make a sacrifice by taking the place of some boy who won't have to be drafted."

The deputy did not want to talk to this guy anymore. "Simms men stand up," he said. "And whosoever's in charge has to have a need for men to look after the boys." He made his way to the door.

"Well, you just stand up and take your place," called Hixson after his back. "Sarah Jane's ma'll tell me all about it soon's she hears. She's always comparing me to you. Don't matter none to her that I know how to make money."

"Lucky that McCormick sold out," said Deputy Simms, the words streaming back over his shoulder.

"Not so lucky," said Hixson. "I've always been in charge."

Deputy Simms's determination grew with every step back to the garage. He had no idea where it came from. He lived in an isolated and backward place in an isolated and backward state. Debates raged in the valley about the cowardice of the men in his state. The governor had issued a call for all able-bodied men to volunteer. His was not a response to the governor's call. That German Foreign Secretary, Zimmerman, had promised the Mexicans territory that included his own state if the Germans won the war. He should have mentioned that to Tom Hixson. Fighting for your own county. For your own state. For your own country. It was reason enough to tell his pa. He needed to talk to the sheriff. Deputy Simms picked up the Model T and headed back to the office.

Still early, yet Deputy Simms would arrive late at the office. By this time, he should have been back from early rounds, at his desk figuring what to do for the day and organizing everything for the sheriff. The sheriff made it in around eight o'clock these days. That November blow was cold, and he expected a warm office.

Beyond a warm office, the sheriff delegated most of the work to his deputies these days. Deputy Simms knew Sheriff Simms assumed nature would pass down the job. Sheriff Simms had been thirty-nine when fate, a form of nature, handed him the job. The deputy had never asked, but the sheriff showed by his action he thought his son ready. It simply was not in the blood to hand over the job. Mark Willford felt ready to take over when his father was sixty-five, after only four years as a deputy. Something about being the grandson of a sheriff makes you ready to be the sheriff.

All of that now seemed mired in complication as the deputy determined to tell the sheriff he planned to sign up. He knew how his father saw things. Stick to your job and take care of your family and your county. True, his grandfather had signed up when Johnson's War threatened the county. Maybe his grandfather gave him his notion of a bigger county, a country.

The deputy knew the sheriff had left his house a little before eight in the morning. He had to walk out his front door, down the concrete sidewalk he had poured, through the picket fence, turn right up the lane, turn right on Main Street, and pass by the Mercantile on the right.

The sheriff had thrown the collar of his heavy wool coat up against the November blow. The deputy could see him approaching as he drove toward the jail in the county's Model T.

"Hey," called out Mark Willford. He motioned to the door of the Mercantile. "Better go in there to have a cup of coffee. I don't have the stove lit yet."

"What in Sam Hill you been doing?" asked his father. He stepped up from the cold-hardened dirt Main Street to the wooden sidewalk.

"I'm enlisting," said the boy out the car door window. He was always the boy when he talked to his father, for sure when he knew his father would not like what he had to say. With the words, he felt guilty. He had not answered his father.

"And leave me without a deputy, I suppose," said the sheriff.

"Nothing much ever happens here," said the deputy. "Woodside'll last forever. Besides, we'll turn up somebody."

The sheriff stood in the door of the Mercantile. The alluring headlines that had drawn in his deputy were wasted on his back. He looked across the wide Main Street and down the one block that remained to walk to his jail. The bright sun seemed to create sparkles in the clear blue sky. New snow leavened the burden of the cold. The sheriff bent to look down at his deputy sitting in the county car.

"Think that somebody could fire up the woodstove?"

"Sure, but why don't you have coffee here while I go back to the office?"

"Old Trueman's a Mormon. He don't know how to cook coffee."

"You're a Mormon, too, Pa. You know how to cook coffee."

"Ain't we all," he said, stamping his feet on the boardwalk. "C'mon, let's go."

The deputy leaned across to push open the door of the Model T and the sheriff sat in. They finished the drive down Main in silence. Deputy Simms made the left turn across the empty street to the rock building that housed the jail.

"You know," said the sheriff, "this wind reminds me we ought to do something about chinking up some of these holes. There's as much blow in that jail as there is out here."

"Maybe your new deputy will be a plaster man," said Mark Willford.

"Maybe," said the sheriff. He thought a moment and added, "It was my father's. He fought for it, but it has bad memories. They should have torn the damn place down when they built the county courthouse."

Sheriff Simms stepped through the door and kept right on going out the front room into the cells. Checking the cells first thing when he arrived was a lifelong habit, prisoner or no. The deputy could feel the tension and amused himself with the thought that if a prisoner had spent the night, the sheriff would have had a hot stove.

"Say it," said the son over his shoulder, stuffing wood into the potbellied stove. "I can feel you want to say something."

"Nope," replied the father before he proceeded to say what he had on his mind. "It's a damn fool idea. Your grandpa had the same idea. My pa and my son, both foolish." The sheriff hung his coat behind the desk. The deputy watched each move and waited for the outburst. The sheriff said, "I got nothing to say."

"Well, then," the deputy bent down in a crouch before the fire he had started in the stove, "it's settled." He spoke between light puffs to help his fire. "The courthouse's gonna be open in about half an hour." Puff. "I'm going to see Pike." Puff. "You know, he's the recruiting officer." Satisfied with his fire, he made the coffee and put the pot on the stove.

The sheriff remained seated behind his desk, his hands in the pockets of his heavy, gray wool pants. He took his time answering. "There's no reason to spend time talking to a foolish deputy, much less a foolish son."

Deputy Simms watched the water start up the riser to the bubble on the top of the percolator. He continued watching the water bubble against the little bulb at the top of the percolator for five measured minutes. He handed the sheriff a cup of coffee. "I saw Ma Carruth's son-in-law at Trueman's. For sure, he ain't goin' to volunteer for no army."

Sheriff Simms bobbed his head up, down, up. He sipped his coffee. "What Hixson does is of little note to me. You're my son and you've got plenty of work to do here. Including keep track of his depredations."

Mark Willford found Enoch Rawlings Pike, the county clerk and the county recruiter, in the courtroom setting up his station as the county court recorder.

"Hey, Scribe," called the deputy to his brother-in-law.

"Hey yourself, Mark Willford." Enoch's warm reply sprang from the deep well of small-town familiarity. Family received no special notice.

"Something for me?" the county clerk asked the deputy sheriff.

"Yep," replied Mark Willford. "Come to enlist."

"What?"

"You heard me."

"Does Sis know about this?"

"Just decided myself this morning."

"What gave you this fool idea?"

"It ain't right. Me sitting up here, doing nothing, while our boys are getting shot at."

"Nobody's getting shot at," said Enoch. Like his sister, he had finished high school. In becoming county clerk, he had fulfilled his name's destiny as Adam's scribe, and he spoke with authority. Since he never put on airs, Mark Willford always accepted Pike knew what he was talking about.

"Well, they will soon," said Mark Willford.

"You going to ask her? There's three kids at home you know."

"I already waited for Frank. He's born now, and I been thinking about it a long time."

"That doesn't answer my question. So, you haven't told your wife?"

"I'll tell her as soon as you take care of signing me up."

"And your pa?"

"He'll do all right. Woodside's still there."

"Barely," said Enoch. "He's nearly as old as your pa."

"Not nearly. Not by twenty years. His son's a teenager," Willford said.

"You're letting your pa down and you know it."

"Naw, I ain't. Woodside and me'll find another deputy for a while. When I come back, I'll be a better sheriff."

"Might be, if you come back. They're killing a lot of boys over there."

"Thought nobody's getting shot at."

"Not our boys yet," Pike reflected a moment, "to speak of."

Everything neat and in place on the court recorder's table,

the county clerk walked to the center of the courtroom and stood in front of the deputy. Tall and trim, Enoch still had to tilt his head up to look in his brother-in-law's eyes.

"You aren't going. I am not going to do it."

"You have to."

"I don't have to. You are thirty years old. You have been deputy sheriff for ten years."

"Twelve," interrupted Mark Willford.

"It's a damn fool idea. You have three children. I have responsibilities to our family. I won't do the paperwork."

"Well, I'll go down to Weber County."

"It's a damn fool idea. And that's a damn fool thing to do. Maybe you're a damn fool."

Enoch Pike took one step forward to stand toe to toe with the taller and bulkier man who married his sister.

"You better hike down there fast. I know the county clerk down there and he has a telephone. Fact is, I know the county clerk in most parts around here."

"You mean you're going to try to stop me?"

Deputy Simms did not want merely to stand in the space he occupied. He set his feet apart and bent his knees. If he had to, he planned to root.

Enoch thought a moment and then said, "It would be unlucky to be on your bad side. Might be worse to be there forever." He made a chuckling, merry sound. "Oh, no. I'm not going to *try* to stop you."

Pike had made no threat. Something the cold did to the dirt in their county. Nobody threatened. Keep a thought to yourself and you still had room. If you say it, you do it. Mark Willford knew Enoch would call every county clerk within a hundred miles. All respected him, maybe some extra because of his name.

"You don't want to find yourself on my bad side," said Deputy Simms.

They walked together up the aisle toward the double doors.

"Already allowed that I don't," said Enoch. "I don't want no damn fool in my family, neither. Not even a dead one."

Deputy Simms stood at the door. His chest heaved at his inability to do what he wanted as he took in the male equivalent to his wife's toughness. He pushed open the door and left the courthouse to walk, the sun a little higher and the blow a little warmer, to the jail. The sheriff, sitting behind his desk, his hands around his cup of coffee, eyed him as he walked in the door.

Mark Willford locked into his father's steady gaze.

"Pa," he said. "In the end, it don't make me no different than that shiftless Hixson."

The sheriff lowered the coffee mug from his lips. "Yeah, it does. We're sheriffs, not soldiers, Simms."

Chapter 20

September 15, 1918

After priesthood meeting and Sunday school, Deputy Simms walked to the jail with the sheriff. A man dressed for the Saturday night dance threw open the door the moment the deputy finished winding the railroad clock, and it bonged eleven. The man held his arms outstretched as if announcing himself before he stepped through the doorway. The September sun streamed around him as he surveyed the room. He looked at the deputy. He looked at the sheriff. Recognition flickered in the sheriff's eyes. It told Deputy Simms to wait and see what happened.

"Ben Pulsipher," the man announced. He thrust out his hand. "Remember me?"

The sheriff nodded slowly. He looked at the hand. Deputy Simms could see the sheriff review all his dealings with this man from some prior time. Slow and quiet he reached out and with a leery note, said, "I do."

Pulsipher threw up his hands and, with hearty good cheer, said, "Best thing anybody ever did for me! Shipping me off to Ogden Military Academy at seventeen."

The deputy guessed at the city-dressed Pulsipher's age. His mental calculation put the events in question at around the time of his birth or a little before. He wondered why Ben Pulsipher had walked into his father's jail. A glance at the sheriff told him he wondered, too. Both waited to find out.

"I'm a lawyer down in Ogden," said Pulsipher. "It won't do for me to say, but I'm quite successful. I've been remiss. I should have come here long ago to thank you."

"Successful lawyers don't drive fifty miles to say thank you," said Sheriff Simms, and in slow measured words, "I'm thinking that's not why you're here today."

"You're right. We are a shameless lot. Unfortunately. I'm the bearer of sad news." He stopped and looked for the signal to proceed he expected from the sheriff. It never came. Without the slightest hint of awkwardness, he resumed. "I'm here to tell you Tom Hixson had a fishing accident. He slipped. I haven't seen him, but I'm told he drowned."

"He what?" exclaimed Deputy Simms.

"First I heard of it," said Sheriff Simms.

"I imagine so," said Pulsipher. "This morning. My clients asked me to tell you."

"Your clients?" asked Sheriff Simms. He lifted his head to give a studied look at the round railroad clock on the wall. Deputy Simms followed his eyes and the quizzical way he held his head. He turned to Pulsipher. "On to eleven o'clock. Still morning. Maybe not early for a Sunday in Coalville, but you're telling me it's late enough for a drowning accident to roust a lawyer all the way from Ogden?"

Pulsipher hastened to pick up the explanation. "Yes, sir. I was in my office. They called and asked me to come straight up. It's early, to be sure, but you do what your clients want. You're from around here, you know men get up early to go fishing."

Deputy Simms had never gone fishing with his father. He doubted his father ever went fishing at all. For sure, he rose early. That'd be as much a part of setting a good example as anything he made sure he did. More to the subject, the deputy doubted that shiftless Hixson rose early a day in his life, much less a Sunday, despite OPP claiming he had charge of the

McCormick ranch and crew.

"Uh-huh," said Sheriff Simms. He waited. Pulsipher volunteered nothing more. "Seein's your clients decided to call you, not me, I suppose there's something suspicious. Where're your clients, now? Did they take off?"

"Oh, no, Sheriff," said Pulsipher. "Nothing like that. They're city boys. The last thing they're going to do is head out in those mountains to be chased down by you in a posse."

"Not going to be any more posses," said Sheriff Simms. "It'd be a car chase."

"It'd still be a posse," said Pulsipher.

The sheriff looked at the lawyer for a moment, then said, "You say they're from Ogden."

"No, I said I was from Ogden," Pulsipher replied.

"Where they from?" asked Simms.

"Out of town," said Pulsipher. "I told you I have a successful practice. OPP gave them my name to contact when they came into town."

"Before the . . . uh, fishing accident?" asked Deputy Simms.

"Well, yes," said Pulsipher. "On general principle. They needed to know how to make it up here. They came into town to have this fishing trip with Tom Hixson."

"Did they plan to have a fishing accident?" asked Sheriff Simms.

"Don't jump to conclusions," said Pulsipher. "They only wanted to know how to get a license and things like that. A point of local contact, you might say. But since this accident occurred, they were right to ask me to come over to tell you about it."

"Lucky they hired an expensive big city lawyer to help them with the Fish and Game Department," said Sheriff Simms.

"I appreciate the compliment," said Pulsipher with a wide smile, "but Ogden is not the big city, and I certainly don't consider my rates expensive."

Deputy Simms had always been at odds with Tom Hixson, but for Sarah's sake, it bothered him. Pulsipher talked about his clients and seemed to pay no attention to the drowned man somewhere unattended.

"Where's Hixson right now?" asked Deputy Simms.

"With my clients, at the fishing hole," said Pulsipher.

"Sitting around together, at the fishing hole?" asked Sheriff Simms.

"Now, Sheriff, don't be like that," said Pulsipher. "My clients recovered the body. I imagine they took a moment to compose themselves, but certainly one of them found a phone to call me. The other one stayed there with the body. I told them both to wait there until I brought you."

The questions built up.

"Why didn't they go to the hotel?"

"The one here in town? Is that still owned by Cluff? They didn't stay in the hotel. I think one of them might have gone there to find a phone."

"So, they drove up here from Ogden this morning?"

"Yep," said Pulsipher. "Like I told you, they called me yesterday and wanted to make an early start this morning."

"It's eleven on a Sunday, and you're already here," said Sheriff Simms. "What time did they call you?"

"I don't honestly remember, Sheriff," said Pulsipher. "But, like you, Sunday or no, I am in my office early for my many clients back East."

"Your clients back East work on Sunday, huh?" asked Sheriff Simms. "Well, do you want to tell me where they are? So, I can go out there and send Kidner out there?"

"Kidner?" asked Pulsipher.

"Undertaker, full-time," said Sheriff Simms. "Seth Parker helped out, part-time, but when his livery became a garage, we needed someone."

"Why don't we all go out there together?"

Deputy Simms remembered discussing with his father how the sheriff tried to avoid dealing with lawyers, even his old friend, Rabbi Slonik. He waited for his father's question. The sheriff asked, "Something about where they are you want to keep secret?"

"Not at all," said Pulsipher. "I'm just trying to be efficient."

"My deputy thanks you." The sheriff pointed to Deputy Simms. "It's his investigation. Tell us where they are, and he'll organize things."

"They're down at the Weber, where the creek comes in," said Pulsipher.

Deputy Simms hoped he had not done a double take. He tried to study the blank look on Pulsipher's face as Sheriff Simms said, "You may be an Ogden lawyer, now, but you're from around here. You know that's a swimming hole, not a fishing hole."

"Well, that's where Hixson took them," said Pulsipher. "Maybe he was trying to fun them. Out there, you'll see whatever equipment they brought for fishing. I told them not to touch a thing."

"Uh-huh," said Sheriff Simms. "That's good of you. And you can tell them the county's paid their hotel for tonight."

"You are arresting them, sight unseen?"

"Nope," said Sheriff Simms. "I'm asking them to stick around for a day so my deputy can get to the bottom of this."

Deputy Simms watched the lawyer who had grown out of the boy his father had banished from the county. Endless seconds of silence ensued.

"That's right good of you," said Pulsipher. "You'll find them more than willing to cooperate. Hixson was their true fishing buddy. Furthermore, they're concerned about his wife."

Their true fishing buddy, repeated Deputy Simms to himself, for a pair who drove up this morning. The question on his tongue disappeared under Woodside's interruption.

"Furthermore?" repeated Deputy Woodside as he walked through the door. He proceeded straight to his desk and stood at its corner taking in the lawyer. "Ain't this old Ben Pulsipher? They taught you big words down at Ogden Military Academy."

"It sure is," said Pulsipher. He stuck out his hand. "You remember me?"

"Ain't much to remember," said Woodside.

"He says Tom Hixson's drowned, up to the Weber swimming hole," said Deputy Simms.

"Didn't hear much," said Woodside. "Heard that."

"He says two men are up there waiting," said Deputy Simms. "We'll go up there and see them." He turned to Pulsipher. "You go fetch Kidner and take him up there."

"And leave you alone with my clients?" Pulsipher shook his head. "No, sir."

"I thought you said they were going to cooperate?" said Sheriff Simms.

"They are, but there's my license to worry about," said Pulsipher.

Woodside gave a laugh. "No bother. Mark Willford, you go out with lawyer Pulsipher, and I'll go to Kidner. He'll be out there, right smart."

"Ride out with me," said Deputy Simms, "in the county car."

"No need," said Pulsipher. "I have my own."

"No doubt," said Deputy Simms. He opened the door. "Best we arrive together."

Their four-mile trip took about ten minutes. Without a single question, Deputy Simms learned Pulsipher had done well at the Ogden Military Academy, had gone to the university, had worked for the first Senator from Utah as a law apprentice and later as an aide in Washington, DC, and had returned to Ogden. Simms then learned how much money Pulsipher had made. Simms learned that last piece of information twice before he pulled the county car to a stop at the flat spot where the road and the Weber meandered closest together. Two men in suits sat around a fire.

"Deputy Simms, Wiley McNabb," said lawyer Pulsipher, gesturing first with some fanfare at the tall man who stood erect, lean and hard edged, then at the round man, not as tall, who slouched, "and Gill Brose. My clients."

"Pleased to meet you," said McNabb, reaching out his hand.

Deputy Simms looked at it, then answered, "Where's Hixson?"

"Over under the tree," said Pulsipher. The deputy responded to the answer with a long look at the lawyer. Pulsipher noticed. "I told them not to move him."

"That's right," said Brose. "He was over there jumping off that low limb into the water."

"Your lawyer tells me you were going fishing. Why was he jumping off that limb?"

"We set out with Hixson to go fishing up to the Middle Fork," said Wiley McNabb.

"Middle Fork?" interrupted Deputy Simms. "That's up to Kamas, nowhere near here."

"Could be," shrugged McNabb. "Wouldn't know about that. It being a warm day, we naturally ended up swimming."

Deputy Simms surveyed the men, the suits, and the fire. "A warm September day wantin' a fire?" He walked over to the tree. He felt some surprise that Hixson did not look any better to him dead than he did alive. "He's wearing his pants."

"Either that or nothing," said McNabb. Pulsipher immediately hushed him.

"And you go fishing in suits?" asked Simms.

"I told you they came from out of town," said Pulsipher. "It don't take much to drop a worm in a stream."

"Uh-huh," said Simms. He looked around. Sure enough, fishing gear lay next to the fire. He walked back to the fire. "We'll wait for Kidner. These your poles?"

"Yes, sir," said Gil Brose. "We brought them with us."

He picked up the poles and gave both a flick of the wrists. "Look like fly rods to me."

"Like they said," inserted Pulsipher. "They brought them. They're from Denver. What can you say? I doubt they know anything about fishing poles used for bait."

Simms let his eyes roam over the entire scene once again: business suits, fly rods, swimming in the mountains in mid-September on a day cold enough to require a campfire, not to mention fishing at a swimming hole.

"I doubt they're from Denver," he said. He turned to McNabb who seemed to be the top dog. "How'd it happen?"

"Hixson said we should all jump in. He took off his shirt and such and climbed out on that limb and jumped. He told us folks around here did it all the time."

That part of the story rang true. "So, why'd he drown?"

"He must have hit his head," said Pulsipher.

"I was asking your man, here," said Simms without looking at the lawyer.

"Well, you know very well, he does not need to answer you," said Pulsipher, the first time this morning he had raised his voice. "But go ahead, Wiley, you may answer."

"He must have hit his head," said McNabb.

Simms turned to Pulsipher. "Thanks."

Woodside arrived. Kidner followed in his hearse. Deputy Simms told everyone to stay at the campfire. He sent the undertaker to inspect the body. Within minutes Kidner motioned Deputy Simms to join him. He bent, tugging the deputy's vest to pull him down, then he pointed to abrasions on the right side of Hixson's forehead.

"Looks like he hit his head on the rocks," said Kidner.

"Can you tell if the rock hit his head for him?" asked Deputy Simms.

"Don't see no other marks on the body," whispered Kidner. "Nothing on the neck or shoulders or rib cage, all the places you'd expect to see violence."

Deputy Simms straightened up and called, "Woodside, put out the fire and look around. Bring everything." He turned to Kidner. "You can pack him up and take him."

"What about the widow?" asked Kidner. "Ain't this the guy married to Sarah Jane Carruth? Does she know?"

Simms nodded. "I'd tell her, but not till after I take these two in. And I have a question for them before you leave."

"I'll swing up there on the way to my place," said Kidner.

The thought of the hearse pulling up in front of Ma Carruth's gate made the deputy hesitate. He had no choice. He said, "Let's finish this part first."

He returned to the campfire and the two men.

"Show me your hands."

McNabb barely lifted his wrists to flop his hands over, front and back. Nothing. No bruises or scrapes, and no calluses either. Brose shot his hands straight out, his shirtsleeve pulling up his arm. Same, except plumper and softer.

"You carry a gun?"

"No."

"No."

"Unbutton your coats."

McNabb and Brose both unbuttoned their coats and held them wide open. Nothing.

Simms looked at Pulsipher who smiled and said, "I told them

to cooperate with you."

"Kidner showed me a bump," said Simms pointing to the undertaker. "On the side of Hixson's head. How'd that happen?"

"Well," answered McNabb starting very slowly, "we thought he bumped his head."

"Enough to knock him out?" asked Simms. He directed a question at Brose. "What'd you do when you saw him bump his head?"

"I didn't even see him jump in," said Brose. "I was still talkin' to Wiley about us gettin' undressed and jumpin' in."

Simms looked at the two men, their suits a little travel weary but not wet.

"Evidently you didn't jump in," said Simms. "Dressed or undressed, didn't you even miss him?"

"That's just the thing," said McNabb. "We decided we didn't want to get all undressed and go in the water and such. So, we both went over to the tree to tell him we weren't gonna do it. We really wanted to stick to fishing." McNabb stopped and looked briefly at Pulsipher. The lawyer nodded. "That's when we found him. Floating there in the water."

"And how'd you pull him out?" asked Deputy Simms. He could see their suits, even their shoes and cuffs, looked dry.

"We didn't know how deep it was," said McNabb. "We thought we could reach him with the poles. We used them to bring him close enough to shore. We dragged him out."

Deputy Simms snickered, "So, you fished him out?"

"You're tricky," said McNabb, "but, yeah, we did."

"How much time did all this take?" asked Simms.

Pulsipher stepped in front of his client to answer, "Don't take long for a man to drown."

Deputy Simms glanced at Ben Pulsipher. Everyone waited. The deputy kicked dirt in the fire. "I'm taking you two to see the sheriff. Pulsipher, you ride back with Woodside."

"Not on your life," said Pulsipher. "I'm going with my clients."

"Those ain't stakes you want to bet," said Deputy Simms. He waved to the two men. "Come over here and turn around." He borrowed a set of handcuffs from Woodside and manacled both men behind their backs. "Go over there and sit in the back seat."

"What about their car?" asked Pulsipher.

"It'll be safe," said Deputy Simms. He started the Model T and climbed in the front seat. He started it rolling. Pulsipher ran and jumped on the running board, then opened the door and sat in the passenger seat. Kidner and Woodside fell in behind him like the line already formed a funeral procession. Kidner turned at One Hundred North to tell Sarah Hixson and Emma Carruth about their loss.

Deputy Simms arrived at the jail, placed each man in his own cell, and recited to Sheriff Simms the story he had been told. The sheriff nodded. He asked no questions about the story. Instead, he asked, "What are you going to do?"

Next morning Deputy Simms arrived at the jail at seven o'clock and made the coffee. He inspected the cells. His two prisoners watched without saying anything. The coffee ready, he poured a cup and pulled up a chair to sit in front of the cells. For an hour before the sheriff arrived, he watched and turned over in his mind a question. Did he really want to charge two men who had somehow rid him of Tom Hixson?

At eight, Sheriff Simms walked through the door, past the stove and the coffee, straight to the cells. He unlocked each cell and held them open without a word.

"Believed us, huh?" said McNabb.

"Not in the question," Sheriff Simms said. "Kidner says death by drowning."

"Where's Pulsipher?" asked McNabb.

"Didn't ask," said Sheriff Simms. "You'll find him. You did before." The sheriff walked to the front door and held it open for them.

Deputy Simms recognized the answer had been taken out of his hands. Sheriff Simms rarely consulted with his deputies about his decisions. This was no different. After Sheriff Simms shut the door behind the last two men to see Thomas L. Hixson alive, Deputy Simms walked over to his father.

"Pa," he said, trying to keep the question out of his voice. "You're not the type to let suspicious things stay that way. They said Tom Hixson slipped and hit his head."

"Jumped," said Sheriff Simms.

"That sure and certain is suspicious."

"You don't say," answered Sheriff Simms.

Deputy Simms looked at him bewildered. Sheriff Simms walked past the stove and poured his coffee as he continued back to his desk. He sat down and sorted papers, clearing off the top.

"Well," said a hesitant Deputy Simms. "Did Kidner tell Ma Carruth? And Sarah?"

"I expect he did. Kidner does his job. You did yours. I did mine." Sheriff Simms finished his mug of coffee. Abruptly he stood up. "I best be gettin to work." He started for the door.

"Do you believe them?" asked Mark Willford to his father's back. "I wanted Hixson to go to war. He wouldn'a died if he'd a gone to war. Leastwise, not in that swimming hole."

The sheriff continued through the door. One step outside the jail he stopped and returned to his son. "Those two men fishing with him said he drowned. Kidner said he drowned. 'Death by drowning.' "

"But Pa, you know what I mean."

"I don't think they were fishing. Tom Hixson couldn't fix for himself, much less bait a hook. We owe Ma Carruth your mother's life," he sighed and shrugged, "but there is nothing I can do. Now she's shut of Hixson, maybe those two did her a favor."

"But, Pa, this is all part of that OPP mess. Something's goin' on we don't know about."

"I'll grant, you should look into that. Still, it's unlikely to change their good story for an accident."

"Well, I didn't like him none, but I will look into it, and somebody ought to go over to talk to Sarah."

"Kidner did."

"I mean from our family. The least I can do is go over there and comfort her," said Deputy Simms.

"Not necessarily." The sheriff turned around and stepped back out the door. "It ain't something I'd do."

Chapter 21

September 18, 1918

Deputy Simms showed up early on Wednesday and looked forward to a few moments of quiet. His father had started his day with the dairy farmers out in Kamas. Woodside had gone to Seth Parker's livery to check on the horses. They were so little used they hardly saw enough exercise to keep them healthy. Deputy Simms had the thought to take Two for a ride, needed or not. The door opened, not so dramatically as Sunday, yet interrupting his joyous solitude. Worse, once again he saw a man standing in the doorway dressed for the Saturday night dance. The September sun streamed passed the lawyer he remembered as Bill Pulsipher.

"Ben Pulsipher," he announced and thrust out his hand. "Remember me?"

The man's question triggered a correction, Ben not Bill. "I do," said Deputy Simms, as slow and leery as he remembered his father's words on Sunday.

He waited to find out what brought Ben Pulsipher to his father's jail a second time.

"My client is Ogden Provision and Packing Company. They have asked me to bring the sheriff notice of an accident." He stopped to let Deputy Simms react. Simms remained still. Pulsipher hunched his shoulders and resumed. "They've had an unfortunate run of bad luck. You know about Tom Hixson, their ranch manager up there. As you would expect, after he drowned, they installed his second-in-command as the new manager. Of course, they did that right away on Sunday to keep things running. I had never met the man, myself. That is until Monday, when I did the paperwork. I understand he's an old acquaintance of Mr. McCormick and he's been around for a while. Of course, he would have been familiar with everything.

"Nevertheless, like any good manager newly appointed, he wanted to survey the domain of his new responsibilities. I do not know any of the details. I haven't been up there yet. About this, I mean. Of course, I was up there on Monday. All I know is what they told me when they called me. The new manager had an accident while he was out inspecting the winter range."

Pulsipher stepped back. He took in the deputy's vest, cotton twill work pants, and boots, and then said, "I suppose I should have worn different clothes. We cannot go beyond the ranch house with the car. You will need a horse. I told them to leave him out on the winter range where he had his accident."

Deputy Simms nodded. "This new manager got a name?"

"Elsemore," said Lawyer Pulsipher. "Like I said, I met him on Monday for the paperwork. The full name is Leonard Elsemore."

Deputy Simms had known and never much liked Thomas Hixson. He had known Leonard Elsemore only by reputation. The two men most responsible for helping Lester McCormick stock the ranch, start butchering, and, after Charlie died, go into meatpacking operations—both now gone. "What paperwork?" asked Deputy Simms.

"I told you, OPP owned the ranch. Hixson managed it and then Elsemore. They needed to give him various authorizations. Strictly routine. Now they don't have a manager."

"Sounds like a dangerous job," said Deputy Simms. "Or payment for past deeds."

"Oh, come now, Sheriff . . ."

"Deputy."

"Deputy. It's a run of bad luck. And you know for sure it is going to get worse. The war's ending. Government contracts are on the decline and we're going to have a recession. People won't be buying much beef."

"They coulda just fired them," said Deputy Simms.

Pulsipher jerked up, startled-like. He stood composing himself for a few moments. "Eventually they would have. We discussed how best to shut down various operations. It was sheer bad luck, like I said, they had these accidents. However, I won't gild the lily. I don't much want to keep driving back and forth between Ogden and Coalville, especially now we're coming into winter. Best thing they can do is sell the ranch."

"What about these two men we had in here on Sunday? They here?"

"OPP employees. I haven't seen them. They might have stayed over at the ranch a couple of days, but I told you I haven't been up there yet this trip, so I don't know where they are."

"Does OPP have a name? Someone I can contact?"

"I work for a manager. I'll confirm who you should contact."

Pulsipher did not seem to be in any rush to leave. Deputy Simms pulled a coat over his vest and headed for the door. "We'll meet you there."

"You know where you're going?" asked Pulsipher.

"We been there before," said Deputy Simms. He and Woodside had ridden out to Park Meadows and the McCormick ranch a few times. This was the first time in the eleven years since Charlie McCormick died at the railroad crossing, and the first time riding out there in a county car. He pulled the door shut behind Pulsipher. "Life's strange. Pa tells me nobody's seen you since he banished you. I never seen you in my entire life, till this past Sunday. Now twice in these three days."

"No need for you to see me. McCormick sold us cattle, then

he sold us the ranch. I didn't need to come up here for that, not even the ranch. I got no family reason. Pa sold his hardware store a long time ago. If OPP listens to me, they'll sell the place to Deseret Land and Cattle and you'll never see me again."

Deputy Simms left Pulsipher at the steps of the jail and walked to the livery, arriving in the middle of the morning's gossip going on between Deputy Woodside and Seth Parker.

"Did you make the coffee?" asked Deputy Woodside.

"Do I value my scalp?" answered Deputy Simms. "It's been the better part of an hour. What you two still gossiping about?"

"Nothing, talking about how it don't look like Tom Hixson had an accident. And poor Sarah. She is still mighty good-looking but now no husband and no kids and she's thirty-six. She'll live there with Emma Carruth forever." Seth Parker's head bobbed with each point he made in judgment of Hixson and Sarah.

"She's better off," said Deputy Simms. "Ma Carruth's a good woman, and Tom Hixson was a bad man."

"Just what we was sayin'," said Seth Parker, stomping his foot and nodding his head. "Did you come down to visit Two, Deputy?"

"In a way, I did," said Deputy Simms. "You got a horse trailer?"

At that, Seth gave an exaggerated laugh. "Now, there's a question. This here's a garage that was a livery, so you might say it's a livery-garage, with horses and cars. It seems logical we'd have a trailer, too."

"That's head-spinning logic, Seth. The county's got a car, and we all got horses, but the county don't have a horse trailer."

"Why do we need one now?" asked Woodside, interrupting the duel.

"That's why I came looking for you," said Deputy Simms. "Ben Pulsipher showed up again this morning. Looking for Pa or you and getting me. Seems the new manager they appointed after Hixson died set out to see their cattle on the winter range and had an accident. Thought you might want to be involved. He's the one you brought in once before, Leonard Elsemore."

"Elsemore's dead?" asked Woodside. "I don't buy it."

"Dead? Or accident?" asked Seth Parker.

Woodside blinked his eyes a couple of times, then lifted his chin in recognition. "First, if Pulsipher's here, it was not an accident. Second, Elsemore was too lazy to ride out to any winter range. They mighta called him the ranch manager, but it's for damn sure he wasn't calling the shots. And third, riding out there in those gullies and washes don't bring enough danger to kill you. It ain't like they keep those cattle in the Uintahs. They keep 'em in the hills. That's why they call it the winter range."

"The county car'll take us out to the ranch house in the better part of an hour," said Deputy Simms. He started to walk to the Model T parked in one of the stalls. "We'll need horses for the winter range. I'd just as soon not use theirs, and Two needs the exercise."

Deputy Woodside insisted on driving. Deputy Simms protested just enough to make Woodside feel good about prevailing and to hide the fact he didn't much like to drive anyway. He felt freer to talk when he was in the passenger seat than behind the wheel.

Deputy Simms wanted to know more about Woodside's past involvement with Elsemore. After they cleared the ledges at the north end of town, across from Woodside's house, he said, "You know, Pa keeps that telegram you sent hanging on the wall above his desk.

'Frisco, Utah, August 9, 1883
Apprehended Elsemore, Johnson's Fort, Monday
Frisco nearest telegraph
Home in a week.'

But he never talks about it, nor anything. All's I know about my grandfather's killing is what I hear around town."

"Plenty o' that," Woodside said. "Same as when we rode out here the first time, Hopt and Elsemore needed Lester McCormick to pull off the express heist. Sheriff Simms figured they would hole up at Charlie's on Porcupine Mountain. We grabbed them inside a day. Well, Lester, the other two got away . . . because of me. When they broke Lester out of jail, Hopt shot Sheriff Simms. Charlie was smart enough to turn Lester in again right away. Elsemore was dumb enough to run. I caught him like the telegram says. That big word was for the benefit of your father's friend, Lawyer Slonik. McCormick stayed in prison four years, and Elsemore sat there fifteen years. Your father stuck at it 'til Hopt faced the firing squad. When the state let Elsemore out, he made his way straight to McCormick. Been working for him since ninety-eight."

"Working for him?" questioned Deputy Simms. He stopped watching the dirty gray sagebrush out the window to look at Woodside. "Or McCormick's taking care of him?"

"That, too," said Woodside, "considering McCormick sold out and became a bishop some seven years ago now."

They drove one hour instead of riding four. The car made its way through the same gate the horses had crossed in the years before Charlie's death. The ranch house looked the same size and shape except freshly painted and with curtains in the windows.

"A woman's touch," said Woodside.

"Sarah moved out here almost from the moment they married, even before McCormick sold." Deputy Simms looked around. He saw two cars in front of the house and a truck near the barn. Strangely for a ranch, he saw no horses, at least none outside the barn. Maybe they were all out to the range. "One of those cars is probably Pulsipher's."

"Yeah, the Buick," said Woodside.

As if hailed, Ben Pulsipher emerged from the front door. He waved them to come on in. Woodside parked the truck and trailer in front of the hitching rail. Deputy Simms watched Pulsipher cross the porch and settle in a chair. He decided the horses needed tending to first.

"Come and sit. Have some coffee," importuned Pulsipher. "Mrs. Hixson has cake, too. It'll fortify us for the trip out there."

Deputy Simms finished with the horse trailer and started talking as he headed for the porch. "You coming? In those city clothes?"

"Don't have anything else, no real need. No need to go out there. An accident, my client is not involved. But I will have to be thinking about a settlement for the widow, and I haven't been out there yet. Maybe not for the reasons you're going, but I better go with you."

Sarah brought a cake platter and a pot of coffee to a small table. As she put the plates in front of them, she caught Deputy Simms's eye.

He finished his cake and his first cup of coffee and announced, "That in the pot's gettin' cold. I'll go bring fresh."

"You okay?" he asked Sarah in the kitchen. "Kidner told me you took it hard on Sunday."

"I'm not my mother," she flashed, an edge in her voice. "Kidner told me my husband was drowned. What did you expect?"

"Nothin'," said Deputy Simms, realizing he had almost demonstrated he thought her better off. "I wanted to know if you're doing better. They treatin' you right?"

"Seems so," she said. "They're gonna sell this place. That was why they had Tom and me come down to Coalville over the weekend. He did not want them to. They had arguments."

"You think they killed him?"

She said nothing.

"Over that?" asked Deputy Simms.

"I don't know what to think, Mark Willford. Sheriff Simms don't seem to think they murdered him."

"No, he said he don't think there's anything he can do," said Mark Willford. "There's a difference."

"Some difference," said Sarah. "Tom's still dead. If they murdered him, they still murdered him." She looked at Deputy Simms for a long moment. "I thought he was exciting. I knew he took risks." She tried for a smile and it dissolved into tears. "What did he do for them that they had to kill him?"

Deputy Simms held the coffee pot in one hand and the mug in the other. He looked to his hands, back and forth, and poured the coffee into the pot on the stove.

"You're not going to tell me, are you?" Sarah asked.

"It would take more proof than we ever turned up," the deputy answered as he poured coffee from the pot on the stove back into the pot in his hand. "He knew a lot." Simms hefted the coffee pot and pointed it toward the door to the porch. "Will they let you stay here?"

"Hard to say. Maybe until they sell it. What's that? A month? Two months?"

"Where'll you go?"

"Wyoming. Evanston probably, maybe Rock Springs. Could go to Green River."

"Family there?"

"Not to speak of. I'll just move there and find a job." She paused. "And a new life."

Deputy Simms took the freshened pot back to the table on the porch. When he set it down, Deputy Woodside said, "Let's go."

"I'm ready to head out," said Deputy Simms. "I've had enough coffee."

"No, back to the jail," said Woodside. "We can't do this."

"What do you mean?" asked Deputy Simms.

"We shoulda figured this out before we set out here. Not more'n five, ten miles from here and you're in Rich County." Woodside turned to Pulsipher and asked, "Do you know where Elsemore's body is?"

"They told me up near the Neponset Reservoir," said Pulsipher. "Plenty of water for the winter, no matter how cold it turns."

"Plenty of water," said Woodside, "from a reservoir in Rich County. They built that dam way last century for the mills along the Neponset River. You're going to have to do this with the sheriff of Rich County."

Pulsipher said, "But our ranch is here, in Summit County. Same as Sunday. Sheriff of the county where the ranch is."

Woodside looked hard at Pulsipher. Deputy Simms could see Woodside thought the lawyer tried to trick him.

"Ranch house. The ranch has land in both counties," said Woodside. "If you're saying he died here and somebody moved him out there to the reservoir, then maybe we could pursue it."

"Oh, no," said Pulsipher. "I'm not saying anybody moved him at all. He died out there, had an accident."

"How do we know that?" asked Deputy Simms.

"Somebody called me and told me there had been an accident."

"Who?" asked Deputy Simms.

"We'll find out," said Pulsipher. "I didn't start any investigation before I came to you. I left my office and drove straight to you. It's enough Summit County's so full of mountains. At least Summit has some people. There ain't nobody in Rich County. Can't be two counties in the whole state with less people."

"The county still has a sheriff," said Woodside. "And the sheriff still has jurisdiction. Sheriff Simms'd raise Billy Hell if somebody came in here to take away a body."

"If the ranch has a phone, we can call them," said Deputy Simms. "It ought to be easy for you to go from here and meet them at Kersey Point. It's right at the end of Kersey Road."

"One more reason," fumed Ben Pulsipher, "for OPP to sell this ranch. OPP couldn't make a go of it with Hixson and Elsemore around, and certainly not now with them not around."

Deputy Simms heard the lawyer's ire and thought it sounded pretend. He looked to see if Sarah had heard. Maybe selling the ranch had been the reason Hixson and Elsemore both had accidents. He did not want to give up the investigation. "Do you want us to talk to the sheriff over in Rich County for you?"

"No," said Pulsipher, "I'll take care of it. I'm going to be stuck up here for days."

Woodside snorted and called goodbye into the kitchen to Sarah.

Deputy Simms walked out to the trailer. He rubbed Two's nose and said, "I was looking forward to that ride, but no exercise today. Maybe we can go somewhere next week."

Driving out through the ranch gate on their way back, Woodside jerked his thumb toward the house and said, "You know, I'm of two minds. I'm just as happy not to be trackin' down Elsemore again. But I don't like not knowin' if that really was an accident."

Deputy Simms bobbed his head in agreement. "I know Hixson didn't drown swimming." He turned to Woodside. "Now I cannot even find those two, McNabb and Brose. Couldn't even prove by me that's their true names. Pa told me there's nothing he can do about it. I don't like it when he says that, but that don't mean it ain't true."

"Let it go," said Woodside.

"That's sorta what he said. He said take Ebby on a picnic before the baby comes, and it gets too cold. If there's anything to work on, it'll pop up."

"Sounds like good advice. You gonna take it?"

"Sure am. At least the picnic part. Sunday. I'm trying to figure out how to take Two along with us."

"Ha," laughed Woodside. "If it's a pick between your wife and your horse, I'd advise you pick your wife."

Chapter 22

September 29, 1918

Deputy Simms had told Woodside of his father's suggestion, but he couldn't believe Sheriff Simms told him to take a day off. In thirteen years, the sheriff had not once shown concern for the load he asked the deputy to bear. In thirty-one years, the father had never acknowledged the son's need for respite from the hard life created by being son of Sheriff John Willford Simms. On Friday morning, not two weeks into the investigation of Tom Hixson's drowning and the men who drove up from Ogden, the sheriff called his deputy over to the woodstove.

"Ebby's due soon. Take the county's Model T and take her up Echo Canyon on Sunday," said Sheriff Simms as he poked wood into the top of the stove. "It'll be the last good day for a picnic."

The sheriff's suggestion had brought great suspicion, but now Deputy Simms thought only of Ebby as he stood in her cousin's kitchen.

The round table had seen many births in a family that arrived with the last handcart company. Even when not in her kitchen, Cousin Blanche attended most of her family's births. The only woman in her family to have girth, her body and her manner seemed to have been given to her to assist that process. Deputy Simms watched Cousin Blanche do her best to help the little girl start life. She entered the world too early in her own journey and too soon after her brother Frank's arrival.

Holding a tiny bundle of wrapped blanket in her hands, Blanche said, her own strong voice thin and broken, "She wasn't strong enough."

"Let me see her," said Ebby. Mother gazed on the still face of her daughter. "She has her color. Rose. She should have a name. When we bury her, we'll bury Rose."

"You're not burying anybody," said Blanche, taking the stillbirth back in her hands. "You think you come through this healthy and strong, but having a baby takes a lot. You're not going anywhere for at least three days."

Mark Willford pointed to the bundle in Blanche's arms, "That'd be Wednesday, I'll take care of it."

"Her," said Blanche, "she was alive until she came here, and no, you won't. Send Mr. Kidner to me, once you're home. Otherwise, take care of your three kids until you come back to fetch Ebby on Wednesday."

Mark Willford never disagreed with his father, the sheriff, and he never disagreed with any woman in his family. That included Cousin Blanche.

Deputy Simms set out for home knowing his Ebby and their Rose would be taken care of by the family of strong women. Better than he ever could. He needed only to worry about the duty his father had discouraged but allowed him. Find out if Tom Hixson's apparent accidental death had been murder.

To return to Echo on Wednesday, he knew he would rely on one more strong woman, his mother. Perhaps the strongest of all, full of energy and working every day at seventy-two, she had encouraged him to follow the sheriff's suggestion to take a day off for a picnic. As her gift to Ebby, she offered to sit with the children. It never came to wonder how she would take care of children seven, three, and one while still working at the

Mercantile. She had raised him.

Deputy Simms cranked the county's Model T and sat in it for lost moments with the sadness of losing Rose. He and Ebby had lost two. Three had lived. More would come. They would not talk about it.

The light above the loading dock flickered on. It broke into his thoughts. He put the car in gear and let it start to roll. Down the front of the loading dock, he thanked his father for the loan of the car even as he returned in it to Coalville, empty, just like when he drove the silver freight and returned home in it empty with his father.

Chapter 23

December 31, 1899

Mark Willford rested the shotgun butt on his right thigh, barrel extended above his head. He held his right hand high on the butt, resting his finger lightly on the trigger guard. He kept his finger clear of the barrel. Mark Willford's posture was as erect and stiff and straight as the shotgun. Sitting next to John Willford, Mark Willford imagined he and the shotgun formed a totem.

Deep blue tissue of dead cold sky stretched high above. Mark Willford followed the sky's edges as far as the eye could carry. Moonlight and white hills combined to provide enough light to see the trail across the frozen rock. He could see they were alone out in the open. Someone could be hiding behind the scruffy sagebrush and scrawny pines up in the foothills. Not much cover, but someone could be there.

Mark Willford's breath streamed out ahead. He measured how he felt inside. Calm. He measured his breath. Normal.

His father held the reins one in each hand. Working on a Sunday, the day before New Year's, not in the official capacity conferred by the star peeking from his vest, he was a man with two families, at the extra job he needed to support Mark Willford's mother. He flicked his wrists and a little ripple traveled down the leather straps to the back of the horses.

The twelve-year-old boy holding the shotgun measured his head and shoulders even with the man wearing the star holding the reins. The lurch of the wagon's roll over a rock brought their shoulders together. Mark Willford's knuckles ached as he opened his hand and closed it to tighten his grip on the double barrel.

Slowly scanning all the way around the horizon, the deep blue had started to change, soon bright. He could see dirt and sage and winter dead bushes all the way to the bluff. No one could be behind those scrawny bushes. He leaned his shoulder into his father again.

"Big day tomorrow," John Willford said. "New century."

"Do we have to work?" asked Mark Willford.

"You won't."

The boy waited for more. The wagon rolled. The sky brightened. The pause lasted. His father had said all he had to say. They passed a mile in silence.

"Mine holiday," said John Willford. Mark Willford found the thread from the long pause. "We'll unload this by noon. You'll miss church, but we'll have you home before dark."

The horses pulled the wagon and the boy with the shotgun and the man with the star another mile over the frozen ground.

"I'll let you go home by yourself," John Willford said in answer to no particular question.

"Okay," said Mark Willford. He cast about for an acceptable way to ask where his father was going. "You need to work?"

"I'll go back to Park City."

"Trouble?"

"Don't expect any," said his father. "A little excitement, maybe, what with the miners and it being New Year's."

"Can I help?"

"You're helping now."

Mark Willford heard the double meaning. His father spoke truth and used it to say no.

Silence settled between them again. Mark Willford felt a thrill talking to his father. He accepted this was the way they talked to each other, punctuated by silences.

They drove on through the narrow ribbon formed by the creek on the left and the sandstone bluffs on the right, horses' hooves on frozen mud the only sound.

Mark Willford pushed the shotgun out in front of his chest with both hands.

"I was thinking more about tonight," he said. "About helping you with the miners."

"I know you were."

Maybe not a mile this time, just a long time quiet.

"It won't be nothin'."

Pause.

"I can help, Pa."

"I know."

They rolled on for another mile in silence while Mark Willford tried to find a way to argue his case.

Like he could read minds, John Willford said, "I like the way you handle that gun, but not tonight."

No matter how Mark Willford tried to control it, the pride grew. Best not to let on; best not to get proud over doing a job you were supposed to be able to do.

"I need the experience."

"That's not how you get experience."

Horses' hooves on silence.

How do you get experience? He knew it was not something to ask. It was something to figure out.

"Your ma needs you tomorrow."

"Aw, Pa, she'll have me tending stove."

"Well, do a good job," said John Willford. "You need the experience."

They continued, Mark Willford trying to figure out how to keep going what passed for talk between them.

John Willford Simms interrupted his effort. "You finished the sixth grade?"

The question surprised Mark Willford. His father knew everything about him.

"You know for sure, Pa. You're joshing. I'm halfway through the seventh."

"You did pretty well, didn't you?"

His father, over six feet tall, was solid like an oak. Mark Willford already measured up at the same height, growing solid like a barrel. He sensed how large his father was without making any connection to his own adult size. He would always be a boy.

"I reckon," said the boy.

Be careful not to say too much. From whatever year marked an earlier age, Mark Willford had learned that you never talked much about how good you were at things you did. That was to risk the wrath of God—and those you wanted to love and trust you.

"Your teacher told me you know how to read and write."

"Of course, I do, Pa," said Mark Willford. Why wouldn't a seventh grader know how to read and write? Then he thought better of the retort forming in his mouth. His father had just told him he had been talking to his teacher. The sheriff talked to the teacher all the time, but Mark Willford never knew the sheriff became the father and talked about him. Best be humble. "The numbers give me trouble, though. And I have algebra this year."

This was a conversation. Questions. Answers. Talk flowing straight ahead out into the cold mountain air.

"Teacher thinks you're doing okay in school. Never mentioned numbers."

"It comes. But numbers is hard."

"Teacher told me you read important things. Like the Greek . . . what'd she call them?"

John Willford edged the wheels of the freight wagon past a wall that the bluff made down to the trail. The question and the maneuvering came all easy. His eyes straight ahead, never moving.

"Classics," Mark Willford said. He slid the shotgun onto his left thigh to hold it in both hands.

"Yeah, the classics," said John Willford. He thought a moment. "Well, maybe she called them something else. Myths. No, epics. The Greek epics."

"Mighta been."

"Anyway, you like them?"

"Sure," said Mark Willford. "There's a whole bunch of 'em. All adventures."

"You say?" said Sheriff John Willford Simms, a tone in his voice. "Adventures, huh?"

Mark Willford wondered at the tone. It didn't make sense for the sheriff to be interested in adventure stories. Boys' stuff. It made him feel uneasy.

"Names are hard though," he said.

"Tell me one," said the sheriff. He added, "One of the adventures."

"Have you heard about the horse?" asked Mark Willford, feeling no less uneasy, not sure where to start, yet happy to show his father what he knew. "The Trojan Horse?"

"That was the one they used to trick them guys, right?"

His father's question caused Mark Willford to throw off a slight shiver. Best to be on guard.

"Say, Pa," Mark Willford said. "I think you're tryin' to trick me, yourself."

"Naw," said the sheriff. Without turning his head, he said, "Maybe I never told you that when we emigrated from Derbyshire to Summit County, we could only bring what we could carry. Ma carried three books, the Bible, the *Iliad,* and the *Odyssey,* all the way across the ocean and across the plain. Coulda been, she read me a few stories."

Mark looked at his father, showing no sign, but it was time to be careful with showing what he knew. "Like I was saying, they're all adventures. You know the story."

"Well, I know what I know," said John Willford. "I don't know what you know."

Mark Willford thought about that. He knew what he knew and one thing he knew was his father expected a man to speak right up. He knew he was expected to face right up to the challenge.

"You're right, Pa. That horse was a trick. What really gets me is you are reading along. Suddenly it makes you stop. You can't keep reading. It *makes* you think."

"I never heard tell that before."

Not so sure he believed the words he heard, Mark Willford took a moment's caution and then jumped in again. "Ya know, Pa, a little bit like you. You're always teaching lessons."

Sheriff John Simms had trained his son well to maintain a straight-ahead lookout. "I thought those stories were just boring old things to kids," he said with a slight smile. "Here, you've made 'em adventures and lessons."

Mark Willford noticed the recognition. "Well, I guess that's why I like to read 'em. This Trojan War was supposed to be about some woman, but that's not it at all." He paused, wanting encouragement, heard none. He carried on. "It was really about selfishness—the selfishness of the guy in charge, some general named Agamemnon."

"How so?"

"He took all the pretty women . . . and the gold . . . for himself. He was a selfish S.O.B."

"Some people are like that. You'll have to learn how to know which ones."

"I know that, Pa," said Mark Willford, "but that's not the lesson."

"How so?"

"The war goes bad for him. He starts to think about the mistakes he has made. Lo and behold, he realizes," the words had started to come in a rush. Mark Willford caught himself, slowed down. "Well, he realizes it all goes back to when he stole Zeus's daughter."

"You don't say."

Mark Willford tensed up, alerted the moment the words floated into the cold mountain air. He better tread with care here.

"You know who Zeus's daughter was?" asked Mark Willford.

"No."

"Folly," said Mark Willford. He looked at his father.

"Keep a sharp lookout," said the sheriff. "Eyes straight ahead."

Mark Willford suffered the rebuke in silence. He wondered was this new information? Or had he discovered something as old as the mountains that surrounded them?

"Zeus's daughter was named 'Folly,' " Mark Willford repeated for emphasis.

John Willford waited a few moments, a lasting silence, and then turned to his son.

"I get it. When that general embraced 'Folly,' that's when all the trouble started."

"Yep."

"Well, I'll be damned."

Mark Willford stood tall in the bucket. Father and son both looked straight ahead.

"I'll be damned."

Horses' hooves on silence.

"Ain't that something?"

Now, that was a compliment.

Horses' hooves on silence.

"Why don't we switch," said John Willford. Mark Willford's face clouded up. The sheriff gave no indication he saw it, but said, "You handle the reins better'n me, best as I recollect."

The trail continued, two long scars scratched in the sandy rocks by wagon wheels, summer or winter, except when there was snow. For one bright day the snow looked like a giant sheet extending all directions that had never been scratched. A wagon trail covered in snow was perfectly beautiful and perfectly treacherous. No way to know where to go and no traction and no way to move the heavy snow. A trail covered in snow did not happen very often. The air was dry and mostly it was cold winter gray.

On the trail about three hours, the cold early morning darkness of the last day of December of 1899 had given way to cold early morning sunlight. By the time Mark Willford dropped his father at the sheriff's office and took the rig back, the sun would be as high in the sky as it was going for the day. It would still have no heat in it.

"You can read, and you can write. You know your grammar, and you struggle with your numbers, but you can do 'em. That about right?" asked John Willford.

Mark Willford risked a peek. He could see his father's eyes moving around, looking in both directions, as they rolled out of the little canyon into a clearing.

"I can add and subtract and do long division and all my multiplication tables. I don't like them. This year is the worst."

Mark Willford would take attention in any form. John Willford was a busy man with his job as sheriff and his first family. He never visited his second family at home. Mark Willford saw his father at church and at work, like today. Still, like before, Mark Willford wondered why all the questions. His father knew everything about him.

"We'll be there soon," said John Willford. Bright clear blue had replaced the dark canopy of sky. They could see for miles around. They could be seen for miles around right out in the open inching a shipment of silver behind two tired horses over frozen scratch marks.

"Like I said, let's us switch." This time the man's voice held no concern for the boy's feelings. "You take the reins and I'll ride shotgun for a while."

Ahead they could see the few rough buildings of the town that had sprung up around the railroad siding. Behind them lay the foothills of the Uinta Mountains, hiding the mine and the small smelter where they had picked up their load and started their day.

Mark Willford started to jump down off the side of the freight wagon.

"Here, let me take this," John Willford interrupted him, reaching his left hand around the double barrel and extending the long gun barrel away, butt toward his son. "Mind the trigger. Now, step down. You know how to handle a gun, don't you?"

"Pa, you said you like the way I handle the gun. You taught me, remember."

Mark Willford remembered. His father pointed out every mistake and just as fast told him when he did right. He was that way with everybody.

What Mark Willford did not know was whether his father believed he had any special, God-given talents. He always listened to hear his father say something like that, but he knew he'd heard about all he was going to when his father said no amount of talent would count for much if he wasn't well trained.

"Pa, I won the rifle competition in the county fair and this July Pioneer Days, they're putting me in with the adults. I ain't won it yet, but I know how to handle a gun."

"Well, then, do it right," said John Willford.

"I was doing it right," said Mark Willford. "I was holding it straight up and down. I know not to have an accident."

"Best know," said John Willford, "seeing's that I'd be on the other end of your accident." He sidestepped to his left and sat down. "Best also know that when you're changing drivers, taking the gun off guard, like you were fixing to do, ain't the way to do it."

"Yes, sir," said Mark Willford. It was like reading those Greeks.

Mark Willford drove a few long minutes in silence to the turn where he entered the streets of the small town and turned toward the railroad siding. John Willford looked far down the street past the siding. Clear. He pointed to a spot.

"Head her to number two down there."

The alleyway next to the siding held a conveyor leading up to and over the ore car. Mark Willford's job was to use the reins to maneuver the horses and the silver wagon right up next to the conveyor. He was not going to admit it was hard work. He was going to do it right. On the first try, he backed into the number two spot.

"You can handle the wagon fine."

"Thanks, Pa."

"It ain't to thank," said the sheriff.

Being told you did a good job was no common thing. You had to thank a person for that gift. Before Mark Willford could disagree with him, the sheriff spoke again.

"It's time to get a job. You best talk to Mr. Parley up here about riding guard for him on these silver wagons."

"Think I could?" asked Mark Willford. He barely paid attention to his own question as he untied the tarp in the back of the wagon.

"You're made of pretty good stock."

That stopped him. Praise came rare as rain and never direct. High praise came when you were measured and told you measured up.

In that moment he realized he would have to leave school—and he learned praise is best used as a salve to pain.

"How much schooling did you get, Pa?"

John Willford took one last look in every direction around the barren loading dock, down the canyon to the west, up the canyon to the east, across the dirt main road to the river, and behind into the foothills. Mark Willford could feel the tension with each careful look, though he expected his father to see no one. He saw no one.

"About third grade," answered Sheriff John Willford, bending to the task of lifting and carrying the heavy metal to the conveyor.

"Is that enough schooling to be sheriff?"

"Evidently."

Mark Willford feared he had overstepped. He wanted to know what he was going to miss. How could he even ask his question? It seemed like he was contradicting.

"Oh, Pa," he said, searching for words, "you know what I mean. How'd it work?"

"Your grandpa left us down in the valley when he was sent up here to settle the mission. They discovered the coal and the very next year the legislature made a county up here. He was already the constable, looking out for the mission, so when they made it a county, they made your grandpa sheriff. He moved Ma and me here, and Ma schooled us some. Did a good job, too. By the time they built the schoolhouse, I was fifteen and already working. I was too old to go back to school.

"Ma was real concerned. She kept talking about all the fine gentlemen in England, all real educated. Pa hailed from there, too. Hell, we all did; but what he cared about was the practical things. He saw she kept me reading and writing and that was good enough for him. I learned as much from her as I ever would have learned in some old schoolhouse."

Mark Willford bent to his share of the lifting and carrying that it took to unload the wagon. After two trips he stopped on the dock and looked at his father.

"So, Grandpa thought you knew enough to become sheriff? That right, Pa?"

Mark Willford knew about himself mostly as the son of the sheriff. And the rest he knew was that he was the son of a sheriff who was the son of a sheriff.

"Keep working. There ain't nothin' to be gained looking at me."

Silence grew between them. Mark Willford lifted and carried and waited for an answer.

"So, how did you become sheriff, Pa?"

"Don't know what Pa thought. Wasn't his way to tell me."

They worked side by side, and the light kept coming up; it was clear the only thing in the foothills was sagebrush, and the only noise was the river across the street. Sweat stains grew down the back of Mark Willford's shirt. The next time he stopped there was nothing left in the back of the wagon to put on the conveyor. He turned to his father and waited for instruction.

"They never expected him to die," said John Willford. He started talking after his last load. "I guess the mayor didn't think I could handle it." He took his gloves off and slapped his leg. "Or didn't want me to. He called me a fugitive sheriff."

"But that was because of the marshals," said Mark Willford.

"Yeah, it didn't have anything to do with whether I could do the job," chuckled Sheriff Simms. "When I was twelve, I turned up a job down in the mine, never even asked my pa. I wasn't the only twelve year old working in the mines. Lucky for me, it didn't last long. They asked me to handle one of the wagons hauling coal.

"Truth to tell, I always thought they gave me that job to stay on Pa's good side. Nobody ever said and I never asked. Rode that wagon 'til I was eighteen, 'til I made deputy."

Something different was going on. John Willford never told him more than what to do and how to do it.

"Didn't you work on the silver wagon, like we're doing now?"

"That wasn't 'til after I was a deputy." The sheriff looked down the street, searching. "I worked the wagon, like we're doing now. Pa never did the silver lottery. We don't seem to know much about how to make money."

Mark Willford heard the "we."

"They gave me that job hauling salt," said John Willford. "Salt is used in the reduction of the silver ore. Until they built the railroads, they had to haul the salt up from the lake where they dried it out. That's how I ended up on the silver freight."

Mark Willford saw the steps. If he could drive the silver freight, he could become sheriff.

"I was eighteen when I asked Pa if I could start working for him. I was driving the silver freight by then. I kept the other job. Had to.

"I worked as deputy a little more than twenty years. I didn't want the job, not the way I got it." He stopped for a moment to look up in the sky. "I had to find the worthless no-account who shot my pa, so I guess I naturally figured I was ready to be sheriff. For damn sure, I wasn't going to let anybody else do it. I put on Pa's star and kept working. 'Cept for him dying, wasn't nothing."

Mark Willford noticed. Everything he had ever learned about his grandfather's death he learned from his mother. That was the first his pa ever mentioned how his pa died.

"I had a lot of law stuff to read there at first," said Sheriff

Simms. "I kept on reading, pretty regularly."

Mark Willford stepped to the front of the wagon. He had wrapped the reins securely around a nail pounded into the dashboard. He slowly unwrapped them and turned back to face his father.

The glint of Luke Willford's star shining bright in the cold morning sunlight flashed in Mark Willford's eyes.

He ignored the deep hollowness that grew with the knowledge he would not go back to school. After all, he was the beneficiary of all the hardships his pioneer family had suffered. He could handle it.

"Expected Mr. Parley by now," said Sheriff John Willford Simms. "Best go down to his office. We cannot leave this load without someone and we can see it from there. You can talk to him, too."

Mark Willford drove father and son and wagon down the frozen little street, the trace of overnight snow swirling in front of them from the morning blow.

If his pa thought it was time to get a job, then today was the day to get a job. After all, he was made of pretty good stuff. Pioneer stock. He had even made it through the sixth grade.

He knew he would be in these mountains forever. That was fine. "Can I become a deputy when I'm eighteen? Like you?"

"That'll be up to you," said Sheriff Simms. "You'll have to ask."

"Well, I'm asking. Swear me in on my eighteenth birthday," he said. "That all I ever want to be. Sheriff Simms, like you."

Chapter 24

September 29, 1918

Deputy Simms felt banished by Cousin Blanche and blessed by her demand that he leave them alone and go take responsibility for his other children and his father. The sheriff gave him the day for the picnic, and he should not be punished with the loss of a deputy for three days. Ebby and her dead baby lay on the table, under the care of family. As he drove, his thoughts ran together and obscured time, from the day he drove the silver freight, to the day he was sworn in and Hixson shot the boy, to last week when Hixson's usefulness appeared to have run out, as well as his life. Distance passed without notice until the Model T's headlights flickered across the screen door and shocked the deputy's eyes in the gloam. His mother on the stoop barely registered. How she could know he had returned gave way to the sense she waited for him. Her hands held something, clasped together at her waist.

Mark Willford scooted across the bench seat and out the passenger door to his mother. "You all right, Ma?"

"Your father's dead." Her matter-of-fact voice sounded drained and thin. "Deputy Woodside came to tell you. I don't think he expected to find me here."

Deputy Simms heard his father say, *take care of your mother,* in such a strong voice, he felt sure he had not heard what his mother said. "What happened?"

"Mr. Woodside told me your father was at his desk, looking

for his star, and . . ."

Mark Willford thought to reach out to hold his mother. He stood frozen and watched her; and her life, not his father's, pulsed through him. She had survived the trek across the plains that claimed her parents. She entered a polygamous marriage as an orphan. She survived years of abuse by the government for the love of her husband. After losing three daughters to the diphtheria, she gave birth to the son watching her. Now she related the death of a man who had not touched her these last thirty-two years. She started to cry. She cried for all those years that John Willford's fear for her health drove his iron resolve to deny them the joy that had been their only treasure in life.

Mark Willford could not recall a time he had ever seen his mother cry. It broke through his paralysis. He reached for his mother and folded her in his arms.

". . . I guess he found his star." She pushed away and opened her closed hand to hold the star up to her son. "He had it on."

Mark Willford pulled her close again.

She pushed back. "The young deputy brought it." She reached up to unpin his deputy's badge. She pinned the sheriff's star through her son's shirt and patted his cheek.

"I always knew I would pin this star on you. I never thought about what it meant." The deputy's mother raised to her nose a handkerchief edged with lace she had crocheted. "Losing your father."

★ ★ ★ ★ ★

II. Sheriff Simms Pins on His Star

★ ★ ★ ★ ★

Chapter 25

Sheriff Simms cradled his mother in his right arm. "I'll take the kids over to Ma Carruth." He whispered into the crisp, night air. "Where do you want to go, there or home?" She clung to him in silence. He said, "I have to find someone to swear me in."

"And take care of your father."

"I didn't forget. I'll find Kidner. It's double duty." He felt his mother tense. She stepped away, and he saw the knowledge in her face. Most families were made of the half who survived. He said, "We lost the baby up at Blanche's."

She started to cry again but caught herself and stood up straight. "How selfish of me. I never thought to ask why you are here without Ebby."

"No need. I planned to tell you, first thing, but for Woodside's news." Mark Willford motioned his head down the street in the deepening evening. "Did he go back to the jail?"

"Yes, I think he went to find Mr. Kidner. I told him to bring John Willford's body to my house. That's where I want to go."

Mark Willford held her in his silent gaze.

"And I don't want to have any discussion about it," she said.

He nodded several times in understanding. "I doubt you will. She's dead six years now. His other children will see it as your place. Or, I'll speak with them. Woodside knows what to do. He's probably already found Doc Crittenden and Kidner'll be wanting to take care of the body. I best be going."

Sheriff Simms took his mother's arm and guided her through the door back into the log cabin. As he crossed the threshold, he remembered his father's help building it when he and Ebby married. His mother found her necessities bag, two loops for handles, hung on finely hewn rods of wood crafted by his grandfather, on a bag decorated with her needlepoint. Sheriff Simms crossed through their room to the door of the children's bedroom. He picked up Frank and called Willford and Thea to go out to the county car with their grandmother. He drove them the few steps across One Hundred North to Emma Wilde Carruth's.

"Ma Carruth, I need you to take care of my children for tonight," he said the moment she opened the door. "Well, until Wednesday." She started to reply, and he held up a hand. "I ain't finished with my burdens." He flicked his head back toward his passengers in the county car. "And help me convince Ma to stay with you until I'm back."

Emma waved her hand and scoffed. "No burden." She took Frank from Mark Willford's arms and stepped onto the stoop to motion his mother and children toward her. She looked at Mark Willford, pointedly focusing her eyes on the star. She said, "I can see you have things to do."

He nodded and reached for Thea's hand. As he walked her past Ma Carruth into the house, he said,"Sorry to be a bother."

"No bother." With everyone tucked in her house, she turned back to Mark Willford. "I'd a been a sight better off if they'd a been my grands."

Deputy Woodside greeted him at the door with Moses Hendershot, one of the county commissioners, when Deputy Simms parked the county's Model T at the jail.

"Figured to see you," said Woodside. "Figured we'd need a county commissioner."

"Pa always told me to count on you." The deputy continued from the door to his father at his desk. "I'll be sworn in here." He pointed out the door. "My father swore me in as deputy on those steps. When his father died, he was sworn in as sheriff here, next to his father. I'll be sworn in here. Next to them."

The three men formed a triangle. Deputy Woodside held the Bible above the body of the man who served the county for thirty-five years over two different centuries, the first four avoiding the U.S. Marshals while pursuing the execution of his father's murderer. He fulfilled vows to two wives as faithfully as he carried out his duties to his county. Lore had it that Deputy Simms's father had said I do, I will, I swear, and let someone fill in the blanks. That is what Mark Willford wanted, but he also knew his father believed in respect for authority, even as he chafed at it. The deputy wanted to be Sheriff Simms as fast as possible, but he patiently followed Hendershot's lead. Upon the final, "I swear," he asked, "Does Doc. Crittenden know?"

"I sent a boy for him," said Woodside. "He has a case in the rooms above the Mercantile. He called and said he'll be over as soon as he finishes and washes his hands."

"He must be getting fastidious in his old age," said Sheriff Simms. With his eyes fixed on his father slumped in his chair, he asked Woodside, "Tell me what happened."

"I had the duty to open the jail and make the fire," said Deputy Woodside. "Being Sunday, Sheriff Simms, uh, your father, told me to come in about noon. He said he wanted to go to church with your mother."

Sheriff Simms nodded. Time together at church on Sunday had been precious to them.

"Sheriff Simms walked in the door promptly at one. The room was warm, and he commented the air smelled of coffee. 'Woodside,' he said, 'from the first day, I knew my pa made the right decision.' "

Woodside grinned, "Your father prided himself on his people judgment."

Sheriff Simms nodded, "That he did." He thought Woodside should be proud and added, "Told me that was the first thing to get right."

"The sheriff started rummaging around in his desk, and I turned to pouring his coffee for him. He asked if I'd seen his star, sort of apologizing that he never took it off, but Saturday was the Stake Dance and your mother insisted. Then he must have found it. He said, 'Oh, here it is.'

"I never paid no attention. He was quiet behind me. I had no hurry to finish. I figured the sheriff was, you know, busy pinning on his star."

Deputy Woodside broke off, looked at his hands while he took in a deep breath.

"When I turned around, he was slumped back, his star pinned on his chest."

"You took his star off him?" asked Sheriff Simms with some disapproval in his voice.

"I thought it best, first thing to swear you in," said Woodside. "I found Hendershot and told him to wait here with your father while I found you."

Sheriff Simms nodded. "Lots to do." He saw Doc Crittenden's face at the window in the door and waved him in, then again, the second wave of his hand faster and bigger than the first.

Doc Crittenden walked across the room to Sheriff Simms in his chair. He looked at him and touched his forehead. "How long ago do you think he died?" he asked Woodside.

"About four hours ago," answered the deputy.

"That's a damn long time," said Doc Crittenden. "What took you so long?"

"I had to go out and round up every one of you," said Woodside, heat in his never ruffled voice. "Most of it waiting for you, Doc. We sent the boy more than three hours ago."

"Did you touch him?" asked Doc Crittenden.

"No," said Woodside. "You've told me often enough not to touch anything. I knew to wait for you."

"What about the star?" asked Sheriff Simms.

"I did take his star off his shirt, if you call that touching."

"When was that?" asked Doc Crittenden.

"More'n two hours ago," answered Woodside.

"And?" asked Doc Crittenden.

"And what?" Woodside answered, his voice edging back to brittle.

Doc Crittenden made no show of answering Woodside. He said to no one in particular, "Even with four hours, it doesn't appear he had a fever."

Sheriff Simms wondered where the subject of a fever came from, and he wondered what was so pressing that his old friend couldn't make it to tend to his father in three hours. He overrode both questions, determined to finish the job in front of them. "Where's Kidner?"

"I talked to him," said Woodside. "Said he couldn't do anything until Doc told him."

"Doc's here now," said Sheriff Simms. "So, he needs to," he thought for a moment about whether to mention his own baby, "come over here and take him to Mother's house. She'll decide all the details."

"As long as she has the funeral no later than Wednesday," said Doc Crittenden.

"Doesn't she have to decide that with the bishop?" asked Sheriff Simms. "Besides, I got my own problems."

"Yes, you do." Doc Crittenden saw his response startled Sheriff Simms. "We'll talk about it later. All I'm saying, being it's Sunday, is he may deserve better, but it's best you and your mother do it Wednesday at the latest."

The language confused Sheriff Simms, a combination of concern from an amiable old friend and a direct command of the sort Doc Crittenden never made. The sheriff looked past Doc and spoke to Woodside and Hendershot. "When Kidner comes, tell him Doc'll give him the paperwork tomorrow. Tonight, his job is to take the body over to Mother's house. Doc and I'll go over there now to see her."

Sheriff Simms pulled Doc Crittenden out the front door. After he cranked the Model T to start, he climbed in his seat and started talking. "There's something I didn't mention in there. Ebby and I lost a baby up in Echo today. I'll need Kidner to take care of it. I'm going up on Wednesday to bring her back."

"Do you want a funeral for the child?"

"No. A simple burial. This is our second stillbirth. A simple burial, maybe with Ma and Ebby's mother. That's all."

"Good, could you do it Tuesday? Evening at the latest?"

"Not sure," said Sheriff Simms. "I was planning to pick up Ebby on Wednesday."

"Best do it on Tuesday. That way you can have your father's funeral over and done with before noon."

"That woulda been Ma's plan, anyway." He put the car in gear and started rolling down Main Street toward Fifty East. As he slowed to make the turn, he asked Doc. "Why?"

"Because there's something I didn't mention in there, too, especially in front of Hendershot."

"What's that?"

"Did you ever hear of the Spanish flu?"

"Read about it. Didn't it start over there in Spain last March?"

"Started somewhere. Maybe not Spain, their newspapers reported it."

"So, what about it?"

"So, it's here. In Utah. In Coalville. I know Dr. Beatty, the

Utah State Health Commissioner. He was a prof of mine in medical school. This boy I'm tending above the Mercantile came back from the fair on the nineteenth. By Thursday, he had a temperature and aches and pains. Now, he has a bad fever, and he's having a hard time breathing. I think he got it at the fair. So does Dr. Beatty. Turns out Beatty was keeping a list before I called him. This is the tenth case."

Sheriff Simms heard concern in Crittenden's voice. "You're worried? Is that a lot?"

"From what I read, it spread fast in Europe and in other places in the U.S., too. In Fort Devens, that's in Massachusetts, I read that six days after the first case, they had six thousand. Dr. Beatty's worried that not all the authorities are pulling together. Last Friday, Dr. Paul, he's the Salt Lake Health Commissioner, told residents that while the disease is highly contagious, it is easily preventable with a little bit of care."

"Was he wrong?"

"Not about the contagion, but tone is important. Dr. Paul may be right if you take out the word *easily* and persuade everyone to think about a lot of care, not just a little bit."

"And that's why you want me to have Pa's funeral on Wednesday?"

"We're going to need to keep it from spreading. After Wednesday, I don't think we'll be having any funerals around here for a while."

"Are you saying, quarantine?"

"I think so," said Doc Crittenden, nodding.

"Like the diphtheria?" asked the sheriff.

"I wasn't around, but from what I've heard, yes, like the diphtheria."

"Neither was I. Ma told me. Pa'd never say anything. He had to enforce it."

"You will, too."

"Yeah, right," said Sheriff Simms. He had lost his father and a second baby on the same day, and he did not know about public health except there were official jobs and important titles to take care of it in Salt Lake. Nothing he would say out loud, but that was the doc's job, and friend or not, he was not going to slip out of it. Besides, the mayor, an ambitious Swede in an English community, would never hear of letting go of his authority for the whole town.

Sheriff Simms brought Ebby home from Echo on Tuesday. Mr. Kidner met them at the family plot. Two grandmothers born in England and the two parents born in these mountains stood alone to bury Rose at sunset.

On Wednesday, Sheriff Simms stepped up to the simple, wooden pulpit behind his father's open casket. He felt nervous. He had avoided the numerous opportunities for a young man to speak in church. This one he could not avoid. He looked out at the faces here to honor his father and remembered his father saw them as all people like him. He could do it.

> "Think about this man. He would never have suggested you do so, but death is liberating, and he is not making the request. Think about this man. Brought here at five, schooled by his mother, made a deputy at eighteen by his father, asked to take an orphan as his second wife at twenty-five, made a fugitive by his country at thirty-nine upon the very day he lost his father to murder.
>
> He survived it all. He fulfilled his calling as father to two families. He captured his father's murderer. He outlasted the marshals and became embraced by the state. He brought common sense and good comfort to his community. He fulfilled his calling to serve as your sheriff for thirty-five years.

His father was a Bible reading man, especially the Book of Matthew. He was not, and neither am I. To top it off, every story I know about him I know from my mother. Because she told me, I believe them all to be true facts.

Because of him, in every way, there's no denying it, I'm lucky to be alive. He and my mother, that woman in the front row you know as Elizabeth Tonsil Simms, had a first baby who was stillborn. The spirit they shared together overcame and over time they were blessed with three beautiful little girls."

A titter rolled across the benches of people come from all over the county.

"I'd say the little house down at the corner of Fifty East and One Hundred North glowed as bright as my ma. They believed they had a complete family.

When those daughters, my sisters, grew to age eight, six, and two, all healthy as could be, the diphtheria came to the valley. It was the first week of March 1879. At first, those meant to be experts thought it to be offspring to unsanitary conditions. But that could not be—not in this community of careful, hardworking, clean-living souls. All death and disease are unfair and the most unfair is the disease that targets children. Nobody really knew that contact was its source and yet they knew not to expose others. Freezing cold weather kept the winter's deep snow piled high long into the spring. Families huddled together. Quarantine kept them apart. The diphtheria trapped in our little valley stayed there, until it died out.

Mother met him at the door and told him she and the girls could not go out. Before he opened the door, she told him if he came in, he could not go out.

The sheriff knew her words were true; he was responsible for enforcing the quarantine. If his children weren't sick, maybe quarantine would be a help; but they were sick. They couldn't breathe and their throats were swelling, and their hearts were beating uncontrollably.

Most of all he was helpless. A helpless man is useless. The star he wore, this star, was worthless. It gave him no power to stop the sickness and death. Not for his family, not for all those other settlers living a black end to ten, or even twenty, years of hard struggle in this dry hot cold place.

For nine days he camped in the yard. He must have felt blessed that the children of his first family had not been exposed and now could be protected by his daily efforts to ensure the town was observing the quarantine. For this dear family, all he could do was speak to his wife each morning through the window.

On the tenth day, God's will brought Sheriff Simms work to do that was more important than observing the quarantine. Each daughter died in her own time. Ma had not discussed with him the details of the first death or the second. They had simply talked to each other through the window and decided to wait to bury all three together.

Mother handed him the little white bundle that was my two-year-old sister. He held the bundle in his arms and carried it to the window and handed her to the sexton collecting bodies for the town. Again. For the six-year-old. And again. For the eight-year-old.

The sexton laid each girl out in a little pine box. My father stepped out and took the hammer from the sexton, and told him, 'I'll do it.' He nailed each box shut.

All the life created by Elizabeth Tonsil and John Willford Simms had been given up. Suffocated. They laid each sealed pine box in the family plot next to Grandma and Grandpa, the pioneers who brought their mother to this merciless place.

Five years of sickness hung like a shroud over the glow of my bright spirited mother. Six years after the diphtheria epidemic, two years after his father was killed and he became the second Sheriff Simms, life forced its will on them again.

He told her he would have been happy enough with a boy, but a little girl, my sister, Clara, was a fine way to finish the family.

You all know my mother. She told him that is not one of the things that falls under a sheriff's jurisdiction."

Sheriff Simms let the crowd laugh. He smiled in anticipation of what he knew was coming.

"When she told him she was pregnant again, she told me he asked, 'How can you be pregnant again?'

And she said, 'You were a party to that party.' "

Another wave of laughter and another smile. Sheriff Simms took a deep breath, pointed each forefinger at his chest, and continued.

"That was me.

Pa being Pa, and you all knew him, said, 'I love you, woman, but this has to stop.'

The night I was born, he kissed Mother and left that three-bedroom house he built after my sisters died, never to return. Some of you may know this and some of you may have figured it out, but for thirty-one years, he never stepped foot in that house again. He loved my mother very much. He kissed her when he saw her at church. He did not need to explain to anybody how much he would deny himself to protect her. And he might thump me when he sees me for telling his secret today."

Eulogy ended, Sheriff Simms and his mother stood next to the casket and greeted people as they filed by. Doc Crittenden caught Sheriff Simms's eye from across the hall and nodded. Doc waited until his mother left. The sheriff thrust out his hand in greeting. Doc Crittenden waggled a finger and shook his head.

"Wow! Some eulogy. I don't remember anyone speaking that frankly."

Sheriff Simms nodded. "I followed your instructions. We buried Rose last night."

"Wise," said Doc Crittenden. "The boy above the Merc is fine, but we have four cases." All the people left the chapel and milled about outside. Mr. Kidner closed the church doors. Only Doc Crittenden and Sheriff Simms witnessed the closing of the casket.

"Why so upset?" asked Sheriff Simms. "Four cases don't seem that bad."

"In two days?" Doc's voice carried concern. "I don't know what's coming, but I think it's going to be more. Worse, I don't know who's in charge."

"The mayor, I'd guess," said Sheriff Simms. "Hixson and Elsemore died just before Pa. Their accidents still must be investigated, even if Elsemore died in Rich County. Hixson was not a swimmer, and Elsemore never went on a hike in his life. Their deaths are related to this meatpacking problem." He paused a moment to make sure Doc listened to him. "I got my hands full. That don't include finding a new deputy."

"Health problems never come at a good time," said Doc Crittenden.

Sheriff Simms distrusted the sound of his oldest friend's words. "I don't think I wanna know what that means, but if I can help, let me know. I'll do what I can."

Doc looked past his old friend as if looking out the closed doors and shrugged. "Your father was an outsized figure around here. He attracted more people to this chapel than the Church ever did."

"Thank you," said Sheriff Simms.

"You won't be thanking me when you hear what I'm asking," said Doc Crittenden. Sheriff Simms waited, watching him look through closed doors. "I want you to send those people home. Tell them not to go to the cemetery. There were more than two hundred people here. We can't have that."

"Why? I did what you said. You told me to finish Pa's funeral today by noon."

Doc frowned. "And I shoulda said, you can't do it at all."

Sheriff Simms trusted this man second to no one. "Doc, I trust you enough to go by your word, but this don't make sense. We had two hundred people in that closed, stuffy chapel and now you want me to tell 'em they can't go stand on a hillside in the sun and the breeze?"

"Like I said, instead of asking you to get it done fast, I should've asked you bury him alone. No use continuing a mistake I already made."

Deputy Simms knew some things had to be done on a word and trust. "Okay. I'll tell 'em Pa wanted a private burial, like the one he was forced to give his father." Doc Crittenden nodded. Sheriff Simms picked up a reticence. "Anything else?"

"Yeah, I told you, who's going to be in charge? I think that has to be you."

"Ha!" exclaimed Sheriff Simms. "First, there's the mayor." He could see no change in Doc's demeanor. "Second, sheriff's a county job. The towns have their own mayors."

Doc Crittenden shrugged again and pushed open the doors, "All the more reason."

Sheriff Simms threw up his hands at Doc's cryptic comment. "What the hell does that mean?"

CHAPTER 26

October 4, 1918

The sun peeked over the Chalk Creek. Sheriff Simms thought he could sneak out back and drop a line for half an hour, maybe catch a couple of trout for breakfast. Deputy Woodside knocked on the door of the log cabin. Young Willford Simms, dressed for school, opened the door.

Looking up at the deputy, he blurted, "Pa said, 'What the hell do you want?' How'd he know it'd be you?"

Woodside chuckled. "Maybe 'cause nobody else'd be fool enough to knock at this hour."

The sheriff's voice carried through the opening from the kitchen. "Woodside, what's so important it can't wait for me to have breakfast before I go to the jail?"

Young Willford ran back into the kitchen, leaving Woodside on the stoop to decide without invitation whether to step inside. The sheriff called out, "Well, don't let in all of outdoors. Come in and close the door."

Woodside followed the instructions. "To answer your question, what's important is what you got to do before going to the jail."

The sheriff stepped through the opening from the kitchen to the front room. "Want some breakfast? I can't offer you some trout, because of you I might add, but Ebby made bread rolls. She makes the best bread rolls in the county."

"Yes, she does," said Woodside, "but Doc Crittenden wants

to meet you at the mayor's office, first thing. He said that means right now."

"No, he don't." Sheriff Simms stood against the doorframe taking a bite out of a bread roll. "That skinny old sawbones don't want to meet me. He wants to get me into something I don't want any part of."

"Sounds about right. He said if you resist, to arrest you," Woodside laughed.

"What's it about?"

"Didn't say. I guess he thinks it's urgent."

"He gets that way, sometimes," said Sheriff Simms.

"Maybe so," said Woodside, "but when Vernon Jr. was down at the university, he said they think pretty highly of him down there."

"They should," said Sheriff Simms. "That don't make him the calmest sort." The sheriff turned back into the kitchen and stepped to Ebby's pan of rolls, chuckling all the way. Over his shoulder, he called, "If all I'm having for breakfast is bread rolls, I'm having another one, but I don't want to get arrested this morning, so tell him I'll be right along."

"Can't," said Woodside standing at the front door talking toward the opening to the kitchen. "He's in the hospital above the Merc. I imagine he's busy. It don't do to bother him. Go to the mayor's office. He'll be there."

"You don't fool me, Woodside. You don't want to go to those rooms above the Merc, and you haven't been there since Doc Crittenden came here and started calling it a hospital."

"No need to. Doc's in charge." Woodside put on his hat and closed the door behind him.

Simms turned to kiss Ebby at the woodstove before he walked to the bedroom. He trusted Woodside's judgment. Avoiding the hospital didn't fall far from the sheriff's thinking.

On the way to the mayor's office, Sheriff Simms stopped at

the little yellow house to check on his mother. No surprise, she had already left for the Mercantile. For a moment he wondered if anything upstairs in the hospital rooms could find its way downstairs to the Mercantile. He shook off the question and continued to Main Street. He approached the trim little building where Doc Crittenden maintained his office, directly across from the Merc. Rumbling started on the steps above the Merc and his friend burst out the door to dash across the wide street.

"My word's not good enough," chuckled the sheriff. "You been watching out the window."

"I been busy. Somebody else watched," said Doc Crittenden. "We have to talk before we go in the mayor's office."

"That's right, Woodside told me about the mayor's office." Doc, dressed in suit and tie, black bag in his right hand, appeared normal enough, but he carried an agitation that threatened to engulf them both. "Well, let's talk right now. Then we can go to his office, if that's what you want."

"Oh, believe me, I don't want to go to his office," said Doc Crittenden, and his next words tumbled out. "We're up to twelve cases of Spanish flu."

"Since four on Wednesday?" asked the sheriff. "Did they all go to the fair, like the boy?"

"And two of them are the mayor and his wife," said Doc Crittenden. "I don't know yet if they went to the fair. We do know a Wyoming man went to the fair and is the one who spread it."

"Jee-sus, Doc," said Sheriff Simms, "we're right next to Wyoming. People come here from Wyoming all the time."

"And go," said Doc Crittenden, "but we can't blame Wyoming. We need to be careful about people. First off, the mayor. When we meet him, he'll be behind his desk. He should stay there, and we'll stand at the door."

"Why do we even have to meet him?" asked Sheriff Simms.

"He can send his instructions out on a piece of paper."

Doc Crittenden gave a sad chuckle. "Haven't you figured it out yet?"

"Figured what out?" asked Sheriff Simms. "You're the doc. I do not know anything about this stuff. Just tell me what to do."

"That's going to be your job."

"What?"

"He's going to put you in charge."

Sheriff Simms pretended not to hear the words. He made his regular survey, up and down the street. This side of Main Street, with the expansive lawns and stately buildings, lay empty in the early morning. On the other side, where the buildings housed the businesses and abutted the boardwalk to make it easier for customers to come and go, activity started to show at seven in the morning. He turned from this routine start of his day to the doc's surprise prediction. "It don't make sense. What am I supposed to do?"

"It makes perfect sense. Take charge," said Doc Crittenden. He started to walk toward city hall and waved his hand for the sheriff to keep up. "What I already said."

Sheriff Simms hustled and caught up with Doc. "And like I already said, I don't know what to do. How can I take charge when I don't know what I should tell folks to do?"

"You'll decide. You'll learn and you'll decide. You know how to make decisions." Doc stopped and looked at the sheriff as if defying him to disagree. "The right decisions."

"Right?" asked the sheriff, his voice reflecting the craziness in the doc's assertion. He held up four fingers. "I been sheriff four days."

Doc nodded. "And deputy to your father thirteen years. I knew your father. Around or not, there isn't much difference in how he expected you to make your own decisions."

"There's a hell of a lot of difference with him not around."

Doc nodded again. "We'll see. Your first decision will be to order the mayor to stay right there in city hall, until tonight. I must examine him, but not in city hall. He can go home tonight, after midnight when nobody's around, and stay there. I'll go examine him and his wife tomorrow. They have four children." He looked up into the cold blue sky. "I'll bet all of them are infected."

Sheriff Simms doubted that last comment had been meant for him. He walked in silence with Doc to the city hall steps. He wondered about the obvious question that Doc seemed to ignore. Taking charge seemed like a tall order. Maybe not as monumental as his pa took on the first day he was sheriff, but decisions that affected the life, even death, of everyone in his county seemed like a tall order. When they stopped at the foot of the steps, he could put it off no longer. He had to ask, "Is this his idea?"

Doc Crittenden smiled as he stepped to the door. "It will be." He knocked, shoved the door open, and with his arm out to form the barricade he had already announced, called into the building, "We'll talk from here."

Sheriff Simms looked down the corridor, two offices on each side and one at the end. "How we gonna do this, Doc? That's his office at the end."

"Axel," called Doc Crittenden, "we're here to meet. You can come to your door, but no further. Stay there."

The doc and the sheriff shared the same towering height, though the doc shaped up lanky and the sheriff like one of the barrels his grandfather built. Neither had met anyone in town whose head reached above theirs, until Johan Axel Valfred came to town with his wife. The mayor now stood in the doorway of his office, his head not two inches below the frame.

"First off, how are you?" called Doc Crittenden.

"Fine. A little hot and sweaty," said Mayor Valfred. "And a

headache. My Pauline won't let me drink the coffee."

"Hot and sweaty on the first Friday in October," said Doc Crittenden. "Feel your forehead. How's it feel?"

The mayor reached his left hand out to take hold of the doorframe and then felt his forehead with his right. "Hot." Pause. "Not very."

"And unsteady, too," observed Doc Crittenden.

"I can take care of that headache," said Sheriff Simms. "Come over. We got coffee."

"You're not going anywhere," snapped Doc. He turned his head to the sheriff. "And you, don't make problems for me."

"I was being hospitable," said Sheriff Simms, holding up his hands in surrender.

"That's the last thing we need right now," said Doc Crittenden. He turned back to call down the corridor. "I talked to Dr. Beatty this morning. We have twelve cases. With our population, that is the worst in the state. Admittedly, you are four of them, but Dr. Beatty thinks we should do everything we can to stop the spread. We have to discourage or stop all public interaction."

"They're singling us out," said Mayor Valfred. "That's not what they're doing in Salt Lake. Dr. Paul thinks due care is enough."

"We got our own problems. We do not need to take on that competition in Salt Lake. Simms here should order every public activity stopped. And people ought to take care with every private activity, too, even stay at home. Simms should say that, too."

"I'm not sure we should be doing all that. I'll have to think about it before making that kind of decision," said Mayor Valfred.

"Maybe," said Doc Crittenden, carrying the word out for a long moment, "in some other circumstances. Perhaps. But you're sick and so's your family and, to boot, we don't even know how you got it. The first decision you need to make is to step aside."

"I don't know." Mayor Valfred started to protest and caught himself. He leaned against the doorjamb thinking and resumed talking as if to himself. "It would take a load off, free up some time." He stood straight and called down the corridor, "Do you truly mean all public activities? There's an election in about a month. Certainly, we have to proceed with our campaigns and the election."

"If you mean the vote on election day, that'll be for the sheriff to decide," said Doc Crittenden, "but for damn sure, I am not going to let you go out and talk to a group of people."

"Well, as mayor, I have to protect our right to hold free elections. I, for one, must campaign. Two years ago, the people elected a Swede in an English settlement. Reelection means approval."

Doc Crittenden turned to the sheriff. "What do you think?"

"I didn't hear Mayor Valfred ask me to help," said Sheriff Simms.

"You didn't hear him ask you to take charge?" asked Doc Crittenden. He chuckled. "You must not a been listening."

"Doc," said Sheriff Simms, "in fact, all I heard was Axel opposing pretty much everything you told me I had to do." He kept to himself that it reminded him of what his mother had told him about his father's first day. The mayor had not wanted to swear his father in. The mayor had not wanted him to do his job.

"Doesn't matter what Axel thinks," insisted Doc Crittenden. "What do you think we should do?"

Sheriff Simms considered long enough to develop his own strategy. It was not the kind of decision he would ever discuss with anyone else. He knew from somewhere he could not name that he had to provide leadership both silent and visible. His voice, firm but quiet compared to his normal all-outdoors volume, carried down the corridor to the mayor's office. "Let's cooperate."

Doc Crittenden smiled. He then turned to look at the mayor and wait.

Mayor Valfred dropped back again and slumped his shoulder against the doorframe, still measuring up about as tall as the doc and the sheriff. "I want to be kept informed." With a slow shake of the head, he added, "And I want to be told what I need to do to campaign."

"We'll send a boy to leave the news at your window. If you need to talk with us, send a note with him," said Doc Crittenden. "Now, stay in that room until midnight, then go home. Stay there. I'll come around tomorrow morning to see you and Pauline and the boys. First, we're going to see if you're up to campaigning, then we'll talk about how you can do it without hurting anyone else."

From the steps the sheriff and the doc walked back to the main sidewalk. Before they parted, Sheriff Simms asked, "What are you telling me to do? Shut down everything?"

"That's the question you're going to face for every door in town."

"I don't know that I've made that decision yet," said Sheriff Simms. Doc Crittenden nodded a form of acceptance and stepped onto Main Street on his way back to the Merc. Sheriff Simms called, "Doc, are you talking quarantine?"

"You're the lawman, but I don't think you can quarantine people who aren't sick." No sooner had Doc finished the words than his face clouded over. "Trueman has it, and he's pretty ill. I saw him early this morning. His wife and baby have it, too, but they're doing well. I told them they need to stay in their home."

"Jee-sus, Doc, you mean my mother might have it?"

"I didn't say that, don't know. It depends on how much she's around Mr. Trueman."

"She works for him. Don't that count for enough?"

"Could do, maybe not. Before you make any decisions, you're going to have to know everyone who has it. Bishop Barber has it, serious, too. He could not make it to your father's funeral. Thank God, as it turns out."

Sheriff Simms stood, wordlessly staring into an understanding of how invisible this disease could be. He had not even noticed that the man responsible for his parents' marriage forty-nine years ago had not been at his father's funeral. The knowledge that Bishop Barber, at his age, had a severe case of the Spanish flu created concern enough for his mother that he found his voice again. "We've got to go over there and talk to Ma. You are coming. You put me in charge, so that's an order."

Doc Crittenden saluted and fell in line behind the sheriff in his resolute march across the broad Main Street to the Mercantile. When they reached the boardwalk, before opening the door to go in, Sheriff Simms said, "Don't make sense. Our little town up here in the mountains with all this sky and fresh air. It can't be worst in the state."

"I'm not so sure how that came about, either. The outbreak at the fair came from that Wyoming man, for sure. Coalville's problems seem to have come from a soldier. So far, the biggest concentration has been at Fort Douglas. It looks like this soldier came through here about ten days ago and visited friends, spent time in the Mercantile, and went over to Bishop Barber's for a shave. That seems to explain these cases, but it may not explain the mayor's."

"Wasted question, I take it back," said the sheriff. "No explanation needed." He shoved open the door. "Not when we don't know how Ma is."

Doc Crittenden grabbed Sheriff Simms by the arm. "I can see you're anxious, but you know, that might be dangerous to barge in there like that."

"Not anxious," said Sheriff Simms. "Nothing's dangerous when it comes to my mother."

"All the same," said Doc Crittenden, "influenza doesn't know you're her son. It'd be best if we wore masks."

Sheriff Simms laughed. "Sure," he said. "You got one?"

"Upstairs, in the hospital, there might be an extra. I've ordered more from Salt Lake."

"There you go," said Sheriff Simms. "You wait here. Or go upstairs." He fingered the kerchief around his neck. "When you live in the desert you have to eat a little sand." He pulled it up over his nose and said through his kerchief, "I'm going in to see Ma. When you find your masks, bring one to me."

Sheriff Simms stepped into an empty store. No surprise, earlier in the morning than he had ever come to the store. People were at work or on their way. He walked back to the butcher counter. Not seeing Mr. Trueman brought a mixture of relief and concern. Trueman knew he was ill and stayed home. Still, sick enough to decide he had to stay home probably meant he spent a lot of time in the store growing sicker before he arrived at that conclusion.

"Ma?" Sheriff Simms called into the empty rows of shelves.

"Mark Willford," his mother said as she stepped out from behind the dry goods shelves and threw up her hands. "What are you doing here? And wearing a mask like a robber."

"Looking to you," said Sheriff Simms. He pointed to his mask. "Doc Crittenden. He told me Trueman has the Spanish flu."

"He does," said his mother. "I sent him home yesterday. Told him to stay there and not come out."

"I asked the doc about quarantine," said Sheriff Simms.

"Speaking from experience," shrugged Mother Simms. "I lived through the diphtheria of seventy-nine, and it seemed like the sensible thing to do."

Before today, Sheriff Simms had only thought about the epidemic that took his sisters as the tragedy responsible for his birth eight years later. Now he realized his mother and other pioneers in town would be a great help to him. "But how did you know it was the Spanish flu?"

"Not sure I knew," she said. "Not sure I needed to know. That was why we had to have your father's funeral on Wednesday. It seemed like a fairly good bet."

He narrowed his eyes and stared hard at his mother. "I been careful in talking with Doc Crittenden. How did you know that?"

"Silly boy." Her eyes twinkled. "How do you think I kept track of you growing up?"

Of course, his old friend had never been careful in his conversations with anyone. Lon Crittenden was a close second to Seth Parker as town gossip. The sheriff chuckled. "You can be a big help, Ma. Looks like I'm in charge of figuring out what to do with this Spanish flu."

"Good," she stepped up and tweaked his cheek. "I shouldn't kiss you, but you've had a pretty big week. If the county cannot have your father in charge of this Spanish flu, they couldn't find a better man than his son."

The sheriff laughed and kissed her. "Whoever *they* is."

CHAPTER 27

Sheriff Simms bent over to kiss his mother goodbye and she turned, pointing to her cheek. He walked out the door of the Mercantile and stood on the boardwalk to review his responsibilities and decide in which direction to take his first step. He told himself to give each responsibility its due. Even if his father had released those two men from Ogden, he felt compelled to turn his attention back to investigating Hixson's death. The money that bought the ranch the rustlers stocked with stolen cattle to sell to the meatpackers came from the robbery leading to his grandfather's death. Rustling took more importance than his swearing in in 1905. Today, thirty-five years later, something that happened in 1883 dictated what the sheriff's office did. Today, each minute he worked on the meatpacking problem and the unresolved history of the money paled in comparison to the Spanish-flu threat every person in his county faced.

Sheriff Simms returned to the jail. "Has Doc already talked to you?" he asked.

"He wouldn't be the doc otherwise," said Woodside. "It don't change much. Tell me what you need."

"Good man," said Sheriff Simms. "There's sheriff's work to do here. I need you to remember that. No matter what I'm doing, make sure you wrap up the investigation on Elsemore's death. I'm going down to Ogden this afternoon to investigate those men before Doc finishes throwing his net around me."

"Don't know about no net," Woodside looked up from his

desk. "But you can't do that."

"Not you, too," said Sheriff Simms. "Why not?"

"You figured out what you got to do yet?"

"That's why I'm going now. I went down once before. Nobody knew nothing. I do not believe that. I figure to try again, fast. After today, who knows when I'll be able to look after it."

"Any thought to keeping strangers out?" asked Woodside.

"Haven't thought about any of it. That's a good idea. Isolated like us, won't take much. We'll work on it, tomorrow. There's only three ways in. I can make us three special deputies. They'll block each one."

"You'd be the one to judge if it'll hold 'til tomorrow," said the deputy, "leastwise, up here, but it ain't so easy for Ogden. They might've already thought about it."

The sheriff stopped. When he was a deputy, he had learned lessons from Woodside every day. That had not changed just because of his star. "You don't think they'll let me in town to investigate."

"Investigate usually means poking around, and you're going to be poking around down at the Ogden Provision and Packing Company. They won't want to give you the chance to infect a lot of men down there." Woodside looked up at the sheriff from under the brow of his hat. "Not to mention, you don't know anything about those people. That's why you're going. Doc Crittenden don't want you sick."

His mother had raised him to be a free soul and his father had demanded he stand on his own two feet. Being told he could not do what needed to be done put a lid on those two principles governing his life, and he wanted to explode. He couldn't. Woodside had called it right. He sat in his chair, his face gaining color each moment. Finally, he looked up and said, "You know what's gonna happen?" He spoke past Woodside into the future. "With the war over, OPP's gonna shrivel up. That's why they killed him. Or some part of that."

"Did ya dig that up in your investigation?" asked Woodside.

"Good question," said Sheriff Simms. "Didn't dig up much of anything. Pulsipher's job is to keep it hidden, and he does a good job no matter what he says."

Woodside nodded. Sheriff Simms continued.

"But you can think it out. Hixson never did an honest day's work in his life, and they been failin' for a good many months now, since the war contracts ended. They don't have any place to sell beef, rustled or no, so when they told him to go packin' because they don't need rustled beef anymore, he threatened to blackmail them. He should'na threatened. That was like a warning, but it's all gonna shrivel up. By the time this influenza is over, whenever that is, there won't be anybody to arrest." Sheriff Simms shifted his focus from the future to his deputy. "There won't be any OPP, and there won't be nobody to care."

All those years learning and waiting to be a Sheriff Simms. Here he was unable to finish a job he had almost wrapped up as a deputy. On his first day as sheriff, he had been asked to do a job he felt unprepared—and inadequate—to do.

"But the special deputies is a good idea, boss," said Woodside. "We need a new deputy, to replace you. So, we only need two part-timers."

Woodside's words broke through the sheriff's uncertainty. Of course, his mother and father had prepared him. They had taught him what to know and what to do and what to expect and, above all, to expect he could take care of anything that came his way. He stood up and headed for the door. "You take care of the special deputies. I'll take care of the deputy."

Halfway out, he turned and stuck his head back in. "And wrap up the Elsemore investigation. It's gonna be tied to the Hixson death, even if I can't work on either one of them."

Chapter 28

Sheriff Simms left the jail, ignored the county car, and walked up Main Street past the Mercantile, all the way to the town's north entrance. Deputy Woodside had built a house across from the sandstone bluffs that guarded the north entrance to town. His small ranch occupied about half the land in the old fairgrounds where Sheriff John Simms had camped from time to time to evade the U.S. Marshals.

In the fall of 1913, North Summit High School opened. From the first football game, Sheriff John Simms committed the county sheriff's department to watching Deputy Woodside's son play quarterback. For three years, Vernon Woodside Jr's skill brought every job and responsibility in town to a standstill on Friday afternoon. One of twelve boys to graduate from North Summit, Vernon Jr. walked on the field and suited up with the varsity down at the university. Coach Norgren saw he could move and throw the ball and allowed as how he could let Woodside stay suited up on the varsity to watch.

Watching was not what Vernon Jr. had in mind to do, certainly not on a team that won three and lost two. After the Utes lost the last two games to schools from Colorado of all places, the three men of the sheriff's department stood around the woodstove reliving the season.

"How did Vernon Jr. hold up," Deputy Simms asked Deputy Woodside. "What'd he say to you after Saturday's game?"

"He said it was damn tough, growing up in the mountains

with a father working for Sheriff John Simms, telling him how the sheriff always demanded you speak your mind."

Sheriff Simms chckled.

Deputy Simms asked, "He shoulda talked to me. How are you going to help him out of his dilemma?"

"I told him when you work with Sheriff Simms you learn how far you can take it, speaking your mind with him." Deputy Woodside smiled at the sheriff and shook his head. "He didn't seem to find that helpful." Now he looked directly at the sheriff. "So I told him it was no different from playing varsity football at a big university where you have to learn to be careful how far you take it with the coach."

"Did that advice help him?" asked Deputy Simms.

"Don't know," said Woodside. "But he'll stay on the team, and next year if the coach tells him to sit on the bench and watch, he'll do it."

Sheriff Mark Simms approached the front door, smiling at the memory. Although Vernon Jr. lettered that year in the final game, a loss to Colorado College at home, Simms wondered who the teacher had been, his father or Deputy Woodside?

The strategy of never giving up and never talking back worked for the kid from a little town up in the mountains. Sheriff John Simms took both his deputies to see Vernon Jr. start for the Utes and win the first game of the season, against Wyoming. Damn it was fun. The sheriff and his deputies expected Vernon Jr. to start varsity all three years.

The Utes won only one more game in 1917. Those losses brought resolve. They had the chance. He had the chance, to be the best ever. Vernon Woodside Jr. looked forward to the 1918 season.

But too many boys suited up for war and too few boys showed up at the university in 1918 to field a football team. Vernon Jr.

had not suited up for the 1918 season and sat on the couch in the dark in his mother's living room, shades drawn against the world, watching the days go by—not because of the war—because he could not suit up.

Sheriff Simms banged on the front door before he opened it and let himself in. "You're late for work, dammit," he thundered.

"Work?" young Vernon repeated from the gloom of the room.

"Can you throw a football?" asked Sheriff Simms.

"If you mean, how's my arm, it's all knitted up, but I can't throw good enough to play."

"So?" asked Sheriff Simms.

"So, no," said Woodside.

"So, are you going back to the university?"

"No."

"So, you're late for work."

"What are you talking about?"

"You're working for me. Get a move on."

"Did Pa put you up to this?"

"Your pa don't know a damn thing about it. I like the idea of a Deputy Woodside and a Sheriff Simms, even if when your pa retires, I'll have a Deputy Woodside who can't use his right arm because he's a goddamn hero."

"I can use it, and I'm not much of a hero," said Woodside. "Those bluffs across the road have always been a place where us boys went lion hunting. I knew it amounted to snipe hunting whenever we heard of a cougar out marauding the livestock. It was such great adventure to grab my gun and go lion hunting.

"When that little girl screamed, it wasn't let's pretend. I tore out of the house. It mighta been on account of that scream. When she saw me, she pointed, for truth, at a mountain lion. It had a scruffy gray and white tomcat in its mouth. It didn't look like it belonged to that little girl or anyone. About then, I realized I hadn't grabbed my gun, but I didn't have time to go back."

"So, you decided to wrestle it?" chuckled Sheriff Simms.

Woodside looked at the sheriff, seeming startled. "Well, I did grab it by the head."

Sheriff Simms nodded a couple more times, a smile still on his face.

Woodside continued, "I held the big cat in a headlock with my left arm. It wasn't doing much but wiggling. I tried to yank the tomcat free. That lion had kind of a pretty face, small and fine featured, about the color of the sandstone. I tried to look under its belly. Best I could figure, it was a female. She mighta weighed, maybe, a tough hundred pounds, not anything more than I could lift if I could wrap my arms around her. Trouble was, she could move every which way. She twisted and wiggled against my arm and hip and leg. There was no picking her up, and she wasn't letting go of that mangy tomcat."

"Wrestlin' a mountain lion over a tomcat?" mused Sheriff Simms. "Maybe I'd best hire a deputy with better judgment?"

"That's how I been seein' it," said Woodside. "Started out I was protectin' that little girl, but she was clear of that lion and just kept pointing to her little cat and screaming. I guess I got just as determined as that she-lion was. One more pull and a head wrenched free, sort of attached to fur." Woodside gave a snort. He held up his right arm. "You might be right. Sitting here, I been thinking it woulda been better to explain to that little girl I couldn't save her cat. I snatched defeat from her jaws."

Sheriff Simms nodded in agreement, no smile.

"Everything was fine. I had the tomcat free, and I let go of my headlock. That cougar took a moment to catch her feet. Maybe she was maneuvering to turn around and race off. Maybe she was still after that mass of fur. Anyways, she reached out and swatted me across my right arm with her paw.

"Like I said, she was about a hundred pounds, nothing but a big cat. I never expected a cat could damn near knock me over with a single swat. That sway felt like three knives tearing my arm open from shoulder to elbow."

Sheriff Simms pointed. "Your arm's healed up now?"

"Not good enough to throw," answered Woodside. "No arm to throw with, no reason to go back to the university down in the big city."

"So, you were too much a hero to make All-American." Sheriff Simms stepped closer to the young version of his valuable deputy. He bent at the waist and looked down at him. "We got bigger problems than to let you sit around the house watching the days go by. Now, git to work."

"When?" asked Vernon Woodside Jr.

Sheriff Simms stood up straight, pointed out the door. "Now! I told you. You're late."

Chapter 29

"Put a clean shirt on," said Sheriff Simms. "You'll see how your pa's dressed, and it's your first day of work." The sheriff waited to walk with Vernon Jr. to the jail. Arriving at the steps of the jail, Sheriff Simms motioned Vernon Jr. to fall behind him. He stepped to the door, opened it, and called.

"Took your advice, Vernon. Brought you a deputy to swear in." The sheriff stepped into the doorway, careful to block any view. "Find the Bible." He stepped aside and motioned Vernon Jr. to step in.

"What the . . ." exclaimed Deputy Woodside.

"Seemed like the best choice to me," said Sheriff Simms. "He can decide about going back to the university next spring. Who knows if we'll be over this Spanish flu by then?"

"And who knows if my arm'll come back," said Vernon Jr. "Probably not."

"We'll see," said Sheriff Simms. "Now Woodside, it seems to me you ought to do the honors. I'll hold the Bible."

After the swearing in, Sheriff Simms said, "Too bad you didn't come with a wife, like Clive. I'm getting hungry. There was talk of making a deal with the Merc to bring us sandwiches, but with Trueman sick, there's no butcher."

"I could do that," said the new Deputy Woodside. "No different from butchering a deer."

Sheriff Simms silently praised his own good judgment. "Go over there now. While you're helping, find someone who can fill in for Trueman. Sort of replace yourself."

A knock interrupted Deputy Woodside's answer. All three looked at the door, but it did not open.

The sheriff stepped up and peeked out the window, "Ma?"

She moved back to the edge of the steps before he could finish opening the door.

"And in a mask?" he said. "You been talking to Doc?"

"Not yet, but if you see him, he can come over to the house. I'm going home. I got a little something in the diphtheria after the girls died, and I got a little something here. I'm going home to take care of myself. At the same time, that way I'll make sure I don't give it to anyone else." She stopped; her breathing labored from the talking. She took a few breaths. "Trouble is, I need to shut the Merc. That bothers me. A lot. People are going to need supplies, even with Trueman and me sick. I hate to burden you more, Mark Willford, but you need to know that. Maybe there's something you can do about it."

Sheriff Simms reached out for his mother. She shook her head, lifted her hand, and waggled a finger. Until that moment, he had not known she was sick with the diphtheria, and now he had to sort out all he had heard. The most tangible task she had given him seemed the easiest to take care of. "Ma, you know Vernon's son Vernon? He made deputy this morning, and his first job was to go over to you this afternoon and spell Trueman. He'll stick with it until he can find someone to take it off his hands."

"Good," said Elizabeth Tonsil Simms. "Here's a key." She gave a little self-conscious laugh. "I expected you'd take care of it."

"What about you?"

She waved her hand again and turned and started down the steps. "First thing is to take care of myself. Second is not to give it to anyone. I'm going to do both, right now." She continued up Main Street toward Fifty East without looking back.

The sheriff turned and stepped back in the jail. He sat at his father's desk—his desk now—for the first time since his father's death on Sunday. He pulled a pad of paper and pencil from the center drawer and scribbled a list.

1. Masks.
2. Don't get sick.
3. Don't make anyone else sick.

"Woodside," he said to his new deputy, "you go over to the Merc right now. You know what you need to do. Be the butcher. At the same time, find a butcher and maybe someone to replace Ma, too. We'll need you for other things." He stood up and turned to the father, "Vernon, keep looking for special deputies, best make it three. Your son's already full-time with the Merc job." Sheriff Simms folded the list, put it in his pocket, and headed for the door. "I'm going to see some people. We need help."

Sheriff Simms crossed the wide Main Street to the business side of town. He found himself grumbling that at least Doc could give him instructions about what to do in this unwanted job. His foot hit the boardwalk and jolted that fruitless thought out of him. The sheriff smiled at how clever his friend was. That was what being in charge meant, figuring out what to do and doing it. Learning by leading. Truth was, Doc knew how to take care of people who were sick. He didn't know any more about how to keep people from getting sick than the sheriff.

His mother had not given him any instructions, but she had told him the two most important tasks to do right now. He smiled. That damn Doc was smart. Sheriff Simms kept that smile and held that thought all the way to the shack that housed the *Summit County Bee* and its owner, Larry Suhler.

"Suhler?" Sheriff Simms entered a small enclosure formed by a wooden railing, twelve inches on either side of each elbow, about double that in front. The closed space separated him from a table that supported the hand-powered printing press. He saw no one at work as the round plate started to move. It kept moving until pressed flat on the table, no longer obscuring behind it the lanky body and white hair of Larry Suhler.

"Who d'ya expect to find here doing this inky job?" Suhler spoke as slow as any mountain man in the county, but he hailed from somewhere that worked a soft drawl into his speech.

"I'll take anyone who does," said Sheriff Simms.

"Not enough business for two of us," said Suhler.

"Well, you look busy," said Sheriff Simms. "That's why I'm here. I need something. If I give it to you tomorrow morning, can you finish it the same day?"

Suhler tucked his chin, catching a laugh in his throat. "You give my business too much credit. It's Friday. Once I finish the *Bee,* I can do it tonight."

"On, my God, the *Bee*. I forgot about that," said Sheriff Simms. He watched the printing press turn out a newspaper while he talked. "Never thought what I've got to do might be news. Anyway, I don't have it finished."

Suhler pulled a printed page off the press and reached for a blank sheet. "What are you talking about?"

"You heard of the Spanish flu?"

"Article about it, right here in the *Bee.*"

"Really, how'd that happen?" asked Sheriff Simms.

"Doc visited, told me we been the hardest hit in the state, and the mayor put you in charge." Suhler rotated the press down and up again. "I filled in the blanks. Wrote the article." He put another blank sheet on the plate. He looked at the sheriff before he pressed down on it. "You want me to write another article?"

"That'd be next week. I want a handbill to circulate a list of things to do today. Two lists really, to take care you don't get sick and to take care you don't make anyone else sick. I haven't made the list yet. I wanted to make sure you could print it for me tomorrow."

"That won't be a problem," Larry rotated the handle that lowered the press. "I got some space. I used it for a house advertisement, you know, filler, but I could put something in there. You know, like a teaser, maybe with a finger pointing at you. 'Do your part!' 'Make sure you don't get sick.' 'Make sure you don't make anyone else sick.' "

"That's clever," said Sheriff Simms. "I'd say, 'Make damn sure you don't make anyone else sick.' "

"I imagine you would," drawled Suhler.

Simms laughed and reached over the wooden railing to shake.

Suhler looked at the sheriff's hand and snickered. He held up his ink-stained hands and said, "Maybe best not. I'll do your list tomorrow and call it a special edition of the *Bee.*"

Back out on the boardwalk, Sheriff Simms looked up and down trying to figure out where to find the president of the Relief Society. Truth to tell, he did not know who had that job. He could hear his pa repeating, *Know your people.*

"Yeah, Pa," he muttered, "I should know who she is."

He looked up to the cloudless, blue October sky and offered a half-guilty shrug as he stepped back into Main Street. As embarrassing as it was, if he wanted masks made, he had to go back to the jail and ask Woodside.

A little after sunset, Sheriff Simms turned the handle of the front door to his mother's little yellow house. Before he could swing it full open, he heard her shout, "No you don't. Out!"

He saw her come out of the kitchen with a large wooden spoon in her hand. She stopped at the table to put on her mask, then kept coming at him waving her spoon. He ducked back out onto the porch and held up both hands in surrender. She grasped the handle and pushed the door closed behind him. "You stay out there till I tell you. I been through this with your father."

"But that was different," said Sheriff Simms through the door. "The whole town was quarantined."

"Take to mind what you're supposed to be doing with the town, Mark Willford. I'm not coming out," she shook her spoon, "and you're not coming in."

"Seems pretty useless to be the sheriff if you can't help your mother."

"I don't need help. There's lots of things out here haven't killed me yet. This won't."

"You see Doc Crittenden yet?"

"Saw him before I left the Merc. I know to take care of myself. He trusts that, but he's a good boy, he'll stop by tonight, sometime."

"Damn well better," huffed Sheriff Simms. "How do you feel?"

"Fever, chills, sometimes both at the same time." She took a sip from her cup. "The cough's the worst."

"Sounds pretty serious to me," Sheriff Simms said through the window.

"Oh, serious enough. I'm treating it seriously," she said and chuckled, "but not deadly."

"You taking anything?"

She held her cup up to the curtains. "Hot lemonade."

"That Doc's prescription?"

"Don't know, but I like it."

"Have enough lemons? That reminds me, I'll go by and check

if young Vernon took care of everything for you at the Merc. I'll bring you some more lemons."

"I don't need extra. Leave them for the others."

CHAPTER 30

October 5, 1918

Sheriff Simms left the log cabin before sunrise on Saturday. No surprise, Doc Crittenden's boy raced up Fifty North and intercepted him before he reached Main Street. Without breaking stride, the sheriff asked, "The Merc or his office?"

"Merc."

At the top of the stairs, Sheriff Simms knocked on the door. Nurse Bullock's hand extended out with a mask dangling from her fingers.

"For me?" asked the sheriff.

"Unless you want to talk through the door."

He put on the mask and tapped the door. Nurse Bullock opened it, waved him into the room, and closed it so fast she almost hit him. He surveyed the four beds, each with a sheet strung up around it. Not sure which sheet hid Doc Crittenden, he pointed at the mask and said, "Woodside asked the Relief Society to make these. They'll have them at church tomorrow."

"There shouldn't be any damn church tomorrow," Doc Crittenden's voice groused from the third sheet.

"The bishop don't agree," said Sheriff Simms.

"Well, he doesn't have a say in it," said Doc Crittenden. "Dr. Beatty called me last night. He wants every public gathering stopped. Schools, movie theaters, courthouse. So, you can just shut him down."

"Whoa," said Sheriff Simms holding a hand up to the sheet.

"How do I do that?"

"Shanks's pony. I told Dr. Beatty not to worry about it. I told him you were a hard worker, and you'd take care of it."

"Thanks," said Sheriff Simms, "since I'm basically doing your bidding."

Doc Crittenden came out from behind the sheet but kept his distance. "Because you're big enough to listen to what I say doesn't mean you're doing my bidding."

"I ain't so sure," insisted the sheriff, "but, for damn sure, you know I can't shut down the bishop. If I can't persuade him, I can't make him close his doors."

"See? What'd I tell you," laughed Doc Crittenden as he slid back behind the fourth sheet. "But if you don't, then you damn well better persuade him. If he keeps up, there won't be enough room in this room. You can quarantine people . . ."

". . . like you said, only those who are sick . . ."

". . . but for all the ones home in bed, there still won't be enough beds here."

"How they fixed over in Park City?" asked Sheriff Simms.

"I'm not the doctor over there." Doc Crittenden emerged from one sheet and disappeared behind another, "but God forbid they have more cases than they can handle. We can't help."

"I have to go over there to see Brimville. This here's gettin' in the way of my sheriff duties, but I'll go as soon as I can. When I'm there, I'll see if they can help."

"These are your sheriff duties," floated the voice from the sheet. "Don't much see how Park City can help, and there's plenty for you to do here yourself. Don't go borrowin' trouble." Out one sheet and into another. "Best make sure they take care of themselves. We're having a hard-enough time of it ourselves. Mayor's got his dander up, but he's too sick to do anything about it. Besides, all he's thinking about is when he can campaign again. Down in Salt Lake, Beatty and Paul don't agree. So, they got all sorts of confusion. Don't let yourself be confused, Mark. Not even by me. That makes for ineffective leadership. Don't let that bishop have a say. What we need more than anything is a clear set of marching orders."

"Even if you don't agree with all of them?"

"I'd have to know what they are, but I imagine there could be some things I don't agree with, as long as there's no confusion."

"The boy'll bring you the *Bee.* Meanwhile, here is what Suhler's printing for me. A list of common-sense suggestions, but you give me an idea."

BEE

Summit County
Special Edition—October 5, 1918

Sheriff Mark Willford Simms asks all in Coalville and Summit County to follow these common-sense suggestions. He asks you to support the community effort to fight the Spanish flu.

1. Take care of yourself.

Wash your hands.

Lots of hot drinks. Hot lemonade if Bishop says no to tea or coffee.

Don't visit anyone who is sick.

Don't go to any meetings.

If you must work, stay away from people.

Don't be embarrassed, wear a mask, please not a bandanna.

2. Make no one sick.

Sick people are sick, not evil.

Follow First Rule: Take care of yourself. Don't violate. Don't encourage violation.

No spitting or coughing or unsanitary behavior.

Stay at home if you are sick or if you fear you are sick.

Don't be embarrassed: tell everyone you are sick.

Don't cause anyone to break this rule.

3. Follow the Rules!

First Offense straight to jail. We only have 3 cells.

"If people don't follow them, I will call them orders. 'Course there ain't none of 'em I can enforce. We're needing to rely on a body's willingness to take care of themselves."

"The spirit is willing, but the flesh is weak," floated out from the sheet.

"That mighta been a different situation," said Sheriff Simms. "Most people will follow their instinct to protect themselves."

"Most, but not all."

"Not all."

Sheriff Simms walked down the stairs and into the Merc to check on his new deputy. It seemed like there were a lot of people for so early on a Saturday. He pulled out his pocket watch. Not much after the normal opening time.

An attractive young woman worked the cash register. Sheriff Simms smiled at the thought Vernon Jr. had already recruited someone. The sheriff touched his hat on his way back to the butcher counter.

"I see the Merc has new help," said Sheriff Simms.

"Linda?" asked Woodside while he concentrated on carving a side of beef.

"Future Mrs. Jr.?"

"Oh, good heavens, no. A high school classmate, that's all."

"Uh-huh," agreed Sheriff Simms with a cluck of his tongue. "D'ya find a new butcher in your class, too?"

"It ain't like that," said Woodside. "And we got bigger problems than a butcher."

"What's that?"

"We're almost out of beef. A fair amount of mutton. Nobody wants it. No pork at all."

"Raise a pig," said Sheriff Simms.

"What's that?" asked Woodside.

"Oh, nothing," said Sheriff Simms. "So many people take care of pigs, some think it's the state slogan. Buy more beef. Ma can figure out how to pay for it."

"That's a problem, too," said Vernon Jr., his shoulders slumping. "Some guy from OPP came in here last night and told me there's new prices on the beef."

"Makes sense. War ending means their business'll drop like a stone." Sheriff Simms nodded his head. "That's probably what got Hixson killed. Makes sense to drop the prices."

"The OPP guy said he was raising prices," said young Deputy Woodside, his voice rising with disbelief.

The sheriff shook his head. "What? He's crazy."

"Who's Hixson?"

"You'll find out. Don't matter at the moment."

"OPP might be crazy, but unless you can roust up some beef, we're gonna run out. I could take it on the hoof. Somebody'd have to slaughter it, but I could take care of it from there."

"Me? You're the butcher, young man." He cracked no smile and waited until Woodside stopped sputtering. "I'm not so sure old Trueman depended much on OPP. He had a good nose. Their operation always smelled a bit, at least around here. He kept mum about where he bought his beef. Best you ask Doc what to do to talk to Trueman."

Deputy Woodside Jr. put down the long knife and picked up the bone saw. "Looks like their plan's working."

"True, for now." Sheriff Simms turned over the mask he had been carrying from the hospital. "Wear this. Your pa has the Relief Society making masks for everybody. If you need to buy from OPP, do the best you can." Before he left, he pulled the bandanna up over his nose. "Breaking my own rules."

"How much should I buy?"

"As little as you can. It's better people decide not to buy than you tell them you don't have beef, or any other food for that matter. They'll panic. You need a butcher more than ever. At least a body to stand behind the counter. Your job's to find someone who'll sell to you, someone who don't sell only to

OPP or hasn't sold out to OPP since Lester McCormick became a bishop."

"What's Bishop McCormick got to do with it?" asked the new deputy.

"Never proved nothing," Sheriff Simms said over his shoulder as he left the butcher counter. He reached the front door of the Merc and turned to call back, "Ask your pa."

Headed toward his jail, Sheriff Simms crossed the wide Main Street, grown dusty in the dry, cold October days. Hixson's death had everything to do with the meatpacking problem and nothing to do with the Spanish flu. Now the meatpacking problem had joined up with the Spanish flu.

Chapter 31

October 8, 1918

Sheriff Simms flopped his left arm across the bed and touched the cool sheet. Sensing Ebby's absence brought him instantly awake. His eyes burst open to twilight, maybe a half hour to sunrise. He swung his legs over the side of the bed and reached for the clothes hung overnight on the straight-backed chair. Three strides took him from the bedroom to the kitchen. Sometimes Ebby arose before him and started baking bread, but she did not bake bread on Tuesdays. He found her sitting in the kitchen.

"Ebby, you all right?"

"Good morning, Willford." The only person in Summit County who did not call him Mark Willford, she smiled at him, weak but a smile.

"My God woman, have you got that flu?"

"Don't think so. I'm not hot, even with my cup of Mormon tea." She pointed to the mug filled with hot water and milk.

"You been up long enough to boil the pot?"

She smiled again, this time with a twinkle. "Well, I didn't watch it."

He looked at her and wanted to help, but if she had the flu, he figured he best not know it.

"There's a whole bundle of quarantine notices out there on my desk. Picked 'em up from Suhler yesterday." He wanted to hold her but stayed standing in the opening to the kitchen. "If you got the flu . . ."

"Then you can't go out either," Ebby said.

"I wasn't gonna say that, but I am gonna ask Doc if I need to lock myself up, too."

"No need," said Ebby. "I'm tired, that's all."

"Tired?"

She looked at him and he could see her chin tremble, but not a single tear formed. "You've been busy. We buried Rose a week ago. Your father, too, come tomorrow. And your mother's sick." Ebby stopped. Willford watched her. She took a sip from her mug.

He waited. After a few moments, he asked, "Is it the kind of tired you can take care of by going back to bed?"

She looked somewhere past him and gave a vague wave of her hand. "If you're worried about that flu, don't. It'll pass."

Unsure what to do next, except to leave her alone in their kitchen, sick or no, he pointed out the window. "Almost sunup. My job is to put up those placards. Will you be okay for me to stop around noon, see how you are?"

She nodded. "It doesn't seem right, like punishing people for being sick."

"Not much I can do. State made the rule. At least, Dr. Beatty."

"State making the rule doesn't change what's right. People will do what's right. That's how they've survived out here almost seventy years. They'll quarantine if they should. It's the sign on the door that's wrong." She waited for him to respond. He didn't. "It'll single people out."

"Maybe you're right," he said, "but the first one goes on Ma's door."

"Strong people can bear singling out," she said. "It's the weak ones get hurt."

It took no more than five minutes to walk to the little yellow house. When he knocked on his mother's front door, she opened the little curtain, making no move to open the door. She smiled at him. "Been here since Saturday, four days if you don't count Friday. The worst has passed, but I can't go out, and you can't come in."

"I know that, Ma," he chuckled. "Sounds like what you told Pa in the diphtheria."

"It does," she said through the window, "because it is."

The sheriff held up one of the placards: **QUARANTINE.** "I gotta put one of these on your door. State issued the order yesterday. They say we're about the worst in the state." He gauged his mother's response. When she made none, he asked, "What do you think about that? Ebby thinks it's terrible."

"I think if I were a bird and I fell out of my nest, I'd want Ebby to come along and find me," she said.

"No denying that," said Mark Willford, "but is this gonna do people harm?"

"It won't harm me," said his mother. "I'll do what my son, who's the sheriff, says, even though my dead husband enforced the quarantine without putting up any signs at all."

"It wasn't my idea," Sheriff Simms said. "I told you Dr. Beatty ordered it."

She shook her head. "Not my meaning. I got the disease. I also got lots of protection. People cannot do me any harm by how they react to me. I already quarantined myself, like before. I even have you. Some people know that and it makes them behave differently. When we're healthy again, I'll go back to my work at the Merc. That's not the same for the weakest, the ones who barely hold on at the edge during normal times. The ones come here to work in the mines, and like it or not, a lot of Indians we haven't driven out yet. Mormon families, too. You best worry about them."

He looked at his mother through the window. "Sort of the

same thing Ebby said. I'm worried about her." He stopped, then added, "and you."

"No need, I'll be back to work on Saturday. Ebby's tired. It'll pass."

"You're rushing it, Ma," said Sheriff Simms. "Young Vernon's doing a good job. He asked Linda Clarke to work up front. Now he needs to find someone to take over butchering."

"That Clarke girl's as smart as they come," said Mother Simms, "and cute, too. Tell them to leave the key at the front door with a note to take what they need and put it on the pad of paper next to the register."

Simms nodded and tacked the quarantine sign up on the siding next to the door. "I best be going." He took a step back to the window. "Dr. Beatty asked yesterday, 'What is it about Coalville?' "

Mother Simms laughed. "It's the Devil's work." She quickly put her finger across her lips. "Don't repeat that. We're a little town, three or four shops, an opera house, a bank, and a church. It don't take much for one visitor to touch every life."

Sheriff Simms shook a no. "Doc Crittenden thinks we had more'n one visitor. Maybe I best figure how to keep strangers out of our county. I'll go up to Echo and make sure they don't let anyone off the train up there."

His mother pulled the curtains aside, "You might want to think about your grandfather's nine principles."

"They're hanging on the wall," said Sheriff Simms.

"They'd be better put to use," said Mother Simms. "We live with intelligent people, hardy enough to last out here on to seventy years. They already lived through one epidemic."

"*The police are the public, and the public are the police.* Pa quoted it all the time."

"You have to ask them," she said. "There'll be a few who throw up their arms and want the mayor or the sheriff to prevent them from getting sick. Especially when someone dies. Death always hits close to home, and that prospect makes it worse for some people than it actually is." She smiled, "Sometimes you have to remind them."

CHAPTER 32

October 12, 1918

It felt like a perfect time to ride Two. Sheriff Simms cleared his head and made a mental list of what remained to be done. That pleasant task disappeared into anxious haste by the time he arrived at Seth Parker's livery, now mostly garage. He could not take the five or six hours to ride her. He did not like admitting it, but his days of riding Two had been over for eight years, except for deer hunting and the rare duty that took him into the mountains where no road had been cut. No riding Two and even the thought of unraveling Hixson's death started to recede. Right now, he had to deal with the Spanish flu, and he had to drive to Park City.

Seth Parker waved Sheriff Simms into the front seat of the county's Model T. "I'll crank 'er," he said over the hood. "A service of the garage!"

The sheriff laughed. "Are you sure, Seth? You must be over sixty-five." The sheriff scooted out of the seat, his left foot on the ground, his right on the running board. "The last thing Pa'd do is have you wait on me."

"Sixty-six, to be exact," said Seth, his eyes fixed on the crank. "For damn sure, he expected me to have his horse ready to go." One more crank and the engine sprang to life. Seth wiped his hands. "I don't see no difference."

"Maybe," said Sheriff Simms, hoisting himself into the driver's seat. He looked at the grinning Seth. "Thanks."

Seth meandered from the front of the car to the open window. "Where you going?"

Sheriff Simms remembered his father's introduction to Seth and the livery—better than a newspaper. Before he answered any question, ever, when he talked to Seth, he asked himself if he wanted the town and county to know his doings. This time, he did. "To Park City. I'm catching up. I ain't been there since Pa died, and I need to find out where they are on this Spanish flu that Doc has me working on."

"Did Doc give you a certificate?" asked Seth.

"A certificate?" Sheriff Simms put the car in gear. "For what?"

"They shut the whole of Park City off yesterday. They'll never let you up the road unless Doc gives you a certificate says you got no signs of flu."

"Yesterday? And you already know that this morning?"

Seth Parker smiled. He took a moment to nurse it, spread his arms wide. "I'm a garage."

The sheriff laughed again. "How'd I forget? Thanks for warning me. They might not know it, but I'm wearing this star. I'll talk my way in. No time to go back to Doc at the hospital."

"They might not take kindly to that," said Seth, rolling his head back and forth. " 'Course you're the sheriff and all. Still, you wouldn't blame a body says you set the rules but don't follow 'em."

"Not my rules," said Simms. "First I heard of 'em."

"So, you only follow the rules you make?"

Sheriff Simms felt ready to explode, but he didn't know whether to laugh or scream. Thundering, "Damn it, Seth," he put the county's Model T in gear and drove to the Merc.

Doc's certificate added forty-five minutes to his forty-five-minute trip. When he arrived at the narrow road up the steep canyon to Park City, three men, deputy marshals he assumed, and two sawhorses blocked his way. He handed over the certificate without being asked.

The deputy who took it made no reference to the star on his chest, but upon reading the first line, said, "Oh, Sheriff Simms, we heard about your father. We didn't know you were coming." Now he noticed the star. "I don't know what to say. Sorry? Congratulations?"

"Thanks," said Sheriff Simms, refolding the certificate and putting it back in his vest.

"You didn't need a certificate," said the deputy.

"So, you say." Sheriff Simms realized words spilled out before thought streamed in. He could not leave those words the last ones he left with deputies doing their job. "Sometimes I don't like all the rules, but to help you boys enforce them, I best observe them."

One car passed the sheriff on the four miles up the single road. He swung off at Ninth Street to make the bottom of Main Street and wondered. Blockade? Or people staying in their houses? He turned up Main Street in front of the bars he had walked past many a night. The county car slowed as the street climbed, but the Model T kept going. Near the top of Main Street, he arrived at the space designed for horses and buggies built with the hotel. Scarcely four years later, the wide turn-in became a car park. Brimville kept the hitching posts.

"Deputy!" rang Curtis Brimville's voice from his gleaming mahogany desk across the bright lobby.

The sheriff stood at the door to consider the reception area, golden-hued to attract the wealthy of a silver town. The few people he saw sat discretely on sofas. His last visit, like all his visits, had been about the meatpacking problem. He had yet to find Brimville cooperative and he feared nothing had changed. He strode up to the desk, "Sheriff now."

"That's right. I had heard that. Forgive me." Brimville walked around his desk, stuck out his hand. "I'll save you the breath. We're still buying from OPP. With this war ending, their prices are coming down. No reason to stop."

Sheriff Simms nodded and looked at Brimville's hand, then put one of his *Bee* handbills in it. "Your personal copy. Suhler has distributed 'em, however he does that."

Brimville looked at the handbill. "Might be useful here, but don't know that it'll make the *Record* all that happy."

"I'll go see 'em. That ain't why I'm here. You say prices are going down, huh? When's the last time you saw someone from OPP?"

"That'd be a week, maybe last Friday. Made my regular order."

"They deliverin'?"

"Right along."

The sheriff looked around the lobby. He waved a hand into the empty space. "Business been good?"

"We're ordering less from them if that's what you're asking," said Brimville. He hastened to add, "but I got no complaint."

"No, of course you don't, and I don't know if you're gonna order from them in the future. I'm here to ask you to make the Imperial an emergency hospital."

"What? That'd ruin my business. What gives you the authority to do that?"

"Don't know it's within my authority, leastwise, not for outside Coalville." He waved again at the empty lobby. "But I don't see much business going on."

"It's just the time of day," protested Brimville.

Sheriff Simms held up his hand. "I'm not asking you because I'm county sheriff. I ain't talked to anybody in charge over here. The mayor's shut down the whole town, but he and Dr. Beatty still had a set-to about the pool halls. I'd bet it's pretty bad over here, too. When you people start to see more sick people than the miners' hospital can hold, it stands to reason, you'll want to send them over to Coalville. You need an emergency hospital right here."

Brimville nodded. "I don't like agreeing with you." He put the *Bee* handbill on the mahogany reception desk. "You go see the people here, and then we'll talk. I might consider it. I could maybe have it done in a week. But I don't want to do it any faster in case they don't go ahead with the camp they're planning."

"Week? I'm thinking Monday. Announce it in church tomorrow."

"I don't go to church," said Brimville.

"The bishop does. He'll announce it. What camp? You turnin' the Imperial into a camp?"

"Sheriff, you forget. We're not a Mormon town. We wouldn't hit half the town if the bishop announces it."

"You only need to tell the mayor and the doctors. So, forget the announcement. Now, what's this about a camp you're avoiding?"

"Again, back to the town. We're a mining town, with lots of foreigners. We don't know how they keep themselves. There's talk of separating them out."

"What's that mean?"

"They want to clean out China Town."

"So, it's really the Chinese, not just foreigners?"

"It's both, but the Chinese already created a separate little enclave. Folks figure it won't be no different to move them."

"Where?"

"You know that grass meadow out where Main Street swings out to the trail to Deer Valley? Pretty little place, lots of fresh air all the time. Folks figure that'd be the perfect place to set up a camp and move the Chinese out there."

"Do they want to move out there?"

"I don't think that comes into the question," said Brimville. "You came up through that blockade on the road?"

"Yes."

"D'you have a certificate?"

"Figured I better," said Sheriff Simms. "Couldn't make it through without one."

"Same difference. Folks is figuring what they need to do to take care of themselves and setting up a camp for the Chinese is one of the things they're considering."

Sheriff Simms heard that phrase, *camp for the Chinese,* and he wondered if he could ignore it if Brimville set up the emergency hospital. He shook his head and said, "Every town in the whole county goes their own way to deal with this thing. People are showing what Ma called frontier spirit. Most people go ahead and do what's needed. A few might die, but the best way to avoid that is to stay calm and take care of yourself."

"No argument there."

"Making rules for other people doesn't help much. That spirit means respecting the reason we came out here in the first place. I wasn't around, but I know my grandpa stared down a whole town fixin' to harm one young Indian boy. The Indians had pretty much done what they were accused of by the Whites. The Whites had for sure done what they were accused of by the Indians, but that didn't justify hurtin' that Indian boy because there were more Whites than Indians."

"Nobody's going to do any harm to them," said Brimville. "The guards may keep the Chinese there, but they protect the Chinese from the rest of the town just as much."

"Guards!" The sheriff's big voice filled the entire lobby. He held himself as steadily as he could and spoke as evenly as his upset allowed. "If there ever is a camp in this state that holds people because of who they are, it'll gainsay the whole reason we have a state."

Brimville said nothing. Sheriff Simms, arms at his side, breathing heavily, shook his head and shoulders, not in anger but to cast off this terrible thought. "This ain't no contest. I'll go find somebody. I'll be back to see if there's any help you need to make this place ready for Monday."

The whiff of boiling Lysol accompanied Sheriff Simms's walk from the Hotel Imperial turnout down Main Street. It seemed like the perfect companion to the caustic mood Brimville had brought on. He thought of visiting the city marshal to stop this camp nonsense. He arrived at city hall and relished the prospect of going downstairs to the first jail they built for his grandfather, dug into the mountain after the silver was discovered. At the door he noticed the Lysol smell followed him. No need to visit the marshal. That poor man had not been the source of the foul decision.

Doc Crittenden's caution from their meeting with Mayor Valfred returned as Sheriff Simms surveyed the three doors arrayed in front of him. No corridor, he would have to open the mayor's door directly. No one had said Mayor Gearailt had the flu. He pushed open the door and stepped in. Mayor Gearailt sat behind his desk wearing a mask.

"Mac," said Sheriff Simms. "Are you sick?"

"Nope, and I don't intend to be," he said, pointing to his mask. "I ordered everyone to wear masks. And they boil them twice a day with Lysol."

"Ah, the smell," said Sheriff Simms.

"Small price to pay," said Mayor Mac Gearailt. "Where's yours?"

"Right here." Sheriff Simms pulled the mask Nurse Bullock had given him from his vest. As he put it on, he remembered Brimville had not been wearing one either. "Makes sense."

"I'm in charge here," said Mayor Gearailt.

Wondering why that needed to be said, Sheriff Simms nodded his head. "Of course. You know Valfred is sick?"

"Is that why you're here?"

"Not really," said Sheriff Simms. "I came over to ask Brimville to set up an emergency hospital in the Imperial. We can't handle any cases from you over in Coalville."

"Not sure it's yours to ask." The mayor waved his hand, dismissing the sheriff's infraction. "It's all right, but it won't be necessary."

"Good to know," said Sheriff Simms.

"Don't doubt me," said Mayor Gearailt. "Did they stop you at the blockade?"

"Sure did. You got good boys there."

"Then you know nobody's bringing that sickness in here. The town fathers are all in agreement, and you know this is not a Mormon town, so there's a lot of disagreement around. We're shutting down schools, theaters, all the public places like Dr. Beatty said. What's more, we're not letting anyone wander around town who's got it."

Sheriff Simms held the *Bee* handbills in his hand, and he didn't like shutting everything down. Like it or not, he had put quarantine signs on afflicted homes, including his mother's. Sheriff Simms said, "All seems reasonable to me. That it? More plans?"

"We're gonna do what we must. Keep this from getting out of hand. We might even set up a special camp."

"Lepers colony?" asked Sheriff Simms.

"I wouldn't say that," said the mayor.

"I imagine not," said the sheriff. His voice took on the tone of exchanging confidences. "By rights, I shoulda gone downstairs to see the marshal about this. I considered it, but like you said, you're in charge." The sheriff paused. "Here." He leaned closer. "Brimville told me the camp is for the Chinese."

Mayor Gearailt sat in his mayor's chair with his arms on the arm rests. He took a few moments before he bent forward and folded one hand over the other on his desk. At length he tilted his head to look up at the sheriff. "It's a town decision. Not fully decided yet. A camp's no different than China Town, except white people don't have to walk through the camp."

"Mac, you're Irish for Christ's sake. The Indians are camped over in Coalville up on the plateau, sufferin' worse than we are, and we got it worst in the whole state. They made the camp. We didn't ask them and didn't put 'em there. The Chinese don't have any flu cases to speak of."

"We aim to keep it that way," said Mayor Gerailt.

"You put 'em in a camp all by themselves and something'll happen," said Sheriff Simms. He leaned on the mayor's desk, knuckles down. "Brimville told me you plan to use guards."

"The details aren't worked out yet, but there's plenty of people treating this quarantine like a big joke," said Mayor Gerailt.

"Chinese?"

"Just being careful."

"Look, Mac, I know about your run-in with Beatty. Now you are tryin' to do him one better. You weren't so wrong about pool halls. Take the same attitude about the Chinese. Can't be too hard for an Irishman to understand that." Sheriff Simms handed him one of the *Bee* handbills. "Have the Boy Scouts hand these out. People will take care of themselves."

"Weak tea," said the mayor. "I done more than this already."

"I know that. You have done a good job. All's I'm saying is being in charge means knowing when to hold off, too."

CHAPTER 33

November 5, 1918

Sheriff Simms and Ebby owned the little lot with the Chalk Creek running behind it. The Chalk Creek brought them to their marriage, and they wanted it running through their life forever. He didn't count that lot or the cabin he built on it when he counted that he owned nothing. Maybe the lot and the cabin on it and the children in the cabin amounted to owning everything. He belonged to the county like the county belonged to him. He had his life, and his life had him. He liked to think everything he did came from his decisions, but he knew otherwise. The diphtheria epidemic brought his life and delivered him to take charge of this Spanish flu epidemic. The blessing of his life delivered responsibility and responsibility made his decisions. Today, life and responsibility meant elections. He completed his rounds of the polling places by seven-thirty.

Sheriff Simms reminded everyone to observe the rules set by Doc Crittenden. He doubted the town or the county, except maybe Park City, faced much risk. Three polling places for a town of about a hundred fifty households made for little activity. It amounted to an exercise in the principle of elections. Everybody but the incumbents dropped out. Mayor Valfred's loud protests to naught, he gloried in being the only name on the ballot. When Sheriff Simms inspected the ballot at city hall, it surprised him to see his name. He had never thought this job, sheriff of Summit County, came as an elective position. He doubted his grandfather, sent here to be the cooper, had either. As to his father, he couldn't remember seeing him shine up to anyone.

With that, he searched out the county clerk, Enoch Pike, Ebby's brother, downstairs in the records room. "Pike, why the hell did you put me in an election?"

"Because that's what it is," said Enoch. His monotone reflected the plain facts he spoke.

"By God, a Simms has been sheriff of this county longer'n it's been a county."

"Of course, that's not possible," said Enoch.

"A calling of God made my grandpa sheriff," said Sheriff Simms. "Do you know what that is?"

Pike, head and shoulders shorter than his brother-in-law, looked up at him. His monotone continued, "With Enoch for a name, you could guess I know the meaning of a calling of God."

Sheriff Simms stared at his talkative, smart-ass relative. "If you have that much Old Testament in you, you coulda left my name off," said the sheriff.

"Now, how does that make sense? And I couldn't. They made Utah a territory. That made your grandpa sheriff, and that gave him elections. Then they went and made it a state. That continued the elections for your pa. And now you are sheriff. You got elections."

Sheriff Simms trusted Enoch to be as competent at his job as any man could be. That did not stop the confusion. He had never seen his father campaign for sheriff, not one day. "So, what happened to the calling of God?"

"I can't say as anything changed. Coulda been God delegated that responsibility to the people when we became a state. I suspect all those years nobody done nothing more than put a name on the ballot like I did for you. Don't know when they started, mighta had elections thirty times by now. I been at this job eighteen years. This is my tenth. You know, we're not talking about politics," said Pike.

"We're not?" asked Simms, bewildered. He tried to make sense of it. "I musta known it was going on, but I never seen my pa ask anyone for anything."

"That may be how you saw it. Your pa had a way of asking that didn't amount to much of a request," said Pike. He waited a beat. His words slowed as his monotone grew in volume. "It is an elective office."

"Well, I ain't about to start," sputtered Simms. "I never asked nobody for nothing. If I asked these people for anything, I'd be beholden to them. That ain't right."

Enoch Pike laughed. "Congratulations. You got it exactly reversed." Sheriff Simms began to work his jaw, chewing on what bothered him. Before the explosion, Pike said, "You are supposed to answer to them. That's why it's an election."

Sheriff Simms did not explode. He continued to stare down at his brother-in-law. *No way you can pound a little guy into the sand, especially if he's your wife's brother, but dammit.* "Answer to them is one thing. I won't be beholden to 'em. It's a job ought to be done right. You take that responsibility when you take the oath. That don't change by gettin' yourself elected."

With his rounds completed, Sheriff Simms felt confident he could answer Doc's fear. Election day would not restart the Spanish flu. Lucky for them they had not faced a presidential election. Wilson had paid no attention to the Spanish flu raging in his country. He spent these past two weeks trying to nurture his Fourteen Points into an armistice agreement. Sheriff Simms had been too busy to have any opinion about the war except the one he always had. His father's death shone a different light on his opposition to Mark Willford's enlistment. Once again, he saw the wisdom in his father's seemingly harsh acts, taken without explanation, but he still felt the sting.

Now Doc Crittenden warned that a big armistice celebration could restart the flu. Sheriff Simms wondered what the doc expected. The old coot had been opposed to the election, too. You couldn't anymore cancel the election than you could close the churches.

No denying that a parade and a city picnic exposed people to each other more than voting in private, and Sheriff Simms admitted that being in the middle made him uncomfortable. He had to protect the people from Doc's extreme care as much as he had to protect them from passing the flu to each other.

With the thought he could now hunker down to real work as he approached his jail, Sheriff Simms spotted the city-dressed man standing at the foot of the jailhouse steps. Simms took in the details of the man's black suit, white shirt, black tie. A big brown bag hanging off his left arm made him look lopsided.

"Hey," called the man.

The sheriff waved his hand and let that cover a few more steps until he came closer. He asked, "Woodside not in there?"

"Don't know. I looked in. Didn't see anyone. Didn't go in. I've been waiting for you."

"Lucky you came today. We've pretty much kept outsiders out."

"I figured as much. Ogden, too. It's election day. You can't restrict access to the polls."

The observation confirmed what the sheriff already knew, he wasn't local. The clothes said, big city. "You from Ogden?"

"I drove up from Ogden. Word has it that the situation is improving," said the man. "Eight nurses who have been isolated for several days at the Dee hospital were much better yesterday." Sheriff Simms couldn't be sure what that information had to do with anything. The man moved toward the door. Before leaving, he turned back toward the sheriff. "If that doesn't allay your concerns, I'm from Salt Lake."

"Uh-huh." Sheriff Simms muttered. "No difference."

"Maybe," the man said in an agreeable tone. He offered his hand. "May I introduce myself."

Sheriff Simms looked at the hand. "You don't wanna do that. Doc Crittenden said he'd cut off any hand I shook. I wouldn't wanna be responsible."

"Well, I thank you for that. Anyway, I'm Carl Stewart Brown, U. S. Attorney for the District of Utah."

"I've heard your name," said Sheriff Simms. The man did not show the usual airs of big-city types, but that did not mean a U.S. Attorney could be trusted. Simms thought it best his words masked his surprise, and he was surprised. "You been around for a while."

"Since Wilson," said U.S. Attorney Brown. "And you are Sheriff Simms. Of course, you all are. I'm told every one of my predecessors had to deal with a Sheriff Simms."

Sheriff Simms evaluated the comment, comfortable to let silence reign. Only his father had to deal with a U.S. Attorney.

"You sound like what I heard about," said the U.S. Attorney.

And *he* sounded like a guy trying to strike a friendly tone. Okay to act friendly, but no Sheriff Simms needed to be friends with a U.S. Attorney. Sheriff Simms waited for Brown to explain.

"I'm here to work on a case of mutual interest. You had a couple of deaths up here. You may or may not know the government is investigating the meatpacking situation. In Utah, that means Ogden Provision and Packing. They're the largest meatpacker and largest employer in the state. I'm investigating two men from Ogden. I'm told they may have been here the day those deaths occurred."

Sheriff Simms nodded, hoping to hide his response to this new surprise. He noticed the careful choice of words about the murders he investigated. He had never thought to ask the U.S. government for help. Not even the Utah government, for that matter.

"I would have been here sooner," said U.S. Attorney Brown, "but they tied me up with allegations that foreigners who work in the meatpacking plant are spreading the flu."

"Don't matter." Sheriff Simms noticed a flicker cross U.S. Attorney Brown's face. "I mean about you coming. It don't matter you're late. I didn't know you were coming."

"Well, I'm here now," said U.S. Attorney Brown. "What can you tell me?"

Way too many things had to be sorted out before he had anything to tell a U.S. Attorney. Election day. Armistice celebration. A case he had not had time to work on since his father's death. A U.S. Attorney offering to help him. A need for the help and a strong doubt such an offer could be trusted.

Sheriff Simms shrugged. "We closed the theater on the thirteenth last month like we was told. The teachers up here been a whole lot more helpful than I hear they were in Salt Lake. I don't know that any of them done nursin', but they all been cooking. The only problem is the bishop. He won't agree to close the church. Lucky for him, Doc thinks we'll see some easing. I haven't been up to talk to Bishop McCormick. No surprise. There's no need of me ever talking to that man. More'n that and you'll need to talk to Doc. Crittenden."

U.S. Attorney Brown waved his right arm for the sheriff to stop. His animated gesture spread across his body to jiggle the arm holding the brown leather briefcase. "Oh, no, no, I am not up here to check on how you're handling the Spanish flu. That wouldn't be a federal matter, anyway. At least it should not be. I'm here to investigate the meatpacking crimes. More accurately, what may be crimes if we find out they are. It all centers on Ogden Provision and Packing. I've been told you had two or three run-ins with them, and now we see you had these two accidents up here."

"More like four or five," said Sheriff Simms, "when I was a deputy." He lifted his eyes and added, "No, more like once a year."

"Starting over," said Brown. "What can you tell me?"

The sheriff pointed up the stairs to the door. "Not much. Leastwise, not me. Hixson drowned. Two men from Ogden visited him the day he drowned. Pa cut 'em loose 'cause he couldn't get anywhere with their story. He allowed as how I could go on investigating if I was a mind to. Then he died." The sheriff paused and looked directly at U.S. Attorney Brown. "Before I could bury him, this Spanish flu came to Coalville. The sum total of what I know is their names. For more'n that, talk to Deputy Woodside. As to Elsemore, their lawyer says he fell off a hiking trail. We don't know if those two men were with him or even if they had anything to do with it. We do know Elsemore, and he wasn't a one to go hiking. I don't know if you heard about the robbery that led to my grandfather's killing, but Elsemore was in on it. That must make him fifty-four or fifty-five. Don't seem likely a man that age would take up hiking for the first time."

"Those the same two men who did in Hixson?" asked Brown.

The sheriff opened the door. Before they both stepped through, the sheriff squared up to the U.S. Attorney and said, "Already told you we don't know. Best keep your mind on what you're doing."

"Your prescription for staying alive?" asked Brown.

"More like my pa's. He's the one had the most to do with you guys. You'd do well to learn it. Like Woodside, here." Sheriff Simms waved U.S. Attorney Brown through the door and stepped to Deputy Woodside's desk. "Woodside, this here's U.S. Attorney Brown. He's gonna work with you on Elsemore's case.

Vernon Jr's still working with Doc, who tells me we ought to see a drop-off come this weekend. If there's no craziness about Armistice Day, maybe Vernon Jr. can help me on Hixson's case, too."

Brown gave Woodside's hand a hearty shake. The sheriff muttered, "A lot o' good I do."

Brown turned to the sheriff. "I didn't ignore your comment. You gave me fair warning. I'll return the favor. OPP's going under. These bad actors might be more dangerous."

"Mmm," noted Sheriff Simms with a nod upward, "my thoughts, in different words."

"Could be," said Brown. "With the war over, OPP's business has started to shrivel. You won't change what this flu does but do what you think you should. If we do not wrap this up before OPP goes under, there won't be any wrapping up."

CHAPTER 34

December 12, 1918

Sheriff Simms stood entranced by the quiet falling snow, oblivious to the rapidly dropping temperature in the log cabin from the open front door. No way he could drive the county car in this snow. The newly created County Public Works Department languished in the confusion and fear of the Spanish flu until the appointment of Sam Francis to Public Works Director. The sheriff trusted Sam would have everything well organized in time, but this snow did not help. He doubted the county owned a snowplow yet.

"Willford!" Ebby's voice interrupted his trance. He stepped out onto the stoop, closed the door, and breathed in the air and the snow. He loved it. In the snow, a horse beat a car every time. He left it to Sam to roust someone to shovel or plow the streets. Until then he would bow to necessity and ride Two, all day, if necessary. He hoped.

When he reached Two in the pen, judging from her vigorous nuzzle, she loved it too. He saddled her, and they joyously high-stepped through the snow to the jail.

Vernon Jr. met him with hot coffee. "Better drink this fast," he said, "Bishop Barber wants to see you."

"On a Thursday?" Sheriff Simms hung his heavy coat on the peg and warmed his hands around the mug. "I think I'll take my time." After he emptied the mug and took it to the rack above the stove, he asked Vernon Jr, "You a good Mormon?"

"Not so's you'd notice. Not as good as my dad."

"Don't matter," said Sheriff Simms. "I was askin' because I thought there's a rule to rotate bishops every eight years. Bishop Barber's been the bishop for fifty years."

"Off and on, maybe," said Deputy Woodside. "If you stop for a while, I think you can be bishop again."

Sheriff Simms pulled his heavy coat off the peg. "Well, we coulda used a different one this last little while." He left the comfort of the warm jail and unhitched Two. He guided her high steps across Main Street at a slow pace. He enjoyed the snow and watched a half-dozen others outside enjoying their slow progress too. He tied Two to the rail in front of the little white shack and opened the door but did not go in. He called, "Bishop Barber, you still sick?"

The bishop stood over one of his customers, mask on, and continued his work as he answered. "No, not at all. Not since Armistice Day."

"You sure?" asked the sheriff. He stepped in but left the door open. "How old are you?"

"Eighty."

"Doc told me that's the biggest risk for you."

"Told me that too, but God gave us this disease. He decides who to take. Didn't take me."

"Yeah," said Sheriff Simms, "your attitude's been helpful right along."

"Chip off the old block," chuckled Bishop Barber. "Thought you'd like to know we'll be telling the Brothers and Sisters they can worship from home during this holy season."

"Two months too late," muttered the sheriff. Then he remembered his father, *never complain about getting what you ask for.* "We're on the way to seeing this end, but until it's over, I'm obliged for any little bit that helps."

The sheriff backed out the open door and unhitched Two. He

considered where to find Doc. *Never complain* might add up to celebrating a closed barn door after the horse has escaped. Still, Doc ought to be told, and he had time before going to see Sarah.

Nurse Bullock sent Sheriff Simms from the rooms above the Merc back across the street to Doc's office where he told Doc Crittenden the bishop agreed to close the church.

"There's something bizarre about people, even bishops," Doc Crittenden chuckled. "Especially bishops. He comes around after the decline has started. Lots of people like him, going the wrong way. Salt Lake's starting to reopen and other communities are shutting down. The cases are going away, and the bishops are telling people they can worship from home. Ogden and Park City are completely shut down, except to soldiers. Hell, everybody knows for a long time, soldiers are the most likely to spread this."

"So, can I start getting back to my real job?" asked Sheriff Simms.

"Not for me to say," said Doc Crittenden. "You're the one's in charge."

"Ha," snorted Sheriff Simms. "In charge like a marionette."

"No different from whatever you do," said Doc Crittenden. He shrugged, taking a long moment, then reached out to pat his friend on the back. "You're sheriff."

"So," said Sheriff Simms, extending the word out in a long transition, "you won't object if I take care of some business I been neglecting. For one, I have to tell Sarah we don't know where those two guys are."

"Sure, always said you should keep on doing your job," said Doc Crittenden. "But check that attitude."

"What's that mean? You never complained before. I ain't changed."

"Go gentle." Doc took a long breath. "This might violate my

code of ethics."

"Can't arrest you for that."

"She's pregnant."

Sarah Carruth Hixson answered the door. Sheriff Simms searched for clues in her face. He tried to see what he could see without looking at what he was looking at.

"Those two guys are long gone. Reassigned according to OPP. I guess like my pa said, 'death by drowning' is enough of an explanation."

"Hello to you too," said Sarah. "Come out of that snow and don't track it in."

Frosty or not, she had been his first friend, and he wasn't about to pussyfoot with her. "Considering. You took that pretty well."

"Considering Lawyer Pulsipher told me when he gave me the relocation money," she said without any change of expression.

"So, you made a settlement with OPP?" asked Sheriff Simms.

"He was pretty clear, repeated a couple of times, this wasn't a settlement. He didn't even ask me to sign anything. Since they sold the ranch, he said it was to help me relocate."

"Uh-huh," said Sheriff Simms. He could hear his father's words, *Nothing I can do about it.* "What you gonna do?"

"Like I told you, move to Wyoming. With what OPP gave me I can set up while I'm waiting for the baby. Then I'll find a job." She smiled at him like she could still outfox him. "Considering . . . Doc already told you."

Denying a fact never seemed a good way to deal with being caught. This time, no different, with the important question being how she would take care of herself and a baby. "May not be the best move," said Sheriff Simms. "Doc says cases are goin' down. They're fixin' to let the movie houses open in a couple of days. He says Dr. Beatty sees a letup by Christmas enough they're opening the schools on the thirtieth. Looks like the worst has passed for us, but I don't know anything about Wyoming."

"You don't need to," said Sarah. "I'm the one's moving."

Her tone startled him but did not lessen his concerns. "You sound like you're fixin' to move right now. When's the baby coming?"

"May," she said. "That's why I'm moving right now."

Something in her tone and attitude, in the very plan itself, did not add up for him. Sheriff Simms said, "Nobody moves to Wyoming in the winter. Everyone from around here knows that. The snow's too deep and the night's too cold to have to rebuild or start over. Every house worth living in is already occupied. I got to do everything I can to keep you here. We're family."

"No," said Sarah, "we're not. My ma saved your ma before we were born. She's the one you owe, not me and not my baby." Her words sounded like anger to Sheriff Simms. He didn't know how to respond. He tried to keep his face and posture from showing it. Sarah took his hand. "Look, Tom's gone. He may not have been the perfect catch, but he's the only one I caught. Now he's gone. I've settled my mind to the thought there's no one to go to for protection . . . or even a caring touch. It makes me short from time to time."

Sheriff Simms tried to make it better. "You'll find somebody up there."

"Fat chance," Sarah laughed. "I ain't looking. Besides, all I'll find up there is sheepherders."

Sheriff Simms felt some dispirited by Sarah's attitude. "I imagine everyone's told you, you had no prize in Tom Hixson. And that don't seem like much of a help, neither."

Sarah glared at him. "And you think my solution is to try to escape it?"

He could see her move to Wyoming as self-reliance. He could

also see she had put her tongue to something he knew better not to say.

"I don't aim to add more to those judgments, but you got to know his death came from the fabric woven by his behavior. I never needed to say you were better off. I wanted to help you as much as I could. I want that to continue."

"Which if I move makes that impossible," said Sarah.

Simms stepped to the back door. He shook his head before he opened it and said, "Pa had a phrase I swore I'd never say. There's nothing I can do."

Sheriff Simms walked out to Ma Carruth's barn. He mounted Two and guided her out into the falling snow. The blessed snow worked its wonders. Two's steps carried a spring to them. He brightened with the partnership they shared on their short ride back to the jail. Sarah's decision threatened to paint gray over the bright truth. They had surmounted the Spanish flu, though the threat lingered.

He did not know what to think. He couldn't keep the Spanish flu out of his county because it arrived before he knew anything about it. Once given the job he had not asked for, he wanted to keep the number of cases as low as possible. He couldn't know if he had reached that goal. Indians had been hard hit, especially the ones who stuck around town. Those who camped out in the country somehow seemed to escape. He had regularly kept tabs on Park City. The camp for relocating the Chinese never happened, but he took no credit for that. Somebody he never met had the good sense to recognize that China Town saw even fewer cases than the rest of town.

He considered. Had he come out ahead or behind? Doc said they almost had it behind them. His mother recovered, and Ebby and the kids never got it. Ahead.

The Coalville Opera House reopened the same night as movie

houses all over the state. *A Dog's Life* by Charlie Chaplin resumed the number one position nationwide, barely beating *Out West* with Buster Keaton, in Summit County. Christmas brought candlelight carols around the tree in the city park. Doc spent time with his family, having only three beds, not four, occupied above the Mercantile. They even planned to open schools for a day and half before New Year.

Not yet gone, but knowing they had the Spanish flu on the run allowed Sheriff Simms to stay home for Christmas with Ebby and the kids. This year they followed Ebby's rule without complaint. Eat breakfast together before opening the presents.

The children's promise to make a fuss over him if he stayed home the whole day lasted through breakfast. He proved no competition to presents. That suited him fine. He silently anchored their day while doing no more than eat the pheasant and venison he had shot and the pies and cake Ebby had baked. Even the entreaties of the county commissioners and the State Prohibition Commission did not overwhelm the blessed easing of the Spanish flu distractions.

Running one election amid the Spanish flu problems left him in no hurry to oversee another one. He didn't see the urgent necessity of the commissioner's fear that Utah would be bypassed in the nationwide referendum on January 16. The towns in his county knew how to run an election. They had proven it eleven times since statehood. Running an election during the Spanish flu pandemic for sure created a bigger challenge than voting yes or no on the Eighteenth Amendment.

All this unnecessary fuss made him hungry. Time for another piece of apple pie.

★ ★ ★ ★ ★

III. Forever Sheriff

★ ★ ★ ★ ★

Chapter 35

January 1, 1919

New Year's Day started late for the sheriff. Woodside covered Coalville. Vernon Jr. roamed the county. The sheriff had the late duty, Park City. He arrived, headed straight for the coffee, and called, "Woodside," He had in mind to send him and Vernon Jr. to visit the polling places to make sure they were staffed, enough to suit the county commissioners with a week to spare.

Hearing no response, he turned around and walked back to his desk. No wonder Woodside had not answered. He sat with an unexpected visitor, U.S. Attorney Brown.

"Attorney Brown," Sheriff Simms saluted with his mug, "Happy New Year. I know why we're here late. Last time was a surprise, but why are you here at all this time?"

"And a Happy New Year to you," said Carl Stewart Brown. "As to Attorney Brown, I am, indeed, an attorney, but I am no longer U.S. Attorney."

"That's news," said Sheriff Simms. He trusted his sense that nothing suggested a problem going on. "Or is it?" He put his mug on the desk and turned to face Brown. "We got work to do for you people, but there's time for coffee if there's things to talk about."

"Not for me, not anymore. I do have things to talk about. I'll take the coffee."

"Hixson?" asked Sheriff Simms as he headed back to the stove. When he handed the filled mug to Brown, he said, "You know, Elsemore's in Rich County's jurisdiction."

Attorney Brown waved his hand. "Not my cases. Believe me when I tell you I am no longer U.S. Attorney. I resigned, effective December 31st."

"Yesterday?" asked Sheriff Simms. "And today, you're here?"

"Always a sheriff," said Brown. He smiled. "It's not so suspicious. I'm on my way to Evanston, or maybe Cheyenne, might be Sweetwater. Anyway, I thought I'd stop by and tell you. Because of my travels I will not be able to introduce you to my replacement, Blair Evans. He was my assistant, and he's a good man, from Ogden and went to Harvard. He's married to Heber J. Grant's daughter."

"Two strikes," said Woodside from his desk.

"Not at all," said Carl Stewart Brown. "You'll like him."

"We don't need to," said Sheriff Simms. "I don't see much need on the Hixson case, and I see less help coming our way. You mentioned things to talk about. Is that it?"

"Advice," said Brown. "I resigned because I want to go into private practice."

"Here?" asked Sheriff Simms, astonished.

Brown noticed and smiled. "No. I want to do some lawyering and some land buying in Wyoming. This eighteenth amendment is coming and if I'd a stayed on, I couldn't leave until who knows when. Maybe, when they toss me out because Wilson's term is over. Things look pretty spoken for in Utah. Who owns what seems decided by a group I'm not likely to join. I'm thinking I could be more certain to make a go of it in Wyoming, if I start right now, start small and maybe grow."

"All right by me," said Sheriff Simms. "I don't know about any of those things, here or in Wyoming. An uncle, my grandfather's younger brother, lives in Rock Springs. He might could help."

"Thanks," said Brown. "I'll look him up. You been around

this OPP operation enough to see what is going on. I think what I need to do is sheep, not cattle. It's the land I'm really interested in. I'm figuring the lawyering and the sheep can add up to a steady income I can count on to buy some land and keep it." He stopped and seemed to survey his thoughts. "Keep it and keep buying more."

Sheriff Simms shook his head and chuckled. "Grow a large ranch on the barren plains of Wyoming. That sounds like a great plan." The look on Brown's face suggested the sheriff's little joke shocked him more than amused him. The sheriff quickly added, "I'd guess sheep are steady. Their name don't tell you, but Deseret Land and Cattle look to be running more sheep than cattle. To settle yourself down permanently, all you need to do is find yourself a woman."

"Oh, I will, Sheriff, I will," said Brown. He laughed softly. "Not that it's like on my list of things to do, but I figure it'll take a little while and once I establish myself, I'll find her."

Sheriff Simms nodded. Brown's confidence seemed reasonable. He watched him stand and make his preparations to leave. The way Brown dawdled, he expected more to come.

"There is one more thing," said Brown. "I think we've wrapped up our investigation of OPP. We'll leave Hixson's death the same as your father's conclusion."

Sheriff Simms nodded. "Nothing I can do."

"What's that?" asked Brown.

"Phrase of my pa," said Sheriff Simms. "Never much liked it. Still don't."

"Well, we had little interest in Hixson's murder," said Brown, "if that is what it was. Now Blair has a choice to make, and the meatpacking problem is no longer a federal priority, not with Prohibition coming. In fact, with the war over, OPP's government contracts have gone to zero. They're shutting down. More precisely, they're selling out to Deseret Land and Cattle."

"We caught wind o' that," said Simms. "And going to sheep."

"Yeah," said Brown. "My guess is until that's done, they're switching from muscling suppliers to muscling creditors."

"No surprise," said Simms. "Things are shrinking after the war. It's gonna clean out the average family. Then these guys don't pay 'em for what they owe 'em from the war." Sheriff Simms could feel the heat rising in his face. "It's no different from rustlin'."

"You may be right," said Brown. "At least for those that sold beef to them."

"What didn't get rustled before," said Sheriff Simms, "will now."

On Friday, February 14th, Sheriff Simms hovered around the front door, trying to make his large frame and barrel chest look inconspicuous as he watched out the little window, looking to catch Vernon Jr. before he knocked. When he spotted the young deputy, he stepped out to meet him halfway down the walkway from the gate to the stoop. His deputy handed him the box of chocolates and said, "Don't seem like you."

"Ebby keeps telling me it's an old English tradition. Ma agrees. Figure'd to surprise her."

Deputy Woodside Jr nodded, "Speaking of surprises, Doc Crittenden wants to see you. First thing, well, right now."

"No, he don't." Sheriff Simms held the box of chocolates in front of him like it was a box of eggs. "Whenever he sends one of you Woodsides, he's trying to get me into something I don't want any part of."

"Sounded pretty serious."

"And he told you if I resist, to arrest me."

Woodside laughed.

"He wants to corral me back into the Spanish flu. I don't like what he's thinking."

"He seemed to think it's urgent."

"He gets that way, sometimes," said Sheriff Simms.

The sheriff waved his young deputy on his way and walked to the door, holding the chocolates behind his back. He walked through the front door directly to the kitchen and without saying a word gave the box of chocolates to Ebby. When she raised her eyebrows and lifted her shoulders in question, he asked "What?"

She rotated the box of chocolates in her hand to look at them. "What are you avoiding?"

Her question surprised him some. She could always see right into him, but he answered a standard. "Nothing."

She punched him and said, "You know you can't get away with that."

"The chocolates are honest for Valentine's Day."

"But you are hiding something," Ebby said. "What is it?"

"Not hiding, avoiding, like you said." He took his hat off the peg and put it on. "I was planning to walk back to the jail until young Woodside came. Whenever Doc Crittenden wants me, he pounces out of his office. He traps me. I can't do nothing but meet up with him."

"So?" asked Ebby. "He's your best friend, only friend."

"Not when he wants something from me. Like he does now," said Sheriff Simms. "Then he's just the doc."

"Could be important," said Ebby. She opened the box and with an impish twinkle in her eye extended it toward him. "You could always hide here and eat chocolates."

He pulled his tan hat a little further down on his head than usual. "Wouldn't that be sweet?"

When Sheriff Simms reached the left turn on Main Street at Fifty North, he considered crossing the street to walk on the opposite side. He gave up the thought, knowing it would not make any difference except to make him look like a coward. Sure enough, before he covered half a block, Doc Crittenden bounded out of his office to set himself in the middle of the sidewalk.

"We gotta go see Mayor Valfred," said Doc Crittenden.

"You maybe," said Sheriff Simms, stepping around his friend. "Not me."

"You too," said Doc, falling in at the sheriff's side. "All four beds over the Merc are full and I sent one home."

"The flu?" asked Sheriff Simms, talking straight ahead and walking straight ahead.

Doc Crittenden pointed his right index finger to his forehead and lolled his tongue out his mouth. "The flu, you ask? Who you kidding?"

"The mayor's healthy. The city reelected him. He should be in charge," said Simms.

"No, he most definitely shouldn't. But I'm not sure we can do anything different with this little resurgence," said Doc Crittenden. He stopped and took the sheriff's sleeve to stop him. "But you're not going to be happy with what he wants to do."

The sheriff made no effort to wrest his arm free. He looked at his friend and asked, "Like what?"

"Like go one better than Mayor Gearailt over in Park City."

Sheriff Simms grunted and nodded.

Doc continued. "They're considered flu-free and Valfred's going to say if what they did worked for them, it's good enough for him."

Sheriff Simms stood for a moment looking at his feet, then looked up at the gray sky. "You'd think on a day like Valentine's Day there could be sunshine." He slowly brought his eyes back to Doc and raised his hands in surrender. "I'll go with you. I'll do what the sheriff needs to do, but I won't take charge."

"That'll be plenty." Doc started off toward city hall.

They walked down the empty corridor and through the door to Mayor Valfred's office and stood in front of his desk until he looked up.

"You still think this flu's coming back?" asked Valfred.

"Don't know about coming back, but some new cases have popped up. That has not happened since November," said Doc Crittenden. "And not just me. I called Dr. Beatty. Salt Lake has new cases, too."

"Well, we must act," said Valfred. "We can't let this start up again."

"Might be prudent to take some precautions," said Crittenden.

"I'll blockade the town and issue an order for people to stay at home," said Valfred.

Sheriff Simms listened to the two men and said nothing. Less said, less likely to end up responsible for the whole damn problem.

Valfred turned to the sheriff. "You take care of that, Simms."

"No." His strategy had not worked, but he for damn sure wasn't going to let them think he would do something he was not going to do.

"I'm ordering you to do it," said Valfred.

"Sounds like it," said Simms, "but I'm county, you're city."

"What do you think should be done?" asked the doc, a smile on his face.

Sheriff Simms could see his old friend's trap, and he took care not to step into it. He said, "I'll send Boy Scouts out to ask if newcomers got symptoms and to hand out something that tells them what we expect in this town, for them to keep healthy and not to make anybody sick. As to those Doc Crittenden says are sick, with three entrances to town, it won't take many, so I'll send the other Boy Scouts around to put up quarantine signs again."

"Not enough," said Mayor Valfred.

"That'll do it," said Sheriff Simms.

"I want more," said Mayor Valfred, "at least until Doc Crittenden tells us there are no more cases."

Sheriff Simms said nothing. Doctor Crittenden jumped in, "Mayor, I think we have a resurgence here, but that might be a little extreme."

"It's what I want," said Mayor Valfred and he pointed at Sheriff Simms, "and I want you to enforce it."

"The county might not be able to stop you," said Sheriff Simms. "I'll have to ask the county attorney, but the county's not gonna do it."

"Then it's time for Coalville to have a city marshal," said Mayor Valfred.

"Couldn't say about that," said Sheriff Simms. "Might be."

Chapter 36

May 31, 1919

Sheriff Simms inched his way past Ebby's kitchen window. He turned his head to sneak a peek. She watched him balance the two-by-fours on his shoulder and grasp a sack of cement in his right hand. He had picked the time with care. The pies in the oven of her woodstove needed more urgent attention than figuring out what he was doing now. He hoped to take advantage of the special pleasure she took in baking, committing herself to its precise rules and careful measurements. He judged himself successful given the no surprise look showing on her face.

Trusting his success, he walked back to the Ford and inched it forward in the narrow plot reserved for the garden. Its knocking motor must have interrupted her count as she cut the cold lard into her pie crust. This time he saw a scowl when he glanced in the window.

He turned the Ford left and crept, boards of all descriptions and sizes tied to top and sides, across the yard behind the house. He cringed when screeching brakes signaled his attempt to bring the truck's slow crawl to a stop. The sheriff leapt from the driver's side, some urgency punctuating a need that he had not discussed with her. He had not the nature to talk about what he had to do. He took it on and Ebby or anyone else found out about it by watching.

He took three trips—right through her vegetable garden—to untie and stack all the boards. On the third, she unlatched the window and set it to the hook hanging from the ceiling.

"Hey, mister," Ebby called, "that's my garden you're traipsing through."

"Winter planted." He barked to hide his guilt. "Nothin's up yet."

He trusted she knew him to be too practical to destroy a bearing vegetable garden. That didn't change the fact no one else in the county could ride on his shoulder and order him around. She half took the job seriously. She whole loved to tease him. Besides, it was the afternoon. Whenever they saw each other in the afternoon, they found it hard not to be playful. He kept his eyes straight ahead and promised himself not to be playful today.

Ebby wiped her hands on her apron and opened the screen. He didn't need to look at her to know her mood challenged him.

Willford retrieved a keg of nails from atop his neatly stacked woodpile, largest and longest on the bottom, smallest on the top. The keg hoisted on one shoulder, he reached in the front seat and grabbed another sack of cement.

"Well," she said. He saw her step off the little wooden stoop and cross to the dirt path. He stood still while she continued to the vegetable garden and moved in close to him amidst the building materials. "I guess you have decided to build something."

"Yep," he said.

"Care to let me in on the project?" she asked.

He stepped back and waved vaguely at the house he had built, simple logs, chinked up to keep the walls solid and the wind out. "Built the cabin," he said. "And all the additions. Just another addition."

"Another addition?" He saw the twinkle. "This house can't suffer comparing. Leastwise not to another outbuilding."

He straightened up and looked at her. That was a surprise. He considered a moment. She held his look. "Nothing to compare." He tossed his head. "Building a chicken coop."

He started pounding stakes in the ground, paying attention to measuring and pounding.

"You know how to do that?" she asked, watching him complete the four corners.

"Built the kitchen, didn't I? Pa taught me."

She sat on one of the stacks of lumber, stifling a laugh. "When'd he teach you how to build a chicken coop? I never heard of chicken farmers in your family."

"Don't need to be."

"Now, there's a truth," she giggled, a simple, little girlish giggle. She pointed to a square in his hands, "Whose stuff is this?"

"Bought some, borrowed some."

He took the shovel and started digging a trench under the string looped around all four corners and pulled taut.

"You fixin' to do this all by yourself?"

When had he asked anyone for help? "Might as well."

"No doubt you plan to raise chickens once this chicken coop is built," she said. He could tell she was a little exasperated. He kind of liked it. "Do you plan to raise these chickens all by yourself?"

"Don't see why not," he said as he continued trenching.

"Me neither. Except, chickens need more care than a husband. Every morning, somebody has to clean up after them and feed them and fetch the eggs."

"That's okay by me."

"Do tell," she said. "It's okay by you, but are you going to do it?"

"Sure am."

"And are you going to kill them?"

"Sure am."

"Must have been something real troublesome," she said. She waited. No response. "I guess you'll even cook them."

"Might's well," he said. He broke into a smile at the absurd thought. He could go one on one with any man in the county, but he could not go on long with this little thing sitting on his lumber. "Aw, hell, Ma, you know you'll do that."

"Do tell," she said. She leaned back. "This chicken coop isn't about raising chickens."

Sheriff Simms offered no response. He knew she'd take her instinct affirmed. She knew he only spoke when he disagreed.

Ebby shrugged. "Since I got plenty to do with three kids, you figure you can learn enough to take care of chickens from some pamphlet down at the agriculture extension?"

"Yep. No reason for me to know all this," he said, carrying wood to each side. "You had chickens. Maybe you should help me."

"Birds that can't lay eggs in nest boxes," said Ebby, "lay them on the floor. The other birds eat them, or they're all fouled with bird doo."

"Won't be much to clean up. The kids need responsibilities, and I'll be here every day."

"You gonna let 'em wander?"

"Some."

"Around my house?"

"Naw. I'll build a little run. I gotta put the popholes in when I build the wall, but I'll keep 'em covered till I build the run."

"That's big of you."

"Keep 'em movin' to keep 'em from peckin' each other." Willford laughed a little and winked. "It ain't much different from other hens. First pecking, right on to cannibalism."

"Wilf," she said, her voice soft. He had hammered up a flat box and started to pour in cement from one of the sacks. Her voice said stop and listen. He stopped. "Why are we taking on a chicken coop now?"

"I had the extra time. It'll all be done today."

"You know I meant why are we taking on chickens right now? You have two jobs, and I have the children and the garden to look after."

"I figure I can make some money. All it takes is a little bit of grain and maybe let 'em peck around the yard for the rest. Those that don't produce, I'll kill. That oughta keep 'em laying. We'll have chickens to eat. That'll save money. And we can sell eggs. That'll make us some money. It'll all help."

"I never wanted to marry no farmer."

"Chickens ain't farming."

"Sure is. Has been since all time. Next thing you'll want cows. Dairy farming and chicken farming go hand in hand," Ebby said.

"You can make fun, but you know we can use the money. I'll sell the eggs and maybe even a roaster or two, down to Trueman's or even to the neighbors."

"Sure will look good. Sheriff out selling eggs," she said.

"Won't bother me none. Wait and see. Don't take much to start. A man says he'll sell me young pullets ready to begin producing eggs, already sixteen weeks old. There's not much time to build this and check the litter is dry and all the feeders and drinkers are in good working order before they arrive."

"My God, how many you figure on having? You're digging up trench enough for lord knows how many birds."

"Hundred-fifty. Maybe two hunnert."

"My word, you're going to become a chicken farmer."

"Not right off. All works out, might lead to that. Figure to start with two dozen. The chicken coop is the only thing I got to build big. I can put in the watering equipment for two dozen birds. Then the nests will be down the wall. Birds don't lay eggs at the same time, so I don't need but a quarter the number of nests that I got hens."

"And light? You know light's what stimulates pullets to lay."

"How you know all this?"

"Like you said, we had chickens. And you forget my first job. Candling eggs."

"Nothing to it," he said. "I'll run a wire out here and hook up a bulb. Turn it on in the morning and turn it off at night."

"Well, you got it all figured. I don't suppose I need to know the real reason you're doing this. I hope you don't bring us no diseases, traipsing in the house from this coop."

"Naw. That Spanish flu is all died down. Doc doesn't think it's going to come back." A thought broke in and he paused. "To speak of. A bird might die now and then, but I'll find 'em every day. I'll keep it clean. That won't let nothing run on."

"Now just tell me again, why you doin' this?"

"I got responsibilities. I figure we need the money."

"Well, raising chickens in your backyard . . ." He watched her struggle with the need to say what she really thought. He trusted the code that created a lifelong habit and left best unsaid that which both knew to be true. He wouldn't have a problem if he didn't take on sending money to the widow Sarah Hixson's family. ". . . could cause a certain amount of disturbance."

"Not if I buy the right type of chick."

"Think the right ones will be quieter, do you?"

"No, Ma. By God, you're an exasperating woman. They'll bring in couple a hunnert bucks or more. God knows we need it. It'll grow. Wouldn't surprise me none if it gets up to near half what I make."

"And the cost? Did you figure that in?"

"Not much. I'll have to pay for the pullets, sure, but that probably won't be but every other year. Rest of it's feed. I can buy chicken feed cheap. For chicken feed, so to speak."

He delivered this last line with his signature monotone, daring her to laugh. She was up to his tricks and outlasted him. Finally, he spoke again:

"We ought to make a hundred-fifty bucks or more. Clear."

"You'll be lucky if you make fifty. First, you sell them to the store at half the price you're figuring, and nobody ever knows what the hidden expenses are, leastwise nobody never been through it before."

"Maybe. You're a wise woman, Ma, and I ain't about to dispute your judgment. My pa held down three jobs, only he was a better man than me. Two families and three jobs."

"You don't have two families, Willford."

"No, but I got to help Ma Carruth take care of Sarah, even if she is up in Wyoming."

She moved right up against him and put her hand on the barrel that was his chest.

"So, that's what it's about," she said.

Willford smiled. She always made him smile, even when she was catching him out.

"You have me all figured out, eh?" he said.

"You'd be surprised," she said.

"What's that mean?"

"People around here seem to want to keep me informed. Your doings is fair gossip."

"Gossip? I don't care what other people say. You know I got responsibilities."

"That you don't need to take on," she said. "I admire your desire to help Sarah, what with Hixson drowned and her boy not a month old. It's an old family obligation, but Sam left Ma Carruth with something and Sarah's young. You can't take care of everybody."

"You know, I never liked Tom Hixson. I didn't like him 'cause I didn't trust him. As cocksure and shiftless as he was, he would have been more careful than to go with those guys if he'd a known the boy was coming. They tried for years, and it stands to reason. Ma Carruth's in her seventies. She needs what Sam left her. There's not much she can do to help her daughter. OPP gave Sarah a little but damn little seein' as they were the ones killed Hixson. She sent herself off to Wyoming with her boy. They need help. I have to do something. I can't stand around and do nothin'."

Ebby dropped her hand, stretched up to kiss him, and returned to her perch on the lumber. "Don't make sense to me. She could live with Ma Carruth."

"Ain't for me to say where they live. I know whenever I hear 'there is nothing I can do,' I can't stand around and do nothin'."

Chapter 37

October 12, 1919

Ogden Provision and Packing Company stopped paying its creditors long before it hid behind a new name. The rustled beef created no obligation to pay the cattle farmers in the mountain valleys. The formula of "buy some, steal some" turned into "pay none" before the symbolic end of World War I arrived on the eleventh second of the eleventh minute of the eleventh hour of the eleventh month in 1918. By the time OPP sold the McCormick ranch to Deseret Land and Cattle, DLC had achieved the distinction of being OPP's biggest creditor as well as the biggest victim of its rustling. Shareholders took over the failing OPP, booted out management, and attempted to pursue a profitable future course. DLC welcomed the suggestion to lease the ranch to the new company created with a name change and the promise of new management by action of the same ownership. Hope springs eternal. DLC hoped to receive lease payments that would recover their future receivables as well as their past losses. The enterprising shareholders also persuaded two Ogden banks to lease back to them the Ogden Livestock Yards taken by the banks in lieu of the loans OPP owed them. The shareholders took a risk and put a little good money after a lot of bad. They counted on the fact that bankruptcy is voluntary—unless three creditors or more act in concert to force it. OPP's three largest creditors viewed continued operation as a better source of repayment than bankruptcy. Out of the ashes of OPP rose the Golden Spike Livestock Show.

On the fourteenth anniversary of his swearing in, Sheriff Simms retired Two. He loved the mare that started out as a loaner and became a birthday gift, loyal and giving everything for four years, not much ridden for ten. Walking back to his jail from the livery, Sheriff Simms spotted someone up the street. He had not seen him in more than two years. He took no joy in seeing him nor recognizing him. Gil Brose had disappeared. The investigation had been dropped. Now he was back. The sheriff wished he had stayed disappeared.

Sheriff Simms quickened his step and called, "Brose?"

Brose stopped and turned.

"In from Denver?" asked the sheriff.

"Not really," said Brose.

The sheriff saw what he remembered, a man short by the sheriff's standards and carrying too much weight to be a workingman. "Isn't that where you and McNabb are from?"

"Not really," said Brose.

"McNabb with you?" asked Simms.

"At the ranch."

"The ranch?" the sheriff repeated, surprised. "Ain't that been sold?"

"We're running it now," said Brose. He lifted carpetbags in each hand. "Needed supplies."

"What's that mean?"

Brose shrugged, "Business."

"Business? I though OPP went out of business."

"Mighta done," said Brose, lifting each bag into the back of a truck. "Golden Spike leased it from DLC. We work for Golden Spike. We run the ranch for the livestock show."

"What Hixson was doing?" asked Sheriff Simms.

"Not exactly," said Brose. He opened the door on the driver's side and Sheriff Simms noticed a golden spike painted on its door panel. "Too bad about him."

"Too bad?" Sheriff Simms could not keep the question out of his surprise. "You still say he drowned?"

"He drowned," said Brose.

Sheriff Simms asked, "Who helped?"

Brose smiled. "Come up. Look around. McNabb would like to see you."

"Not unless I have to," said Sheriff Simms.

May 1, 1920

Sheriff Simms stood at the foot of the steps to his jail, coat off, face up, taking in the early morning May sun. His vest and pistol belt provided warmth, and the sun chased away the morning chill. He breathed the first air with no trace of snow, none on the ground nor in the offing, since October. Winter in a town almost six thousand feet high called for partnership with snow. People accustomed to life on ground closer to sea level called the accommodation hardship not partnership. Once every few years, like the biblical seven years, snows flew so early, so heavy, and lasted so long that the eight hundred souls in town, including Sheriff Simms, blessed even the threat of floods that came with the sun. His joy in Saturday's sun ended when he recognized the squat frame of Gil Brose for the second time in a year. The unwelcome figure appeared to come from the Cluff Hotel headed straight for him.

Brose stopped next to the sheriff at the foot of the steps, his head barely above the sheriff's star. He pointed and said, "You know how to use that pistol?"

"I practice on field mice," said Sheriff Simms. "When they come out from winter."

"Well, I got a warrant here," said Brose. He nodded toward the sheriff's hip. "You'll need it for a rat."

"Warrant?" Sheriff Simms threw his coat over his shoulder, freeing his hands.

"I went to court yesterday. The judge issued it. He told me I'm a judgment creditor, and I had to take the warrant to you."

Sheriff Simms frowned. "I was hoping we was through with winter."

"What?" asked Brose.

"Nothing," said Sheriff Simms. "Let me see it." He reached out one hand. "Those things don't turn out well."

"I don't know nothing about that." Brose handed over the warrant and started up the steps toward the door. "The judgment's against McNabb. That's why I asked if you could do anything with that pistol besides wear it. He's a son of a bitch."

The sheriff watched Brose pass him through the door and held up the warrant to read it. "Is this list of stuff the creditor's claim?"

"My stuff," said Brose. "That's all I want. He fired me and I just want my stuff and get the hell out of here."

"Fired you?" The sheriff climbed the steps. "I thought you two was partners."

"Me, too. He didn't." Brose looked around the empty jail and sat down at the chair next to the sheriff's desk. "Turns out, he was boss. He knew it. I did not. We had a fight. He told me to get off the land. Wouldn't let me take anything. I had to go to court for my own things."

"How'd you get here?"

"I took a car."

The sheriff raised an eyebrow. "You stole a ranch car?" He looked at the warrant and thought he'd call the judge, but why bother? He knew the judge's signature. He looked at Brose, "I don't like doing this."

"Don't imagine he expects it. He thinks he can push me around."

Sheriff Simms doubted he could legally put conditions on serving the warrant, but he had never expected Gil Brose to walk in his office needing something from him.

"I'll do it, if you'll tell me what happened with Hixson. Truth."

"He drowned," said Brose, his smile a shade too broad. He tapped his finger on the warrant on the sheriff's desk. "You know you got to serve that. I'll pile my things in the truck and that'll be that."

"I can't," said Sheriff Simms. "It'd still be the ranch car. I can help return it, not steal it."

"Truck," said Brose. "So, I'll leave it there. You can give me a ride back to town."

Sheriff Simms left a note to tell Vernon Jr. he'd be back by noon. Simms felt a fleeting annoyance. He had wanted to be there when Deputy Woodside announced that his morning rounds had been a blur of people in too good a mood from the blue sky and clear streets. No mischief to be found.

Gil Brose drove the Golden Spike truck through the north end of town, onto the now called Lincoln Highway, up past Wahsatch, and on through the same tall gate Woodside had led then deputy Simms, fifteen years before. This time Wiley McNabb stood on the porch of the ranch house and waved them in. Brose drove the truck behind the barn and parked it with the other ranch vehicles. Sheriff Simms pulled up to the hitching post in front of McNabb. Simms left the truck running and set the brake. He reached for the Winchester 73 left to him by his father. He distrusted pistols, like all Sheriffs Simms, but he remembered Brose's caution. Like his father, he wore one.

McNabb noticed the rifle and raised his two empty hands to his chest. "Do we need to go to the ranch office?" he asked.

Brose ambled around from the barn and stood ten feet away.

"When did you get back in my county?" asked Sheriff Simms.

"What?" asked McNabb with a scrunch of his face. "We been

up here since Golden Spike leased the ranch from the Mormons."

"That'd be DLC," said Sheriff Simms.

"Yeah," said McNabb. "Better part of a year. Pulsipher told us he informed you Golden Spike took it over."

"Well, he did that," frowned Sheriff Simms, thinking his pa had pegged Pulsipher right. "What he didn't tell us is that Golden Spike brought you two to manage the place."

"You're forgettin' I told you," said Brose.

Sheriff Simms pinched the bridge of his nose, closed his eyes, and shook his head, "Yeah I guess I did forget that."

"That might explain why we never seen you," said McNabb. " 'Course, we been busy. It's fixin' to be good times and we're restarting it good."

Brose stepped in closer and said, "I told you McNabb was my partner, now he wants to force me out."

"Is that why you're here?" asked McNabb.

"You threatened to kill me if I didn't leave. I'm willing to leave. I can work lots of places for Golden Spike, but you won't give me my stuff." Brose turned to the sheriff. "He'd say I stole 'em if I took my own things so you can see why I had to ask the judge for a warrant so he can't say I stole my own things."

The sheriff watched them both. Not a hair's breadth to choose between them. He held the rifle with his finger at the trigger guard. He did not trust either one. "Go ahead, get your things." The sheriff turned to McNabb, "I saw to it he brought the car back. It's behind the barn. I'll drive him away."

McNabb nodded, remained on the porch. "All the same, I ain't lettin' him in my house."

"It's best you come," said Brose. Simms didn't move. McNabb didn't move. Brose blurted, "He's the one did Hixson. You could use that to keep him from acting up."

"He's lying," McNabb said. "I want him out of here, but I

ain't lettin' him in my house. I'll go get his things."

McNabb turned and walked through the front door. Inside of five minutes he bumped the screen door open with the carpetbag in his left hand. He stepped sideways out onto the porch with the carpetbag toward Brose.

Sheriff Simms saw the shotgun come up in McNabb's right hand. McNabb dropped the bag and stepped toward Brose.

"No!" Sheriff Simms yelled, plunging his rifle toward McNabb's gun.

The shotgun exploded in Brose's face, and McNabb whirled, firing the second barrel. Searing pain cut through the sheriff's left arm. He held the stock and through the pain he raised the arm to hold the rifle steady.

"That's two," he yelled at McNabb. "You're out. I shoulda shot you already, and you best not risk I'll hesitate a second time."

McNabb stared at him with the empty shotgun in his hand.

Sheriff Simms gestured with his rifle. "You're down for two murders, but from family, I know how long it takes to put you before a firing squad."

"Never," yelled McNabb as he jabbed the shotgun butt forward at the sheriff's face.

Sheriff Simms let the rifle slide through his hand enough to gain a firm grip on the barrel. He leaned inside the butt of the shotgun and swung the right hand holding the barrel to bring the stock against McNabb's neck.

Standing over McNabb, hand around the neck of the stock, finger on the trigger, he said, "I'd a better saved the county time and money."

He took the handcuffs in his useless left hand. "Stay on your stomach and reach your hands behind your back, or I will."

Five months later, moments after the judge gaveled recess for lunch in McNabb's trial, Sheriff Simms felt a tap on his shoulder. Before he could turn around, he heard, "Let me buy you lunch."

The sheriff pushed himself out of the chair and turned to recognize Carl Stewart Brown. "Don't recall that anyone ever bought me lunch. Don't aim to start now."

"Of course not," chuckled Brown. "You're the sheriff. But it's personal, not business."

"It's never not business," said Sheriff Simms. He took a moment and let a recollection percolate up. "Besides, didn't I hear you're a judge now?"

"True," Brown drew the word out a long moment, "riding circuit in Wyoming. Out of your jurisdiction, so you can't influence me. Like I said, the subject is personal. I'm thinking we can go across the street, to the Cluff Hotel."

"Pretty fancy," said Sheriff Simms.

"It's the only hotel in town," said Brown.

"Still fancy." Brown made a gesture for the sheriff to walk down the aisle to the courthouse door.

The sheriff held off. "What do you want?"

"Always the sheriff," mused Brown. "Nothing." He stepped back and again waved the sheriff up the aisle. "Except to talk."

"Depending on what you want to talk about," said Sheriff Simms, still holding back. "That's not nothing."

"My love life," laughed Brown. "Does that qualify as enough of nothing to you?" He stepped back and tried once more to wave the sheriff up the aisle.

Sheriff Simms walked with Carl Brown to the Cluff Hotel. Mrs. Cluff gave him a menu. He felt overwhelmed when he sat down. The sheriff could not recall ever having ordered from one. Every item had a price. He spent no time looking at the description of what the prices bought. He picked the lowest price on the menu, Salisbury steak.

"That's hamburg," said Carl Brown. "Order a real steak. It'll be good here."

"Wouldn't surprise me," said Sheriff Simms, "but since I don't know if you're payin' 'til I hear what you want to talk about, I best stick to what I ordered."

"That's easily solved," said Brown. "I met a family friend of yours." He stopped there to let the sheriff ask. He didn't. Brown resumed. "Since Pulsipher dragged me down here on a trumped-up idea my testimony would be good for his client, I thought it would give me a chance to ask you to put in a good word."

"Who you talking about?

"A fat man from Tennessee named Tom Roberson is the proprietor of an all-night establishment on Front Street in Evanston. He gave Sarah Jane Hixson a job tending bar."

"Yes, he did," said Sheriff Simms. "I didn't know his name, but she told me she had a job bartending."

"She's trying to take care of her boy. It's lousy pay, but she keeps all her tips."

"How'd you meet her?"

"There," said Brown. "No denying, she's a good-looking woman. Her clothes fit her well, you might say. But she made it clear, she works at a bar and all she's selling is what you can drink. Can't sell Becker's beer, it's Prohibition." Judge Brown's friendly smile widened. "So, they sell Becker's Best. That'd be a nonalcoholic grain beverage.

"She didn't know she was talking to an officer of the court, but that wouldn't have mattered. Sarah Jane's pretty much settled her mind to the thought she has no one to go to for protection or a caring touch. That makes her a bit short from time to time."

"She mighta said the same thing to me. Did she tell you that?" asked Sheriff Simms.

Brown answered with a smile. "The first time I saw her, I couldn't help but make the mistake of asking, 'How long have you been working here?'

"She didn't bother to tell me. I could see her getting hot under the collar. She continued setting up glasses on the counter in front of the mirror. She could see my reflection. I had been loading my sheep all day, and I was dressed for that kind of work. To make up for looking like a sheepherder, I might've left too large a cash tip. She could see it next to my glass. She stared at herself in the mirror for a long time. I could see her eyes move to take in the tip. She didn't say anything. She watched me watch her struggle with her thoughts.

" 'Go ahead, take it,' I said, 'I'm a sheepherder, but I can afford it.'

"She turned around. 'I'm not interested in sheepherders,' she said. I could tell from the way she looked at me, she thought my words didn't square with being a sheepherder.

"I returned every Thursday, so on the third night, third week, and third Thursday I put a cash tip down for my Becker's Best. She left it in the space between us. I assumed she picked up the first two each week after I left the bar. I did not ask. I started to tell her what I did for a living.

"She never talked to the men at her bar, including me. She never asked any questions, nothing personal, nothing about business. People worry about being in debt, especially women, so I volunteered I borrowed the money to buy the sheep. I told her, like I told you when I came through last January, it's a simple formula. I invest the profits from the sheep back into the land.

"I think the debt kind of rocked her. She saw Roberson bringing food from the kitchen to a customer and ran to help him. Listening to stories might've been her job but learning too much about the personal details of one man probably struck her as just not a good idea. She walked the length of the bar, checking for refills. She returned and I called for another. I paid with a fresh bill that left more cash on the counter. I watched her set Roberson's nonalcoholic grain beverage next to the first one I had barely touched.

" 'You never order two,' she said.

"I said, 'I'm a fine catch, you know.'

"That night, pretty much my usual, I wore a coat and tie. I admit that didn't exactly square with being a sheepherder, either. She might have thought there was a problem with age. My guess is she's older'n me, maybe five years.

" 'I don't want to be caught,' she said, 'I've done that already with a younger man, wild and exciting. You don't seem right. I can't imagine I'd best let a sheepherder in debt catch me.'

" 'Let me buy your time for an evening, and I'll convince you.'

" 'Well, there you have it,' she said. 'Don't know what to make of you, but men are all the same.' "

Sheriff Simms laughed. "Sounds bleak."

"That's why I wanted to buy you lunch," said Brown. "Ask your advice."

"That all?" asked Sheriff Simms.

"Well, it wouldn't hurt if you put in a good word for me. I understand you're old family friends."

"Can't do that," said Sheriff Simms.

"Put in a good word?"

"Let you buy me lunch. What I seen o' you is a lot better than what I saw of Hixson. I don't follow what you're doing, but you seem to be working hard, lawyering and sheep farming. How you got to be a judge, I don't know if I want to know."

"All part of my plan. When I started last year, I figured it'd take four years. If you asked me, I'd say I'm on schedule. Well, not exactly. I didn't expect to meet Sarah Jane until the end of the four years."

A shrill whistle pierced the hotel's dining room and interrupted any thought Sheriff Simms might have had to comment on Brown's progress with Sarah. He looked to see Mrs. Cluff run to the front of the room to scold young Deputy Woodside. She pointed to their table.

"Don't know what 'couth' means," said Woodside, nodding his head toward Mrs. Cluff, "but I couldn't see you with all these tables. The whistle did what I needed doin'."

Sheriff Simms liked the boy as much as he liked his father, not something to let on now. "And that'd be?"

"The jury's comin' in," answered Woodside. "I thought you'd be interested."

"Only if he's guilty," said Sheriff Simms.

Chapter 38

August 1923

Noon and August hot. The last Monday should not be this hot. Sheriff Simms left the jail to go home to wash his face and enjoy a good meal with Ebby. He could cool off and lift the heavy business of this Friday's firing squad for McNabb. He felt great pride knowing that his state still allowed the condemned to pick the method of execution and required that justice be carried out in the county where the deed took place. McNabb deserved the firing squad he faced. Still, Sheriff Simms almost felt gratitude for the man's taking care of Hixson. He did not like that feeling. In truth, he wanted to walk home more to help him think straight than to cool down.

He liked walking home. He liked the feel of the stretch in his back and his hips. He liked being on the streets, seeing the people. He liked surprising Ebby. A surprise visit at lunch brought Troy, born last month. Troy's birth did not erase Rose's death, but it raised their spirits.

His father and his grandfather both faced a murder in their county. Each one tracked down a desperate character. All three brought in their man. Like them, he bore the responsibility for carrying out the sentence.

Five months passed before the trial that found McNabb guilty. Thirty-six months rolled on in arriving at execution. For the three years since the sentence that was his to carry out, he had not thought about it—not once. Until today. He did not think about what he did not think about. Except today. What he did not want to think about he thought about a lot.

Out the door, up the little alleyway behind the courthouse to Main Street, turn right one block to Center Street. Sheriff Simms stopped at the corner in the bright, hot, dry air and looked both ways on the empty street. He hoped for someone to see. He did not like to talk to people. He liked to see them and watch what they were doing. It ended there. He would walk across the street to avoid a conversation.

The sheriff turned right. After two blocks of enjoying the trees they had planted along Center Street during the war, one thought flickered. He had to pass Jay Hinckley's house. His pa's training came in handy. Eyes straight ahead, without moving his head he saw Hinckley on his porch and kept walking.

"Hey, Sheriff," Hinckley called and threw open the door to the big screened-in porch.

"Hey, yourself," answered Sheriff Simms without breaking his stride.

"Hold on a minute," Hinckley leaped from the top step to the sidewalk and made the gate about half a step behind the sheriff. "Come on in and have lunch."

Sheriff Simms stopped to answer. "Nah, you ain't Ebby." He looked up into the trees but did not turn around.

"These young trees have grown high," said Hinckley. "They have big leaves, create a nice cool shade. We could have lunch on the porch."

Simms considered Hinckley standing in his starched shirt and tie. A few years younger than the sheriff and friendly enough, maybe more friendly than their acquaintance called for, but did the man not hear?

"Thanks, Ebby's expecting me," said Sheriff Simms.

"Easy enough, Willford, I could run in there and call her," said Hinckley. "We need to talk about the bank."

Only one person in the county could call him Willford, and he was going to have lunch with her.

"No," said Sheriff Simms. "We don't need to talk about that at all."

"You know, Willford," continued Hinckley, "many individuals made fortunes from the Park City mines. They took their wealth and built mansions down on South Temple."

Sheriff Simms could hear a rehearsed argument but stood still to hear him out and said nothing. Not that he thought Jay Hinckley a bad man. He seemed to be a hardworking sort, and he always looked to be on the verge of some success. The sheriff had simply thought him not someone to make the space to know, except to keep track of. For sure, he had no mind to be Willford to this man. Being familiar didn't come natural to Sheriff Simms.

"Well, isn't that important to you?" Hinckley's impatience prompted the question and broke through before the answer. "Throw in with us and you can have that. It's time we had another bank in town. You're thirty-six. It's time to think about making your fortune."

"Old Emery never built no mansion down on South Temple," said the sheriff. Emery Crittenden had been the only banker in town for as long as Sheriff Simms had known him or Doc or breath.

"That's not the point. The point is we want you to join us. Be one of the founders on the bank application."

Sheriff Simms started to walk again. "Nah, I'm late for Ebby's lunch."

"There's gonna be good times. They're starting to call it the Roaring Twenties. Our backers think it's a good bet," said Hinckley. He took a few steps beyond the gate in the little picket fence and fell in next to Sheriff Simms. "You won't need to put up any capital."

"I ain't taking nobody else's money."

"No, no, not like that. They'd sell you some stock at a special price. You'd be in on the ground floor. Mostly we just want you." Simms laughed. Hinckley kept talking. "You got good judgment. People'll think twice about missing their payments with you around. Your good judgment will bring us business."

"Yep," said the sheriff, continuing to the corner of East One Hundred Street.

"Will you at least think about it?" called Hinckley.

Sheriff Simms turned to walk further north, waved his right hand over his shoulder, and said, "Nope."

Sheriff Simms did his best to sneak up behind Ebby.

"Willford?" she asked. "Is that you?"

No matter how often he tried, he couldn't catch her unawares. He comforted himself with hearing a note of surprise in her voice.

"Yep." He put his arms around her and squeezed. She twisted to look over her shoulder, raising an eyebrow. She swiveled in his arms and wrapped her arms around his neck. Her kiss set him to thinking she was tired of baking.

"Maybe this will be a real nice lunch," he said.

"Maybe," she said, relaxing in his arms. She started to hum again. Ebby baked every day. Today was Monday, pies. She didn't hum every day. Ebby wriggled out of his embrace and removed a pie from the flat board across the sink. After spreading flour on the board, she dropped a mound of dough in the center.

"Okay," he said, a little suspicious. "Why're you humming?"

"Why're you here today?"

"Well, woman," he said, "it ain't for the reason you think."

"Now, don't go saying that, Willford." She grabbed a handful of flour from her rolling board and threw it at him.

"Seriously, Ma," he said. "I'm home to enjoy Troy." He caught himself, "and you," he added for fear he might have said something wrong. "I shoulda been more careful. On the way, Jay Hinckley corralled me about their new bank."

"You worry about money. That'd solve your worries, you know." Ebby placed the rolling pin at the top edge of the circle of dough growing under her expert touch. She turned and smiled, and he heard both persuasion and support. "Those boys at the new bank still need you."

"Yeah, to talk sense to 'em," he growled. "They're crazy. I don't know nothing about banks. Neither do they. Lest why would they be asking me, of all people, to join up with them? It makes no sense."

"Like you said, to talk sense to them. You have sound judgment. Everyone in town would trust putting their money in a bank where you work."

"I ain't so all fired sure this town needs another bank," Simms declared. He eyed a piece of pie. His voice slowed from its normal slow pace as he started cutting the pie. "My job don't pay much, but it'll be there ten years from now."

"I'm happy with what we got," Ebby said. Her eyes twinkled, "What with all the extra money from raising chickens." She caught her breath. "We'll be all right. I know it'd be an ease to your worries to be making more money."

"That it would," said Simms. He put his piece of pie on a plate and held it to his nose. "Strawberry, ain't it?"

"Yes. They're a little early. A bit hard and sour." Her eyes lit up. "Like you."

"Well, you sweetened 'em up," he said. "Like me."

He took a bite and waved dismissal of the subject with his fork. "I know I like your pie," he said. "I don't know nothin' about banking."

"You're just durn stubborn," she said.

"I ain't stubborn. I didn't graduate high school, and I been a guard or a deputy or a sheriff all my life. Besides," he sank his fork into the last of the pie on his plate, "you can thank Prohibition for these good times. Ain't gonna last. Neither one."

"No tellin', maybe it's progress," said Ebby. "You can't hold back progress."

"Ma, all I know about banking is how to guard one. Good bankers got to have a certain gift. Not many do, and the gift ain't cheating. I don't have it. Even if you can't know beforehand, I don't have it."

Trees. Come Friday and he could only hear trees. He looked up and saw the rustle of aspen leaves. In a month they would be gone. Sheriff Simms listened but heard nothing else, only trees. He had set the chair in front of the corral and paced out the distance. With his toe he drew a line, scuffing away weeds grown in from disuse. He stood behind the line and looked to the chair. It would suit. The sound of cars and trucks grew behind him. He turned to see the caravan coming through the tall posts that formed the ranch gate. Deputy Woodside drove McNabb in the lead car. Doc Crittenden drove his own car and carried three members of the firing squad. Vernon Jr. drove the county truck and two more members. Sheriff Simms made six.

Doc Crittenden parked his Buick and walked over to the sheriff. A rattling noise drew their attention to Kidner's once horse-drawn black wagon as it drove through the gate.

"Seth did a good job fixin' Kidner's old hearse up with a motor," said Sheriff Simms.

"Kidner's all you needed," replied Doc Crittenden. "You didn't need me."

The sheriff held him steady. "Nope. You're the doctor. He's the undertaker. From what I read, that makes you the coroner."

"Modern," said Doc Crittenden. "What'd your father do

with no doctor in town? It sure doesn't sound like the Old West."

"Not my aim," said Sheriff Simms. "My Grandpa Simms died four years before I was born. Everything I know about him, I been told. My pa wasn't a talker, but he told me about how he rode in on a posse after a boy who rustled his uncle's cattle. They tracked him down and shot him. Ma told me a few stories, too, but most of the stories about my grandpa and my pa come from people in town, friends and such, who want to make sure I know what they did. I ain't sayin' I believe all of them, but I wanted to believe every one of 'em was real. What it amounts to is I ain't that big. Some because my problems ain't that big and some because, well, maybe this isn't the Old West. Maybe it wasn't the Old West when it *was* the Old West. Fact is, I'm not living some story, and I ain't that big. I'm doing my job and it turns out," Simms looked into the sky, calculating in his head, "what is it, sixty-nine years since the territory made Grandpa Simms the sheriff? It's smoothed out some, but it turns out it's still pretty much the same."

"Some men, like McNabb, came west to choose their own trail to Hell," said Doc Crittenden. He watched Kidner maneuver his hearse to park at the side of the corral, a respectful distance from the chair. "Some, most all of us, came to find a road to Heaven." Doc turned to consider the sheriff. "If it be sixty-nine years, that'd be when you Simmses started to protect the ones from the others."

The sheriff laughed a response. "Might be a bit highfalutin, Doc." He kicked a clod on the ground. "Best just say we took what the duty gave us."

"Is this your worst duty? Ever?" asked Doc Crittenden.

"Not in the question," Simms lapsed into silence. "Leastwise, nothing I ever think about." That started him to thinking. He let the silence grow, then added, "There've been worse. Like that silly cigarette act."

"You're funning me." Doc Crittenden pointed to the chair. "I'm asking a serious question."

"Not even a little. That cigarette act made for worse duty than doing any hard job *right,*" Simms snickered. "I might could say the same about this Prohibition. They started that eighteenth amendment rolling, and lawmakers down at the state capitol figured they could make a man perfect by passing a law. Too much never counted enough. They passed that law to ban cigarettes in 1921. I never smoked 'em myself, but there was no damn law sillier than that. This Prohibition thing may have started it, but it ain't as silly as that was.

"Right off, everybody forgot about it. So, the legislators rigged up with the State Prohibition Commission. They had this law and now they had a commission. The commission sent a memo. 'Your Responsibility as a Law-Enforcer.' I don't see how they figured I didn't know my responsibilities, and that commission didn't help none.

"People kept selling cigarettes and people kept smoking cigarettes. Now they had a reason to start bootlegging them." He pointed at McNabb. "Rustling makes people dangerous. Bootlegging makes people dangerous.

"When I put on this star, I swore to enforce all the laws. That law was damned foolishness. Compel obedience. Bullshit. Somebody better'n me brought it to an end. I don't know who he was, but after two years of this nonsense, he found the way. I think he was state police, and he was smart enough to arrest some good citizens in the Vienna Café down in Salt Lake, right in the same room where the governor and his bodyguard were smoking a cigar."

"Why smart?" asked Doc Crittenden. "It doesn't seem fair, the state police arresting a regular guy smoking when the governor was doing the same thing."

"That's just it," chuckled Sheriff Simms. "The uproar, scandal you might say, put that hypocrite Governor Mabey to work. It wasn't much more'n a month till he got that law repealed."

"March of this year," said Doc Crittenden. He smiled, "So, the guy who enforced that law did what it took to rid us of it. That's what you're trying to tell me?"

"Not trying to tell you nothing," said Sheriff Simms. He waved Vernon Jr. over. "I just tried to treat a dumb question like it weren't."

"Even so," said Doc Crittenden, "this can't be easy for you."

"Easy ain't what we're talking about," said Simms. "He did the thing in my county, so I have to organize his firing squad. I picked out here where he shot Brose because I didn't want a bunch of onlookers that I can't stop coming. We're doing justice to someone who did wrong."

Young Deputy Woodside stepped up and held steady for the sheriff's attention. Simms tipped his hat, "Set all the members behind that line. Doc'll take care of McNabb." Woodside nodded. "You give 'em their shells?"

Woodside nodded again. "One blank in the six rounds, but they're still gonna know."

"Of course, they are." Sheriff Simms turned to Doc Crittenden. "Go ahead."

Doc stepped to Deputy Woodside and the prisoner. He grasped McNabb's wrist and took his pulse. He felt McNabb's forehead, then led him to the chair. Deputy Woodside fixed his ankles to the legs with leather and drew his arms behind to snap on handcuffs. Doc Crittenden pinned a patch of red cloth to his shirt on the left side of his chest. Finished, Doc stepped back. "Mr. McNabb. Do you have anything you wish to say?"

McNabb craned his head around to Sheriff Simms. "Not such a high price to pay for sparing this world of Brose. Now that he's gone, the most bitter of my enemies are forgiven. I am ready to go."

Sheriff Simms stepped to his place, sixth on the line. Three appeals and three years of examination by the state were undertaken to determine McNabb's psychological state. After blasting his business partner in the face and turning on Sheriff Simms to do the same, he had been found "irresponsible and only 60 percent normal" but still sane.

The sheriff struggled to hold no opinion. Trying to ignore the pain in his left arm that never went away, he wanted to believe he simply had his job to do as sheriff. He never discussed the rage he felt against McNabb. That felt about right. His father never discussed what he must have felt against Hopt. It was that simple. He had his job to do. He looked down the line and shouted his first command.

"Ready."

Six men lifted their rifles.

"Aim."

Six men steadied their breath.

"Fire."

CHAPTER 39

1924 New Year's Eve

Sheriff Simms watched the glow of the slag heaps ooze down the mountain. The snow that started in the backcountry gave the miners an excuse to come down early. They streamed off the mountain into the saloons on Main Street. Congress in Washington and legislators in Salt Lake passed laws to make the behavior of these working men perfect in their eyes. Now the sheriff shouldered the duty to enforce a bad law and reap the contempt of people who worked for a living while the politicians congratulated themselves and bathed in virtue. Enforcing the law had a habit of coming before family. He sat cramped and cold expecting the night to hold worse than any Saturday night. He thought of Ebby at home.

"Watch out for trouble," she warned him.

That's what he did. Trouble seldom comes from unexpected sources. He watched out for rattlesnakes because they were rattlesnakes. He figured to take the same care with the saloons that lit up Main Street almost day bright on New Year's Eve.

Like any other night when celebrating threatened to create more trouble than fun, he left his car to walk up the boardwalk. Crossing Main Street, he looked over his shoulder to the mountain glowing silver above the town. He smiled at the thought the glow emerged from inside the mountain, rather than from the moon on the snow-swept slopes. He didn't begrudge men turning dirt from Park City into mansions on

South Temple. He didn't know how to do it. He believed anyone who did deserved to be respected, but being respectful didn't mean he thought the mansions were as beautiful as the mountain devoured to build them. Useless stuff though it may be, that beauty counted for the snow, too. Struggling with the snow cost everyone a lot of difficulty, but Simms considered it a minor payment for the beauty on those hills.

The sheriff started his slow progress up the boardwalk looking to the usual trouble spots. Everyone in Park City knew he was there. One sure advantage to a wooden sidewalk. He never used the sheriff's office right across the street from the Town Hall and the jail. If people thought he was in the office, they would not behave as though he'd walk in any minute.

He walked to the top of the boardwalk thinking about Prohibition. Crossing over where Main Street disappears into the mountain, he returned down the right-side thinking Prohibition is a proposition designed to make people rich. Seemed to work for some, but for him, it only served to make him wonder *why I'm so damn limited.* Some force controlled his mind. He could see only what was at hand, taking care of his little mountain county. Except for trying to sign up to go to war, all he ever wanted to do was follow his father and grandfather, stay right there, and take care of trouble.

No trouble came from the expected spots. Back in his car, he sat cramped and cold, thinking how limited he was for on to two hours. He repeated his rounds and thoughts, followed by another two hours of the same cramped and cold sit in his car.

One of Mother Urban's girls ran down the boardwalk to his car, her screams arriving long before she did. He knew he would not have a third two hours of calm and climbed out of the car to meet her.

She yelled, "Two guys, up to the banker's bar, is waving guns at each other."

The thought of sitting cramped and cold for another two hours took on a whole lot more pleasing prospect than what he knew he had to do. He left Mother Urban's girl to return at her own pace and ran up the center of Main Street to the banker's bar.

The sheriff pushed inside, one step away from being directly between the two men waving their guns. "You're not bankers," he hollered, "just sons of bankers." Strictly speaking, not a banker's bar but a bar set in an old bank—and not a legal establishment. "I know your daddy," he said to young John Boyden Jr., son of John Boyden, the banker in Park City.

He didn't so much mind they were both waving their guns, even at him, but worse, they didn't look like men—or boys—who knew what they were doing with guns. He could hear his father's words, *take care*. Before he rapped 'em good, he'd talk.

"What the hell am I to do here? You know it's illegal to buy booze. You're not supposed to drink. And goddammit all to hell, it makes me real mad when you call attention to your illegal drinking by waving a gun in my county." Sheriff Simms watched their drunken bodies wave their guns more than he could tolerate. He stuck his hand out, "Now, gimme those."

"You may know my old man," said young John Boyden, "but you ain't taking my gun."

Sheriff Simms offered no response. It didn't take but a hard elbow in the stomach of the one standing next to him. His face slammed into the table. That made it easy for the sheriff to come up with his gun. He raised the gun to eye level.

"Now, John Boyden, do you want to give me that gun?" He held out his left hand and nodded toward it. "I ain't too good with my left hand. So, I could miss you altogether. But then again, you're close to me. For a pip-squeak, you're large enough to make an easy target."

"What ya gonna do?" asked John Boyden.

"What I wanna do is dunk your head in Silver Creek until you're sober."

"You can't do that," said Boyden. "Poison Creek'd kill me."[4]

"If you don't sober up fast, them's the wages of sin," said Sheriff Simms.

While the sheriff talked, he edged behind Boyden's buddy, right hand holding his face on the table, pulled his arms back, and cuffed him. Finished, the sheriff took half a step and hit Boyden a straight right in the face. "Done talking."

"Cain't do what I want," he told Boyden, now spread out on the floor. He took Boyden's gun and had both guns in his left hand. He dragged Boyden by the foot to the door. He returned to Boyden's buddy and dragged him by the handcuffs. "Up, both of you."

The sheriff pushed them both out the door. "I'll tell you," he said, chatting as he walked down the boardwalk, "I feel an uncharitable delight sending you boys down that hole under Town Hall. I like that jail. My grandfather needed a jail and the town fathers thought in a mining town it made more sense to dig one than to build one. The cell has a lock on it. At the foot of the stairs, there's a lock on the door of the room that holds the cells. And up the stairs, one way out, and the door is locked. I put you down there, you're gonna be there when I come back."

Sheriff Simms marched them downstairs and into the cell, clicking each lock he had told them about. He stood back from the cell door. "I'll fetch you tomorrow afternoon." He chuckled. They'd gripe at him tomorrow, but tonight, they were too dumb drunk to hear a word.

Sheriff Simms climbed back up the hill to the banker's bar. He wrote out a summons and shut Johnston down. Everybody knew the rules. They even called it "Urban's Tax." Mother

4 Silver Creek was nicknamed Poison Creek because of the runoff that was dumped in it from processing silver ore.

Urban kept her houses for the men. She depended on the sheriff to keep order. When trouble arose, he'd arrest Mother Urban. She made the profit; she accepted being arrested. She paid double her fine and went back to her houses. It kept her in business, and it kept Park City afloat. Old Johnston owned that bar. He had a great smile and met the sheriff with it when he held out his hand to receive the summons. He paid his fine and opened for lunch on New Year's Day.

New Year's Eve brought neither fights nor risky gun-toting nor further troubles to Sheriff Simms after the fracas at the banker's bar. Yet action jammed the street.

A limitless desire to dance streamed with music out of every saloon into Main Street. The young girls, wearing short dresses and bobbed hair, followed the jazz music like the Pied Piper. Sheriff Simms considered their near to scandalous outfits, perhaps perfect for the touch-tight crowded bars, none too bright in the wide-open cold and snow. The boys dragged behind by the girls had the good sense to wear long pants and coats. The girls wore scanty things held on by the merest strap covering their shoulders with skirts designed to flip the short skirts up, well, to their waist, by the dance they did, kicking their legs back and forth, front and back. Seeing them, he remembered Vernon Jr. had told him about a dance craze, the Charleston, that started in some Broadway show by the name of *Runnin' Wild.* That seemed to suit the Park City crowd as they jammed Main Street in the snow and cold on New Year's Eve.

Sheriff Simms patrolled, walking up and down the street, and watching, until about five in the morning. Still winter dark, he sensed the party thin out and knew it would soon end. The nonstop music displaced displays of bravado that accompanied the alcohol consumed. Not that good sense emerged to dominate the revelers. These young women wore even less by the way of shoes than they did by the way of clothes. He expected and feared they would end up exposed, frostbitten, and in the hospital. The sheriff did not know what to do with that concern. It had not happened in the first five hours of watching over them. He settled for hoping it would not happen in the next hour.

The sheriff arrived in his quiet little town about six o'clock, a good long hour before twilight started to lift the darkness off New Year's Day. The empty streets surprised him none. For caution's sake he slowed down as he drove past the one saloon in town and gave a careful look. It seemed quiet, nigh on to dark. A couple of blocks further up Main Street, despite the early hour and dark sky, he turned on Fifty North. He planned to stop by his mother's house and wish her Happy New Year. Six o'clock and dark on a holiday meant nothing to her; she would be up and busy.

When he saw no light through the front window, he drove around to the back and parked in front of the shed. No doubt he would see a light in the kitchen.

He did not. Perhaps planning New Year's Eve coverage had made him inattentive to evening plans told but not really heard. Maybe his mother had dinner with Ma Carruth and simply stayed overnight at her old friend's house to avoid walking home in the snow and dark. Just as likely she had gone to his house to provide Ebby holiday company since he had left her alone for his duty in Park City. He opened the back door and stepped in. He could see his mother had not been up and working in her kitchen.

Sheriff Simms walked into the little front room that had been the original house and snapped on the lamp he had expected to see through the window. He crossed the floor to the opening of his mother's bedroom. The pulled curtains seemed normal, except for the hour.

He stepped through, leaving the curtains closed. Light seeped in from the living room.

The sheriff did not need to shake his mother awake at this late hour. Not a reveler, and she had not spent the evening with Ma Carruth or Ebby. She was not asleep.

The sheriff stood over his mother. She lay on her back, the covers where she had pulled them to comfort her night's sleep. The room was cold. No surprise, she liked to sleep in a cold room. He gently touched her cheek. It felt cold. He could not tell when it had stopped warming itself. It had been more than an hour ago.

Sheriff Simms returned through the curtains, switched off the light, and headed out the back door. He hesitated to crank the Model T and make a noise that would offend this quiet moment. He turned on the street and continued the short distance to his house. Before he opened the door, he stood on the stoop and looked through the little window. He saw the light in the kitchen and breathed relief. Ebby was up baking.

He entered quietly, crept up behind Ebby, and kissed her on the neck, "I stopped by Ma's house. She died in her sleep."

Ebby spun around, "Oh, Willford."

He shook his head. "She looked peaceful, and she was busy yesterday."

"That doesn't make it any easier," said Ebby.

"Not the fact," he said, "but it eases the thought." Ebby twisted and pushed away from his arms, then laid her head on his chest. He said into her hair, "She was seventy-six. She said she expected to die three times already. I'm thinking she'd take this without much fuss."

"I expect," said Ebby. Without raising her head, she asked, "What will you do?"

"I'll call Kidner in a minute," said Sheriff Simms. "I'm thinkin' tomorrow's enough for her to be laid out. We'll bury her Thursday."

In the same church, to the same size crowd, Sheriff Mark Willford Simms rose on Thursday, the same as he did with his father, to deliver the eulogy marking his mother's passing.

> "If you're in this audience, I'm guessing you know about my family. You know my grandfather emigrated to Zion and to this mountain valley as a cooper. That wasn't enough for Brigham. He wanted him to be the constable and that made him sheriff when we became a territory. You know my father was born in England and came here with his mother and father to grow up to be his father's deputy and raise a fine family. That didn't satisfy the bishop. He wanted him to marry an orphan and take her off the hands of the Church and the community. Both John Willford Simms and Elizabeth Tonsil were reluctant, but I for one can say I am happy they overcame their hesitation.
>
> That orphan girl had courage, spunk, style, and willpower. She withstood the snows of Hilliard. She lived through and then with the diphtheria deaths of her three daughters. She suffered the risk and recrimination of her adopted country because she and her husband wanted to live out their barren life together in the manner they had bargained for. She even sacrificed all the rest of her years of loving touch to give life to the man standing before you today trying to do justice to her remarkable life. She supported herself by work. She supported everyone who hears my voice by love. She will be completely forgotten by all but those few who follow my sister Clara and me. Truth be

told, there will come a time when they too completely forget her.

She died with the New Year as if by going to bed and saying goodbye. She had not been sick. She had not talked of death. To be sure, she never talked of hardship. Any hardship. They arrived, she lived through them, and she continued.

The difference exists only in us, in how we endure hardships.

Death came. She embraced it. She has moved on."

Sheriff Simms allowed no receiving line at the reception by the Relief Society in the little yellow house. Ebby held their fourth live child, six-month-old Troy, and Simms did not want her to stand all that long. He led the other three children, now twelve, eight, and six, to assist the Sisters in cleanup. It always amazed him how everyone could find their way to the tables for food but not to the sink with the dirty dishes. He banished the thought. This was a day to let them celebrate his mother.

The sheriff spotted Sarah Jane Carruth Hixson Brown dressed in a yellow dress like the one his mother used to wear. Talking with a group of ladies all dressed in gray, Sarah looked fresh and saucy. He knew it was her way of paying tribute to Elizabeth Tonsil. The sheriff stepped up to the group, saluted an imaginary hat with two fingers, and said, "Ladies, I need to hear my old friend's doings since she moved to Evanston." He took Sarah Jane by the elbow and moved her into the little front room.

"I met Attorney Brown two or three times before he became your husband," said Sheriff Simms. "I haven't seen you since."

"It's nice to see you again, too, Mark Willford."

He paused a moment, a little dumbfounded, not sure if he

had been rebuked. He said, "I never heard about it. That was kinda fast."

"Not so fast," said Sarah Jane. "We married last summer. I met him soon after I moved up there. That'd be four years this month."

"He told me he had a four-year plan." Sheriff Simms cocked his head, calculating. "That'd be even before he met you."

"I suppose I cut a year off the hunt," chuckled Sarah Jane.

"D'ya think that's what it was? He was in the hunt for you?"

She laughed. "I know I was. I had the boy, and a boy needs a father." She touched his hand. "You helped out, but I wanted a husband. Not to say anything bad about Tom, especially to you, but I wanted someone different from him. I had no idea how to get one. I knew I didn't figure to find the husband I wanted after-hours."

"He told me he met you at the bar."

"He talked to you about me?"

"At McNabb's trial. He tried to bribe me to put in a good word to you."

"Bribe?" she smiled.

"He called it lunch at the Cluff Hotel," said Sheriff Simms. A short silence preceded his conclusion. "Apparently he didn't need a good word from me." Another silence followed. Before it grew awkward, he asked, "Does saving you from the Relief Society ladies justify telling me all about it?"

"That does merit a reward," she laughed. "He kept leaving tips that were too big. One night, he took my hand and said being as we were already in Evanston where kids cross the state line to marry up, we could go to the Justice of the Peace."

"Sounds romantic," said Sheriff Simms. "Did you?"

Sarah looked at him as though he had said something strange. "More plain foolish than romantic," she said. "He didn't know anything about me, and I knew I was losing, well, losing what must have been attracting him in the first place. I was certain I could never be a mother again. You know, age and past and such. I told him pretty much all of this."

"He didn't even listen," said Sheriff Simms.

"He said, 'I know you have a boy who's four today and who's been giving you troubles lately.' Well, that did it. One fact, and it told me he knew everything.

"The Justice of the Peace married us. He took me in this car called an Auburn to a little house he owned in Evanston. It slipped my mind to ask how a sheepherder came to own an Auburn and a house in Evanston.

"Next morning, he took Marion and me to breakfast at the Evanston Hotel. While he cut Marion's flapjacks, he said he might not a told me all of it. He had told me he borrowed money to buy the sheep, but he said I needed to know he owed a lot of money. He worked fifteen hours a day to make the bank payments.

"I figured I shoulda guessed it. From a shiftless husband to a broke one. I told him I wanted a father for Marion, not for anyone to take care of me. I'd work.

"He almost spit out his coffee. He said, 'Oh, it's not that. I have offices in Laramie and Cheyenne, and I work such long hours, I, well, I mean, we, have houses there, too.'

"I couldn't understand any of what he was telling me.

"I put down my fork and asked him straight out. 'You mean you're telling me you're a lawyer making enough money to pay the mortgage on four houses. And you're a judge?'

"He smiled like I had caught him. 'Yes'm. And I own a little land and some sheep.' "

"Quite a story," said Sheriff Simms, grateful that Marion now could be well-taken care of, and no one had to rely on that line of the McCormick ranch—Ogden Packing and Provision—Golden Spike Livestock. It felt like the end of forty-one years of burden and pain. Maybe some new trials would emerge to test him, but for right now, he wanted to deliver Sarah Jane to Ma Carruth and retrieve Ebby.

Ebby held Troy in her arms. Willford and Frank stood with her, watching the sheriff approach. Thea had undoubtedly taken over the kitchen and given instructions to the Sisters.

In wishing this reception over, Sheriff Simms looked back over the funerals in his life. He attended his grandfather's through the story his mother told him. At his grandmother's, his father's wish that he would become sheriff came in his father's prediction he would be the last Sheriff Simms. He sandwiched his father's funeral between the murderous OPP and the murderous Spanish flu. His first duty had not been to find the killers but to keep people from killing themselves. Now his mother had died and with her all links to the century that brought them here.

He gazed at his wife and three boys. None of the boys were destined to become sheriff. The absent child was the most suited to it, but a girl. The job would not be hers. He had not yet served his calling six years, and he wanted to do the best he could in every moment left to him, for he would be the last of the Simms sheriffs.

Forever.

The Sheriffs Simms Genealogy

Founding Sheriff

Luke Willford Simms b. 1827 England d. 1883 Coalville	Mary Ann Opshaw b. 1824 England d. 1906 Coalville	Thomas Tonsil d. 1869 Coalville	Lissy Hatfield d. 1869 Coalville	James Pike b. 1827 England d. 1909 Coalville	Margaret Robertson	John Rawlings	Elizabeth Brown

Fugitive Sheriff

John Willford Simms b. 1844 England d. 1918 Coalville	Elizabeth Tonsil b. 1846 England d. 1924 Coalville	Franklin Dewey Pike b. 1852 England d.1928 Coalville	Sarah Ann Rawlings b. 1852 England d 1948 Coalville

Forever Sheriff

Mark Willford Simms b. 1887	Elizabeth Pike b. 1890

Willford John b. 1911	Dead Female b. 1913	Thea b. 1915	Frank b. 1917	Dead Female b. 1918	Troy b. 1923	Cybil b. 1925	Dead Female b 1926	Hector b. 1929

ABOUT THE AUTHOR

Stern pioneer stock bred to survive in the high mountain desert mated with good-humored optimism escaped from Southern poverty to create the determination and reverence for education that have guided **Edward Massey's** life. Great universities and an exciting business career fired the kiln that molded his calling to write. *Forever Sheriff* brings the fifth published novel, and the third with this great publisher, to his writing career. Edward writes every day. Consulting and speaking support Anne and him in Connecticut and Maine. See edwardmasseybooks.com.

The employees of Five Star Publishing hope you have enjoyed this book.

Our Five Star novels explore little-known chapters from America's history, stories told from unique perspectives that will entertain a broad range of readers.

Other Five Star books are available at your local library, bookstore, all major book distributors, and directly from Five Star/Gale.

Connect with Five Star Publishing

Website:
gale.com/five-star

Facebook:
facebook.com/FiveStarCengage

Twitter:
twitter.com/FiveStarCengage

Email:
FiveStar@cengage.com

For information about titles and placing orders:
(800) 223-1244
gale.orders@cengage.com

To share your comments, write to us:
Five Star Publishing
Attn: Publisher
10 Water St., Suite 310
Waterville, ME 04901